Discover why everyone's talking about Charlotte Betts

Praise for *The Apothecary's Daughter*

'A colourful story with a richly-drawn backdrop of London in the grip of the plague. A wonderful debut novel'
Carole Matthews

'Romantic, engaging and hugely satisfying. This is one of those novels that makes you feel like you've travelled back in time'
Katie Fforde

'A vivid tale of love in a time of plague and prejudice'
Katherine Webb

'If you are looking for a cracking good story and to be transported to another age, you really can't beat this'
Deborah Swift

'A thoroughly enjoyable read which will keep you enthralled until the very last page'
Jean Fullerton

Multi-award winning author **Charlotte Betts** began her working life as a fashion designer in London. A career followed in interior design, property management and lettings. Always a bookworm, Charlotte discovered her passion for writing after her three children and two step-children grew up.

Her debut novel, *The Apothecary's Daughter*, has won several prizes including the RoNA award, Historical Category, in 2013. Her second novel, *The Painter's Apprentice*, was also shortlisted for Best Historical Read at the Festival of Romance in 2012.

Charlotte lives with her husband in a cottage in the woods on the Hampshire/Berkshire border.

Visit her website at www.charlottebetts.com and follow her on twitter at www.twitter.com/CharlotteBetts1

Also by Charlotte Betts:

The Apothecary's Daughter
The Painter's Apprentice

The Spice Merchant's Wife

Charlotte Betts

piatkus

PIATKUS

First published in Great Britain in 2013 by Piatkus

A CIP catalogue record for this book is available from the British Library.

ISBN 978-0-7499-5927-2

Printed and bound in Great Britain by
Clays Ltd, St Ives plc

Papers used by Piatkus are from well-managed forests and other responsible sources.

Piatkus
An imprint of
Little, Brown Book Group
100 Victoria Embankment
London EC4Y 0DY

An Hachette UK Company
www.hachette.co.uk

www.piatkus.co.uk

To Isabella Rose
and Florence Elizabeth,
with love.

Chapter 1

London
August 1666

The summer had been swelteringly hot with barely any rain to wash away the dust and stench and I was not alone in wishing it at an end. The city was as hot and dry as a tinderbox and all anyone could do was to find a shady place and sit very still, waiting.

Mother Finche, plump, with a fair, faded prettiness, chatted desultorily with her two friends about the recent outbreak of the plague in an apothecary shop in Fleet Street and the scandalous doings of our French Catholic neighbours. At our feet silky pools of claret, purple, acid yellow and marine blue damask suitable for lining the parlour walls lay across the Turkish carpet, left by the draper for her consideration.

A fly buzzed irritably at the window and a languid breeze carried in the reek of summer drains together with a suspicion of rotting fish from nearby Billingsgate. Outside, the relentless clatter of wheeled and shod traffic grinding over the cobbles on Lombard Street set my teeth on edge.

I was suffering from the kind of heat-induced headache that even oil of lavender couldn't ease and the conversation washed over me like the lapping waves of a warm sea. Longing to escape from the stifling parlour my thoughts drifted to my long-held daydream of being mistress of my own household. And, at last, after long years of misery and loneliness, my wish might soon be realised.

'Katherine?' Mother Finche touched my hand to draw my attention. 'My son's bride is *such* a dreamer,' she said to Mistress Spalding.

Mistress Spalding fluttered a fan in front of her flushed cheeks, wafting the tang of stale perspiration across the room. 'Who can blame her? This terrible heat is exhausting.'

Mother Finche fingered the purple silk damask. 'This is very rich, don't you think?' she mused.

'Might it be too dark?' I ventured.

'Nonsense!' she said. 'Why, the Duchess of Lauderdale has exactly this colour and she is a lady of excellent taste. Besides, I shall have borders of yellow fringing.'

'I shall be most envious of you,' said Mistress Buckley.

'That's settled then,' said Mother Finche, satisfaction in her voice.

While the ladies gossiped, the clock on the chimneypiece ticked on as steadily as a resting heartbeat, measuring out the seconds. How many hours of my life, I wondered, had I spent in someone else's home waiting and listening to the ticking of a clock? When would it all come to an end? It wasn't that my husband's parents were unkind to me but I'd lived in limbo with these near strangers for what felt like an eternity. Seven months married and my husband had been away for six of them.

I went to the window and rested my aching forehead against the casement. After rubbing away the city dust from the glass, I watched the people in the street below moving as slowly as treacle in winter, keeping close to the walls to avoid the sun. The black dog was back again, I noticed, nosing in the filth of the drain.

Bessie carried in the rattling tea tray. I caught the greasy odour of the kitchen on her coarse hair and saw the half-moons of sweat under her arms as she wearily set out the silver teakettle, spoons, dainty china cups and a ginger cake drizzled with honey.

Mother Finche began the ritual of measuring out the costly tea leaves and pouring the hot water. As the wife of a prosperous merchant, she had quickly embraced the fashion for tea parties, which the Queen had brought with her from Portugal. Mother Finche was always looking for new ways to impress her rich friends.

'A street boy brought a note,' said Bessie, taking a folded paper from her pocket.

Mother Finche held out her hand.

Bessie shook her head. 'It's for Mistress Robert.'

'For me?' I didn't have any friends or family to send me notes. I unfolded the paper and the blood surged up into my cheeks. The *Rose of Constantinople* had docked and the long wait was nearly over.

I murmured my excuses to Mother Finche and her friends, slipped out of the parlour and ran down the stairs before she could stop me. Six months overseas and at last my husband was returning to me. I was nervous of this husband that I hardly knew, apprehensive and excited at the same time. He was the key to everything; the home and family of my own that I'd longed for ever since I was orphaned and sent to live with hateful Aunt Mercy.

Sultry heat rose from the ground and pulsed from the walls of the buildings in Lombard Street as I hurried by. Fly-covered mounds of stinking mud and rubbish prevented the sluggish trickle of water in the central drains from carrying the detritus of the streets away. My feet kicked up little clouds of dust, making a dark rim on the hem of my skirt.

I paused at the edge of the road to allow a heavily laden dray pass and saw a man emerge out of the shadows on the other side of the street and step into the harsh sunlight. Dressed in a feathered hat and full-skirted coat of sea green with waterfalls of white lace to his shirt, he looked as cool as a mountain stream. He carried a long, silver-headed cane in one hand and clasped an ornate glass bottle in the other. He walked slowly, not unusual in such heat, but there was something curious about the slight hesitation to his step and the way he swung the cane in small arcs in front of him.

It all happened so quickly that later I was hard-pressed to remember the exact sequence of events. I saw the man stop dead and cock his head as if listening. And then I heard the rumble of coach wheels approaching fast. Too fast.

Two black horses came galloping into view, their hooves striking sparks from the cobbles as they dragged a wildly swaying coach behind them. The coachman, clinging to the roof, attempted to regain control of his runaway steeds, while a pack of street dogs snapped and snarled at their hocks.

The man in the green coat was standing directly in the coach's path.

Horrified, I shouted, 'Look out!' expecting him to leap aside, but he appeared frozen to the spot. I dashed across the street, arms outstretched, and thumped him in the chest, sending him sprawling in an undignified heap.

A rush of horse-scented air lifted my hair as, flecked with foam and their eyes rolling, the horses thundered past in a swirling cloud of dust.

Gasping, I clutched a hand to my chest.

The man was raising himself from the ground, his elegant brocade coat smeared with grime and the foam of white lace at his cuffs blackened with dust. A trickle of blood ran down his handsome face.

'I have cause to be grateful to you,' he said. The timbre of his voice was deep and smooth and I noticed that he was very tall, a little over six feet, I guessed.

And then I became aware of a whisper of an enchanting perfume drifting on the stifling air, teasing me with the fresh, outdoor promise of a spring day. A dark stain had spread out on the ground between us and shards of broken glass sparkled in the sun like diamonds.

'Your flask is broken,' I said.

He pushed back his thick blond hair with fingers that trembled a little but his expression was impassive.

Bending down to pick up his wide-brimmed hat, I noticed the delightful perfume again. Powdery and sweet, it brought to mind rain-drenched violets growing on a mossy bank. 'Was that perfume in the flask?'

'It was.'

'It's delightful.' His eyes were an unusual light green but he didn't meet my gaze. I felt a flash of annoyance at his rudeness and wondered if it was vanity that had caused him to match his coat so perfectly to the colour of his eyes.

'I fear my client will be disappointed,' he said. 'I was on my way to Bishopsgate to deliver it.' He inclined his head. 'Gabriel Harte, perfumer, at your service, Miss . . . ?'

'Mistress Finche. Katherine Finche.'

'Finche? Would that be the spice merchant Finches of Lombard Street?'

'The same.' I held out his hat but he didn't take it. Wrong-footed, I stood there with the hat in my hand feeling foolish.

'I dropped my cane,' he said. 'Would you oblige me by looking for it?'

Irritated that he made no attempt to look for it himself, I glanced around and spied the cane on the ground a few feet away. Again, he didn't move to take it from me. 'Your cane, sir!'

'Thank you.' Slowly, he reached towards me, moving his hand from right to left until it connected with the cane.

It was then that I realised he was blind.

He must have heard my indrawn breath because he gave me a half-smile. 'I would have been in difficulties if you hadn't come to rescue me.'

Contrite at my earlier annoyance, I said, 'And I have your hat here, too.' I touched it lightly to the back of his hand and he took it from me. 'There's blood on your cheek. Shall I wipe it away?'

'If you would be so kind.'

Slightly embarrassed at such close proximity to a stranger, especially one so well favoured, I stood on tiptoe and reached up to wipe his freshly shaven face with my handkerchief. His skin carried a pleasant aroma of lemon balm and rosemary.

It was strange to look at him from close quarters, knowing that he couldn't see me. 'You had a lucky escape,' I said. 'When I saw the horses racing towards you, I feared the worst.'

'I might have been frightened, too, if I had seen them.' He smiled properly then as if he had made a good joke.

'Can I take you somewhere?' I offered.

His smile froze. 'Thank you but no.'

'You've had a shock . . . '

'I can make my way home to Covent Garden perfectly well, thank you.'

'But that's on the other side of the city!'

'Why, so it is!' His tone was amused. 'But I have been finding my way across the city, with only the help of my cane, for many years now. I thank you for your kindness, Mistress Finche.' He bowed and then set off, his cane swinging gently in front of him. Then he stopped and turned towards me again. 'Mistress Finche?'

'Yes, sir?'

He hesitated. 'Would you describe your appearance to me?'

'My appearance?' I frowned.

'Forgive me. I know from your voice that you are young and that you are small and slender because your footsteps are light and quick, but I should like to know your colouring.'

I stared at him but his face gave nothing away. It didn't appear to be an impertinent enquiry. 'Why, sir, I have dark hair and hazel eyes and my skin is fair.'

His unseeing eyes stared into the distance somewhere over my left shoulder. 'Thank you,' he said. 'I believe I have your picture now.' After a moment he gave a decisive nod. 'And I hope your headache improves before very long.'

How did he know I had a headache? Puzzled, I stood there with the scent of violets suffusing the air and watched until his lean figure disappeared into the crowd.

Once he'd gone, I put my crumpled handkerchief into my pocket and encountered Father Finche's note, prompting me back to the matter in hand.

Making haste down Fish Hill, I felt the faintest stirring of a breeze and this increased as I turned into the hustle and bustle of Thames Street. I skirted around a dray, whose driver was having a noisy altercation with the owner of a cart laden with timber. Jostled by sailors, coalmen and chandlers and the air full of the keening cry of seagulls and snatches of conversations in different languages, I cut through one of the alleys down to Tower Dock, from where I could look east along the river.

The tide was coming in and the river was crowded with ferryboats, barges and wherries carrying passengers from Gravesend to the city. A salty breeze was freshening from the east. Several boats were berthed and I hurried past the Custom House and turned into Wiggins Key. My heart skipped when I saw the *Rose of Constantinople* towering above me. Sailors ran up and down her gangplanks with baskets of goods on their shoulders and the wind rattled at the furled sails and lifted the pennant at the top of her mast.

Queasy with anticipation, I stood on the quayside, shading my eyes from the sun and squinting up at the *Rose*, looking for Robert amongst the hubbub. I couldn't see him so, taking care not to trip over coiled ropes snaking across the quay, I made my way to Father Finche's warehouse.

Matthew Lunt, the clerk, came to greet me.

'Is Mr Finche here?'

Matthew mopped his freckled face with a handkerchief and nodded at the office.

I peered in through the open door to see my father-in-law sitting at his desk. He'd taken off his wig and draped it on top of his globe.

Pink and shiny-faced in the heat, he glanced up at me. 'Katherine, my dear!'

'Thank you for letting me know that the *Rose of Constantinople* has docked.'

'I knew you'd be anxious to see your husband again.'

I looked at my shoes, while I tried to recall what Robert looked like.

'As a merchant's wife you'll have to become accustomed to his long absences,' he said. 'But you'll have children before long to keep you occupied.'

I felt the blush race up my cheeks.

Father Finche smiled kindly at my embarrassment. 'Once Mother Finche had Robert and Sarah to keep her busy, the months when I was overseas flew past. She doted on our children. What a shame she had such a disagreement with Sarah.' He sighed. 'To tell the truth, I shall miss my travelling days. Not the sea voyages perhaps but visiting strange lands and peoples and the excitement of discovering exotic new merchandise.'

'I look forward to hearing about Robert's adventures,' I said.

Father Finche leaned forward conspiratorially. 'Don't tell my wife but I've taken a gamble on this last venture.'

'A gamble?'

'Usually I'm exceedingly cautious, but this time I've invested every last farthing of my own funds, as well your dowry, and persuaded all my friends and acquaintances to invest in the venture. Once all the goods are sold, I shall hand over the business to Robert. It's time for youth and energy to step forward.' Father Finche patted my hand. 'Go on home now, my dear. Robert's still aboard overseeing the unloading.'

‘Oh! But . . . ’

‘He won’t want to be interrupted now but we’ll return in time for dinner.’

Disappointed, but at the same time relieved to postpone meeting Robert again, I made my way back to the Finche house.

The great orange sun was beginning to sink behind St Paul’s by the time I heard voices downstairs. Mother Finche and I had been sitting in the parlour for hours, listening to the clock tick while we toyed with our embroidery. I’d changed my dress three times and my stockings twice. My nose was dusted with powder but I had no need of Spanish cochineal paper to heighten the colour in my cheeks.

Dry mouthed, I listened to the cadences of my husband’s speech as he came up the stairs.

The door opened. Father Finche strode in, followed by Robert’s stocky figure, their strident laughter filling the elegant room.

‘Well, here he is, Katherine, my dear!’ said Father Finche, smiling widely at me.

Mother Finche ran forward to embrace Robert and smile at him with a softness in her eyes I hadn’t seen since Robert left. ‘Welcome home, my dear.’

Robert and I looked at each other uneasily. I remembered the line of his jaw now, a sharper version of his father’s chin. His skin had darkened in the Turkish sun and his brown hair had lightened a little. He assessed me with cool grey eyes and I became uncomfortably aware that he probably hardly remembered me, either. Then he smiled. One of his teeth had a small chip to one corner but they were white against his tanned skin.

‘Katherine.’ His cheek was prickly against mine as he kissed me and he carried with him the smoky smell of tar and of sweat overlaid with the salt tang of the sea.

'Welcome home, Robert.' He carried two parcels under his arm and I wondered what he'd brought. 'How was your voyage?' I asked. 'Were there any pirates?'

'None we couldn't frighten off with a cannon shot across their bows.'

I shuddered at the thought of it. 'And the *Rose of Constantinople*?' I asked, full of hope and expectation.

'The warehouse is stacked to the gunnels,' said Father Finche with satisfaction. 'And Robert has brought back some excellent merchandise.'

A knot of tension loosened somewhere under my breastbone. The quality of the goods Robert had bought with my dowry would determine our future.

Robert handed one of the parcels to me. 'This is for you, Katherine.'

I unwrapped it and a bundle of shimmering silk slid to the floor. Exclaiming in delight, I gathered up the slippery material. Tiny gold peacocks were embroidered over the topaz silk, which was shot with moss green so that it looked topaz when I held it one way and then green if I tilted it the other. 'It's beautiful,' I breathed.

'I chose it to match your eyes,' said Robert.

I smiled tentatively at him and he smiled back.

'And I brought this for you, Mother,' he said.

She shook out her bundle of midnight blue silk and kissed her son with loud exclamations of delight.

'Shall we go straight in to supper?' said Father Finche.

I watched Robert as he ate cold beef and bread, the last rays of the sun slanting through the window and sparking golden flashes of fire off his knife. He became very animated as he told us the tales of his voyage.

'If you think it's hot here in the city you should have been with me in Aleppo. Or Smyrna. The sun on the top of a man's head can turn him mad. I took to wearing Turkish robes in Constantinople, like the natives, and found they served me very well. Perhaps I should adopt that way of dressing here while the weather is so warm?' he teased.

'That would cause a stir in church on Sunday!' laughed Mother Finche.

'I've brought you Damascus raisins and nutmeg for our puddings and some Moroccan leather to re-cover Father's smoking chair.'

'And the rest of the merchandise . . . ' I ventured.

'Never fear!' said Father Finche. 'I have looked over all Robert's purchases very carefully. Your dowry has been well spent and before long we will begin to see the return on our investment.'

'How long?'

'So impatient!' said Father Finche, his grey eyes amused. 'Has your time here been so onerous?'

'No, indeed! You have been kindness itself . . . '

'Ah well, I remember how urgently my wife wished to leave my father's house and set up her own household when we were newly-weds.'

'There's no hurry for them to set up their own establishment yet,' said Mother Finche. 'Robert has only just returned to us and we will wish to enjoy his company for a while before he thinks of a new home.'

I dropped my gaze to the table in case she saw the sudden animosity in my eyes. More than anything I longed for a home of my own.

'In any case,' said Father Finche, 'we need to keep the goods in the warehouse and sell them little by little so that we don't flood the market.'

My throat constricted. *How long?*

'Don't look so stricken, Katherine!' Father Finche laid a heavy hand over mine. 'You can start to look for a rented house. And when you find a suitable property, I'll buy you new furniture to start you off.'

'Thank you, Father Finche!' I kissed his sweating cheek and he patted my hand again.

'What happy days are to come!' he said. 'The warehouse is packed with the choicest silks, nutmeg, cinnamon, cloves, pepper and indigo. I'm never easy until a ship has safely docked. But now I can forget the bad dreams of sudden storms, shipwrecks and pirates that have plagued me over the past weeks.'

Robert yawned widely. 'It's been a long day for me and the ground is still rolling under my feet.' He looked at me sideways. 'But tonight I shall sleep in my own bed.'

'Why don't you retire early?' said Father Finche with a half-smile. 'You and your wife must have a great deal to talk about.'

The heat flooded my face and I could not look at him. All at once I didn't want to be alone with the stranger who was my husband.

Robert picked up our wine glasses and kissed his mother. 'Goodnight, Mother. It's good to be home.'

'It's wonderful to have you back.' She patted his cheek.

'Goodnight,' I said and followed Robert from the room.

Glancing back through the open door I saw Father Finch smiling knowingly at his wife.

Upstairs, the maid had left a jug of warm water and Robert stripped off his shirt and washed, while I undressed behind the screen.

Fumbling with the ribbons of my nightshift, I took a deep calming breath. We had consummated the marriage on our wedding night but the month of preparation before Robert's voyage had been busy and we'd had little time to learn to know each other. Unworldly as I had been and with no mother to advise me, my marital duty had surprised me somewhat but I hadn't found it too disagreeable.

'Katherine!' called Robert.

I tied my ribbons and then loosened them again and arranged my curls over my shoulders. I was under no illusion that this was a love match. The Finches had been looking for a bride with a good dowry to allow them to expand their business and when Aunt Mercy's man of business made discreet enquiries in the city, they had been happy to arrange a meeting. For my part, I would have accepted a hunch-backed, cross-eyed dwarf to escape from my miserable existence cloistered in Aunt Mercy's cheerless house in Kingston.

'Katherine!' Robert called again.

Slowly, I left the shelter of the screen.

He lay on the bed, looking at me. 'Come to bed,' he whispered.

Chapter 2

I awoke early the following morning to find Robert lying spread-eagled across the mattress. I raised myself on my elbow and studied him, while I had the opportunity of doing so unobserved. His breath came in regular puffs and one tanned hand twitched slightly. Dark stubble shaded his chin. A pleasant but unremarkable face, neither handsome nor ugly.

The sun began to creep in through the shutters and the church bells rang the hour.

Robert took a deep breath and stirred. He stared at me with unfocused eyes.

'Good morning, Robert.' What had happened between us the previous night had been in the dark and now I couldn't quite meet his gaze by daylight.

He yawned widely and sat up, scratching at the bristles on his chin. 'We didn't have a great deal of time together before I left, did we?'

I shook my head.

'There were nights,' he said, 'lying on a bedroll on deck and looking up at the stars, that I thought about you and couldn't remember your face. It troubled me.'

'I found it the same myself!'

He kissed my hand. 'Now that I'm home we shall change all that.'

The tension of the past months began to ease a little and I smiled back at him.

'Why don't you call on me at the warehouse this afternoon, Katherine?' he said.

'I should like that very much.'

After dinner, while Mother Finche rested, I set off to the warehouse. The heat assaulted me as soon as I opened the front door. The black dog lay on the step again, gnawing at his haunch and I pushed past him, stepping over our neighbour's stinking rubbish, left out for the dustcart. Further down the street, an oily stain marked the ground where the perfume flask had broken. I wasn't sure if I imagined it or not but I thought I could still detect the faintest hint of violets hanging in the air, despite the pervading stench of decaying vegetables. Fleetingly, I wondered if the handsome Mr Harte had returned safely to Covent Garden. And how *had* he known that I was suffering from a headache?

When I reached the warehouse I found Robert with his head bent over his desk.

'Am I interrupting?' I whispered.

He glanced up at me. 'I've been making the last entries recording the new stock. Would you like to see the merchandise?'

He took my arm and unlocked a door from the office into the warehouse.

The dark and cavernous space of the warehouse soared above us but my overwhelming impression was of the sweet, pungent aroma of nutmeg and cloves, so intense it made the inside of my nose prickle.

Narrow ribbons of light crept in through the roof's wooden shutters but the warehouse was full of shadows. The walls were lined with racking and laden with crates and bales of cloth. A number of rickety ladders leaned against the walls and nets full of goods hung from the rafters. Barrels were piled as high as a man in the centre of the warehouse, allowing narrow alleyways between. Our footsteps across the beaten earth floor were curiously muted, as if the very fabric of the building sucked all sound away from us.

'The high ceiling makes it feels like a church,' I whispered. 'And the spices smell like incense.'

'You don't need to whisper,' said Robert.

'Are all these goods ours?'

'Father hires out some of the warehouse space to one of the chandlers who stores his timber and pitch over there. We deal in spices and Damascus raisins but there's money to be had in importing silk, cotton cloth and curiosities, too.'

I stared around at the vast quantity of goods. 'Did you bring all this back with you?'

'Some stock has been here for years, waiting until the moment, and the price, is right to auction it to the highest bidder. I've bought some handsome maroquin leather of the finest, softest quality but I shan't sell the skins yet. They'll be an investment for our future.' Robert thrust a hand into his jacket and withdrew a key. 'I'm going to take you to Mincing Lane. One of Father's acquaintances has a house there available to rent and I've borrowed the key.'

I couldn't suppress a squeal of delight and Robert laughed.

Mincing Lane was but a stone's throw from the wharves and conveniently close to the warehouse. We stood in the street and looked up at the house, an ancient half-timbered building, three storeys tall, with the first and second floors projecting out over the street. The thatch was new and the windows in good repair.

The prospect of having a home of my own so soon made my heart beat like a drum.

Robert unlocked the door and I followed him inside. On the ground floor there was a serviceable kitchen and a stillroom, several storerooms and a cellar. A narrow staircase led upstairs to a charming oak-panelled parlour and dining room, each with a hearth. I ran my finger over the polished panelling and then opened the diamond-paned window at the back.

'Robert!' I called. 'There's a garden.'

He came and peered over my shoulder. 'Look at the old apple tree; it's laden with fruit.'

Upstairs were one large and two small bedchambers. The floors sloped and you had to be careful not to knock your head on some of the beams but I loved it.

'What do you think, Katherine?'

'It's perfect!' In my mind's eye I saw embroidered bed curtains and soft rugs on the elm floorboards and a carved press for our clothes. I wanted desperately to make it into our home.

His expression was doubtful. 'It's not very large; certainly not as large as either of us are used to.'

'But it's cosy!' I couldn't bear it if Robert didn't want it. 'And it's only a step away from the warehouse.' I held my breath.

'At least there are three bedchambers. We could have a maid and there would still be one left for a nursery.'

It was as if he'd read my mind. 'Robert, you cannot *imagine* how I have longed for a house of my own. Living with Aunt Mercy was ...' I swallowed. How could I put into words the absolute misery of my previous life in the guardianship of a woman who hated me?

'Was what?'

'There was no laughter or sunshine,' I said slowly 'Only hours spent in silence learning my catechism. Or being beaten for some imagined misdemeanour and banished to my chamber for days on end.' Shuddering, I recalled her birch switch. I could still see the fine white scars across my buttocks from her frenzied beatings. 'I *long* to have a family of my own. I want to make us into a family as happy as the one I lost.' There, I'd told him what was in my inmost heart. I glanced up at him, afraid I'd said too much.

'Were you so very unhappy as a child?'

I nodded, the memory of it making my stomach churn.

He tipped up my chin and kissed me on the lips. 'I'll give you lots of babies, if that will make you happy.'

'Oh, it will!'

Robert's hands ran down my back and then encircled my narrow waist. 'What a shame there's no bed here. We could start making a baby straight away.'

'Robert!' I pushed him away, scandalised, but at that moment, if there *had* been a bed nearby, I would not have denied him. Our marriage may not have been a love match but all at once I was brimming with confidence for our future.

Later, I left Robert in his office and, my head full of plans for embroidering bed curtains and cushions for the little house, I walked back through the hot and dusty streets to Lombard Street.

Mother Finche was waiting for me in the parlour.

'Robert asked me to call on him at the warehouse and then –' I couldn't contain myself '– he took me to look at a house in Mincing Lane.'

'A house?'

'Yes. We have decided to rent it.'

'But it was agreed you would both stay here for a while!'

'Robert likes the house.' I judged it wisest not to say how much I loved it.

'Then I shall take a look at it to determine if it is suitable.'

'It is perfectly suited to our needs,' I said, surprised at how firm I sounded. Over the years I had learned never to argue with Aunt Mercy. Old habits are hard to shake off but this house was too important to me to capitulate to another's whims.

Mother Finche sighed. 'Tomorrow we'll make a visit to the Royal

Exchange. There was some very pretty wallpaper in one of the shops, which may do for your parlour.'

A surge of self-confidence flowed through me. I'd never dared to state my desires so clearly before and I was astonished at how easily my mother-in-law had accepted it. Nevertheless, I merely smiled meekly and said, 'Thank you, Mother Finche.'

A firm rat-a-tat sounded upon the street door.

Bessie's heavy footsteps came up the stairs and the door creaked open. 'Mistress Robert, there's a gentleman to see you.'

'A gentleman?' said Mother Finche, giving me a sharp look. 'For my daughter-in-law?'

'Mr Harte,' said Bessie.

A moment or two later Mr Harte paused in the doorway and I was struck again by how elegantly he dressed.

'Mr Harte,' I said, standing up. 'May I introduce you to Mistress Finche, my husband's mother?'

'Katherine told me about your brush with a runaway coach,' said Mother Finche. 'Please take a seat.'

He hesitated for a moment and I touched his sleeve lightly.

'There is a chair a few feet in front of you,' I said.

Sweeping the ground with his cane, he located the chair and sat down, crossing his long legs. I noticed that he wore cream silk stockings and fashionable red-heeled shoes with fancy silver buckles.

'Are you quite recovered?' asked Mother Finche.

'Perfectly, thank you.' He reached inside his coat, pale fawn today with a daring scarlet lining, and withdrew a small bottle. 'I've brought this for the young Mistress Finche for her kindness.'

The pretty bottle was made of pale greenish glass with white satin ribbon tied about its narrow neck. Carefully, I removed the stopper and sniffed at the contents. 'Oh!' Delighted, I rubbed a drop onto my wrist and then offered the bottle to Mother Finche. 'It's lovely!'

'What can you smell?' asked Mr Harte, a half-smile upon his face.

I brought my wrist up to my nose and inhaled again. Closing my eyes, I let the scent of it take me back in time. 'Roses. Those dark red ones that are very nearly black. And lavender. Honeysuckle?'

'You have a good nose,' he said.

'It reminds me . . .' I broke off, suddenly overcome with almost unbearable sadness. All at once I recalled my mother's hand stroking my hair as I sat upon her knee one summer's eve in the garden of our family home in Oxford. That last summer before she and my father were snatched away from me by the sweating sickness.

'What does it remind you of?' prompted Mr Harte.

'A summer garden,' I said. 'A beautiful summer garden.'

He smiled. 'I like that. This is my latest formula and, until now, it had no name. I shall call it Summer Garden.'

Mother Finche rubbed a drop of the perfume on the back of her hand. 'It smells divine,' she said. 'I should be happy to buy some from you.'

Disappointment made me draw in my breath. I wanted this perfume, my summer garden perfume, all to myself.

Mr Harte leaned forward in his chair, his hands resting upon his silver-headed cane. 'Madam, may I suggest something a little different for you? Perhaps you would care to call on me in Long Acre by Covent Garden?' His voice was rich and persuasive, like honeyed mead. 'For someone of your sophistication I might suggest Flower of India or perhaps Promise of the East. Two ladies in one house should wear different perfumes, don't you think?'

Mother Finche returned the bottle of Summer Garden into my outstretched hand. 'Long Acre, you say? Is that by any chance the House of Perfume?'

Mr Harte nodded. 'You've heard of it?'

Her pale blue eyes opened wide. 'What lady of quality has not? Your perfumes and pomades are displayed on the dressing tables of all the smartest boudoirs in the city.'

'May I expect you then at the House of Perfume?' asked Mr Harte.

'I should be delighted.' Mr Harte had Mother Finche simpering like a girl.

He stood up. 'Until then, dear lady.' Turning to me, he said, 'Perhaps you would be so kind as to see me to the door?'

He took my arm as lightly as a feather and I led him downstairs. I opened the front door and a blast of heat and sunlight came bursting into the shadowy hall with all the subtlety of a blacksmith's furnace.

'Thank you for your gift,' I said, looking at Mr Harte's hair, as thick and golden as a field of ripe wheat in the light of the sun.

He lifted my hand as if to kiss it but then turned it over and delicately sniffed my wrist, sending a disturbing shiver up my arm. 'Summer Garden complements the natural scent of your skin.' He smiled conspiratorially. 'And I understand perfectly your wish that your mother-in-law shouldn't share it with you.'

'Perhaps that's selfish of me?'

'Not at all.' He put on his hat. 'Is your headache quite better?'

I laughed. 'You aroused my curiosity. How *did* you know that my head ached that day?'

Smiling, he said, 'I am a perfumer, Mistress Finche. Oil of lavender is a favourite cure for ladies' headaches. And I heard something in your voice that indicated you were in pain. Wear Summer Garden every day while the sun is so fierce and the lavender in the formulation will keep headaches at bay.'

'I will.'

He bowed and turned to leave.

'Be careful!' I warned. 'There are steps ...'

'Three.' He located the top step with his cane. 'Is the dog still there?'

'No, he's gone. He usually returns in the evening. I think our maid feeds him scraps from the kitchen.'

Mr Harte navigated his way down the steps. 'Good day to you, Mistress Finche.'

I knew better than to offer to guide him this time. 'Thank you again for the perfume. It will bring me a great deal of pleasure, especially while the city is so overheated and full of noxious odours.'

'Wait a while until the top notes have evaporated and then sniff your wrist again.' He said. 'You may find it surprising.' He replaced his hat, bowed and set off down the street.

I watched him go, intrigued as to how a blind man managed to dress so stylishly. A wife perhaps, who took pride in making sure that her husband was always well turned out?

Robert came home early that evening. 'It's all arranged,' he said at supper. 'I've agreed to rent the house in Mincing Lane for a year.'

I jumped up from the table to hug him. 'Thank you, thank you, Robert!'

'It would seem you've made your wife very happy, my boy,' said Father Finche, reaching for the wine bottle. 'A toast! To your new home!'

Dazed with happiness, I drank my wine too fast and choked. Robert thumped me on the back and when the commotion was over I saw that Mother Finche's eyes were bright with tears and my own happiness filled me with compassion.

Reaching across the table, I took her hand. 'Mincing Lane is only a few streets away. Robert and I will often ask you to join us for dinner and I shall be very glad of your advice on furnishing the house.' The latter was a barefaced lie but she looked so sad.

Mother Finche sighed heavily and squeezed my hand. 'Since my daughter has forsaken me, Robert is all I have left.'

'But you shall see Robert whenever you wish.' There was no malice in Mother Finche, only a little vanity and an inability to let her son go.

She sighed again and I was relieved when Bessie came then to clear the plates and bring in sweet wine and candied apricots.

Chapter 3

That night I sat at the dressing table in my nightshift while Robert undressed.

'What happened between your mother and your sister?' I asked.

'Sarah married beneath Mother's expectations.' Robert pulled off his shirt and dropped it on the floor. 'James is a curate on a small income and Mother wouldn't give them her blessing. They married anyway but Mother refused to attend the wedding. Sarah has never forgiven her. She doesn't write or visit and it's broken Mother's heart.'

'How sad.'

'I've attempted to persuade Sarah to invite Mother to stay but they are each as stubborn as the other, I'm afraid,' said Robert, unbuttoning his breeches and stepping out of them.

Slowly, I smoothed a few drops of Summer Garden on my wrists and behind my ears,

Then he stood before me, naked as the day he was born.

'Of course, what Mother needs,' he said, 'is a grandchild to dote on.'

I stood up, aware that the candle on the dressing table behind me silhouetted my body through the thin cotton of my nightshift. 'I'm sure you're right,' I said.

Later, while Robert snored gently beside me in satiated sleep, the wind began to tease the shutters. Hot and sticky, I couldn't sleep. Our lovemaking had been over very quickly, leaving me strangely unmoved, but Robert had seemed satisfied. Smiling a little into the dark, I wondered if his seed had already taken root within me. Perhaps, God willing, by next May there would be a baby in a cradle under the apple tree at Mincing Lane?

The wind began to rise and the shutter banged back and forth. I slipped out of bed and went to the window, allowing the breeze to lift my hair and cool my naked skin. The street was dark and empty, lit only by a few glimmering lanterns hanging in the doorways. I always liked that time of night, the secret time, while the city slept.

Footsteps echoed along the street and then the night watchman called out, 'One of the clock and all's well!'

I shrank back so that he couldn't see my nakedness and latched the shutters.

Sliding under the sheet a waft of Summer Garden drifted towards me and I detected a richer, deeper perfume under the top notes of rose and lavender. Puzzled, I lay quietly in the perfume's warm embrace, remembering that Mr Harte had said it would surprise me. Then the answer came to me: jasmine. Once the perfume had warmed on my skin, the intense base note of jasmine came to life after dark, just as it did in a summer garden.

Smiling, I yawned and then slept.

A loud bang woke me and I sat up in the dark. The shutters must have worked loose again. But it wasn't the shutters.

'Master Robert!'

Hastily, I shook Robert awake while I scrabbled into my night-shift just in time to preserve decency as the bedchamber door flew open.

'Master Robert!' Bessie's agitation caused her to spill wax from the candle onto her wrist and she nearly dropped the candlestick. 'The church bells ringing backwards woke me up. It's a warning! There's a fire down by the river and your father wants you to go and see if it's near the warehouse.'

Robert was out of bed and pulling on his breeches in a second, heedless of his nakedness and of Bessie's wide-eyed shock.

'I'm sure it's nothing to be concerned about,' he said. 'I'll be back by breakfast.'

I drifted into uneasy sleep, waking again at dawn. The bed beside me was still empty. Unlatching the shutters, I leaned out of the window. There was nothing to see, since our bedchamber faced north away from the river but there was a faint acrid smell in the air. I dressed and hurried across the passage to the guest room, which looked south. A drifting cloud of smoke hung over the houses in the distance. It seemed to me that there was a great deal of smoke for a house fire. Disquieted, I went downstairs.

Father Finche was already in the dining room, drinking coffee.

'There's smoke towards the river,' I said, pouring coffee for myself, 'and I thought Robert would be home by now.' I sipped the bitter brew and burned my tongue. Father Finche always liked his coffee as black as soot.

'I'm going to see what's happening, Katherine.'

A couple of hours later, I was worn to a frazzle with Mother Finche's unending anxious questions and made my escape to the kitchen to ask Bessie to bring more coffee and some bread and cheese.

Bessie and the cook, Mistress Higgins, were standing by the back door gossiping with the coal man and his boy.

'It's terrible!' said Bessie, her greasy hair escaping from her cap. 'More'n three hundred houses are on fire.'

'And London Bridge is burning and no one can escape to the south of the river.' The coalman's eyes shone with fevered excitement. 'You can't imagine the heat of the flames and the choking smoke, all stirred up by the wind. The great waterwheel under the bridge has caught alight,' he said, shaking his head. 'It's fallen off its axle into the mud.'

'But how will we manage?' said Mistress Higgins, her face pink with indignation. 'The master doesn't pay six shillings and eight pence a year to the water company to fill our cistern for me to have to fetch the water from public conduits.'

'The fire's taken a hold and no mistake,' said the coalman, wiping his nose on his sleeve. 'Ah well, best get on; we've coal to deliver.'

Mistress Higgins cut a slice of bread and took a wedge of mouldy cheese from under an inverted bowl on the dresser. She trimmed it deftly with a sharp knife and then whistled out of the back door.

A black dog appeared as quick as a flash and sat at her feet.

Mistress Higgins threw the cheese into the air and the dog leaped up and caught it between its jaws with a snap.

'This is the dog that often sits on the front doorstep, isn't it?' I said.

'It's not doing any harm,' said Mistress Higgins, folding her brawny arms and looking at me with the light of battle in her eye.

I looked at the dog and he looked at me. He was an ordinary street dog of no particular variety with a white blaze on his chest, but his brown eyes were full of intelligence. Tentatively, I held out a hand for him to sniff and then patted his head.

'Better the dog has the scraps than the rats,' said Mistress Higgins.

Bessie put a pot of coffee on the tray and I followed her back upstairs.

I opened the parlour window and hung out over the sill. A heat haze still shimmered above the ground and a lowering cloud of black smoke hung above. There were an unusual number of loaded carts rumbling over the cobbles and people in a hurry, some pushing handcarts, dodged in and around them. Uneasy, I closed the window to keep the smoke out.

Later, Mother Finche and I picked at our dinner.

'I'm so worried,' she said. 'Surely John and Robert should have returned by now?'

'I can't settle to anything,' I said. 'I'm going to the warehouse to see what's happening.'

Lombard Street was crowded with pedestrians, carts and carriages. Turning into Gracious Street I struggled against a flood of people hurrying in the opposite direction. Smoke whirled in a mischievous wind that snatched at my hair, whipping it across my face.

'You can't go that way, miss.' A man bent half double from the weight of carrying a large backpack blocked my way. 'The houses down there are all ablaze and a spark landed on the roof of Saint Laurence Pountney and the fire caught under the lead. The church went up almost at once, even before they could take out the church plate.'

I stared down Gracious Street and saw a pall of thick black smoke. 'But I must go down Fish Hill.'

'You can't,' the man said.

Reluctantly, I retraced my steps and turned east into Fenchurch Street and then south into Mincing Lane. But my apprehension grew when clouds of choking smoke made me turn back.

Frightened now, I pushed through the crowded streets until I found a way through Seething Lane and into the eastern end of Tower Street. The noise and confusion was terrible; children cried, dogs barked and all the while carts overloaded with household possessions rolled along like a retreating army. Jostled from side to side, I was terrified of losing my footing and being trodden underfoot.

Then, down one of the alleys into Thames Street, I caught a glimpse of a wall of orange flames and over the shouts and screams came the roaring of the inferno. Horror struck, I turned back and cut through the web of lanes that led down to the river.

At last I came to the warehouse. Barrels, boxes and bales of cloth were piled high in the yard but there was no sign of either Robert or Father Finche. I was standing in the doorway calling for them when two shabbily dressed young men ran into the yard, tipped one of the barrels onto its side and began to roll it away.

'Hey!' I called. 'Where are you taking that?'

'To the river,' one of them shouted back over his shoulder.

They ran off, laughing raucously.

Realisation dawned and a tide of anger boiled up from the bottom of my shoes. They'd stolen the barrel; the barrel of goods that had been bought with *my* dowry!

'Stop, thief!' I screeched. Snatching up a stone from the dusty ground, I flung it after them but they didn't even look back. My unsuitably flimsy shoes slipped and slid in the dust as I ran and I barely kept the scoundrels in sight as they hurtled along, rolling the barrel between them. They gave quarter to no man as they thundered along the wharf knocking pedestrians aside.

I threw another stone at them with the full force of my anger, exulting in the bellow of rage when it caught one of the miscreants on the back. Nearly expiring with heat and gasping to catch my breath, I heaved in a lungful of smoke and leaned against a wall, coughing. Both men and the barrel disappeared into the swirling smoke.

Flakes of ash drifted down like snow. The myriad of wooden houses, boat sheds, fish shops and chandlers' yards crammed together by the waterfront only fifty yards away were burning fiercely, fed by the maritime stores of rope, hemp and tar.

A never-ending stream of people hurried down to the river, which teemed with boats. Large and small, they were all heavily laden with boxes of cooking pots, bundles of bed linen and crates of chickens.

I hurried back to the warehouse, where I found Robert and Father Finche heaving more barrels into the yard. Dabbing perspiration from my top lip, I said, 'Two men stole one of our barrels. I chased after them and threw stones at them.'

'Did you, by God!' Robert gave a shout of laughter.

'We've more to worry about than losing one barrel,' said Father Finche, red faced and sweating. 'I sent Matthew to hire a boat so we can take the goods to safety. Why doesn't he come?'

'I doubt there's a boat left,' I said. 'The river is so thick with boats that you could walk to the opposite bank using them as stepping stones.'

'The fire is coming closer by the minute,' said Robert, glancing over his shoulder at the smoke.

'It won't reach the warehouse, will it?' But even as I asked the question I knew that it was a strong possibility.

'William Holland's warehouse is still between us and the fire,' said Robert, nodding at the roof of the warehouse looming over the yard wall.

'What can I do?' I asked.

The three of us worked together in silence carrying whatever we could from the warehouse into an untidy heap in the yard while the smoke became so thick that we had to tie handkerchiefs over our noses.

A couple of hours later my arms and back ached from the unaccustomed physical work and when Robert and I dumped yet another crate into the yard I stopped to stretch out my back. 'Will we be able to fit all this on a boat?' I asked.

Robert wiped perspiration off his forehead with the back of his hand. 'We don't even know if there is a boat.'

'There has to be,' said Father Finche, his face set. 'The goods are barely any safer in the yard than in the warehouse.'

'I can't believe the fire will reach us,' said Robert. 'This warehouse was here before I was born and it'll still be standing when there's moss growing on my gravestone.'

'Don't say that!' I said, shivering suddenly, despite the heat.

Running footsteps made us turn to see a man sprinting into the yard.

Father Finche sighed in relief. 'Matthew,' he said, 'where have you been? What news?'

'For the love of God, come and help!' Matthew cried. His carroty hair had pulled free from its confining ribbon and curled wildly around his face. 'William Holland's warehouse is afire. The timbers are so dry it's burning fast.'

'Did you find a boat?' Father Finche gripped his clerk's shoulders in a grip of iron.

'There are none to be had.'

Father Finche's face blanched.

'I couldn't even hire a handcart or a boy to push it,' said Matthew, his freckled face red from the heat and the effort of holding back tears. 'There are no horses and the whole city is on the run. Hurry, we must go now to put out the fire at the Holland warehouse or we'll be lost. The wind is blowing sparks far and wide and everything is so dry that they catch wherever they land.'

Without another word we ran after Matthew. At the waterfront a chain of men passed buckets of water from hand to hand from the river to the Holland yard. Ladders leaned against the warehouse and men took it in turns to clamber up and throw water onto the flaming thatch of the roof.

'It's hopeless!' said Father Finche, shouting over the roar of the flames. 'You might as well try to piss the fire out.'

A sudden spurt of flames shot high in the air and scattered fire-drops over us. I gasped as a cinder landed on my shoulder and I felt it sting before I had time to brush it off.

The roof timbers collapsed into the warehouse with a loud groan, echoed by the men who stood by watching in horror. A great blast of hot air followed, scorching our faces.

'Holland's warehouse is full of casks of brandy and olive oil. They'll feed the fire,' shouted Father Finche.

Almost before the words were out of his mouth an explosion rent the air. I screamed, clapping my hands over my ears as a searing blast rocked us and flaming brands shot over our heads.

I saw Robert, open-mouthed, as he watched a mass of blazing thatch fly in an arc above us over the wall onto the roof of the Finche warehouse. 'God help us,' he whispered.

Father Finche yelled for help and the men abandoned the Holland warehouse, dragged the ladders to the wall and scrambled over it to Finche's yard.

Hampered by my skirts, I ran the long way round down to the waterfront and up the alley, the breath sobbing in my throat. Stones cut through the thin soles of my shoes and I was limping by the time I reached the yard. A quiver of ice-cold shock ran through me when I saw that the Finche warehouse roof was already on fire.

Shouting directions, Father Finche organised a chain of men down to the river and I pushed myself into the middle of it, ignoring the men's surprised glances. It was hot, heavy work and my palms soon blistered. I allowed my mind to go blank as the leather buckets flew from hand to hand, refusing to acknowledge that the fire was growing fiercer by the second.

Another explosion roused me. The warehouse roof was alive with great dancing flames and a plume of black smoke poured from one end.

'There's no hope for it,' said Matthew Lunt. He put down his bucket and wiped sweat and tears from his eyes. One by one the rest of the men gave up and dropped their buckets before leaving the yard.

Robert, Father Finche and a small group of men stood in a silent huddle before the warehouse watching it burn.

'I forgot the maroquin hides!' said Father Finche. 'And the embroidered silks! I know just where they are . . . '

'Are you out of your senses!' shouted Robert.

His father ignored him and ran off.

Robert raced after him and I followed. By the time I reached the back of the warehouse the two men were wrestling with each other. Then Father Finche punched Robert in the face with such force that he fell to the ground, a hand clasped to his bleeding nose.

Father Finch shook off my restraining hands, unlocked the rear door of the warehouse and went inside.

I pulled Robert to his feet, exclaiming at the blood gushing from his nose. Before I could stop him, he'd followed his father inside.

I glanced up at the blazing roof. There was still time. I stepped over the threshold.

The warehouse was full of smoke and I pulled up my overskirt to make a thick pad over my nose. The popping and spitting of the fire was dreadful as the greedy flames licked high up through the roof, reaching for the sky. Golden sparks dropped continuously, setting afire the chandler's stacks of timber and pitch stored beneath.

Then I glimpsed a movement through the billowing smoke. 'Robert! Father Finche!' Coughing, I felt my way forwards. Burning debris fell from the roof as I crept closer to the fire.

The air began to fill with the pungent smell of roasting nutmeg, cinnamon and cloves, even stronger than the acrid smoke, making me cough and my eyes water. Row upon row of spice barrels were ablaze, burning with sudden fizzing flares of rainbow colours.

A creaking and a groaning above made me look up and I squealed and jumped back as the roof caved in, crashing to the ground. An avalanche of flaming thatch and glowing timbers followed.

A scream cut through the raging clamour of the fire and my stomach turned over in fear. Crawling on hands and knees across the earth floor, I was able to creep under the worst of the smoke.

I found Robert, struggling to lift a heavy roof beam and cried out in horror when I saw that Father Finche lay underneath it, trapped by his legs. The other end of the beam was glowing red and flames leaped up towards the hole in the roof.

'I can't lift it!' Robert's voice was high-pitched with terror. 'I don't know what to do.'

‘Help me!’ screamed Father Finche. ‘For God’s sake get me out before I burn!’

‘You need a lever.’ I crawled across the floor again and pulled a sturdy plank off the pile of the chandler’s timber. Suddenly blood-curdling shrieks came from behind me and, whimpering with dread, I crawled back to the others, dragging the plank with me.

Father Finche’s clothes were alight and Robert, blood still dripping from his nose, was trying to beat out the flames with his bare hands.

I dropped the plank and threw myself on top of Father Finche, muffling the flames and his terrible screams with my skirts. After a few minutes the flames were extinguished but Father Finche still shrieked in pain and terror.

‘Thank God!’ said Robert. He snatched at the plank and levered the beam up a fraction. ‘Pull him free!’ His eyes bulged and his arms quivered as he strained.

I slid my hands under Father Finche’s shoulders and hooked him with my forearms, pulling with all my might. I ignored his pitiful cries as, coughing and choking, I heaved again. Desperation gave me strength and after what seemed like an age, I felt him shift a tiny amount. ‘Just a bit more!’ I shouted.

Robert grunted, the beam gave a little and I fell backwards as Father Finche slithered free. Shutting our ears to the poor man’s moans, Robert and I pulled at his arms. Half carrying, half dragging Father Finche and coughing fit to burst, we fell through the door into the yard.

Chapter 4

Mother Finche was frantic. She screamed when she saw Father Finche's burns and Robert's blood-smeared face and clothing. Wild-eyed, she ran her hands over her son until she had assured herself that he was only a little singed.

She sent Bessie to fetch water, bandages and burn salve and wiped her menfolk clean, exclaiming aloud at every new cut and blister.

Father Finche groaned, crying out when his burns were bandaged.

Afterwards, Robert took hold of his mother's hands. 'There's no easy way to tell you this, Mother. We've lost the warehouse.'

She stared at him, uncomprehending. 'But the new cargo is stored there.'

'Not any more,' said Robert, grimly. 'And the city is burning out of control.'

'Then it must be stopped!'

Robert ran a hand through his hair, his face ashen. 'All we can do is pray for a miracle.'

Suddenly inexpressibly weary, I left them to their lamentations and went upstairs to take off my clothes, which were ruined beyond mending. My skirt was filthy and in places holes had been burned right through my chemise and petticoats.

Shivering and shaking from delayed shock, I stripped completely and scrubbed at my skin to remove the bitter smell of the smoke. The warehouse had gone, taking with it my hopes and dreams.

Sitting on the edge of the bed in that luxurious bedchamber, it was hard to comprehend that the terrible fire was raging only a short distance away. I couldn't shake out of my head the cloyingly sweet smell of our fortune going up in flames as cloves, cinnamon and nutmeg fizzled and flared in bright flashes of indigo, violet and orange.

Robert came into the bedchamber as I was about to put on a clean chemise.

His eyes were bloodshot. 'Father would have died a terrible death if you hadn't been there today, Kate. I didn't know what to do and I can never thank you enough for your bravery.'

'I only did what anyone would have done.' I sat on the bed while he stripped off his own stinking clothes and washed.

Downstairs in the parlour Father Finche sat in a chair muttering, while Mother Finche kept up a bright flow of inconsequential conversation. She looked up in relief as we entered the room.

'Robert,' she whispered, snatching hold of his sleeve, 'your father isn't in his right mind.'

'It's the shock,' I said. 'He'll be all right after a good night's sleep, I daresay. Perhaps,' I ventured, 'perhaps we should have some supper and then go out to see how much the fire has spread? It may be that we need to pack up whatever we can carry in case the fire heads towards us.' I spoke the words calmly but I could not still the shaking that seized me as I thought about the consequences of the fire reaching Lombard Street.

'Here? To the Finche house?' Mother Finche's cheeks flared scarlet. 'It won't spread this far! Will it?'

Robert's silence answered her and she burst into a storm of weeping.

I murmured soothing words until her tears abated. 'Let us go to the kitchen and ask Mistress Higgins to prepare our supper.'

But Mistress Higgins wasn't in the kitchen. Bessie, however, was at the table covering a basket with a clean cloth.

'Cook's gone,' said Bessie, 'and I'm off, too. My family lives in Bearbinder Lane and the fire's coming closer. If I were you I'd pack up and leave before it's too late.'

'You can't just go!' said Mother Finche.

Bessie raised her eyebrows and tossed her hair. 'Have you not looked out of the window today, mistress? There's a fire and the smoke's blacker than a pirate's heart and ashes are falling like snow.' Without another word, she hoisted her basket on her arm, opened the back door and was gone.

Mother Finche and I looked at one another.

'Shall we see what we can find for supper?' I said. 'The men haven't eaten all day.'

Mother Finche nodded and I set out some trenchers onto a tray and searched for knives and salt.

'Well!' Mother Finche's mouth pursed in indignation as she stood in the doorway to the pantry. 'That pert little madam has gone off with the chicken pie. There was more than half of it left after dinner yesterday.'

'I suspect that's what she was packing into her basket,' I said.

'Well, she certainly needn't look to *me* for a reference,' said my mother-in-law.

A search of the pantry revealed only a lump of mouldering cheese, half a loaf of stale bread, an onion and a few withered carrots.

'Why don't you go and keep Father Finche company and I'll do what I can here?'

Sighing, I set to work to make soup. While it was simmering I cut the bread and scraped the mould off the cheese. Opening the back door, I whistled and within a few moments the black dog appeared to eat the scraps.

He looked up at me, his brown eyes full of hope and I patted his skinny ribs before pushing him outside into the smoky air and shutting the door firmly behind him.

When the soup was ready I carried the supper tray upstairs, my blistered palms smarting.

'I'm going to see how far the fire has spread,' said Robert, a worried frown crinkling his forehead. 'If there's any likelihood at all of our house burning we need to be far away before we're trampled in the rush.'

'It's growing dark,' I said.

'I must at least see which way the wind blows.'

I went downstairs with Robert to speed him on his way. 'Don't take any risks, will you?'

I returned to the parlour with a heavy heart.

Father Finche had fallen into a restless doze and Mother Finche sat beside him holding his hand.

'I don't think we should wait for Robert to return with news,' I said. 'We should pack up whatever we can carry in case we have to leave quickly.'

Mother Finche's bottom lip trembled. 'I can't believe this is happening.'

'Don't think about it at all,' I said, taking pity at her woebegone face. 'There's time for that later. For now we must keep busy and, most of all, safe.'

Taking a deep breath, Mother Finche squared her shoulders. 'You're quite right, Katherine. I'm going to pack any money we have in the house and my jewellery. If the worst happens we may need to sell it.'

'Perhaps, if there's time,' I said, 'we should make bread? It's soothing to knead the dough and there's nothing else in the house to eat. Bread may be in short supply for a while. I'll set the dough to rise before we start to pack.'

Mother Finche sighed. 'I'll come and help. There's comfort in company, don't you think?'

Kneading the dough was a mindless task, which took our thoughts away from the terror stalking the streets outside. While the bread was rising, Mother Finche went to the parlour to look in on her husband while I packed a few kitchen essentials into a flour sack. I'd no idea how long we might be away, or if indeed we should ever be able to return. I carried all the silver down to the cellar in the fragile hope that if the house was burned the flames might not reach down so far.

Upstairs, I looked out of the guest chamber window but the glow of the fire and the sky full of black smoke only served to increase my fear. The street below was all hustle and bustle, as if the whole city was on the move. I packed a change of clothing for Robert and myself, including stout shoes, as I feared we might have to walk for some distance. Hesitating only a moment, I tucked my bottle of Summer Garden perfume and the lovely topaz silk into the bottom of the bag. As an afterthought I added a pot of burn salve and a large piece of clean linen that could be torn up to make bandages.

Robert returned just as the bread was coming out of the oven.

'We must leave now,' he said. A tic twitched at the corner of his eye. 'It's becoming impossible to move through the streets because they're so jammed with carts and people. I'm concerned about moving Father, but if the fire does come this way it will only be worse for us if we wait.'

'Mistress Buckley and her husband have gone to the country but we can stay with Mistress Smedley in Wood Street,' said Mother Finche. 'It's out of harm's way and then we'll return here when the danger is over.'

'We must bar all the windows and bolt the doors,' I said. 'There will be thieves out tonight.'

Robert and I started upstairs, locking the shutters. Drifts of smoke still weaselled their way in through the cracks.

In the kitchen, Robert hammered the shutter bar into the sockets with his fists. 'I tried to hire a cart,' he said, 'but it's impossible. One man asked me for forty pounds for a cart you'd usually hire for only a few shillings. Can you imagine!' All at once his face crumpled. 'I don't have forty pounds, Kate. The warehouse has gone and we're ruined. What are we going to do?' He covered his face with his hands.

I watched his shoulders heave and fear for the future gripped me. 'We must take your parents to safety; that's the *only* thing to think of now.'

He nodded and blinked back his tears. 'I'll go and see if Mother is ready.'

I bolted the kitchen door and shook it hard to check that the bolts were fast. Outside, I heard the black dog whining and scratching at the door.

'Go on home!' I called to him.

I wrapped the warm bread in a cloth, tied it across my body and gathered up the flour sack.

In the parlour Robert roused Father Finche and pulled him to his feet. The poor man looked about him, utterly bewildered.

'We must go, Father.'

'Where are you taking me? My leg hurts.' He touched his cheek and winced. 'What happened?'

'You were burned,' I said, taking his hand. 'Don't you remember?'

He shook his head but allowed himself to be led downstairs.

We gathered in the hall and I lit the lanterns. Mother Finche took one look at our pathetic bags of possessions and burst into tears.

'I don't want to leave!' she wept. 'We've lived in this house for twenty years and I couldn't bear it if anything happened to it.'

'Perhaps the wind will die down,' I said, 'and the fire will burn itself out.' But I'd seen the great leaping flames and felt the furnace heat of it and knew it would destroy everything in its greedy path.

'Come, Mother!' said Robert gently. 'Take Father's arm.' He opened the front door and ushered us out into the smoky street.

Mother Finche looked back at the door, her eyes brimming.

The sun had set and the darkening street was heaving with pack mules, coaches, drays and carts and not one of the people in the crowd hurrying by were without a bundle on his back.

A hot wind blew in sudden gusts, carrying with it flakes of ash and blowing my hair across my face so that I could hardly see where I was going. Bells rang, children cried and squealing pigs ran past, but there was nothing to do but launch ourselves into the noisy flow.

Jostled and pushed, we were swept along with the tide. Mother Finche screamed as Father Finche tripped and Robert only just managed to save him from being crushed under the wheels of a coach.

It was hard to see where we were going, with only our flickering lanterns to light us. Each step into the dark took us closer to an uncertain future and with each step the panic rose in my throat. I forced the thoughts away and simply carried on putting one foot in front of the other.

Almost bent double with the weight of the baggage tied to my back, I stopped in the shelter of a doorway to ease the load. Something nudged my knee and I looked down to see the black dog.

'It's no good following me,' I said to him, 'I've no food to spare. Go away now! Shoo!'

He sat on the ground and fixed me with earnest brown eyes.

'Hurry up, Kate!' said Robert.

'Perhaps I shouldn't have brought so much,' I said, readjusting the bundle of bread tied across my chest. 'After all, Mistress Smedley is sure to have enough food to keep us for a night or two.' I wasn't prepared to contemplate what would happen if we couldn't return to the Finche house after that.

The smoky wind buffeted us, snatching my skirts and making the lamp flicker. At last, battered and bruised we came to Wood Street near the city walls.

Mother Finche cried tears of relief and exhaustion as we approached Mistress Smedley's house. 'I don't care if we stay in the meanest servant's attic tonight on a lumpy mattress. All I want is to do is curl up and sleep,' she said.

But the Smedley household had already fled from the fire and the house was in darkness with every door locked and barred.

It was all I could do not to join Mother Finche in a fit of weeping.

A sorry party, we set off again by the pale light of the moon to rejoin the great press of people attempting to leave the city by Moor Gate. Chains barred the gate to prevent the carts pouring in from the countryside, whether to help carry the city-dwellers to safety or merely to make a profit, I wasn't sure, but the result was that no wheeled traffic could pass. Fights broke out amongst the desperate travellers and the smoky air rang with shouts and screams.

Weary and footsore, we finally reached Moor Fields in the middle of the night and sank down onto the dew-covered grass amongst the other families who had fled from the fire. Babies wailed and women wept but at last, in spite of the cold, hard ground and the howling of the wind, we slept.

Chapter 5

I dreamed the old dream again of Aunt Mercy whipping me with her birch switch, each lash across my naked buttocks making me scream in agony. She dragged me by my hair and threw me, sobbing, into the cellar where creatures scuttled over my feet in the total darkness.

The sound of a crying child woke me. I lifted my head, unsure where I was. A sharp stone dug into my hip and there was a crick in my neck from the sack of kitchen goods I'd used as a pillow. My clothes were sodden with dew. It was barely light but the heavy cloud above glowed with a nightmarish blood-red hue. And then I remembered the events of the previous day and my heart turned over, as cold as a stone.

Looking about me, I saw that the whole of Moor Fields was packed with a vast sea of people. Here and there a small fire flickered in the grey light and a few men wandered aimlessly about or stood staring back towards the smoke pouring from the still-burning city. Ash and pieces of burned paper whirled in the gusty wind and deposited themselves all over the inhabitants of the field.

A vision of the blazing warehouse and the choking stench of the burning spices came back to me in all its horror. I cried then, hot, silent tears of despair, seeping from under my closed eyelids.

At last I wiped my eyes on the hem of my skirt. Robert and his parents still slept. Father Finche, burns seared onto his cheeks, moaned in his sleep.

My own need became pressing and I picked my way in the half-light over sleeping bodies towards a clump of bushes near the edge of the field. I wasn't the only one who'd had the same idea and I found a dozen or so women lifting their skirts in the incomplete privacy afforded by the scrubby bushes. The men had taken themselves a little further off but, after all that had happened, modesty seemed to be of little consequence.

The others were awake by the time I returned.

Robert knelt on the ground with his arms around his weeping mother, while Father Finche limped up and down.

'A lifetime's work and my son's inheritance has all gone up in smoke,' he raged. 'How could I have been so *stupid*?' he berated himself. 'I borrowed from everyone I knew to bring home a cargo twice as large as usual. I risked *everything* so that I could cease work myself and hand the business over to Robert. And now . . . ' His face twisted in anguish.

'What do you mean, you risked everything?' asked Mother Finche. 'You're always so cautious. Whenever I suggested you purchased more goods than usual, you always said it was wise never to put all your eggs in one basket.'

'If only I'd heeded my own advice!' He gave a sudden vicious kick at his backpack. 'I wanted one last throw of the dice before I stepped out of the business.'

'Is nothing left?' Mother Finche's face seemed to have sagged in on itself and her hand trembled as it rested on her husband's arm.

Father Finche shook his head, unable to lift his gaze from the ground.

Robert's stomach growled with hunger. That at least was

something I could help. I took a loaf and a flask of ale from the flour sack. 'You must eat something,' I said, offering it to him.

He took it from me without a word and ate it with his eyes turned towards the burning city.

As Father Finche took a morsel of bread from me something touched my leg and I saw that the black dog was back again. I couldn't resist the appeal in his hungry eyes and gave him a little of the crust from my bread. He wolfed it down and then curled up on the ground beside me with his head on my knee.

All the while we ate our meagre breakfast more and more people arrived at Moor Fields, half fainting with exhaustion and shock. The fields became so crowded that there was barely room to sit down. We arranged our baggage around us and Mother Finche and I spread our skirts to lay claim to our little patch of grass.

During the following hours I dressed Father Finche's burns as well as I could. He had ceased to speak and appeared increasingly indifferent to his surroundings.

Mother Finche escaped from her grief by curling up on the ground and sleeping with her shawl over her face.

A family arrived, pushing an overloaded handcart of household goods and set up camp near us.

'What news?' asked Robert, glancing over his shoulder at the black smoke still surging from the city.

The young father rubbed his eyes, leaving white trails in his sooty face. 'Our home in Watling Street has gone. A hundred houses an hour are being consumed.'

'What about Lombard Street?'

'The fire raced up Gracious Street and then into Lombard Street.'

'The Lord save us!' whispered Robert. 'Our home is there.'

'I'm sorry to tell you the houses there all tumbled down, one after the other from end to end, thatch afire and walls crumbling from the heat of the inferno.'

'What is to become of us?' Wild-eyed, Robert clutched at his hair and glanced at his sleeping parents. 'However will I tell Mother and Father?'

Fear turned me to stone. I couldn't take it in; my head felt as if it were full of fog.

'I'm sorry for your trouble,' the man said, 'but there are thousands in the same state, including myself. All the places we know in the city are blazing. Even the Royal Exchange has gone.'

'But I was there only the other day,' I said.

I couldn't imagine that palace of delights, where every mercantile need could be met, turned to rubble. 'What about Mincing Lane?' I asked, frightened to hear.

'All gone.'

I pressed my hand to my mouth as I pictured the avaricious fire racing along the lane and engulfing the little house that I already loved. I imagined fingers of flame insinuating themselves through every little crack they could find and breathing its heavy, scorching breath onto the oak panelling in the parlour until it glowed and caught alight, forcing itself into every secret place and consuming everything until there was only a pile of ashes left.

'God knows what we're to do now,' said the man, an edge of panic creeping into his voice. 'I've three children and a wife to feed and my brewery's gone. The barrels burst when the fire boiled the beer and it ran out in a steaming river down the street.' He wiped his hand over his face again and turned back to his family.

I cannot bear to recall Mother and Father Finche's sorrow and fear when they understood that, as well as their business, their home of twenty years had gone forever.

'We're ruined,' mumbled Father Finche. 'I wish we'd perished in the fire for there is nothing left for us now but to live off the parish.'

'I'll not let that happen,' said Robert. 'I'll find work and support you.'

'But what are we to do until then?' Mother Finche looked at her son with tragic eyes.

'And who will employ you, Robert?' asked Father Finche. 'Businesses and homes have been destroyed and fortunes lost by so many. There may be no work.'

'If I have to empty cesspits I'll find *some* kind of work,' said Robert, fiercely.

My hand crept into his and I leaned against him. I think I loved him, just a little, in that moment.

A great groan of distress went up all over Moor Fields at eight o'clock that evening as the news came that St Paul's Cathedral was alight. A wind-borne spark had crept under the leads and the timber roof beams had caught fire. Jackdaws circled the spire as the roof hissed and spat as the lead began to melt and run out of the water-spouts, pouring into the street and making a river down Ludgate Hill. The sound of the stones cracking in the extreme heat was as loud as pistol shots and the coloured glass in the rose window liquefied. The heat and smoke were so intense that a jagged fork of lightning streaked down from the smoke cloud hovering above the blazing cathedral, followed by a deafening crash of thunder.

The crowd stared in horror at the conflagration in the distance, lamenting at the sight. Voices called out to God to forgive them their sins since Judgement Day was surely nigh.

Mother Finche gripped my hand until I winced. 'Pray that I will be forgiven, Katherine,' she wept, 'for I know I have been proud and covetous. I wish I'd never boasted to my friends of how much that purple silk for the parlour would cost!'

A rumour spread that it was foreigners who had started the fire and the crowd's anger grew. Someone said that fifty thousand Frenchmen had invaded and were coming to murder us and loot what remained of the city.

During the night the call of 'To arms!' woke us. Several men, made mad with fear and rage, armed themselves with sticks and brave words and set off for the city to seek out the bastard French and batter them to death.

We were woken again later that night when the King's troops marched the men back again and stood guard over us to ensure there was no more trouble.

But the following day the wind died down and before long we began to receive reports that the fire was no longer burning out of control. Some fell to their knees and prayed. Ship's biscuits were distributed from the naval stores, but they were hard as stone and so full of weevils that I retched at the sight. The black dog that still followed me about ate his fill though.

Later that day a stir ran through the encampment as a group of horsemen trotted across Moor Fields.

'It's the King!' went up the cry.

Roused from our misery, we stood up to gain a better view and I saw a tall man with a swarthy complexion and a hooked nose seated on a great black stallion. The King kept his mount under control as it pranced sideways, ears back and the whites of its eyes showing. Behind him smoked the ruins of St Paul's.

'The judgement that has fallen upon London is immediately from the hand of God,' he said, in a firm, clear voice, 'and no plots by Frenchmen or Dutchmen or Papists have any part in bringing you such misery.'

'He would say that, wouldn't he?' said Mother Finche. 'After all, his mother was French.'

'I have found no reason to suspect connivance in burning the city,' the King continued. 'I desire you all to take no more alarm. I have strength enough to defend you from any enemy and be assured that I, your King, will by the grace of God live and die with you and take a particular care of you all.'

The King ended his speech by promising to send five hundred pounds worth of bread to us the next day and the day after that and then, as the crowd gave a ragged cheer, he galloped away with his retinue, back to his palace for dinner no doubt. Meanwhile, we passed another wretched night in the open among the restless and fearful refugees.

Over the next couple of days the smoke ceased to rise in such volumes from the city and some of our number began to pick up their belongings and leave.

'Robert?' I said.

He turned towards me, his grey eyes red-rimmed and his chin bristly for want of a barber.

'We can't stay here.'

'Where do you propose we go?' he said. 'To our home in the country, perhaps?'

I flushed at the sarcastic tone of his voice. 'I've heard that army tents are being erected at Gresham Palace,' I said.

'I can't think about where we might go,' said Rob, a hand over his eyes. 'I can't think straight at all.'

Apprehension gripped me again. If I couldn't rely on my husband to be strong for us, what hope was there for our future?

'I'm told my home has tumbled down and burned but I must see it for myself . . . ' Robert looked away from me, blinking back tears.

Nothing I could say would ease his sorrow. Tentatively, I touched his sleeve. 'Shall we go then?'

We left Mother and Father Finche to guard our possessions and set off towards the city.

At Moor Gate I exclaimed aloud when we found that the heavy iron chains that had barred the way a few days before now lay twisted and melted on the ground. The air was still smoky and overheated, becoming hotter as we walked through a street of charred and blackened houses with their roofs open to the heavens. Venturing further into the city, we fell silent, barely able to comprehend the dreadful scene of utter devastation laid out before us.

The scorching air nearly suffocated us as we clambered over mounds of smouldering rubble. Almost all the houses had gone, leaving only the brick-built chimneys standing sentinel. An eerie silence had fallen over the ravaged ruins of the city; not a church bell rang, no horses' hooves or coaches' wheels clattered over the cobbles and the usual bustle of daily commerce was absent.

Beneath our feet the ground was still roasting hot and our shoes singed as we hopped from foot to foot. Here and there fires still burned brightly in the coal cellars of ruined houses. We came across a dead cat, its stiffened body dried out like a piece of old leather. Sheets of paper whirled in the heated air and I caught one as it twirled towards me. The bookshop owners and the printers had stored their books, paper and presses in St Paul's, believing that they would be safe there but the fire had respected no man or his treasures.

'How can we possibly find the house?' wept Robert. 'Nothing remains in this wasteland except the great ruin of St Paul's to guide us.'

I wiped the perspiration off my face with my forearm, far beyond caring that it was unladylike and that my clothes and person were filthy. 'You can see from one end of the city to the other,' I said, surveying the smoking ruins. 'It looks like some terrible desert landscape of Hell.'

'Oh, Kate, whatever are we to do?' Robert covered his face with his hands. 'Where can we go? How can we live?'

He clung to me with the terror of a drowning man as he sobbed and all the while flakes of ash drifted slowly down to the smoking ground to cover it with a blanket of sorrow.

Chapter 6

June 1667

I dreaded my regular visits to Lambeth. Clutching my basket over my arm, I rang the bell and waited. Footsteps clumped along the passageway and the peephole in the door scraped open. A bloodshot eye regarded me.

'State your business,' said a hoarse voice.

It was the same every time; you would imagine Dobbs knew my business by now. 'It's Mistress Finche, come to visit my father-in-law,' I said, heart-weary even before I entered the chilly confines of the debtors' prison.

The great iron bolts screeched, setting my teeth on edge, and yet again I vowed to bring some oil with me next time I visited.

Dobbs stood in front of me, his fat legs spread and hand outstretched. 'Well? Where's my garnish?'

I took the half-crown from my pocket and reluctantly handed it to him, avoiding the touch of his calloused fingers.

He tested the coin by biting into it and grunted in satisfaction. His smile revealed blackened teeth. 'Wouldn't want your ma and pa to end up in the Hole, would you?'

I shivered at the mention of that terrible, dark and stinking place he'd shown me beneath the cellars and followed him down the gloomy stone passage, damp even in June.

It was hard to believe that less than a year ago the Finches had lived in a fashionably furnished house in a smart street and were now brought so low. I shuddered at the memory of how we had taken shelter in an encampment of tents in the grounds of Gresham Palace. Living conditions had been harsh until Robert had secured himself a position as a clerk and we were able to rent a single room in a crooked house near Smithfield. But even then our troubles weren't over.

Dobbs lifted the ring of keys hanging from his belt, unlocked another gate and creaked it open. Light flooded into the passage. 'Twenty minutes,' he said.

Blinking, I emerged into the courtyard.

A boy raced past me, bowling a hoop. He was followed by a raggle-taggle of screaming children and I had to step back quickly to avoid the dust cloud rising in their wake. The courtyard was teeming with people, some walking arm in arm and others clustered in groups or sitting on the benches that surrounded the walls.

I searched the crowd and saw Mother Finche, now as thin as a rail; her careworn appearance almost unrecognisable from nine months ago. I remembered again how, one by one, Father Finche's creditors had come knocking at the door, demanding to be paid. Robert earned barely enough to feed us all a daily crust and there had been no question of settling the debts. Then, one dreadful morning in November, men came to carry Father Finche off to the debtors' prison.

Mother Finche glanced up and her face cracked into a smile of welcome. 'Katherine, my dear.'

Her clothes smelled fusty and her hollow cheek was dry and papery against my own. Already her eyes were on my basket.

I removed the cloth and showed her the contents. 'Bread, fresh-baked this morning and half of the carrot and turnip pie I made last night. There's a little piece of cheese and . . . ' Triumphantly, I withdrew the treasure. 'A whole gingerbread!'

Mother Finche was barely able to resist snatching it from my fingers. Her eyes welled with tears. 'Whatever should we do without you? The soup here grows thinner by the day with never a bone to flavour it any more. And then sometimes . . . ' She twisted her fingers together, her mouth working in her distress.

'Sometimes?' I prompted.

'John isn't strong enough to fight his way to the front of the queue to collect our fair share. A group of men here organise everything and if you don't please them life can be very hard.' She leaned forwards and whispered, 'Some of the younger women are prepared to give favours. They remain plump and pretty as long as they continue to please.'

'It's very hard for you, Mother Finche.' I handed her the neatly folded clothes from the bottom of the basket. 'Shall I take the dirty washing away with me?'

She gave me a wavering smile. 'If I can stay reasonably clean I can endure it.'

'Where's Father Finche?'

She shrugged. 'Where is he always? Lying on his bed and staring at the wall.'

We pushed our way through the crowd and Mother Finche led me to the foetid cell they shared with twenty others. A small, barred window high up in the wall allowed a sliver of light to penetrate the shadowy recesses of the chamber. The mossy bricks of the vaulted ceiling dripped moisture onto the wide wooden shelves lining the walls that served as bunks. A rat scuttled across the floor and hid behind a stinking bucket in the corner. I knew better than to wince at the sight and smell of the dungeon, ever since Dobbs had taken me to visit the unspeakable horrors of the Hole, I was aware that it was Paradise in comparison.

Father Finche lay curled up on his bunk under a thin grey

blanket. Full of pity, I saw how the flesh had fallen away from him and how his fingers lay claw-like upon his chest. Slowly, he turned his head to look at me.

'Any news?' he whispered through cracked lips.

'Robert is still trying to find a buyer for the building plot,' I said. 'But it's difficult. There are so many others whose houses have burned but who cannot afford to rebuild so land is cheap. And the plot still needs to be cleared of the rubble, which deters buyers.' I didn't want to tell him that the highest price he'd been offered so far wasn't nearly enough to pay off Father Finche's debts and release him from the debtor's jail.

It was time for Robert to face his father and tell him how hopeless it was. Each time I begged him to visit his parents he turned away, saying he couldn't bear the stink of the prison. We often argued about it and, increasingly, I felt little respect for a man who would put his own sensibilities above those of his suffering parents.

Father Finche coughed and turned his face to the wall again.

Mother Finche placed the provisions from the basket in the wooden box I'd brought her on one of my previous visits. Rats had already gnawed at the corners, deep parallel grooves showing pale against the dark stain of the wood. She tucked the box under her husband's blanket. Thieves, driven by starvation, abounded and it wasn't wise to display your riches.

'Dobbs will be shouting for me soon,' I said. 'Goodbye, Father Finche.' He didn't stir.

We returned to the courtyard and I took Mother Finche's hand. 'Why don't you come home with me?'

She shook her head. 'You know why. He'd never eat anything at all if I didn't drip a little soup between his lips every day.' She caught my arm. 'Tell me about Robert. Is he well?'

I nodded.

'Ask him to come and see us again, will you? It's been so long.'

'He's been working hard,' I said evasively. I couldn't tell her how much he hated to visit. 'Perhaps he'll come this Sunday.' I would do my utmost to persuade him.

'And how is Robert's work?'

I shrugged. 'Elias Maundrell is a mean old skinflint and makes Robert earn every halfpenny of his pittance. He's at the office from first light until after dark most days.'

'We had such hopes for him,' she said, shaking her head. 'I can hardly believe he holds only a lowly position as a clerk.'

'He's lucky to have work. Hundreds have nothing. I count myself fortunate that I manage to earn a little from my sewing.'

'And Sarah? Has there been a letter yet?'

I shook my head, sad to see the hopeful light fade from Mother Finche's eyes. I'd written to Robert's sister twice, hoping she would come to comfort her parents but it seemed the rift between herself and her mother was too great for forgiveness.

We stood by the gate waiting for Dobbs to let me out.

'You're a good girl, Katherine,' said Mother Finche. 'Strangely, even if John didn't need me, I don't want to leave this place. While I'm here I can imagine going from room to room in the Finche house, looking at all my lovely furniture and I can dream of walking down Lombard Street to the Exchange to buy myself some trifle that I have no need of.' She sighed. 'If I go outside I will have to face the horror of it all again.'

I hugged her, overcome with pity. I, too, often went to sleep at nights imagining the little house in Mincing Lane that was nothing but a dream any more.

I heard the rattle of Dobbs's keys in the other side of the gate. 'I'll come back soon.'

She clung to my hand. 'Bless you, my dear.'

A few minutes later I was outside the jail, breathing deeply to rid my nostrils of the stench of several hundred people cramped together without adequate sanitary arrangements. The smell seemed to cling to my clothes and hair, saturating me in hopelessness and despair.

I didn't have long to wait for a wherry and sat with the wind in my hair and the sun on my face, making me feel clean again, as the boatman pulled downriver towards Blackfriars.

I made my way northwards through the western part of the ruined city towards Dolly Smethwicke's house to see if she had any more sewing work for me. The city was still a bleak and forbidding landscape pitted with open cellars to trap the unwary. Not a church steeple stood and the ruin of St Paul's, its stones cemented together with melted lead, was a crumbling memorial to its former beauty. Carts ceaselessly trundled hither and thither carrying away charred timber, stone and debris.

Dolly's home in Aldersgate was adjacent to some of the last houses that had burned in the fire and she still relished telling the tale of how she'd watched the flames licking across the rooftops until the wind changed and her house was saved. It might have been better if her mean little hovel *had* burned. Several tumbledown houses were crammed together in a gloomy court where a group of ragged children were attempting to tie a bucket to a cat's tail. The poor creature yowled piteously and I shouted at the wretched urchins, who ran off shrieking.

Dolly chuckled and folded her arms over her ample stomach. 'Back again, then?' she cackled. Moon-faced with straggly white hair, her piggy little eyes missed nothing. 'I've been expecting you.'

The last time I'd seen Dolly we'd argued over the price she'd paid me for the chemises I'd completed for her. Years of manning a market stall had given her a sharp tongue and a keen eye for a bargain

'I heard you're looking for outworkers again,' I said.

She sniffed. 'Maybe.'

I ducked through the low opening and followed her inside. Half a dozen orphan girls sat around a table, sewing petticoats in silence by the dim light of the grimy window. The table was piled high with folded lengths of linen and baskets of finished petticoats were stacked against the walls.

Dolly rummaged around in one of the baskets and pulled out a bundle. 'Nightshifts,' she said. 'Ruffles and drawstrings around the neck. Gathered sleeves with frilled cuffs.'

'How much?' It was always best to get straight to the point with Dolly.

She sucked what were left of her teeth. 'Four pence the dozen.'

'The sun must have addled your wits, Dolly. I'll do them for a shilling.'

Dolly cackled. 'And you think the sun has addled *my* wits?'

'You know the quality of my work. I'll not rush them so that the seams come apart the first time they're worn. Eight pence the dozen.'

Lips pursed, Dolly squinted at me and I shrugged and turned to leave.

One of the orphans whispered to her neighbour and Dolly was onto her in a flash. 'Didn't give you leave to speak,' she snapped, slapping the back of her hand against the girl's head.

I opened the door.

'Six pence.'

I turned and looked at her. 'Half now.'

We stared at each other for a long moment until Dolly gave the smallest of nods.

I stood in silence while she wrapped up the bundle of nightshifts in a piece of clean cloth and waited, hand outstretched, while she grudgingly counted three pence into my palm.

'No later than Thursday, mind!'

Not deigning to answer, I left.

I walked through Smithfield but the market was over, leaving the reeking ground slippery with dung. Even though the hour was late the makeshift stall at the corner of Shoe Lane still had some carrots and turnips left and I used some of my earnings to buy our dinner.

It was as I hurried along Holborn that I saw Gabriel Harte. Dressed as elegantly as if he were about to attend a party, he walked with his silver-topped cane swinging gently before him. I hesitated and then remembered that he wouldn't be able to see my shabby clothes or the bundle of nightshifts in my arms.

'Mr Harte!' I called.

He lifted his head and smiled, his teeth very white.

'It's Katherine Finche,' I said, remembering all at once how handsome he was.

'I recognised your voice.' His expression became sober. 'I heard that the Finche warehouse and your home in Lombard Street burned. May I offer my sincere condolences to your family?'

'Thank you, Mr Harte.'

'For my own part, I never cease to be thankful that conflagration didn't reach as far as Covent Garden. How do you all fare now?'

'Pretty well. My husband has found employment and we have accommodation.'

'I'm pleased to hear that. There have been terrible times for so many and since I'd not heard of your whereabouts I feared the worst.'

'We all survived,' I said. 'Though I fear my husband's parents will never be the same again from the shock of it.'

'Will you bring your mother-in-law to visit me at the House of Perfume?' He smiled again. 'There is nothing so elevating to a lady's spirits as a new perfume, I'm told.'

'Perhaps,' I said, knowing that such a thing would never be possible.

'I must hurry away to an appointment,' he said, 'but I'm truly delighted to hear that you're safe and well.'

I took his proffered hand. 'Goodbye, Mr Harte.'

'Until next time.'

I watched him walk away and experienced a peculiar pang of sadness as he returned to his life and I to mine.

Nell's baby was wailing as I turned into the narrow alley where we lived, the sound drifting from the upstairs window. Then the black dog appeared from nowhere and danced around my feet, jumping up to lick my face. He'd refused to leave me ever since the fire and, somehow, I'd managed to find him scraps to augment what he could find by foraging in the streets. I called him Shadow since he tried to follow me wherever I went.

The front door of the house was ajar and I frowned; one of Nell's gentlemen callers must have left it open again.

I pushed open the door of our room and kicked off my pattens. This small, shabby room was no palace but it was a great deal better than living in the encampment at Gresham Palace.

Now, in the summer, our room was adequate, if noisome from the drain outside. In the winter the wind had howled through the shutters and blown down the chimney until Robert and I had been forced to huddle together, teeth chattering, and wearing all our clothes at once to prevent us perishing in the freezing air. It had been the coldest winter in living memory and the Thames had frozen over.

The door swung open and a pretty, fair-haired girl stood on the threshold.

'Charlie's crying again,' said Nell. 'And there's a gentleman expected.'

'Do you want me to take the baby?'

Nell nodded vigorously, a smile lighting her guileless blue eyes. 'I've made his dinner.'

I followed her upstairs and reeled back at the smell of an overflowing bucket as we entered her room. At fifteen, Nell was too young to be a mother without a family to support her. 'You haven't washed Charlie's breech clouts again,' I said.

The baby lay on the tumbled bed, screaming himself scarlet, and I picked him up, holding him at arm's length since his clothes were soiled.

Wordlessly, Nell handed me a bowl of grey-looking pottage and I retreated downstairs to my own room.

Too upset to feed, the baby screamed, pushing his fists into his mouth as I tried to comfort him. Poor Shadow hid under the table, terrified by the noise. I took off Charlie's wet clothing, and walked the floor patting his back until his screams turned to sobs.

Heavy footsteps went along the passage and clumped up the stairs. I heard Nell's girlish giggle in the room above and a man's deeper tones.

I sat on the settle and fed Charlie while, upstairs, the bed creaked rhythmically. Nell's gentleman caller must have been desperate for female company to put up with the foetid reek of her room.

Soon after, the booted footsteps clattered downstairs again and Nell knocked on my door. Charlie had fallen asleep in my arms.

'Is he all right?' she asked, her eyes anxious.

'Perfectly.'

'Thanks for having him. It's hard when he's not asleep . . . ' She lifted a shoulder and glanced away from me. 'You know . . . The gentlemen don't like it.'

'He's ten months old now, Nell. You need to find another way to earn a living.'

'Can't get no work as a servant with a littl'un.' She held out her arms.

After Nell had gone, I prepared the vegetable stew while Shadow sat by my feet watching me as intently as a hawk.

I wiped the table before opening Dolly's bundle of cambric and sorting out the pieces that made up each nightshift.

'Shall we sit outside while the sun is bright, Shadow?'

His ears pricked up and he followed me into the tiny yard, currently hung with the O'Brien family's washing.

Several hours later the shadows had lengthened when I heard Robert calling me. 'I'm in the yard, Robert!' I flexed my fingers and stretched out the knots in my back.

Robert emerged from the back door. 'Isn't dinner ready?'

I stood up too quickly and my scissors clattered to the ground. 'It'll only take a minute to warm up.' Glancing at his face, it appeared it was going to be one of those evenings when nothing would satisfy him. Giving up his comfortable position as heir to the Finche wealth had been hard for him and working for Elias Maundrell hadn't improved his temper. 'I have some more sewing work, 'I said, keeping my voice light and cheerful as I held up one of the nightshifts.

'How much?'

'Sixpence the dozen.'

'Couldn't you have got more?'

'Dolly only offered me four pence at first. How was your day?'

He shrugged. 'Miserable old skinflint docked my pay because I made an ink blot on the ledger. It wouldn't have happened if he'd let me have a new pen when I asked for it.'

I watched him clenching and unclenching his fists at the memory of Elias Maundrell's mean-spirited action.

Elias Maundrell was set to make a fortune, I reckoned, since his business was in buying and selling building materials and the whole of the city needed rebuilding. Of course, the war with the Dutch was still making it hard for supplies to reach London but that wouldn't last forever.

Robert ate his stew in silence punctuated only by sighs. When we finished I lit the tallow candle, washed up the bowls and put them away.

'I'm going to bed,' said Robert.

My heart sank. Robert was always tired these days but he couldn't sleep if I kept the candle burning. I knew I must continue with my sewing if Dolly was to have her order by Thursday but couldn't manage without the light.

'I ought to finish this nightshift.'

'Do it in the morning.'

I glanced at his face again and decided not to argue. I would rise as soon as it was light and work a little faster to make up for lost time.

A short while later I blew out the candle and slipped into bed beside Robert. Hesitantly, I reached out and touched his arm. Perhaps tonight . . .

He shook off my hand. 'Don't, Kate!' he warned.

Cheeks scalding, I withdrew my hand as if I'd burned my fingers. 'I only wanted to give you comfort,' I whispered.

'Two minutes of comfort and then there'd be a child to feed. You know we haven't enough money for that.' He heaved the sheets over his shoulder, turned his back to me and was asleep almost immediately.

I lay in the dark listening to the rats scuffling in the walls. Putting my hands over my ears, I distanced my mind as far as possible from the dreary existence that we lived. Again I imagined myself in the house in Mincing Lane but the life I craved seemed to be further away from me than ever.

Chapter 7

March 1668

The ale sizzled and spat as I took the poker out of the fire and plunged it into the tankard. I sprinkled a pinch of powdered ginger into the foaming ale and handed it to Nell.

She wrapped shaking fingers around the steaming tankard and sipped the contents. 'I suppose it's for the best,' she said, looking up at me with tear-drenched eyes.

I couldn't help but agree with her but merely wrapped my cloak around her shoulders to dispel the chills. In any case, the babe she'd miscarried that morning after a too vigorous visit from one of her gentlemen callers the previous night would soon have made it impossible for her to continue earning her living in that way. 'You have Charlie,' I said.

Hearing his name, the toddler looked up from where he was sitting on the floor and offered me a bite of the crust of bread smeared with honey that I had given him.

Shadow moved in, watching the little boy closely in case he dropped it.

Nell sniffed and wiped her nose on her wrist. 'I would've liked a little girl.'

'But you would have liked her to be healthy and not want for anything.'

'My Charlie don't want for nuffink!' She glared at me in indignation and I thought it would be heartless to remind her that without my help Charlie would often go hungry.

'Why don't you leave Charlie with me for a while and go and have a sleep until you feel better? And, Nell . . . '

'What?'

'You shouldn't receive any gentlemen for a week or two. You need time to heal.'

'But I've got to work. There's no money for bread.'

I sighed. 'Nell, you really must try and save a little for difficult times. I'll feed Charlie for a few days but you'd better not let my husband know. And when you've had a rest you can take yourself off to the Hind's Head and ask for work in the taproom. I've heard they're looking for a serving girl.'

After Nell had gone, Charlie sat by my feet playing with a cooking pot and a skimming spoon and I opened my wooden chest and delved inside. Right at the bottom lay my treasures. The bottle of Summer Garden perfume was cool in my hand and I recalled Gabriel Harte's conspiratorial smile as he persuaded Mother Finche to allow me to keep it for myself. I placed the tiniest drop on my wrist and sniffed at it. Closing my eyes, I summoned up the garden in Oxford and the soft tones of my mother's voice as she stroked my hair. Then, pulling the length of topaz silk from the chest, I held it against my breast and peered into the precious piece of broken mirror that I'd found in the ravaged city. The sheen and rustle of the silk was so beautiful it made me want to cry. I could see no occasion to wear such finery in this life.

Sighing, I put my treasures away and set to work, sewing as fast as I could before the light faded.

Later, Nell put her head around the door.

'Are you feeling better?' I asked.

She yawned and nodded. 'I'm going to the Hind's Head like you said.'

'I'll put Charlie to bed and keep an eye on him if they'll give you a trial.'

Impulsively, Nell hugged me. 'See you later then!'

I gave Charlie his bread and milk and nuzzled his neck. A yearning for a child ached in my breast. A baby of my own to love would be compensation for my loneliness and disappointing marriage. I sighed before blowing raspberries onto Charlie's skinny little tummy until he laughed fit to burst.

Humming as I carried the toddler about on my hip, I tidied up and collected carrots and a small piece of ox liver from the cupboard and placed them on the table ready to prepare supper. I covered the liver with a cloth; it was too precious to allow the flies to share it with us.

Charlie yawned and rested his head on my shoulder. His body became warm and limp in my arms.

Then footsteps ran down the passage, the door burst open and Robert erupted into the room. 'Kate! Guess what happened today?'

Charlie whimpered.

Robert stopped short. 'What's the whore's brat doing here?'

As quick as a flash I put my hands over Charlie's ears. 'Don't say that! Nell's gone to find work at the Hind's Head. I said I'd put Charlie to bed.'

'Well, hurry up then! I've something important to tell you.' His face was wreathed in smiles and he appeared in an uncommon good humour.

Curious, I hurried upstairs. It only took a moment for me to settle Charlie and then I returned downstairs.

Shadow sat at Robert's feet, resting his chin on his master's knees and gazing up at him adoringly.

'What's the important news, Robert?'

He withdrew a small package from inside his coat and put it on the table with a flourish. 'Open it!'

Shadow transferred his attentions to me as I pulled back the paper. I gasped when I saw two large mutton chops. We rarely afforded meat, except for the odd scrap of offal. 'Where did you get them?' I glanced up at him anxiously. 'You didn't steal them?'

'No, I did not, you saucy minx!'

'How then?'

'Bought them in the market,' he said, his eyes teasing.

'Robert! Tell me!'

He settled back in his chair. 'I'll have a tankard of ale to whet my whistle first, Mistress Finche.

'It was like this,' he said, a moment later, wiping foam off his top lip. 'Now that the Port of London is open again Pinchpenny Maundrell went out to inspect an order of timber from Norway.' He leaned forwards. 'I tell you, Kate, the Norwegians will warm their pockets for a long time as a result of the Fire of London. We'll take all the timber they can supply and be glad of it. Anyway, Maundrell was out of the office when there came a visitor to negotiate an order of bricks. I sat him down to wait and he began talking to me.'

'What about?'

'This and that. He's a big man, built like an ox, but he wears fine clothes and carries a silver snuffbox. His name is Standfast-For-Jesus Hackett and the world will hear more of him in the future, I'm sure. He has a compelling way of speaking that makes you feel he's destined for great things.' Robert's eyes gleamed with fervour. 'It transpired that Mr Hackett wished to place a large order for bricks and timber. He mentioned that he's looking for land to buy in the city and enquired if I knew of anybody who wanted to sell. So I told him about how the Fire ruined us and told him of the Finche plot on Lombard Street.'

'And is he interested in it?'

'I've sold it to him!' said Robert, triumphant. 'He gave me five pence a foot for it.'

'Will it be enough to pay off your father's debts?'

Robert shook his head. 'But we can pay off Anthony Sharpe, who's pressing me so hard every day.'

'But there isn't enough to release Father Finche from the debtors' jail?'

'Not yet but I haven't finished my tale. Listen, will you?'

I folded my hands in my lap.

'Mr Hackett said he could use a man like me in his office.' Robert stood up and paced the floor, elation making it impossible for him to sit still. 'He said my business experience was wasted as a mere clerk and a man of my worth should be elevated. Times are set to be very busy indeed in the building trade and he needs a right-hand man to help him purchase the materials and to sell his houses once they are built.'

I held my breath.

'And he's offered me the job for almost twice as much as old Maundrell pays me.'

'That's wonderful!'

Jubilant, Robert swept me up in his arms. 'So, on the strength of that, I bought the mutton chops. And if my wife would stir her stumps we might even have them for dinner tonight.'

'What about the liver?'

'To hell with the liver!' Robert snatched it up off the table and threw it over his shoulder.

Shadow took his chance, leaped into the air and snapped it up before it hit the ground.

'We could have had that tomorrow!' I said. 'When do you start?'

'On Monday. So I can tell Elias Maundrell to poke his rotten job up his arse, for all I care!'

'You won't,' I said, shocked.

'By God, I will! And if we continue to live carefully, we can put some by to pay off Father's debts. In a few years I'll be able to start up the business again.'

Privately, I wondered if Mother and Father Finche would survive the hardships of even one more year in jail.

Later, the room still rich with the smell of mutton fat and our stomachs comfortably full, we slouched on the settle with another glass of ale.

Robert belched quietly. 'That was the best dinner I've had since . . . ' He trailed off.

Since before the fire, I thought.

Robert went into the yard with a pipe of tobacco and I took the opportunity to run upstairs and peep at Charlie.

Downstairs in our room again, I undressed. Hopeful that tonight might be different, I lifted the lid of the chest and took out the little bottle of perfume and applied a drop to my wrists and throat.

Robert came in shortly after and blew out the candle before climbing into bed beside me. 'It's cold in the yard,' he said, shivering. 'There may be a frost again tonight.'

His breath was smoky on my cheek as he curled himself around me, seeking warmth. His hands slid under my nightshift and, as his breathing quickened, he suddenly turned me on my back, pushed his knee between my thighs and entered me. A few quick thrusts but, in spite of my hopes, he withdrew from me at the last moment and spilled his seed on my thigh. There would be no baby yet but perhaps we were about to move on to better times.

Chapter 8

June 1668

Humming to myself, I smoothed out the beautiful topaz silk over the kitchen table. Carefully, I marked out the pattern with a piece of chalk and then picked up the scissors. As I was about to make the first cut, the door opened and Charlie toddled in, followed by Nell.

Nell reached out to stroke the silk. 'Where did you get it from?' She looked askance at me.

'I didn't pinch it, if that's what you're thinking,' I said. 'It's one of the few things I saved from the fire and I've been keeping it back for something special. Robert and I have been invited to dinner by Mr Hackett and I'm making a dress to wear.'

Nell's blue eyes were wide with admiration.

'I think Mr Hackett wants to inspect me.'

'Well, anyone can see you're a lady, whatever you're wearing.'

'Why thank you, Nell!' I glanced at my hands, rough and reddened now from doing the laundry and scrubbing floors. I'd have to do something about that before I was presented to Mr Hackett.

Nell leaned forwards and whispered, 'There's this man that comes into the Hind's Head of an evening.'

'Ah! And he's caught your fancy?'

Nell blushed prettily. 'He's a stonemason, older than me, but he has such a merry twinkle in his eye. He's asked me to go to the playhouse with him tomorrow afternoon before I go to work. Would you look after Charlie?' Nell sniffed and wiped her nose on her skirt.

'Of course I will.'

Her face blossomed into a wide smile. 'He's called Ben Perkins and . . . ' She wrapped her arms tightly around her skinny little body. 'Oh, Kate, I do like him so!'

'I'll lend you my chemise,' I said, eyeing the greyish cotton frilled out over her stained bodice.

Her delighted smile illuminated her face. 'And will you teach me how to behave like a lady?'

'Well, you can stop blowing your nose on your skirt for a start.'

She nodded and then began to twist her hands together. 'I wish . . . ' She broke off again and muttered something I couldn't hear.

'What is it you wish?' I asked her.

Her lashes sparkled with tears. 'I don't want him to know about the gentlemen callers.'

That could certainly be a bar to the path of true love running smoothly. 'You haven't had any visitors for some time now.'

She shook her head vigorously. 'And I don't want no more. It was difficult after Mam died.' She avoided my gaze. 'I never liked going with any man who turned up on the doorstep but Charlie and I had to eat, didn't we?'

'It's different now.'

'But I couldn't work at the Hind's Head if you didn't look after Charlie because I'd never leave him on his own. I couldn't manage without you, Kate.'

I hugged her, thinking that she was nothing more than a poor motherless child.

'Better get on,' said Nell.

A few moments later the door closed behind them and I picked up the scissors and made the first cut into the topaz silk.

The following week I stood in front of the shard of mirror coaxing my hair into ringlets. I'd worn curl rags all day and was pleased with the result. My poor work-weary hands had been smoothed with goose grease and rosewater and I fizzed with nervous excitement at the prospect of meeting Mr Hackett and his guests.

I took the pair of cream stockings and shoes out of the chest and put them on. They were second hand, of course, but the small darn on the right stocking was too high up on my calf to be seen and the stain on the satin slippers was barely noticeable. The topaz dress lay on the bed and I slipped the bodice over my best shift. I hadn't worn a boned bodice with back lacing since the Fire because a front fastening dress was much simpler to manage now that I did my own cleaning and baking. It was a struggle to lace myself up the back without help and I found I automatically adjusted my posture to prevent the long point at the front from digging into me. I glanced into the mirror and smiled at how the wide neckline and the full sleeves flattered my shoulders.

The cool, slippery weight of the silk rustled luxuriously as I stepped into the skirt. Slowly, I walked across the room listening to the whisper of silk around my ankles. I opened the bottle of Summer Garden and dabbed the perfume between my breasts and behind my ears until the lovely scent floated in a flowery cloud around me.

I peered into the sliver of mirror again, angling it this way and that to try and see all of my reflection at once. My hazel eyes sparkled, my cheeks were pink with anticipation and I thought I looked very well.

There wasn't long to wait before Robert came home.

He took my hands and held me at arm's length, before giving a low whistle of approval. 'You've wrought a miracle with that length of silk, Kate. It's as fine a piece of workmanship as any French tailor could make.'

Praise indeed, from Robert! 'Would you lace me up more tightly? I can't reach the back properly.'

'I'm not sure how good a lady's maid I'll make,' said Robert with good humour, 'but I'll do my best.'

'You're certainly stronger than a lady's maid,' I said as he heaved on the laces. 'Just a little more. You can stop when I can't breathe any more. That's enough!' I glanced down to see that my breasts now looked as plump as pigeons.

Robert washed in the basin of warm water I'd prepared for him while I took out of the chest the handsome claret coat and figured waistcoat I'd bought in the same second-hand shop where I'd found my shoes and stockings. I watched him dress and was disappointed he didn't notice that I'd sewn ruffles onto the cuffs of his shirt, risking Dolly's displeasure if she realised that the last batch of petticoats were shorter than usual.

'I look quite the gentleman again, don't I?' he said, preening himself.

'Indeed you do,' I said, but in my eyes, the mark of a true gentleman lay in the manner in which he treated others rather than in his dress.

Nell and Charlie peered at us down the staircase as we prepared to leave. Nell clasped her hands to her breast. 'You look like a princess,' she breathed. 'And Mr Finche looks like a prince.'

Robert ignored her comment, turned his back and brushed a hair off the sleeve of his coat.

'Knock 'em dead!' said Nell, sticking out her tongue at Robert's back.

I smiled at her. 'I'll tell you all about it tomorrow.'

Chapter 9

Mr Hackett's house was an imposing new brick and stone mansion in Hatton Gardens.

'It's even grander than I expected,' said Robert as he lifted the heavy brass doorknocker.

The babble of conversation drifted down from an open window above and I tightened my hold on Robert's arm. 'I've attended so few parties,' I said. 'The only gatherings I went to with Aunt Mercy were funerals.'

Robert smiled. 'I hear that Mr Hackett entertains lavishly. We're certain to have an excellent dinner.'

A manservant in scarlet and gold livery opened the door, ushered us across the marble hall and up a sweeping staircase into the drawing room, richly decorated with gold damask, gilded cornices and mirrors.

We stood for a moment in the doorway, overawed by the splendour of the room.

'Here's Mr Hackett,' whispered Robert.

Head and shoulders above his chattering guests, Standfast-For-Jesus Hackett, a veritable oak tree of a man, strode towards us, the floor juddering under his heavy footsteps. Swarthy of face, with a narrow moustache like the King's, he wore a black wig arranged in glossy curls over his broad shoulders. Attired in a coat embellished with a great quantity of gold point work across his barrel chest, he cut an imposing figure.

'There you are, Finche!' His hoarse voice boomed out as loudly as a costermonger's as he enveloped Robert's hand in his own and gave him a playful punch to his arm.

Robert staggered slightly. 'May I present my wife, Katherine?'

Hackett took my hand and lifted it to his full, red lips.

I smiled politely, shivering a little as his moustache pricked the back of my hand.

'You're a dark horse, Finche! You've been hiding this lovely lady away from me.' Hackett's dark eyes gleamed as he looked me up and down. 'Let me introduce you to my guests. I've invited some of the richest men in London and we need to make good use of them. Move amongst them, Finche, and warm them to my business plans. Take your pretty wife with you to ease the conversation.' Taking my arm in a firm grip, he led us into the room.

Hackett introduced us to a number of guests and very soon my head began to swim as I tried to remember all their names. More guests arrived and Hackett went to greet them, finally letting go of me. I glanced down to see that the fine silk of my sleeve was creased and dark with sweat where he had clutched my arm.

'A most amiable man, isn't he?' Robert whispered in my ear.

'He's very . . . ' I watched him greet one of the new guests, with loud exclamations of delight and a great deal of back-slapping. Despite his fine clothes, there was something not quite gentlemanly about him.

'He's very what?' asked Robert, irritably.

'As you say, he's most amiable.' But Robert had already left my side to speak earnestly of Hackett's business ventures to a Mr Snodgrass, whose attention wandered as his gaze searched the room over Robert's shoulder for more worthy company.

'So, you see, there are interesting opportunities for investment in Mr Hackett's ventures,' said Robert, finally grinding to a halt as Snodgrass stared out of the window and took a pinch of snuff from his silver snuffbox.

'If I wish to invest in Hackett's enterprises –' Snodgrass whisked a filmy handkerchief from his coat to catch a gargantuan sneeze '– then it is Hackett I shall speak to,' he said, wiping snuff from the front of his velvet coat.

We were saved from any further awkwardness when I heard someone speak my name.

'Mistress Finche?' Gabriel Harte stood before me, with a fair-haired lady on his arm.

'Indeed it is, Mr Harte,' I said, my spirits lifting at his friendly smile. I noticed that he wore again the sea-green coat that so perfectly matched his eyes.

'I thought it had to be you since I could detect a hint of my Summer Garden perfume in the air. I made only a small quantity of that formulation and it suited you so well that I felt it wasn't right to allow other ladies to wear it. Please, allow me to present my wife, Jane.'

I took the lady's hand and she gave me a sweet smile. Her top teeth protruded slightly, and her deep-set eyes were grey. Curiously, she wore a plain gown of brown silk and no jewellery. Since her husband dressed in such finery I would have expected her to wear a more decorative gown herself.

'This is my husband, Robert Finche,' I said.

Mr Harte stretched out his hand to Robert. 'I made your wife's acquaintance when she did me a kindness some time ago.'

'Oh?'

'Mistress Finche helped my husband when a runaway coach nearly knocked him over,' said Mistress Harte. Her features were plain and she was in no way a beauty, but her figure was slender and her voice soft.

'A runaway coach? When was this?' asked Robert.

'In another life,' I said, 'the one we had before the Great Fire.'

'Many lives and fortunes were lost or changed forever by the fire,' said Mr Harte. 'A terrible, sad business and I heard of your troubles. How do you fare now?'

'My family lost everything,' said Robert, shortly.

'I am very sorry to hear that,' said Mr Harte.

'But my husband has lately become employed by Mr Hackett,' I said, hastily, 'who, I believe, has a great number of interesting plans with regard to the rebuilding of the city.'

'I suspect that is why we have been invited here tonight,' said Mr Harte.

Then a servant announced that dinner was served.

The dining room was magnificent. Crimson silk covered the walls and two glittering chandeliers, each a man's arm-span wide hung over a long table laid with crisp white linen and silver bowls of hot-house flowers. The beeswax candles were already lit, a gross extravagance since it was still light outside.

I glanced at Robert as we were shown to our places and experienced a moment of unease when he was directed further down the table, but then Gabriel Harte was seated on my left. I was relieved that I should know at least one of my dinner companions. A portly man with a grizzled grey wig and a florid complexion sat on my right.

'Charles Clifton, magistrate,' he said, his eyes firmly fixed on my bosom. 'And who might you be?'

'Allow me to present Mistress Finche,' said Mr Harte.

I barely had time to respond before there was a fanfare of trumpets and a dozen servants filed in, all carrying platters held high. My eyes opened wide at the array of roasted meats, a baron of beef, whole lambs and suckling pigs, haunches of venison, several roast peacocks prettily dressed with their tail feathers and quantities of golden quails and chickens on silver dishes.

'The venison smells most delicious,' Mr Harte said. 'Let me

guess . . . ' He sniffed at the air. 'Chicken. Lamb, of course, and pork. But there's something else . . . ' He shook his head.

'Another bird,' I said, entering into the game.

'Roasted swan?' He tapped his fingers on the table, frowning. 'No, you'll have to help me.'

'Like many birds, the male of the species is dressed very fine while the females are unobtrusive.' I glanced at his wife, contrasting her plain brown dress with the rich fabric of her husband's coat. 'The gorgeousness of his feathers may make him consider himself to be the king of birds,' I said.

Mr Harte's frown cleared and he laughed. 'You have given away too much, too soon, Mistress Finche. It must be the peacock!' he declared with triumph.

The roasted meats had barely been placed upon the table before the next wave of dishes arrived: pies, rabbit fricassée, oysters, several varieties of salads and ten poached pike on a bed of watercress.

The guests fell upon the feast. I described the dishes to Mr Harte and passed to him those that he wished to try. It fascinated me how well he managed to cut his meat, rarely fumbling or spilling any of the rich sauces. I noted how he lightly touched the tablecloth with his little finger to locate a clear space on the table before putting down his wine glass.

'Are you watching me, Mistress Finche?'

I started. 'Oh no. Well, that is . . . I was simply admiring how well you manage.'

'I had a good teacher in my youth. My uncle had been blind for many years before I began to lose my own sight.' He ran his thumb around the edge of his plate and then stretched out his remaining fingers until they touched his wine glass. 'You see, I always take particular care to place my glass in exactly the same location and at the same distance from my dinner plate, no matter where I dine, so I can always find it.'

Then Charles Clifton caught my attention, asking me to pass him the salt. 'Haven't seen you at one of Hackett's parties before,' he said.

'My husband is only lately employed by Mr Hackett.'

Clifton waved his knife at me, dripping gravy off the blade onto the snowy tablecloth. 'Mark my words, Hackett will go far! Tell your husband from me that he should invest in his employer's schemes. I certainly expect a handsome return.'

Clifton turned his attention back to his wine, while I reflected that it would be years before we cleared Father Finche's debts and had any funds to invest in anything except our most fundamental necessities.

Some time later, I surreptitiously eased my bodice, wishing I hadn't asked Robert to lace me so tightly. Glancing down the table I saw that he was absorbed in conversation with Sir Robert Viner, reputed to have advanced thirty thousand pounds towards the cost of the King's coronation. What exalted circles we were moving in now! I suppressed a giggle at the thought of the expressions on the faces of Mr Hackett's illustrious guests if they knew that we had been waved off for the evening by a whore and her bastard.

'Is something amusing you?' Mr Harte's voice broke into my reverie.

'Oh! No indeed . . . ' Mortified at the prospect of having to explain myself, I changed the subject. 'May I pass you some of the apple and quince pie?'

Mr Harte dabbed his mouth with his napkin. 'I think not or I may have difficulty in buttoning my coat tomorrow. Hackett certainly knows how to put on a banquet.'

The footmen moved amongst us on silent feet and trays of marchpane sweets and candied fruits were placed before us, together with glasses of sweet golden wine.

Mr Hackett pushed back his chair with a loud scrape and stood up, towering over us. He banged on the table with the handle of his knife and waited until all conversation stopped.

'Ladies, gentlemen!' He held his arms out like a preacher in the pulpit. 'I welcome you all here tonight and thank you for your presence in my humble home. But now I beg your indulgence for a few moments.'

Mr Harte leaned towards me. 'Now we come to the true purpose of the evening,' he whispered.

Hackett's voice was sombre. 'Those of you who were in London in September sixteen sixty-six and witnessed the savagery of the Great Fire as it raced through our beloved city, ferociously consuming everything in its path, will never forget the sight and sound of it. The great pall of black smoke, carried as far away as Oxford, the wicked roar of the flames and the screams of the homeless is engraved upon our hearts and still haunts our dreams.' Hackett's voice reverberated around the dining room and his guests were silent, each alone with his own memories of that dreadful time.

I glanced at Robert and saw that his face was set and his knuckles white as he gripped his hands together on the table.

'And afterwards . . . ' Hackett passed a hand over his eyes as if the memory was almost too much to bear. 'And afterwards, when the ravenous flames were quenched at last, the city was a smoking ruin unrecognisable as the vibrant, bustling place we all knew and loved.' He paused and several of the ladies present dabbed their eyes.

'And what of the homeless?' continued Hackett. 'Left to fend for themselves without a roof over their heads or a crust to feed their starving children.' He turned to gesture at Robert. 'See Finche here! The educated son of a wealthy merchant, his family lost everything. Now his father is in the debtor's prison, through no fault of his own, except perhaps for foolish speculation. A debtors' prison! It could have been any one of you around this table.' He fixed a stern gaze on one after the other of the guests.

I felt the heat rise up my throat, consumed with a sudden rage at this man who was using the Finche family's misfortunes and humiliation to further his own ends. I tasted blood as I bit my tongue, the only way that had ever kept my temper under control when Aunt Mercy berated me for my inadequacies.

'Robert Finche,' said Hackett, 'has never done a day's wrong in his life and his prospects were destroyed by the fire.' Hackett gave a wry smile. 'Perhaps he's been luckier than many since I have taken him into my employ, but what of the *thousands* of Robert Finches out there with no homes to live in?'

Robert still kept his unwavering gaze on Hackett's face while I fumed silently.

'And, most importantly,' continued Hackett, 'are we all going to sit by and watch while the homeless, who must live somewhere, move out of the city? If there are no homes the city will die. Can you imagine it? There will be no one to work in your businesses. There will be no baker to bake your bread. No markets and no shops. The churches will be empty on a Sunday. Wind will blow the dust down deserted streets. Already hundreds have gone to the country. *They will never return.* If we don't do something very soon our city will become a wilderness for ever.' Hackett sat down and wiped his face on his handkerchief while his guests began to murmur amongst themselves, their consternation evident.

Mr Harte turned towards me and spoke in an undertone. 'It was unforgivable that he used your family's misfortunes to add colour to his argument but it's evident that Mr Hackett's father has taught his son well.'

'His father?'

'A non-conformist minister, full of fire and brimstone.' Mr Harte smiled. 'A great orator, even if I didn't hold with his views. I heard him speak once and came away full of terror that the sky was bound to fall in upon me if I didn't repent.'

'He's standing up again,' I said.

'And no doubt will provide us all with the answer to this vision of a deserted city,' whispered Mr Harte.

I took one look at the cynical curl on his lips and knew that his feelings for Hackett mirrored my own.

Hackett held up his hand until there was silence again. 'But none of this may come to pass if we all work together,' he said. Taking a deep, sighing breath, he paused until everyone's eyes were fixed upon him again. 'And –' his voice rose to a crescendo '*– and just as the phoenix arose from the ashes, our great city is poised to rise again*!'

Several of the guests cheered.

'Already the King's surveyors have marked out the streets.' He held out his arms. 'We must build new homes. And we must build them quickly.' He thumped his hand down on the table, making the cutlery rattle. 'The land is available and I have made it my business to purchase as much as I can. I have the workforce to hand; men made homeless by the fire and desperate for work.'

A man in a blue velvet coat called out, 'Cut to the chase man! How much do you want from us?'

Hackett waited until the laughter died down. 'You are perfectly correct, sir. I do want your money. As much as possible and as soon as possible. I have building plots all over the city just waiting for investment. All of you gathered here tonight are wealthy and if you invest in my rebuilding schemes not only will you benefit the homeless but I can make you wealthy beyond your wildest dreams.'

He paused for effect, his eyes gleaming and the colour high in his cheeks. 'Gentlemen, believe me when I say this is a once in a lifetime opportunity. And the city that we build between us will stand for a thousand years.' His voiced boomed out. 'Invest your money with me and together we will make the city rise again!'

A great cheer rose up and the men stood up, banging their fists on the table.

Hackett smiled benignly at his guests until, at last, the furore died away. 'And now,' he said, 'enjoy another glass of wine before the musical entertainment. Should you wish to discuss an investment in one of my schemes, come and talk to me or to my man, Finche.'

As Hackett sat down I saw Robert push his chair back and rise to his feet. 'Ladies and gentlemen!'

I bit my lip. Was Robert going to be angry with Hackett over his earlier comments? He had every right, but whatever I thought of the man's manipulative tactics, we couldn't afford to run the risk of angering him. But I needn't have worried.

'Please raise your glasses in a toast to Mr Hackett,' called Robert, his eyes shining. 'The city needs more magnificent men like him. He has generously given me the chance of a new life and I can never thank him enough. I have observed how his original and inventive mind sees the possibilities in a situation to make fortunes and I sincerely hope you will all grasp this wonderful opportunity to join with him and be a part of the rebuilding of the city.' Robert, his face glowing with hero-worship turned to his employer and raised his glass. 'To Mr Hackett!'

The guests rose as one and raised their glasses.

'Well,' said Mr Harte, once they had all sat down again. 'I'm pleased to see that your husband clearly didn't find Hackett's references to his family's misfortunes as unacceptable as I did.'

'It would seem not,' I said, barely able to conceal my astonishment and distaste for Robert's craven stance. I put down my glass of sweet wine since it suddenly tasted sour.

'Would you aid and abet me in a crime?' asked Mr Harte.

'A crime?' I said, startled.

'Only a very small one, I promise you. My son, Toby, is four years old and has a very sweet tooth. I wondered if you would choose one of those delightful little marchpane sweets for me to wrap in my handkerchief and take home to him?'

I laughed, relieved that such a request was unlikely to have me clapped into leg irons. 'Now, let me see,' I pondered as I studied the dish of sweetmeats. 'This one is in the shape of a heart or there is a date stuffed with marzipan and almonds.'

'Either would please, I'm sure.'

'And perhaps two would be doubly pleasing? My mind is made up; he shall have both. May I have your handkerchief?'

The crime committed and the now rather sticky handkerchief stowed away inside Mr Harte's coat, he offered me his arm and we left the table for the drawing room.

Darkness had fallen and the glittering light of the drawing room chandeliers cast a warm glow over the room, which buzzed with conversation. We paused for a moment in the doorway. Robert was deep in discussion with a group of gentlemen but then I saw Mistress Harte talking to an expensively dressed young woman with elaborately curled blonde hair and led Mr Harte to join her.

'This is Mistress Arabella Leyton,' she said. 'Mistress Leyton, may I present Mistress Finche and my husband, Mr Harte,' said Jane Harte.

I found myself being regarded by a pair of ice blue eyes but Mistress Leyton's gaze quickly moved to Mr Harte.

'How do you do?' She smiled, showing sharp little teeth like a fox's as she looked him up and down in a way that set my own teeth on edge. I caught Jane Harte's eye and an unspoken alliance was formed between us. There are some women who are dangerous and Mistress Leyton was one of them.

Mr Harte bowed. 'Delighted to make your acquaintance, Mistress Leyton,' he said, oblivious to her décolletage and fluttering eyelashes.

I realised then that Arabella Leyton hadn't yet realised that Mr Harte was blind.

'Mistress Leyton was just telling me that she is soon to be married,' said Jane Harte.

'I have been so unfortunate in my husbands,' said Arabella Leyton, 'since they both suffered untimely deaths, but I have great hopes for Mr Goddard.' She nodded significantly at an elderly man talking to Mr Hackett. 'He is in possession of a very comfortable income.'

'And do you have children?' I asked, uncomfortable at her mention of such private information.

'Five. The sweetest little angels you could imagine.'

'Then Mr Goddard will be doubly blessed to find his life so enriched,' said Mr Harte.

'Indeed he will! Let me take you to meet him.' Mistress Leyton slipped her arm through Mr Harte's and led him away.

'Well!' I said.

Jane Harte giggled. 'Isn't she dreadful?'

'Two husbands buried already!' Encouraged by the laughter in Jane Harte's eyes, I whispered, 'I can't help wondering if it was a blessed release for them to be snatched up into the arms of their Maker before their time.'

Spindly gold chairs had been set out for the guests and the musical quartet installed in front of the fireplace began to tune their instruments.

'I'm hoping that the musical entertainment won't last for too long,' whispered Jane. 'I have a new nursemaid and I'm not at all sure that she is entirely suitable. I discovered her in the garden with the butcher's boy last week.'

'That must be a worry for you.'

Jane sighed. 'It's not easy to find a girl I can really trust. But then, finding good servants has never been easy, has it?'

I had no servants to concern me but was saved from making any response when Mr Hackett came towards us.

'Two lovely ladies!' he said, rubbing his hands together.

The delicate chair creaked dangerously as he sat down. He was so large he overflowed it and I moved my own slightly closer to Jane.

The music was enjoyable but I was constantly aware of Mr Hackett's presence since his thigh pressed so hotly against mine. There was something unnerving about the man. He emanated not only a strong aura of power but of intense masculinity, which was somehow untamed. I didn't like it.

I glanced across the room to see Gabriel Harte swaying gently as he listened, eyes closed and totally absorbed in the music. Clearly, his blindness was no detriment to his enjoyment.

'Pretty passable, eh?' said Mr Hackett as the final violin solo drew to a close. 'The musicians play for the King's Theatre, but I made it worth their while to entertain us this evening,' he said, rubbing his thumb and forefinger together.

'It was delightful,' I said, as Robert appeared beside us.

'I've had very interesting discussions with several of your guests, Mr Hackett,' said Robert. 'A number of them will call on you over the next day or two.'

'Good work! I'll have them signed up and take their gold in a trice once they sit down with me.' He picked up my hand and patted it. 'Been talking to your wife, Finche.'

Made uncomfortable by his close scrutiny, I concealed my blush by looking at my shoes as Mr Goddard and Mistress Leyton came to say goodbye to their host. Arabella Leyton managed to offer me the tips of her fingers and then swept her husband-to-be away. I felt rather sorry for him.

'We must say our farewells, too,' said Jane Harte.

'I enjoyed the music,' said Mr Harte, shaking Mr Hackett's hand. 'It encourages me to practise my violin more often.'

'It has been a great pleasure to meet you, Mistress Harte,' I said.

Mr Harte bowed and whispered, 'And Toby will be a happy little boy when he sees what you have procured for him.'

'I wondered if you would care to take tea with me, Mistress Finche?' Jane Harte said. 'Come any afternoon to the House of Perfume in Long Acre.'

'I should like that . . . ' My smile faded. If I visited Jane Harte I would be obliged to invite her to my home but I couldn't possible ask her to visit me in the shabby little room where we lived.

The Hartes left and the remaining guests were calling for their carriages.

A short while later we were out in the street and walking behind the link boy, who Mr Hackett had insisted on calling for us to light our way.

'A most successful evening!' said Robert, linking his arm through mine. 'I count myself truly fortunate in my new employer. He's splendid, isn't he? And he never spoke a truer word when he said that if I hung on to his coat tails I'll go far.'

But in what direction, I wondered.

Chapter 10

Rain hissed down outside and I was glad to be indoors. The fragrant scent of cinnamon began to tease my nostrils and I dropped my sewing and hurried to the fire. Pressing a finger gently in the middle of the cake I smiled in satisfaction as it bounced back. It seemed that Maggie Kinross, Aunt Mercy's cook, had taught me well. I pictured her for a moment, a scrawny woman with a mouth that looked as if she'd been drinking vinegar, but she'd had a soft spot for me and made the most exquisite cakes.

I returned to my chair by the window. The luxurious party at Mr Hackett's house the previous night seemed like a dream now that I was back home. My lovely silk dress had been packed away and I doubted I'd ever have cause to wear it again. Sighing, I glanced around. Petticoats in various stages of completion were laid out on the bed as if a grand society lady had tried on every one she owned and then petulantly cast them aside in a chaos of ruffles for her maid to tidy away. It was hard to imagine a greater contrast than Mr Hackett's opulent gilded drawing room and this shabby room with its damp-stained walls and bare floorboards.

The thud of hooves along the alley made me glance up as a

momentary shadow darkened the window. I glimpsed a great black horse pass by and Shadow began to bark. A few moments later there was a loud tattoo on the street door.

Soon afterwards came a sharp rap on my door and I went to open it, grasping the dog's collar. 'Quiet, Shadow!' His barking subsided into a deep, throaty rumble.

'Visitor for you,' Mistress O'Brien said, shifting one of her innumerable runny-nosed toddlers from one hip to another and looking at me through narrowed eyes. 'It's been a while since we had gentlemen callers in this house and I'd prefer to keep it that way, Mistress Finche.'

I flushed scarlet as I took in her meaning but before I was able to refute the charge I saw my visitor crowding the passageway behind her. 'Mr Hackett! I did not expect ... Leave the door open, if you please! My landlady ... ' Helplessly, I gestured at Mistress O'Brien, still standing immovably in the passage.

'Has a nasty, suspicious mind.' He frowned at her.

Mistress O'Brien opened her mouth but closed it again as Mr Hackett, dripping with rainwater, loomed over her.

'Run along and wipe that child's nose,' said Mr Hackett, closing the door firmly in her face.

Hurriedly, I gathered up the half-finished petticoats from the table and bundled them onto the bed.

'I was riding past when the heavens opened and look for shelter.' He removed his hat, shook his head and raindrops flew off his wig. He unbuttoned his riding cape, leaving a puddle on the floor. It smelled of sweat, horses and damp wool.

I took his cloak and hat and hung them over the clothes airer by the fire. Shadow sniffed at Mr Hackett's breeches, while I wondered how I could possibly make conversation until the rain passed.

'May I offer you a glass of ale?' I asked.

He nodded, all the while looking around the room in a way that made me feel as if he'd caught me in my shift. I poured the ale and set it on the table.

He drank deeply and wiped his moustache on the back of his hand. 'Something smells delicious.'

'Honey and spice cake, if you'd like to try it?'

He smiled broadly.

I cut the cake and he ate it in two bites. Silently, I passed him another thick slice.

The small room was overwhelmed by his presence; he seemed too large to fit and the air crackled with the energy he emanated.

'Excellent!' he said a moment later as he licked his finger and mopped up the last crumbs from his plate. Suddenly, he reached out and imprisoned my hand.

Rigid with apprehension, I stared as he stroked his thumb over my palm and calloused fingers and then turned my hand over and ran his finger over a broken nail.

'Your hands are well shaped, but they are as red and rough as those of the poorest scullery maid,' he said. 'A lady like you should have a cook and servants to wait upon you.' He sighed. 'How that husband of yours can subject you to live like this, I do not know.'

I snatched my hand away from him. 'As you pointed out so eloquently to your guests last night, he is fallen on hard times through no fault of his own. You cannot imagine we would choose to live here if there were any alternative?'

Hackett threw back his head and laughed. 'Ah, you're not so meek as I thought then? And, you must admit, my guests were moved by my little speech last night? Already I have investors queuing at the door.'

Rage rose up in my breast. 'Then you have benefited greatly from our misfortune, Mr Hackett, and I do not like it. I do not like it at all. I trust that your great benevolence to the poor homeless of the city may extend to my husband?' I tasted blood as, too late, I bit my tongue. My heart began to thud as I realised the extent to which I'd let my anger overcome my manners. What if Hackett sacked Robert on account of his insupportably rude wife?

Hackett stared at me, his face expressionless, and then shook his great head from side to side.

A shiver ran down my back.

All at once the door burst open and Charlie plodded into the room, followed by Nell.

'Charlie smelled the baking . . . ' Nell stopped.

'Nell, this is Mr Hackett,' I said as evenly as I could. 'My husband's employer.'

Nell bobbed a curtsey.

Charlie, a determined expression on his face, reached over the edge of the table, picked up the knife and waved it at the cake.

'I'll take Charlie . . . '

'No, do stay, Nell!' I seized the knife from Charlie's little fist and cut them both generous slices of cake. 'Mr Hackett was just leaving.'

Hackett's malevolent stare turned me cold. He snatched his steaming cloak from the clothes airer and swirled it around his shoulders. 'We'll continue our conversation another time, Mistress Finche.'

'Perhaps,' I murmured, opening the door.

I held my breath until I heard the front door slam and a moment later a dark shadow passed over the window again as he cantered past.

'Blimey!' said Nell. 'He's a big bugger.'

I sat down, my knees suddenly weak. 'Oh, Nell! I do hope I haven't cost Robert his job.'

She shook her head. 'He fancies you. You can tell by the way he looks at you.'

'I was very disrespectful.'

'Men like a bit of spirit now and again.' She sighed. 'And believe me, I know what men like.' She looked thoughtful for a moment. 'Wouldn't put him past a bit of rough handling.' Nell still looked to be little more than an undernourished child but her knowledge of such things made the expression in her eyes wise beyond her years.

'Robert thinks very highly of him.'

Nell shrugged. 'Ben is taking Charlie and me to visit his mum tomorrow afternoon.'

'He must be serious then.'

She nodded, her face split by a wide grin. 'And there's more. We were getting on so well and Ben has taken such a shine to Charlie that I decided to tell him the truth.'

'The truth?'

'You know –' she lowered her voice, glancing at Charlie '– about the gentlemen. I'd been worrying about it but in the end decided I had to tell him.'

'And?'

'He already knew. You could have knocked me down with a feather!' She scowled. 'A man in the Hind's Head had a skinful one day and called me a light-skirt. Ben took him outside. He said no one was going to bad-mouth his girl and gave him a pasting. So then the gent told him he'd been one of my callers.'

'Oh, Nell!'

'Ben said he knew me well enough that I wouldn't of done it unless I'd had to. And I wouldn't of. He knows I've been working hard to make a fresh start. Besides –' her cheeks flushed a rosy pink '– we haven't . . . ' She shrugged. 'You know. I'm not doing that again unless I'm married.'

'Quite right too.'

Later, after Nell had left, I went back to my sewing. The afternoon dragged by while I fretted over my impetuous behaviour towards Mr Hackett. The memory of the way he'd stared at me with his eyes as hard as stone kept flashing through my mind. I jabbed the needle in and out of the petticoat and caught the thread into a tangle. In spite of his fine house and the lavish dinner, Hackett was no gentleman but, nevertheless, he held our future in his hands. Distracted, I pricked my finger and blood spotted the white cambric. Furiously, I scrubbed at the mark with a damp cloth and watched as it spread into a rusty stain. I threw the petticoat down in a temper. Damn Hackett!

Robert was late home and I grew increasingly anxious wondering if Hackett had taken him to task but at last I heard footsteps. Cautiously, I opened the door.

'Is dinner ready yet?' Robert asked.

I let out my breath in relief. It would appear that nothing too dreadful had occurred.

I ladled our turnip stew into bowls and cut the bread. 'Did you have a good day?' I asked.

'Busy. There were a great number of callers at the office after last night. What about you? Did you visit Mother and Father?'

'The rain was so heavy that I didn't go after all. I baked a honey cake for them but Mr Hackett called by and ate most of it.'

Robert looked up from his stew. 'Mr Hackett? He came here?'

I nodded. 'He came to take shelter from the rain.'

'But I've always been careful never to let him know exactly where we live.' Robert's face flushed. 'I didn't want him to know just how poor our lodgings are.'

I frowned for a moment while I thought. 'Then he must have tipped the link boy to tell him after he lighted us home last night.'

'What did he want?'

'I'm not sure,' I said, evasively. 'Nell and Charlie came by and he left.'

Robert groaned and put a hand over his eyes.

'Did he say . . . ' I faltered, 'anything?'

'He wasn't in the office all afternoon.'

'Only . . . ' Best to confess and get it over with. 'Only he said that I ought to have a servant to do the rough work. And I –' I swallowed '– and I said it wasn't your fault that the fire had ruined us. Then he boasted that his speech about you last night had resulted in extra business . . . '

'It did,' said Robert.

'And I said that I didn't like it that he was benefiting from our misfortune.'

'Kate! You didn't!'

I nodded.

'What did he say to that?'

'Nothing. That's when Nell came by.' I twisted my hands together in my lap. 'But, Robert, he gave me such a hard look.'

'Then heaven help us.' Robert pushed away his half-eaten stew. 'By all that's holy, Kate, how could you? He's a good employer but he won't be crossed. Let's hope to God you haven't ruined it for us.'

'I'm sorry,' I said helplessly.

He scraped his chair back and stood up. A minute later the door slammed behind him.

Robert returned from the Hind's Head well after midnight, reeking of ale, and lurched into bed beside me. He fell into a deep sleep and his rumbling snores kept me awake half the night. In the morning he ate his oatmeal in brooding silence before leaving for work.

I baked another honey cake and scrubbed the floor with all the energy I could muster, believing that hard work was the best way to chase away my worries.

Later, Shadow and I went to deliver the completed petticoats to Dolly. She docked my pay by a penny as her sharp eyes noticed the small bloodstain straight away. There was little point in arguing with her. I took another bundle of sewing and went on to Lambeth to deliver the honey cake to Robert's parents.

'Did Robert not accompany you again?' asked Mother Finche.

'He's working,' I said, hoping it was the truth and that Hackett hadn't turned him off.

I returned to our room with dragging steps, dreading that I'd find Robert at home but there was no sign of him. Shadow flopped down on the floor and sighed as I wearily unwrapped the new bundle of piecework and laid out the pattern pieces. Bodices were time consuming to make as they needed narrow pockets for the whalebones and then there were all the holes for the lacing, which needed to be carefully worked to stop the fabric from fraying. Still, I'd negotiated a good price for them.

A couple of hours later I'd made good progress on the first bodice when the front door slammed and I heard running footsteps. The door to our room burst open and Robert stood framed in the doorway, heaving for breath.

Heart knocking, I rose to my feet. I didn't dare to ask him what had happened and waited until he'd caught his breath.

'Put on your hat, Kate! We're going out.'

'Going where?'

His face split into a wide grin. 'A carriage is waiting for us.'

I untied my apron and put on my hat.

Robert caught hold of my hand and pulled me behind him. We skittered up the alley and out into Fetter Lane where a carriage drawn by a pair of matched greys with red ribbons in their manes waited for us.

'Robert, what's happened?'

He didn't have time to answer before the coachman stepped down and opened the door of the carriage for us. As I climbed in I saw that Mr Hackett was seated inside and my heart sank.

'Good afternoon, Mistress Finche.'

Robert sat down beside me and I was grateful for his presence. The thought of being alone in a carriage with Mr Hackett made me shiver. The smell of his wig pomade and the tobacco on his breath pervaded the enclosed space and I murmured some kind of a reply while I attempted to regain my composure.

Hackett, an amused smile on his fleshy lips, watched me closely as I squirmed under his scrutiny. 'Well?' he said.

The carriage gave a lurch and rolled away.

Robert gave me an encouraging smile.

'I believe I may owe you an apology, Mr Hackett,' I stuttered. 'Perhaps I made discourteous remarks to you yesterday.'

'No perhaps about it,' he said, stretching out thighs as sturdy as tree trunks.

He reminded me of the bull in the field next to Aunt Mercy's house that had terrified me as a child. I half expected him to paw the ground and blow down his nostrils before charging at me.

'Then I apologise,' I said, crossing my fingers under my skirt.

Hackett raised his eyebrows. 'I'm disappointed,' he said. 'I believed you to be a woman of some spirit.'

'I find too much spirit in a wife undesirable and will not have it,' said Robert.

Hackett laughed and clapped Robert on the knee. 'Then you're a better man than I thought you were!'

Incensed, I opened my mouth to make a sharp retort but then pinched my lips together and stared out of the window whilst planning seven kinds of hell for all men but for Robert and Hackett in particular. After a while, curiosity won the battle over outrage. 'Where are we going?' I ventured.

'Ironmonger Lane. I'm taking you to see one of my houses. Your husband thought it might interest you to see how I spend my investors' money.'

I gave Robert a sideways glance and saw that he was smiling with amusement. Suddenly I felt vexed that there was some kind of secret being kept from me. 'Ah, yes!' I said. 'The investors whose consciences you stirred to take pity on the poor, while you plied them with rich food and fine wines?'

'Exactly so!' The adversarial glint was back in Hackett's eyes again.

I decided not to push my luck any more and sat demurely with my hands folded in my lap, looking out of the window, while the carriage bumped along. I saw that we were entering the burned area of the city and there were few landmarks to see except for some half-completed houses, hurrying pedestrians and several carts trundling along the dusty roads. After a short while the carriage jolted to a stop.

A newly built house stood before us, its yellow bricks bright in the sunshine and still unsullied by the sooty London air. An adjoining house was encased in scaffolding. Workmen swarmed over the site, carrying hods of bricks on their shoulders as they scrambled up rickety-looking ladders. I saw one of the men, sitting on a pile of sand and eating a chunk of bread, nudge his mate and pick up his shovel before nodding at Mr Hackett.

'I'm building these houses on the Dutch model,' said Mr Hackett. 'As you can see, the house is narrow but tall, allowing more houses to be built on smaller plots of land.'

'That's very clever,' said Robert, admiringly.

'And more profitable,' I added, longing to kick him for his fawning tone.

Mr Hackett smiled. 'Shall we go inside?'

We followed him up the pale stone steps to the front door, gleaming with fresh paint. Inside, the house was quiet and smelled of new wood, wet plaster and paint. Mr Hackett's heavy footsteps echoed as he walked through the hall and opened a door into the parlour. We stepped inside and he pointed out the carved fireplace and the superior quality of the glass in the windows.

We followed him from room to room, as he extolled the virtues of the house. Robert hung on his every word, nodding his agreement so often that I wondered his head didn't fall off. After the tour Hackett led us back into the parlour.

'What do you think of it?' he asked me, with an insufferably smug smile.

I looked around, taking my time. I shivered a little, the plaster had not yet completely dried out and the air felt damp, reminding me of the mean little room that was now our home. But then a sudden stab of jealousy for the lucky family who would inhabit this clean new house pierced my heart.

'This room is of a modest size, but I suppose it is perfectly adequate for a small family,' I said, aching to wipe the complacent smile off Hackett's face. 'It's a shame the timber panelling is not well finished but I daresay it will improve with several years of careful polishing.' I noticed with satisfaction that Hackett's smile had wavered a little. 'The fireplace is rather small,' I continued, 'and there are a great number of knots in the floorboards.' I caught Robert making angry faces at me from behind Hackett's back and became conscious that I'd allowed myself to go too far. I reined back the sharpness in my voice. 'But the windows are large and the house light.'

'At last something pleases her ladyship!' said Hackett. 'But despite the apparent failings of this house in your eyes, you must agree that it is a far superior dwelling to your current lodgings, Mistress Finche?'

'But you must remember that our current lodgings are not at all what we have been accustomed to. Until recently, both my husband and myself have lived in luxuriously appointed homes.'

Robert's face turned pale and his eyes beseeched me to be silent.

'I see,' said Hackett. 'So you would not care to live in this insignificant little hovel? I had thought that it would suit you. In fact, I suggested to your husband this morning that I might allow you to live here for a peppercorn rent. But, as it is too poor a dwelling for one used to greater things, we'll say no more about it.' He turned and began to walk towards the front door.

Aghast, I glanced at Robert, who had covered his eyes with his hand. Yet again I had let my impulsive behaviour lead me into worsening our situation. In an agony of indecision, I hesitated before swallowing my pride. 'Mr Hackett,' I called to his retreating back.

He turned to face me, his expression bland but the light of triumph in his eyes.

'Mr Hackett, I had no intention of appearing impolite . . . '

'Again?'

A large stone seemed to have lodged itself somewhere under my ribs, perhaps in anticipation of eating an enormous slice of humble pie. 'I simply meant that perhaps what this house lacks is a woman's touch.' I forced a smile. 'Someone who will love it. A little beeswax polish and some hard work would make the panelling and the floors gleam and a vase of flowers and the scent of honey cake baking would soon make this house feel like a welcoming home.'

I held my breath and waited while Hackett enjoyed my discomfiture. Dust motes drifted in a shaft of sunshine and outside a workman broke into a snatch of bawdy song.

'And could that someone be a lady, such as yourself, perhaps?' he said at last.

I served myself another helping of humble pie. 'I should, of course, consider myself very fortunate if this were to be our home.'

'I should think so! Especially in your current circumstances.'

I bowed my head. Damn the man! Was I going to have to lick his boots?

Robert cleared his throat. 'Mr Hackett, sir, you must know how much in your debt we should be if you were to permit us to reside in this fine house?'

'But do you think your wife is fully aware of that debt, Finche?'

Robert glanced at me, his mouth in a thin line. 'Yes, sir, I do believe that she is.'

'I wonder.' Hackett looked at me, unsmiling. 'And how would you propose to make me aware of the depth of your gratitude, Mistress Finche?'

I looked right back at him, determined not to let him see how my hands trembled at the thought of losing the opportunity of leaving our miserable room and living in such a house as this. 'I should make you one of my honey and spice cakes that you so enjoyed last time we met, Mr Hackett.'

I heard Robert draw in his breath sharply and I wondered if I had misjudged Hackett, but then he let out a shout of laughter.

'By God, Mistress Finche, I've never met such a woman as you. You look as meek as a kitten but you're not afraid to show your claws.' He spat on his hand and held it out to me. 'Make it two honey cakes and we'll have a deal.'

Slowly, I held out my hand, schooling my expression not to show the distaste I felt. 'Two honey cakes it is,' I said.

Chapter 11

A few days later I prepared a special dinner for Robert. I waited until he'd finished the steak and kidney pudding with plenty of rich gravy served with a dish of buttered carrots before plucking up the courage to speak.

'Robert, something has been worrying me,' I said.

'How can anything possibly worry you when our fortunes are about to change?' he asked with a smile. He burped gently and blotted his mouth with his napkin.

'It's Nell,' I said.

'What about her?'

'I'm worried what will happen to her when we move to Ironmonger Lane next week. She won't be able to work at the Hind's Head if I don't mind Charlie. I'm fearful that she'll be forced to take in gentlemen callers again.'

Robert shrugged. 'She shouldn't have allowed herself to get with child in the first place.'

'It's not as simple as that! She's a good girl, but she was very young when her mother died and left her destitute. Our new home has plenty of room.'

'That's not what you said to Mr Hackett.' Robert's mouth set in a mutinous line.

'We'll need a maidservant and I thought that Nell . . . '

'No!' Robert pushed back his chair. 'I'm not having a common street jade in my house. And besides, we cannot afford servants. There are still my parents to consider and every penny we can save will go towards paying back their creditors.'

'But what will happen to little Charlie?'

He stared at me in disbelief. 'Are you really asking me to support a whore's brat when my parents are imprisoned in a debtors' jail?' His face was crimson with anger as he threw his napkin down on the table. 'You really are the most selfish person I've ever met, Katherine.' He turned on his heel and a moment later the door slammed behind him.

Outraged, I kicked the table leg. If he was so concerned about his parents, the least he could do was to visit them once in a while.

It was beginning to spot with rain by the time I'd visited Robert's parents in Lambeth and started home. I had my head down, watching my step in the potholes and worrying about Father Finche's persistent cough, when I glanced up to see a familiar figure walking along the road, holding a small, flaxen-haired boy by the hand.

'Mr Harte?' I called.

He stopped and turned, his head cocked. 'Mistress Finche?'

I smiled, pleased that he had recognised my voice. 'Indeed it is. And might this young gentleman be your son?'

Mr Harte smiled and bent to whisper to the child.

Toby stepped forwards, swept off his hat and made a stiff little bow. 'At your service, madam.' He glanced up at me with wide eyes as green as his father's, thickly fringed with blond lashes.

'Mistress Finche was the kind lady who chose the sweetmeats for you when Mama and I went to Mr Hackett's party last week,' said Mr Harte.

'I hope you enjoyed them, Toby?'

He nodded solemnly.

'My wife has been hoping all week that you'd call on her,' said Mr Harte.

'We're moving house and I've been busy,' I said.

Toby pulled on his father's hand. 'It's raining harder, Father. And you need to help me count the steps to the next corner.'

Mr Harte bowed. 'Do visit us very soon, Mistress Finche.'

I watched as they set off together, Mr Harte's silver-topped cane sweeping from side to side and Toby counting their steps. The rain began to fall in earnest then and I, too, made haste towards home.

I was towelling my hair dry when Nell knocked at the door. My heart sank as I knew I couldn't delay any longer in telling her that we would be leaving. I noticed that she'd brushed her hair and her cheeks were pink. It grieved me to have to make her unhappy.

'Kate, such a thing has happened! I couldn't wait to tell you. It's Ben.' She clasped her hands to her breast. 'We're going to be married!'

'Married? But that's wonderful news!'

'I keep pinching meself.' Nell's face shone with happiness. 'Ben wants to look after me and Charlie. He'll bring him up as his own and never make no fuss about it. We're to be wed in three weeks. Me and Charlie'll move in with Ben and his mum. She'll look after Charlie in the evenings while I work until . . . ' Her cheeks flushed a rosy pink. 'Until there's another little one on the way.'

I hugged her, delighted to hear about her turn of luck and relieved that I wouldn't let her down, in equal measure.

After Nell had gone I set to my packing with a lighter heart, only spoiled by the niggle of unease about being beholden to Mr Hackett. Still, I was sure that he would extract his money's worth out of Robert and meanwhile my dream of a proper home of my own was about to come true.

The next week, Ben Perkins, dark-haired with a ready smile, brought his cart to assist me with the move since Robert was at work. It didn't take long for our few sticks of furniture, a trunkful of clothes and our pots and pans to be loaded onto the cart.

Nell bid me a tearful goodbye as I climbed up to sit beside Ben. 'Don't forget,' she said, 'the wedding's on the second Sunday of next month at St James's in Clerkenwell.'

Ben flicked the reins. As the horse quickened his pace, I glanced behind to wave again and check that Shadow loped along behind.

The cart trundled down the alley with its swaying load. The sun was warm and I began to feel excitement welling up inside me as we entered the burned part of the city and neared my new home. Dust on the unmade road whirled in little eddies in the breeze, covering us in gritty particles as other carts, most piled with bricks or timber, passed by.

'Will you be able to find Ironmonger Lane?' I asked, suddenly anxious that there were so few landmarks and I wasn't sure how to find the new house again.

'Lord love us; no difficulty at all,' said Ben. 'Why, I'm delivering cart loads of stone all over the city 'most every day now. I even supplied your Mr Hackett with the Portland stone for the quoins on your new house.' He made a wry face. 'Drives a hard bargain that one. I crossed him because I only sell the best quality. I said to him, what's the point in building a new house with second-rate stone that'll crack after a season?'

Everywhere I looked there were marked-out building plots beside the road and I took careful note of whatever landmarks I could see. Then Ben nodded at a post stuck in the ground on the corner of the road with 'Ironmonger's Lane' roughly painted onto it.

My heart began to thud furiously as the cart juddered to a stop outside the house.

Men working on the scaffolding next door stopped what they were doing and watched us curiously. I went up the steps and, with hands shaking with excitement, opened the door. The hall was narrower than I remembered but the sunlight followed me in and I couldn't help a wide smile spreading across my face. I had waited for this moment for as long as I could remember.

Ben came puffing up the steps with a trunk on his shoulder and I hurried to help him. The rest of the morning passed in a blur as we unloaded the cart. One of the workmen stuck his shovel in a pile of sand and came to help carry the table and the bed up the stairs, while I hurried up and down with bundles and boxes. At last the cart was empty.

I poured Ben a tankard of ale from the flagon in my basket.

'Reckon I'll be off then,' he said, wiping sweat from his forehead.

'Thank you so much,' I said, holding out to him the bag of coins Robert had given me earlier.

He recoiled. 'I didn't do it for money,' he said. 'After everything you've done for my Nell, I'm pleased to help.' He touched his finger to his forelock and smiled. 'But don't disappoint her. You will come to the wedding, won't you?'

'I wouldn't miss it for the world!'

Ben smiled. 'God bless you.' He jumped up onto the cart and drove away, stirring up a cloud of sandy dust behind him.

I called to Shadow and went back inside. After closing the front door, I leaned against it. My very own home. A wave of exhilaration flooded over me and I skipped into the parlour, whooping with delight before lifting my skirts and running up both flights of stairs with Shadow snapping at my heels.

Breathless with laughter, I flung open the window in the attic bedroom and hung out over the sill. The sky was a huge dome over the flattened city, so different from the old days when often there was only a sliver of sky to be seen when you looked heavenwards through the narrow gap between the houses. If I turned my head to the right I could see the river, crowded with boats, and to the left I caught a glimpse of London Wall. In front of me was the wasteland of the burned city with the squat silhouette of the Tower on the riverbank in the distance. Here and there partly finished houses projected out of the flattened rubble like broken teeth. How long would it be before all the houses, shops, taverns and churches had been rebuilt and once again the city would resound to the incessant ringing of church bells, costermongers' cries and the clatter of traffic?

My stomach rumbled, reminding me that I would have to go out to buy something for supper. I hurried downstairs to the kitchen to unpack the pots and pans.

The pantry hadn't been whitewashed inside and I found a trail of rat droppings leading to a large crack in the plaster under the shelves.

'Perhaps we should have a cat, Shadow?' I said.

He regarded me with bright eyes and one ear cocked.

I swept up the rat droppings, tipped the kitchen utensils out of their travelling home in the bucket and made my way down to the cellar. A sliver of light filtered down from a small window at the top of the wall and I felt my way around in the gloom until I found the cistern, which was half full.

Mr Hackett had been proud of the fact that he'd connected the house to the network of elm pipes that still lay under the city. In their panic during the Great Fire, citizens had feverishly dug up the roads and punctured the pipes, seeking water to quench the flames. The water supply was still erratic, even for those who could afford it. Heaving a sigh of relief, I dipped the bucket into the cistern. It was a long walk to one of the public conduits outside the city and I doubted that water carts were frequent visitors to Ironmonger Lane.

I carried the dripping bucket upstairs and vigorously scrubbed out the pantry. I would stop up the crack where the rats came in and whitewash the walls but for now that would have to suffice. I untied my apron, snatched up my basket and set off for the market.

Providentially, Leadenhall market had escaped the fire and was within easy walking distance. The new streets were staked out and several building sites swarmed with men but it was strange to walk along the dirt roads without being continually jostled by crowds or having to step out of the way of waggons. I missed the hustle and bustle of the old city.

Walking along Cheapside and Poultry, I came to Cornhill and the junction of Lombard Street. It gave me a peculiar feeling to know that the Finches' home in Lombard Street had gone forever. Shivering a little, I continued my journey along Cornhill. There were more people going about their business there and several horse-drawn carriages and a dustcart rolled past. Before long I could hear the market vendors' cries and catch the faint scent of animal blood and rotting vegetables on the breeze.

The flesh market was still busy. Men hurried past in sacking aprons, carrying great sides of beef on their shoulders as if they weighed no more than a small child. The air was saturated with the metallic smell of blood that ran from every stall, forming clots in the sawdust on the ground.

I bypassed a stall where a cow's head, black with flies, twirled slowly from a hook in the full sun and bought a piece of stewing beef from a butcher whose apron bore less bloodstains than most.

Screeching seagulls circled low over the fish stalls, waiting for the fishwives to throw the guts behind them as, knife glinting in the sun, they sliced mackerel and withdrew the innards with a swift flick of their wrists. I bargained hard with one of the hoarse-voiced vendors and bought two smoked fish for our breakfast for the following day. Strawberries from a fresh-faced country girl's basket, carrots, onions and a bunch of thyme completed my purchases.

Once I returned to our new home there was only time to put the stew onto the fire and comb my hair before Robert returned. I stationed myself by the parlour window and as soon as I saw him coming, ran out to meet him.

'Welcome home!' I said.

He smiled as I dragged him up the front steps and before I knew what was happening he'd swept me up in his arms. 'I shall carry you over the threshold.'

'Robert! You've caught up my skirts,' I said, trying to pull my petticoat over my bare knees.

'There's no one to see.'

It was true; the street was deserted and the workmen had gone home for the day, so I stopped struggling and began to giggle as he made a show of huffing and puffing as he staggered into the hall.

'Well, Mistress Finche,' he said, 'thanks to Mr Hackett's generosity, now we are truly home.' He planted a kiss on my mouth.

Elated, I slid my arms around his neck, happy to respond to his kisses, which soon became more urgent.

'I think it's time for you to show me our new bedroom, don't you?' he whispered.

'The stew is on the fire . . . '

'To hell with the stew!' he said, pulling me upstairs.

In the bedroom he fumbled with our clothing, loosening laces and undoing buttons, leaving a trail of stockings, breeches and petticoats as we half fell through the bedroom door and onto the bed.

His eyes were shut tight in concentration and I studied a hairline crack in the ceiling as he moved within me, wondering how it would be to be so absorbed in the moment.

At last, passion spent, Robert let out a long sigh.

I experienced sadness, disappointment almost, that he didn't want to talk but fell straightaway into a doze. I wondered if other wives felt the same after fulfilling their marital duties. It wasn't until then that I realised that Robert hadn't withdrawn from me to spill his seed on my thigh, as usual. I smiled to myself.

Chapter 12

I've never liked to be indebted to anyone, a legacy I suppose, of always having to be so very grateful all the time to Aunt Mercy. So it was in a resentful frame of mind I set to work in my new kitchen to discharge my debt to Mr Hackett. Once the two fragrant honey cakes were cooling on the table, however, my mood become sunnier again.

I changed into my green dress, one of the few possessions I'd saved from the fire. It was patched and worn now but it suited me. I dressed my dark hair so that it curled becomingly around my face and then, hesitating only a moment, drew out my satin slippers from the trunk.

The men working on the adjoining building site called out a cheery greeting as I left the house and, although some might have considered their catcalls disrespectful, it put a spring in my step.

It was in this happy frame of mind that I came to Mr Hackett's chambers in Holborn. A young clerk let me in and showed me to an antechamber to wait. Raised voices came through a half-open door.

'We had an agreement!'

'The situation has changed, Maundrell,' said Hackett in rumbling tones.

My ears pricked up at the mention of Robert's previous employer's name.

'I've invested in my own brick manufacturing company in St Giles in the Fields now and my bricks cost far less than yours,' continued Hackett.

'We had an agreement,' persisted Elias Maundrell, 'and I turned away all other orders since you promised to take every brick I could bring you.' There was a note of desperation in his reedy voice.

I sat, rigid with embarrassment, while the altercation continued. Much as I had never liked Mr Maundrell, I didn't care for him to find me listening to his humiliation.

'I haven't time to sit hear all day listening to you bleating,' said Hackett. 'Hogg will see you out.'

'But I . . . '

'Hogg!' bellowed Hackett. 'Come and remove this person from the premises.'

A weaselly-looking man with thinning hair hurried into the anteroom and pushed past me to enter Hackett's inner sanctum. A moment or two later he reappeared, ignoring old Elias Maundrell's protests as he dragged him away by his collar.

I shrank back and turned my face away. Soon afterwards the front door slammed shut.

I remained on my chair, eyes downcast, when Mr Hackett strode into the antechamber with a face like thunder.

He stopped short when he saw me. 'To what do I owe the pleasure of your visit, Mistress Finche? Come to needle me again with your sharp comments?'

'Not at all,' I said, wishing I were somewhere else. 'I've come to keep my side of our bargain.' I uncovered the two honey cakes in my basket. 'These are for you.'

His frown disappeared and he gave a snort of laughter before delving into my basket with fingers as fat as a butcher's best sausages. 'You'd best come in to my office.'

'I don't wish to disturb . . . '

'Nonsense!'

Reluctantly, I followed him. I had planned to discharge my debt as quickly as possible and be on my way.

He sat down heavily beside his desk and nodded at the visitor's chair. 'Drink?'

'Thank you, no . . . '

'Of course you will.' He opened a cupboard beside his desk and took out two glasses and a bottle of rum.

I watched in horror as he poured two full glasses and then pushed one towards me. I had never drunk rum before and didn't like the smell of it.

Hackett gulped down half of his drink and then took a knife from inside his coat and hacked off two slices of cake. He tossed one to me and I caught it awkwardly. 'Just like my old mother used to bake,' he said, mouth bulging. 'Except that hers were nearly always burned.' He laughed loudly, enjoying his joke and showering the desk with crumbs. 'So, how do you like the house? Not proving too small and mean for you, your ladyship?'

'Quite the contrary,' I said. It really wouldn't do to upset this man. 'We have so little furniture that there's plenty of space.'

Hackett drained his glass and cut another slice of cake. 'By God,' he said, 'I'd soon become fat if you were my wife.'

Repressing a shudder at the thought, I sipped at my glass of rum and ate the cake, hoping it would offset the strong drink.

'My wife was a poor thing. Pretty as a picture, but too delicate to survive the rigours of childbirth.'

'I'm sorry to hear that,' I said politely.

'Don't be. I'd already tired of her.' Hackett poured himself another glass and waved the bottle at me. I shook my head, wondering how soon I could leave.

Hogg sauntered into the room and leaned against the wall with his hands in his pockets. 'I seen Maundrell off,' he said.

Silently, Hackett filled another glass for him. 'Don't suppose he gave you any trouble?'

Hogg laughed. 'He won't be back.'

'Jumped-up little toad.' Hackett looked at me. 'Finish your drink, Mistress Finche. Or shall I call you Kate?'

I avoided answering his question by taking a large mouthful of rum, holding it in my mouth for as long as possible but in the end I had to swallow it. I pushed the glass away.

'I shall take offence if you don't drink with me,' said Hackett, his eyes gleaming.

'I must take my leave,' I said, standing up. 'I have another call to make.' I swayed slightly, steadying myself against the edge of the desk while my stomach churned.

Hackett laughed. 'Come and see me again. Or perhaps I should call on you one afternoon? An afternoon when your husband is at work, maybe?' He opened the door. 'Finche!' he bellowed.

A moment later Robert appeared. His eyebrows shot up in surprise when he saw me.'Your wife has been paying me a social call.'

I shook Mr Hackett's hand and left with as much dignity as I could muster.

'What are you doing here?' hissed Robert.

'I brought Mr Hackett's honey cakes,' I said, hiccoughing slightly.

'Oh.' He looked at me suspiciously. 'Have you been drinking?'

'Rum. He made me have it. Robert, Elias Maundrell was here and that man Hogg threw him out.'

'Maundrell?'

'Hackett reneged on his agreement to buy bricks from Mr Maundrell.'

'Serve him right!'

'But Robert . . . '

'Go home, Kate.' He opened the street door and I found myself on the other side of it.

My feet and my head ached by the time I reached Covent Garden. I knew I should have worn sturdier shoes but I'd succumbed to vanity and worn my satin slippers as more suitable for a social call. Still, the walk had settled my uneasy stomach.

Walking in the cool shade under the arcading around the piazza, I stopped at one of the fruit stalls to purchase two apples, taking my time to select perfect specimens, all flushed with scarlet. I ate one of them as I walked, hoping it would remove the smell of rum on my breath.

From the gravelled piazza it was but a step along James Street to Long Acre, a wide tree-lined street. There I found several smart shops, interspersed with coachbuilders' yards and a number of large houses set within sizeable gardens. The sign of the pomander and the rose swung gently in the breeze, hanging from a tall, double-fronted house with a columned portico, all set behind railings.

Mr Harte must be richer than I'd imagined, I reflected as I climbed the graceful steps curving up to the front door. I pulled on the iron ring set beside it and heard the bell jangling in the distance.

'Yes? Can I help you?' A young man, unusually short but with sleek black hair and an impressively large nose, opened the door and stood looking up at me. Then I realised that he was not a child or even a dwarf but had a crooked back.

'I wondered if Mistress Harte is at home?' I said.

He regarded me with dark beady eyes and I tried not to giggle at the sudden thought that, in his silky brown coat and russet waistcoat, he looked exactly like a robin.

He cocked his head. 'Is it Mistress Finche?' He didn't wait for my answer. 'Yes, of course it is. The lady of the house has been expecting you. The mistress is in her closet, if you'd care to follow me?'

I stepped inside the high-ceilinged hall and at once I became aware of an intensely beautiful fragrance: the delightfully musky perfume of dried roses with spicy undertones mixed with something I thought might be verbena. I remained still while I inhaled the air, searching for the source of the scent and then realised that the manservant had already crossed the stone-flagged floor and started up the carved oak staircase.

I hurried to follow him and waited on the landing, while he tapped on a door and opened it without waiting for an answer.

Jane Harte sat by the open window in the sunny little room, embroidering a cushion cover. She looked up and gave me her sweet smile. 'Mistress Finche, how very delightful! You don't mind sitting in my closet, I hope?' She leaned forwards. 'We can be comfortable here as it's less formal than the drawing room.' She turned to the manservant. 'Jacob, will you ask Ann to bring us some tea?'

Jacob inclined his head and withdrew.

I sat on one of a pair of pretty Venetian armchairs covered in flame-stitch embroidery worked in shades of coral and cream. The walls were hung in a delicate shade of duck-egg blue damask and above them was a painted frieze of hummingbirds and twining woodbine. A glass bowl of scented white roses sat on a cabinet. 'What a charming room!' I said.

'It's my secret hideaway,' said Mistress Harte. 'This house belonged to my husband's uncle and it remains furnished exactly as he left it. When Gabriel and I married I promised never to change anything without his consent because he can remember it all in his mind's eye. But this room is my domain and I have permission to make it exactly as I choose.'

'It's delightful,' I said. I placed the apple I'd bought in the market on the side table. 'This is for Toby.'

'How kind! He still talks about the marchpane sweetmeats you purloined for him. I'll call him in to pay his respects.'

'I should like that, Mistress Harte.'

'Oh! Please call me Jane.' She smiled warmly at me.

'And I'm Kate to my friends,' I said, thinking that apart from Nell I didn't have any friends.

The door opened and a neatly dressed maid carried in a tea tray. She placed the tray on a small table at Jane's side and left as quietly as she had entered.

'Ann is my new maid,' said Jane, 'but I think I am going to be pleased with her.'

'The last time we met, at Mr Hackett's party,' I said, 'you weren't entirely happy with Toby's nursemaid.'

'There's a frivolity about her I do not care for.' Jane sighed as she poured the tea. 'Do you have children?'

I shook my head and her searching look led me to say what was in my heart. 'But I long for a child above everything. I lost both my parents when I was eight years old and want so very much to have a family of my own.'

'I do understand how terrible that can be,' said Jane. 'My own mother died when I was ten and my sister eleven.'

'Are you close to your sister?'

Jane's eyes filled with tears. 'Four years ago, Eleanor died, too.'

The old sadness welled up in my breast but I took a little comfort from the fact that Jane really understood the pain I felt. 'The sorrow of losing your family never leaves you, does it?'

She sighed. 'I was reminded of it again the other day when a house in Rochester Court burned to the ground. A mother and four children perished.'

'How very dreadful!'

'I can't stop thinking about the children that survived. Worse than that, some say that the house was burned down deliberately.' Jane shook her head in disbelief. 'The downstairs shutters were forced open in the dead of night and flaming torches thrown inside.'

Shocked, I put down my teacup. A memory of the billowing smoke and the heat of the inferno in the Finche warehouse flashed through my mind as I imagined the terrified screams of the children trapped in the blazing house.

I blinked as a child's sudden shriek snapped me out of my reverie.

Jane called through the window down to the garden. 'Toby! Come and say good day to Mistress Finche.'

A few moments later, footsteps clattered up the stairs and the door burst open.

'Toby!' Jane pulled the boy to her side and brushed mud off his breeches. 'Look at you! What have you been doing?'

'I was fighting the Dutch soldiers. And then the French.'

'Did you win the battle?' I asked.

He nodded solemnly. 'I always win.'

I reached for the apple on the side table. 'I brought this for you.'

He thanked me with a beaming smile. 'I'd better go back to the garden now or the bloody French will have overrun it again.'

'Toby!' Jane pulled at his arm. 'Who taught you to say such a thing?'

'What?' He looked up at his mother with innocent green eyes.

'What you said about the French.'

'Jacob says we mustn't give them an inch or they'll take a mile. Damned French started the Great Fire, Jacob says.'

'We don't know that for sure, Toby. Now run along and play.'

'Yes, Mama.' He smiled at me as he polished the apple on his sleeve. 'Will you come again?'

'Perhaps next time you'll come and visit me?'

He took a bite of the apple. 'I shall bring my hoop and let you play with it. I'd better go and see what the blood–' He glanced at his mother. 'I'll go and make sure that the wicked Frenchies aren't climbing over our garden wall.'

I smiled at Jane as he skipped out of the room. 'I envy you,' I said. 'He's delightful.'

'That child spends far too much time with Jacob Samuels,' she said. 'I know Gabriel finds Jacob to be a most devoted servant but his influence on Toby is not always what I would wish.' Jane sighed. 'Ah well! Gabriel tells me you have a new home.'

'Mr Hackett offered us the opportunity to rent one of the houses he's built.'

'Perhaps he feels remorse for the embarrassment he caused you?'

'Robert said that Mr Hackett would prefer the house to be tenanted rather than risk the homeless rabble breaking in. Besides, the adjoining house is not yet completed and there's a deal of noise and dust, which might deter any potential purchasers.'

'But how delightful to have a lovely new house.'

Churlishly, I remembered the deep crack in the pantry wall where the rats came in. I laughed. 'Everything echoes at present since we have so little furniture.'

'But now you have the opportunity to choose whatever you like to your own taste.'

I shrugged. 'Over time, perhaps. We're saving all that we can to help Robert's parents.'

Jane bit her lip. 'There is a table and six chairs banished to the attics by Gabriel's uncle. They're old-fashioned but well made and I wonder if you'd like them? I can arrange for them to be delivered to you.'

Embarrassment made my toes curl. 'I'm afraid I cannot offer to buy them. It's Robert's parents, you see . . . '

'The only payment I ask is an invitation to supper one evening so that I can see them being put to good use.' Jane smiled.

I smiled back, full of excitement at the prospect. 'Then I'd be most grateful to receive them and will look forward to you dining with us,' I said.

'And I'll ask Gabriel to bring his violin and flute to entertain us after supper,' she said.'

When it was time to leave, Jane said, 'Shall I see if Gabriel is receiving visitors?'

We went down to the hall and Jane knocked on a door and

waited, while I searched again for the source of the musky rose perfume.

The door was opened by Jacob Samuels. 'Yes?' he said.

'Is my husband busy, Jacob?'

Unsmiling, Jacob said, 'I shouldn't like to disturb him.' The door started to close but then there was the sound of footsteps and the door was snatched open wide.

'Thank you, Jacob,' said Gabriel Harte. He held out his hand to me. 'Mistress Finche, welcome to the House of Perfume.'

'May we come in?' asked Jane.

'I should be disappointed if you didn't,' he said.

My first impression of the room was of its faint but delightful perfume. Indefinable, it was a mixture of a myriad of flowers but with underlying notes of citrus, spice and the fresh green scent of herbs. The room was full of light from the tall window overlooking the street and oak panelling the colour of honey lined the walls. High-backed chairs were placed around a glass-topped table, all set upon a silky Persian carpet. Another door stood ajar and I glimpsed the gleam of glass bottles in the shadowy workroom beyond.

'This is the Perfume Salon, where Gabriel greets his clients,' said Jane. 'Society ladies visit and take tea while they make their purchases.'

Mr Harte opened both the doors to a cupboard with a flourish and I went to look at the silk-lined shelves containing a variety of decorative bottles of perfume all tied up with satin ribbons.

Jane led me to the shelves that lined one wall, filled with a profusion of scented candles, lace sachets and pomades.

'How very tempting,' I said, filled with longing. 'In fact, I should like to purchase this pot of lavender beeswax. The panelling in our parlour is very new and I have resolved to polish it every week until it mellows.'

Mr Harte named a price I thought very reasonable.

'I couldn't help noticing the beautiful fragrance that greeted me in the hall,' I said as I counted out the coins and placed them on the table.

'That will be the sweet jar.' Gabriel Harte smiled. 'Or rotten-pot as it is also known. We collect flowers from the garden, starting in the spring, and layer them with salt in a pot with a perforated lid. The flowers ferment a little and we add roses, lemon balm and lavender all summer.'

'I thought I could detect lemon balm!'

'You have a good sense of smell,' said Mr Harte. 'And then in the autumn we add spices and ground orris root. It smells sweet now but in the winter, if we place the jar close by the fire, then you truly benefit from the perfume.'

'I must try that,' I said, 'although I'll have to plant a garden first. We've moved to a new house in Ironmonger Lane and at present there's only a small patch of earth full of bricks and rusty nails.'

'I'll bring you some cuttings from our garden,' said Jane.

'You've already been kindness itself,' I said, 'and I must take my leave of you before I outstay my welcome.'

Mr Harte closed his cupboard of fragrant delights and then held out a candle tied with rose pink ribbon. 'A gift for you. It will scent your new home with tuberose.'

I said my goodbyes and left the House of Perfume, bubbling with elation. I hadn't had many friends in my life, Aunt Mercy hadn't allowed it, but I was as sure as I could be that Jane would become the friend I had always longed for.

Chapter 13

The sandy ground was full of lumps of old plaster and charred timber but I set to work with a spade borrowed from the builders next door. Shadow watched me with a wagging tail and then entered into the game by digging several holes in the stony earth before falling asleep in the shade of the wall.

Later, I stretched out the ache in my back, leaned on the spade and planned where I would plant roses. I dug up several bricks and set them aside to mark out the boundaries of my herb garden. I would plant rosemary, mint, parsley and sage to begin with and edge it with lavender.

The sunshine was so warm at midday that I sat outside to eat my bread and cheese. Apart from the hammering of the men on the building site next door and the occasional cart rumbling by, it was as quiet as a country garden. But then I realised that because there were no trees or flowers in the burned landscape, there was no bird-song and no drowsy sound of bees about their business either. It was hard to imagine that this house was in what had once been a teeming city. Idly, I wondered how long it would be before noise and clamour would be heard again over the garden wall.

A while later, I heard a loud rat-a-tat-tat of the doorknocker. Brushing earth off my skirt, I hurried to open the door.

A burly man with a jaunty red neckerchief stood on the doorstep.

I took the proffered note and glanced behind him to see a laden cart. A youth in a sacking apron was untying the ropes and removing a tarpaulin to reveal Jane Harte's dining table and chairs. My heart leaped with excitement.

'Where do you want them?' asked the carter.

As I directed him to the dining room I realised that, in addition to the table and chairs I'd been expecting, there were two large trunks, a ladies' writing desk, a small table, a clock, several bundles tied up with string and an assortment of cooking pots. Once the men had gone I opened the note.

My dear Kate

I hope you will not be offended that I have sent you a few additional items.

I enjoyed your visit yesterday very much and look forward to calling on you once you have settled in to your new home. Toby asks me to thank you for his apple and says he will not forget to bring his hoop.

Your friend,

Jane

Smiling, I untied the bundles to find some pretty crewel-work curtains and matching cushion covers, together with a set of bed hangings and a counterpane in raspberry damask. Amazed and delighted at such riches, I hastened to open the trunks and discovered a selection of glassware, an embroidered linen tablecloth, several serving dishes and a fine pewter jug. I spent the next hour contentedly arranging the furniture.

The dining table and chairs had the warm patina of age and the new oak panelling appeared raw by contrast. Opening the pot of beeswax polish I'd bought from Gabriel Harte, I began to apply it with a rag.

Later that afternoon, I stepped back to admire my handiwork. The oak had begun to glow with a mellow sheen and lavender scented the air. The sound of the workmen packing up their tools before the end of the day drifted in through the open window and Shadow came to sit at my feet, looking up at me expectantly.

'Yes, I know it's your suppertime. And it's time I cooked our supper, too.'

Robert came home as I was draining the potatoes. He slumped down at the kitchen table.

'Tired?' I asked. My spirits sank. Robert's moods always hung over us like a black cloud.

He shrugged.

'Will you bring up some ale from the cellar and then supper will be ready.'

A short while later he reappeared. 'Have you let some meat spoil down in the cellar?' he asked.

'I don't keep meat in the cellar.'

'Something smells,' he said, wrinkling his nose. 'It can't be the cesspit; we haven't been here long enough for it to overflow.'

'I'll take a look later,' I said, impatient to share my excitement about the new furniture with him. 'We're going to eat in the dining room tonight. Will you carry the jug of ale?' I led the way upstairs and opened the dining room door with a flourish.

I had set the table with clean napkins and the new glasses. The tuberose-scented candle was already lit and the perfume mingled pleasingly with the aroma of lavender and beeswax polish. 'What do you think?' I asked, delighted with the fruits of my labours.

Robert stared at the room. 'Where did all this come from? I told you we cannot spend my earnings on fripperies while my parents are in need.'

'But I didn't!' I said crestfallen. 'Jane Harte cleared out her attics.'

'The blind man's wife?'

I nodded, though I thought it insensitive of him to refer to Mr Harte in that way.

'I don't want other people's charity.'

'But Jane said she had no use for them. Besides –' I swallowed, my happy mood entirely evaporated '– I promised to invite her, with her husband, to share our supper one day soon.'

'Without asking me?'

'I thought you'd be pleased.' I blinked back sudden tears. 'I wanted everything to be perfect for you tonight.'

Robert sighed and sat down at the table.

Silently, I poured him a glass of ale.

He drank it down in one and wiped his mouth on the back of his hand. 'It's hard sometimes to accept our altered circumstances and I don't like being an object of pity.'

I opened my mouth to say that he didn't seem to mind when his precious Mr Hackett drew attention to our plight in front of all his guests but thought better of it.

That night Robert was already in bed by the time I came upstairs. I undressed and lay down beside him.

He turned his head to kiss my cheek perfunctorily. 'Work was wearisome today and I spoke sharply. I can see that you're doing all you can to make our home comfortable. Send that supper invitation to your friends.'

'Thank you, Robert.'

He sighed again and turned his back on me.

The day of Nell and Ben's wedding dawned fair and clear and I was pleased that I'd managed to cajole Robert into attending the event, even if he'd never understand why I was fond of Nell.

We sat on the pew behind Mistress O'Brien and her tribe of children, who had been bribed into a semblance of good behaviour with a segment of orange to suck. We were the only representatives for the bride but Ben Perkins's side of the church was full. I truly hoped that Nell would find in the Perkins clan the replacement family she craved.

I was delighted to see how happiness had transformed Nell from a skinny waif into a pretty young woman. I wasn't the only one in the church who watched the couple exchange their vows through a film of tears, although I was distracted somewhat by the O'Brien boys turning around in the pew and pulling fearsome faces at me with vampire teeth made of orange rind.

After the ceremony we all repaired to the Dog and Duck for eel pie, mashed potatoes and copious quantities of ale. Nell, glowing with joy, kissed my cheek and went to dance with her new brother-in-law.

Ben Perkins, his eyes shining, shook my hand. 'Happiest day of my life,' he said, 'and I've you to thank for helping my Nell to climb out of the pit she fell into.'

'She wasn't in it for long enough to spoil her, thank the Lord,' I said.

'Just you remember,' said Ben, his merry eyes serious for once, 'any time you need help, Ben Perkins is your man.' He hugged me tight and kissed my cheek. 'No disrespect, missus,' he said, 'but my heart is overflowing today.'

'No offence taken,' I replied.

'There's just one thing . . . ' He hesitated. 'It's hard for me to say, you being so happy in your new home and all.'

'What is it, Ben?'

'A word to the wise about that Mr Hackett. He's a bit of a tricksy one. Your man should find another place of work if he can. Being in the building trade I hear things sometimes. Only whispers, mind.'

'What kind of whispers?'

He scratched his head. 'Hackett's always on the lookout for a quick profit. Sometimes that means his supplies and methods aren't always the best.'

'I'm not sure I understand.'

'You tell Mr Finche to keep his eye open for another opportunity is my advice. That's all I'm saying.'

Ben's comments served to underline my own unease concerning Mr Hackett but I dreaded the thought of having to speak to Robert about it.

Robert and I joined in with the dancing, accompanied by a gipsy violinist and one of Ben's numerous cousins with his penny whistle. An hour or so later, the company was very merry from the ale and we slipped quietly away.

'Nell's fallen on her feet there,' said Robert as we walked through Smithfield. 'There aren't many who'd take on a retired whore and her bastard.'

'Ben's lucky to have them,' I said.

'She looked well enough today,' said Robert, grudgingly.

'Ben mentioned something which worried me,' I said. 'He's heard people whispering about Mr Hackett. He thought you should look for a new position.'

Robert stopped walking and pulled me around to face him. 'A new position? Has he any idea how difficult it is to find work? I for one am grateful for what we have and so should you be.'

'I am but Ben says . . . '

'I don't give a tinker's cuss what Ben says! He's only a carter, after all. Don't for the Lord's sake stir up trouble, Kate.' Robert's face was white and his jaw tense. 'Do you really want us to be out in the street again?'

'No, of course not but . . . '

'Then keep your mouth shut!' He gripped my arm and shook it violently.

I gasped at his sudden fury and he stalked off, too fast for me to catch up with him. Shocked at the vehemence of his response, I followed with dragging steps.

When I arrived home I stood outside on the dirt road, looking up at our house. The new yellow bricks were stark and the house and its half-finished neighbour seemed uncomfortably tall and thin against the barren landscape. It may not have been quite the home I'd dreamed of but even the suggestion of losing it felt like a hammer blow. Robert was right, of course. It wasn't wise to poke a stick at a hornets' nest.

Chapter 14

August 1668

The evening before our planned supper party Robert returned from work with the news that Mr Hackett was to join us.

'I was going to make the supper a simple affair,' I said, in dismay. 'We've been eating beans and potatoes all week so that I could save enough from our housekeeping budget for the supper but if Mr Hackett is coming . . . '

'You shall have enough money so that we won't be shamed,' said Robert.

'I don't know how to cook fancy dishes like swan or peacock.' I twisted my wedding ring around my finger, suddenly anxious.

'Mr Hackett likes plain cooking. In fact, when he heard that we were holding a supper party that's when he invited himself. He said he hoped to enjoy some of your fine baking.'

'I see.' How very like Hackett to invite himself. 'Then it's lucky we have a dining table large enough to seat us all, isn't it?'

I arrived at Leadenhall market early to avoid the August heat and paid six pence for a leg of beef, an unheard of luxury over the past two years, and two plump chickens and a glistening pike before purchasing vegetables and a magnificently ripe cheese. The knowledge that Mr Hackett would be our guest put an entirely different complexion upon the evening. I felt comfortable with Jane and Gabriel Harte, but now I was distinctly nervous. What if I burned the pie or curdled the custard?

I baked the apple and quince pie and a cinnamon and raisin cake, then prepared the vegetables, poached the pike and dressed it with lemon and watercress sauce. The kitchen was hot and, fearful the fish would turn, I carried it down to the cellar since the pantry was already full.

The smell hit me as soon as I opened the cellar door. Gagging, I retreated. I managed to fit the pike in the pantry after all, balanced precariously on top of the muslin-draped cheese, before lighting a candle to go and investigate the problem in the cellar. It was soon apparent that the floor was awash with seepage from the cesspit. I didn't understand it. We hadn't been in the house long enough for the cesspit to need emptying.

I closed the door firmly behind me and marched outside to the building site next door.

'Who's in charge here?' I demanded of a youth mixing mortar in a bucket.

He nodded at a man sawing a plank of wood.

'Excuse me,' I said.

The man continued sawing until I tapped him on the shoulder.

'There's a problem in my cellar,' I said.

He pushed his hat onto the back of his head and stared at me.

'I said . . . '

'What's that got to do with me, missus?'

'You built the house, didn't you?'

'That's as maybe but . . . '

'There's sewage rising up in my cellar and don't you dare tell me it's nothing to do with you!'

'Ah.' He scratched at his head. 'I did tell Mister Hackett he ought to of emptied the old cesspit before we built on top of it. The foundations must of broken through into the old pit.'

'Let me be clear. You built a new house on top of an overflowing cesspit?'

'That's about the size of it. Nothing I can do, missus.'

'Mr Hackett is to be my guest for supper tonight and I shall speak to him about it.'

He laughed. 'Good luck with that, is all I can say.' The foreman made himself busy with his saw again.

Fuelled by anger, I swept and polished the house within an inch of its life, beating the rush mats outside in the garden and sweating over the ironing of the napkins. I laid the table carefully, setting out the new glasses and the crisply starched napkins. Since I had no flowers in the garden, the scented candle given to me by Gabriel Harte took pride of place in the centre of the table.

At last, the leg of beef was on the spit over a low fire and I judged it safe to leave it unattended while I went upstairs and changed. I had laid out my silk dress ready on the bed, together with the satin slippers and silk stockings. Stripping to my shift, I washed away the grime of a day spent sweeping, cleaning and cooking, paying special attention to my fingernails in case the odour of onions and fish lingered. Suddenly tired and headachy after all my exertions I sank down on the bed, wishing I had twenty minutes to close my eyes and doze but knew I daren't risk the leg of beef burning.

Sitting in a semi-daydream, combing my hair and smoothing cream onto my work-roughened hands it suddenly occurred to me that my courses were late. I sat bolt upright and counted the days on my fingers since the last time I'd bled. Thirty days! Perhaps a baby was already growing inside me? Suddenly remembering the beef, I hurried to dress and then rubbed a few drops of Summer

Garden onto my temples, although, magically, my headache had disappeared.

I was hurrying down the stairs when I heard Robert's key in the lock.

'I can smell something cooking,' he said. 'Is it all right?'

'Heaven preserve us, the beef!' I rushed downstairs to the kitchen.

The leg of beef was a trifle overcooked on one side but I cranked the spit and turned it over. After hurriedly putting on an apron, I made myself busy cooking the remaining dishes and it wasn't long before the doorknocker sounded. I was relieved to find Jane and Gabriel Harte standing on the doorstep. At least I wouldn't have to make stilted conversation with Mr Hackett until the others arrived. I noticed that Mr Harte carried his violin.

Jane's delicately perfumed cheek was cool against mine as she kissed me. 'I've brought you these,' she said, handing me a bunch of pink and cream roses. 'And some rosemary cuttings. I remember you said you were making a herb garden.'

I buried my nose in the roses to inhale their sweet scent. 'How lovely! I've already planted some herbs but I lack rosemary so your gift is very welcome.'

'And here's a housewarming present from me,' said Mr Harte in his deep tones. He proffered a jar, glazed in shades of soft green.

I took the jar from him and removed the lid. Inside was another lid, perforated with small holes and at once the same bewitchingly musky perfume arose from it that I recognised from the hall at the House of Perfume. 'Oh!' I said, delighted. 'It's a rotten-pot.'

Gabriel Harte smiled. 'So you remember that?'

I hoped fervently that my present would mask any unpleasant odour from the cellar.

Robert came to greet our guests, engaging Gabriel Harte in conversation while Jane exclaimed in delight at our new home.

'I cannot thank you enough for your gifts,' I said. 'We had so little furniture but now it feels like a real home. And it's extremely fortunate that we now have a dining table because Robert has invited Mr Hackett to join us.'

Jane wrinkled her nose. 'I hope you don't mind me saying that I'd hoped it would be just the four of us?'

'Mr Hackett invited himself and Robert isn't in a position to refuse him.'

Jane patted my wrist. 'We shall just have to make the best of it.'

Then the sound of the doorknocker resounded through the house.

Mr Hackett was dressed in a coat of a garish shade of lime green. 'I can smell something delicious even before I step over the threshold,' he said.

'I hope you won't be disappointed,' I said. 'I have no Italian cooks to serve a dinner as fine as you are used to.' I took him into the parlour and slipped away to the kitchen.

The chickens were now basted to a glistening copper and the leg of beef rested on one of the fine serving dishes Jane had sent to me. I hurried upstairs and placed the dressed pike on the dining table and then trotted up and down the stairs several more times until all the dishes were arranged. I lit the candle and went to announce that dinner was served.

I needn't have been anxious about the simple fare I offered. The beef was crisp on the outside and rose pink within and the pike poached to perfection. Jane said that the apple and quince pie melted in her mouth.

'Heard you were coming tonight, Harte,' said Mr Hackett. 'Wondered if you'd thought any more about investing in my schemes for the rebuilding of the city?'

Mr Harte placed his wine glass carefully on the table, a finger's width from the edge of his plate. 'It may be a better time to invest now, since the war with the Dutch is over and building materials are more readily available.'

'In any case, I have my own brickyard so I'm able to keep costs low.'

'It's a pity that the great visions for the city as presented by Sir Christopher Wren, John Evelyn and Robert Hooke have not been realised,' said Mr Harte.

'To be sure, those grandiose schemes with their piazzas and boulevards appeared to be an opportunity to redesign on the model of the great cities of Italy and France but they were impractical and unaffordable.' Hackett speared a thick slice of beef with his knife. 'So our beloved city will rise again but as a vastly improved version of its ancient self. The rat-infested slums have gone. Those trades producing noxious smells will be banished from the centre of the city and the churches, guildhalls, businesses and homes will be built to a new model.' He pointed his knife at Gabriel Harte. 'A better model, just like this house.'

'Losing the slums was the only good thing to come out of the Fire,' said Robert.

'There's a once in a lifetime opportunity for investors now,' said Hackett, ignoring Robert's comment. 'Out with the old and in with the new, I say! A chance for good roads and affordable houses with proper drains for the masses.'

'Very public spirited of you.' Gabriel Harte raised his glass. 'And I'll drink to the health of those who move back into the city and make it come alive again.'

'Hear, hear!' replied Robert, draining his own glass.

'A very fine supper,' said Mr Hackett, helping himself to another chicken leg and a substantial slice of pie.

'You have a good cook,' said Jane.

'We don't have a cook,' I said.

'No cook?' Her grey eyes opened wide.

'Nor any other servants.'

Hackett laughed. 'Mistress Finche is a most capable woman if a little, shall we say, high-spirited at times.'

There was an edge to his voice that made Robert's lips tighten.

'How do you manage?' asked Jane.

'I've had to learn,' I said crisply. 'Since the Great Fire we have endured many challenges.'

'Finche's father is still in the debtors' prison,' said Hackett casually, chewing on his chicken bone.

I seethed, only just biting back a sharp retort.

'You made a point of mentioning that before,' said Gabriel Harte. 'Unnecessarily, I believe.'

'I'd no idea you had no servants,' said Jane. Her expression was concerned. 'What a great deal of trouble you have been put to! Not even a scullery maid?'

I shook my head. 'But I'm delighted you came tonight.' I put my hand to my mouth. 'Oh! I forgot the cheese,' I said. 'Let me take away some of the empty dishes and I'll fetch it.'

'I'll help you,' said Jane.

'Is there no more wine?' asked Mr Hackett.

'I'll go to the cellar,' said Robert.

Mr Hackett lumbered to his feet, belching under his breath. 'As there are no servants,' he said with a pointed glance at me, 'I'll save you the trouble.'

'No, really . . . ' Robert stood up, his cheeks scarlet.

I bit my lip. Dare I let Hackett go down to the cellar? But how could I resist? 'I'm sure Mr Hackett can find the wine, Robert,' I said, smiling sweetly.

'Sit down, man!' Hackett pushed Robert down onto his chair. 'I've no airs and graces,' he said, following Jane and me from the room.

'You know where the cellar is,' I said as we reached the bottom of the stairs.

'I should do, seeing as it's my house.'

I pursed my lips and went into the kitchen.

'Shall I scrape the plates?' asked Jane.

Standing close to Jane, I noticed again her subtle perfume, flowery and sweet without being cloying.

Then Shadow, ears cocked, materialised beside us, looking longingly up at Jane as she held the plates.

Whilst Jane was making friends with Shadow I opened the pantry door and removed the muslin from the cheese. Aghast, I stared at it. Mice, or rats, had nibbled all around one side of it. I bent down to look at the wall under the shelf and saw that the crack, which I'd filled with leftover mortar begged from the builders next door, had widened and there were rodent droppings on the floor. Hastily, I trimmed the cheese with a sharp knife. It looked a little lopsided so I put it on a large serving dish and surrounded it with apples.

It was then that I heard the roar of rage.

Jane and I hurried to the top of the cellar stairs to find Hackett clasping a bottle of wine, standing on one leg and shaking stinking liquid off his foot.

Robert and Gabriel Harte came running from the dining room stairs to discover what had happened.

'Mistress Finche!' Hackett snatched hold of my wrist. 'What the hell is going on in your cellar, woman?'

Gabriel Harte raised his eyebrows. 'Perhaps you should phrase your question more politely to Mistress Finche?' His words hung like frost in the air.

'It's perfectly simple,' I said. 'Mr Hackett built this house, and the one next door, I expect, on top of an old cesspit. Unfortunately, he decided not to empty it first and the new foundations have broken into it. There's an unfortunate problem with seepage.'

'That's appalling!' said Jane, holding her handkerchief to her nose.

'A regrettable oversight,' blustered Hackett, glancing at Gabriel Harte. 'I'll arrange for the night soil men to call upon you at your earliest convenience, Mistress Finche.'

'How kind,' I murmured, noticing Robert's mouth was pinched

with anger. 'And now shall we return to the dining room to finish our supper?' I said.

The ripe cheese barely masked the appalling stench coming from Hackett's shoes, overpowering even the sweet perfume from the rotten-pot and the scented candle. Any of the party who still had room for cheese quickly lost their appetite and we retired to the parlour.

'I can't help noticing your perfume, Jane,' I said. 'Is it orange blossom?'

She nodded. 'Gabriel made it especially for me when Toby was born. He says no one else will ever have this formulation.'

All at once I felt a prick of jealousy. I couldn't imagine Robert making such a romantic gesture for me. But then, I sighed, we hadn't married for love.

'Society ladies are always asking Gabriel to create a unique perfume for them but he's rarely persuaded,' said Jane. 'I can only remember him making a special formulation for a select few in recent years: his grandmother before she died, my sister, bless her soul, and one poor lady whose husband beat her.'

'What a shame!' I said. 'It's a waste of his talent not to make such lovely perfumes, don't you think?'

'I'm not so sure.' Jane smiled. 'It drives the ladies wild – so used to having their own way in most things – that they cannot persuade him to change his mind. Meanwhile they buy from the standard ranges, which are delightful, whilst remaining constantly tantalised by the hope that today will be different.'

'He's an astute businessman, then,' I said, glancing at Hackett, holding forth loudly upon what the King and parliament were doing wrong and how much better, in his opinion, he would rule the country himself if only he had the time.

I suppressed a yawn. After all my hard work in preparing for the supper party, now that I had sat down and the anxiety over cooking the dinner had passed, I was suddenly overcome with exhaustion. I wondered if this tiredness was a sign that I was indeed expecting a baby.

Jane flickered a glance at me as we listened to Hackett's voice booming on and on. I didn't like him but he had such a powerful presence that his energy filled the room, making him impossible to ignore. In an attempt to prevent Hackett from monopolising the entire evening I clapped my hands and called upon Mr Harte to entertain us with his violin. We discovered that he was an accomplished musician and it was a pleasure to listen to him.

At last our guests took their leave.

Jane kissed my cheek and murmured that we should meet again before too long.

'I've wrapped up some slices of raisin cake for Toby,' I said.

'Raisin cake?' said Mr Hackett. 'I'll have a slice or two of that, if you please, Mistress Finche.'

I did not please but was in no position to refuse and wrapped up his portion of cake and handed it to him with as good a grace as I could muster.

'An excellent dinner and entertaining company,' said Gabriel Harte, bowing to me.

I glowed with pleasure, happy that my efforts were appreciated.

'She's a fine cook, Finche,' said Hackett, punching Robert's arm in a playful fashion. 'But I couldn't abide a wilful wife, myself.'

Robert gave him a sickly grin.

I lifted my chin and smiled at Hackett. 'I trust you will remember your promise and send the night soil men to us tomorrow?' I said.

A flicker of annoyance passed over his face. 'I said I would, didn't I?'

'Thank you so much,' I said, smiling sweetly.

The door closed behind our guests and then there was the sound of carriage wheels rolling away.

I yawned. 'I'm too tired to clear up tonight. Shall we go straight to bed?' Then I saw that Robert's face was tight with fury.

'What possessed you to let Mr Hackett go down to the cellar when you knew the cesspit was overflowing?' he hissed.

I stared at him. 'We didn't have a great deal of choice in the matter.'

'You knew the cellar was awash!'

A small spark of anger ignited in my breast. 'I doubt if I could have prevented him. And *you* certainly didn't!'

'He's not a man to be crossed!'

'He was in a tolerable good humour when he left us. Besides, he's promised to rectify the problem.'

'But at what cost?' Robert turned away from me and strode across the hall and up the stairs.

A moment later the bedchamber door slammed.

Undecided, I stood motionless in the hall. Should I go after him and apologise? Annoyance pricked at me. Tired as I was, I knew I was too irritated to sleep. Why did Robert always have to cast a pall of discomfiture over everything? Sighing heavily, I returned to the kitchen.

Two hours later the kitchen was spotless. Shadow lay fast asleep under the table. Wearily, I carried a candle outside to the privy. It was then that I discovered that my monthly visitor had arrived and I was not to have a child after all.

Chapter 15

Jane Harte, holding Toby by the hand, arrived on my doorstep the following morning.

'I know it's impolite of me to arrive so early but I worried about you after we left last night with all the clearing up to do on your own,' she said.

'So we came to help you,' chimed in Toby.

I stretched out to take Jane and Toby's hands. 'How very kind! Come in and I'll make you some refreshments.'

'Is there some raisin cake left?' asked Toby with a hopeful smile.

'Come down to the kitchen and we'll see.'

'Will Shadow be there? Mama told me about him.'

'Shadow is never far away. That's how he came by his name.'

In the kitchen I opened the pantry to fetch a bottle of cider while Jane exclaimed because everything was cleaned and neatly put away.

'I knew I wouldn't sleep easily last night until it was all done,' I said.

'You must be very weary today?'

'All the better for seeing you.' I opened the back door and called to Shadow, who came bounding up to greet my visitors.

Toby laughed with glee as Shadow greeted him, tail wagging furiously.

'Watch this, Toby,' I said. 'It's a new trick I've been teaching him.' I fixed Shadow with a stern stare. 'Shadow, die for King Charles!'

Shadow rolled over and played dead.

'How very obedient he is!' said Jane.

The effect was spoiled somewhat when Shadow leaped to his feet and thrust his nose into my hand. 'He's supposed to remain lying down until I give him the command,' I said. 'He's expecting a treat now but he hasn't really behaved well enough.'

'May I train him?' asked Toby eagerly.

'Why don't you take him outside into the garden? I'll give you some little pieces of bacon rind to bribe him into good behaviour.'

After Toby and Shadow had trotted outside, I poured cider and cut slices of cake and put them on a tray to carry upstairs.

'Do let us stay in the kitchen, Kate,' said Jane. 'It's so easy and comfortable here. Besides –' she glanced at the open door '– I like to keep Toby in earshot when he's in the garden. I'm sure you'll feel the same when you have children of your own.'

She must have seen my expression change since she reached out and took my hand. 'I'm sorry, did I say something to offend you?'

I shook my head. 'It's just that . . . ' I sighed. 'I had hoped that I was to have a baby but then, last night, my hopes were dashed.'

'I'm sorry. But there will be other opportunities.'

'Robert . . . ' I hesitated but Jane's grey eyes were kind. 'Robert doesn't want a child. Not at present, at least. Since his parents are in prison, we save every penny we can to clear their debts. Until that day, Robert doesn't want another mouth to feed.'

'But that might take years!'

'I know.'

Jane squeezed my hand. 'God moves in mysterious ways and His plans for you may be different from those of your husband.'

'That's what I pray for,' I confessed.

Our conversation moved on to other matters: my plans for the garden, the new row of houses being built opposite, Jane's forthcoming visit to an aunt in the country and the continuing difficulty of finding a good nursemaid for Toby.

We were so absorbed in our conversation that it was only when Toby came indoors that we realised it was past noon and Jane said that they must leave, despite Toby's protests.

'Do, please, come to visit me again,' I said.

'Call on us at the House of Perfume when I return from the country,' said Jane.

I was about to pack up a basket of food to take to Mother Finche when there was a knock at the door. Drying my hands on my apron, I hurried upstairs. I opened the door to find three of the workmen from next door. Two carried pickaxes and the other a shovel.

'Dick Lewis,' said one of the men, doffing his battered hat and winking at his mates.

'Have you come to see the cellar?' I said. 'The old cesspit has overflowed.'

'Stinks worse'n a tanner's yard. Let the dog see the rabbit, then,' said Dick with a cheerful grin. 'And seeing as I'll be busy down there for a while perhaps you'd be persuaded to give us something to wet our whistles, missus? Mighty hot work, digging out a vault.'

Silently, I showed them to the cellar door and they descended the stairs into the evil-smelling gloom.

I fetched three tankards and took them to the top of the stairs. 'There's a barrel of ale on the shelf. And I expect to find enough left for my husband's supper tonight.'

'Got a lamp, missus? It's like the pits of Hades down here.'

I sat in the kitchen sewing petticoats for the remainder of the afternoon, listening to the thud of pickaxes and the scrape of the shovel on the cellar floor. Each blow of the pickaxe sent such vibrations through the house that the plates rattled on the dresser.

At last the men emerged and stood in my kitchen, their boots dripping with filth. The stench made me want to retch.

'Right, missus. That's us done for the day,' said Dick Lewis.

The dung cart arrived soon after and the night soil men traipsed up and down the stairs with their buckets, complaining about the August heat all the while.

'Grand new house this may be,' said one of the men, 'but they shoulda put a back gate in your garden, missus, so we could go through the kitchen door and save us going up and down two flights. The place is all stairs!' He wiped his sweating brow on his forearm.

'Watch what you're doing, please!' I shuddered as stinking effluent slopped out of the bucket and dripped down the stairs. Somehow it made it all the worse that it wasn't even our own sewage.

Doors banged and booted feet clumped incessantly up and down all afternoon. Shadow didn't approve of the strange men invading his house and had to be shut, barking, in the garden to stop him nipping their ankles. The stench was overpowering and, even though I opened all the windows, it hung over everything.

Unable to watch any longer, I took myself off to the parlour to polish the panelling. Irritably, I rubbed at the oak but not even the scent of lavender and beeswax soothed me. Muttering under my breath, I worked the polish deep into the grain and then stopped in consternation. A crack, wide enough to push a finger into, had opened up in one corner of the room.

At that moment one of the men banged on the parlour door. 'All done, missus. Here's the account.' He proffered a grimy piece of paper in a dirt-ingrained fist.

'You must render your account to Mr Hackett.'

The man tipped his hat onto the back of his head. 'Don't know nothing about that.'

'In any case,' I said, my face flaming, 'I have not the means to pay you at present.'

He sucked his teeth. 'Put it all back again, shall I?'

'You wouldn't!'

He cocked his head and raised an eyebrow at me and I longed to slap his impertinent face. I squared my shoulders. 'Leave the account with me and I will pass it to Mr Hackett for payment.'

'I'll come back tomorrow evening.' He smiled, showing blackened stumps of teeth. 'Be a shame if the dung cart upset itself all over your front steps, wouldn't it?' Without another word, he left.

Later, I was in the kitchen, reheating the last of the pie when Robert returned from work.

'The house reeks,' he said, putting a hand to his nose.

'Mr Hackett's men have been here all afternoon, digging up the cellar. And then the dung cart came. It smells so dreadful that I've carried two chairs and the small table outside so we can have our supper in the garden.'

The garden was quiet again since the workmen had gone home for the day. Sun slanted over the wall and I saw some of the tension drain away from Robert's face as he ate his supper.

'I have such plans for the garden, Robert,' I said. 'Can you imagine an apple tree, or a plum if you prefer, over in that corner? And honeysuckle trained over the walls.'

'I spent many a happy hour in the garden in Lombard Street,' sighed Rob. 'It's hard to imagine that it's all gone.'

I was about to encourage him away from melancholy thoughts when the doorknocker sounded.

Robert frowned. 'Are you expecting visitors?'

I shook my head then hurried upstairs as the knocker banged again, more insistently this time. I struggled to open the door as the latch had become unaccountably stiff and was surprised to find Elias Maundrell waiting on the step.

'Is Finche at home?' Without waiting for a reply, he surged across the threshold. 'It's urgent that I speak to him. Fetch your master at once, if you please!'

Chagrined, I realised that since I'd answered the door he thought I was the serving maid. 'My husband is at his dinner,' I said, standing firmly in his path.

'Nonetheless, I will speak with him urgently.' His nose twitched and he glanced down to check the soles of his shoes.

I opened the parlour door. 'I'll tell him you're here.'

Heaving a sigh, Mr Maundrell stepped into the parlour and began to pace back and forth.

Down in the garden, Robert wiped his mouth on his napkin and pushed back his chair. 'I'd better see what the old misery wants.'

A short while later I heard voices raised in a heated argument and crept up the stairs to listen.

'Finche, I insist you speak to Hackett! You must appeal to him before it's too late!'

'Don't you dare tell me what I must or must not do!'

The parlour door was ajar and I glimpsed Elias Maundrell grasp Robert by his collar.

'I'm telling you, those bricks are dangerous!'

'And I'm telling you to leave this house.' Robert shook off Maundrell's hand and strode towards the door.

Hastily, I retreated downstairs as their staccato footsteps crossed the hall.

'You mark my words, Finche!' Maundrell's angry tones reverberated around the hall. 'You'll never be able to live with your conscience if –'

The front door slammed, shaking the house to its very foundations.

I waited for Robert to return downstairs, wondering what had passed between the two men. After a while I went to find him.

He was in the parlour, staring out of the window.

'What did Maundrell want?'

'Nothing to concern you.'

'He sounded –' I sought for the word '– desperate.'

'He's full of sour grapes because Mr Hackett didn't want to buy his bricks and sent him off with a flea in his ear. Silly old fool!'

'What did he mean, saying that the bricks are dangerous?'

He spun around to face me, scarlet with rage. 'Were you listening to my private conversation?'

'You were shouting!'

'I'm warning you, Kate –' he slammed his hand against wall '– if you know what's good for you, don't you dare nag me about something you know nothing about.'

I took an involuntary step back, frightened by the fury in his face. Without another word, I retreated to the safety of the kitchen.

The next morning Robert left for work without saying goodbye. Tight-lipped, I packed my basket and set off to visit Mother and Father Finche. As I made my way through the city, I observed how many more houses were now completed. Here and there the unmade roads had been paved and the whirling dust that had blown over the wasteland for the past two years had begun to settle. The sound of horses' hooves, wheeled traffic grinding over cobbles and the occasional cry of a knife-grinder or costermonger made me smile. The city was beginning to awaken.

Father Finche's cough was worse again. I propped him up and fed him chicken soup. Mother Finche watched me, an anxious question in her eyes, while I kept up a flow of bright conversation.

'I suppose there are always problems that arise in a newly built house,' I said. 'The plaster is still drying out and I'm thankful for the warm weather or I'm sure our clothes would be growing mushrooms by now.' I sighed. 'At first I worried that the house smelled as damp as a crypt but now it smells like a midden.'

'It's lucky the overflow didn't happen in the autumn,' said Mother Finche. 'All your preserves and smoked meats would have spoiled.'

Mother Finche wiped soup off her husband's chin. 'John, will you try a little of Kate's bread? I could dip it in the soup to make it soft.'

'So tired,' he whispered, closing his eyes.

'We'll leave you to doze a while,' she said.

Arm in arm, we walked around the courtyard.

'Kate, I'm worried about John.' She wiped away a tear on a corner of her apron. 'Even if we are released from this place, I can't imagine that he'll ever be really well again. Oh, Kate, what is to become of us?'

Helplessly, I patted her back while she cried on my shoulder. 'We're doing all we can to settle the debts.'

Mother Finche heaved a sigh. 'You're a good girl, Kate. Forgive me; I have the toothache again and it makes all seem worse than it is. But I do so wish Robert didn't have to work so hard that he never has time to visit us.'

I could say nothing but it made me angry that Robert remained obdurate about visiting his parents and I was forced into the uncomfortable position of having to make constant excuses for him. Unpleasant though the jail was, surely he could put aside his distaste to give them a little comfort?

It was late afternoon by the time I reached home. I'd collected a bundle of nightshifts from Dolly and then gone to the market so my arms were full as I struggled to unlock the front door. It seemed to be wedged and I had to put my packages on the step to grapple with the key. The lock had become exceptionally stiff and, once I'd heard it click, I was surprised that the door still wouldn't open.

It was hot and I was already anxious that the fish in my basket would turn if I didn't put it on the cold slab very soon. I continued to push at the door, tears of frustration welling in my eyes, when I saw the dung cart coming along the road. It drew up in front of the house in a cloud of dust and the driver jumped down and advanced on me.

'Come to collect my money, missus.'

'You'll have to wait,' I said. 'The door's stuck.'

'Well, now. My cart is full to overflowing.' He scratched his head and smiled wolfishly at me. 'I've got a terrible thirst on, but I shan't have time to wait and empty the load at the laystall on the edge of the city if I'm to go to the alehouse. Of course, if you was to pay me what you owe, I'd be happy to . . . '

'How can I pay you?' I said peevishly. 'The money is inside and I can't open the door.' I gave the door a kick. It didn't budge, but I yelped as I stubbed my toe. 'Don't just stand there,' I said, through gritted teeth. 'See if you can do it.'

Obligingly, he put his brawny shoulder against the door and pushed. Nothing happened.

'Oh, for pity's sake! I'll fetch the workmen from next door.' I marched down the steps and onto the building site. A piercing whistle came from the scaffolding above me, followed by raucous laughter as I stuck my nose in the air and picked my way through piles of sand and bricks towards Dick Lewis, who was busy mixing cement.

'My front door is stuck tight fast,' I said.

Dick leaned on his spade with beefy forearms brown from the sun.

'Please will you open it for me?' I was reduced to giving him a winning smile.

He winked. 'Seeing as it's you, missus.'

He followed me back to the house and he and the night soil man tried without success to push the door open. Three more workmen brought a roof beam with them and, with a great deal of grunting, they united forces and used the beam as a battering ram. After several attempts the door splintered and then crashed open.

'Whatever made it stick so badly?' I asked. 'There hasn't been any rain to swell the timber.'

Dick Lewis ran his hand over the damaged door and inspected the frame. 'New houses sometimes take time to settle,' he said.

'I'll send my lad over to plane down the door and give it a lick of paint.'

'Never mind that,' said the night soil man, placing himself squarely in front of me. 'Where's my money?'

Wordlessly, I fetched the coins Robert had given me the night before. I hoped that he would recoup the sum from Hackett or we'd be without housekeeping money the following week.

Later, after they had all gone, I noticed new cracks running from floor to ceiling in the hall.

Chapter 16

September 1668

On the second day of September there was a fast day in remembrance of the Great Fire. Robert and I walked down Lombard Street on the way to attend a remembrance service at All Hallows. He clenched his teeth as we passed the flattened area of ground where the Finche house had been. Hackett hadn't yet started to build on the plot, though the rubble had been cleared.

We sat in silence in All Hallows, both of us recalling the terrible days of the fire two years ago when our lives had changed so dramatically. Afterwards, we returned home and went supperless to bed. Robert turned his back on me again. Lonely, I lay awake in the darkness berating myself for not being happy when I had a husband and the home I'd dreamed of for years.

The next day, in an attempt to shake off my fit of melancholy, I visited Jane Harte. We had met several times in the past month and I had grown to look forward to her company.

Jacob Samuels opened the door to my knock. 'The mistress is in the garden,' he said, looking up at me with his piercing black eyes.

I noticed that he carried a lace-trimmed handkerchief scented with a dark and musky perfume. I was disappointed that there was no sign of Mr Harte, but I heard the lilting sound of his flute coming from behind the closed door of the Perfume Salon.

I followed Jacob through the house, smiling a little to myself when I saw he wore high-heeled shoes with intricate silver buckles. A hunchback he may be, but that didn't prevent him from a degree of vanity.

Jacob opened a door to the garden and waved me through.

'Follow the lavender walk,' he said, 'until you reach the fountain. You'll find Mistress Harte in the arbour.'

I set off along the path, taking pleasure in the neatly kept flowerbeds and stopping at the pool where a dolphin spouted water and fish lazed in the sun-warmed water. Then I heard a small cry and turned to see Toby trip and fall from his hobby horse.

'Are you all right?' I called.

He brushed gravel off his knees and his face lit up into a wide smile as he saw me.

He ran towards me, his arms outstretched, and I caught him up in a hug. 'Did you bring Shadow?' he asked.

'Not today, sweeting. But I have brought you this.' I pulled back the cloth that covered my basket and showed him the glistening saffron buns that nestled inside.

He drew in his breath with delight and then we heard footsteps as Jane appeared.

'You spoil him, Kate,' she said, smiling fondly at her son.

'May I eat them now, Mama?'

'Come and sit on the bench beside us and you may have one.'

The leaves were already turning russet as summer faded into autumn and it was very pleasant to sit under the honeysuckle arbour. To Toby's delight, a robin came to peck at the crumbs from his bun.

Jane wiped his mouth with her handkerchief. 'Now run along and play while I have a gossip with Mistress Finche.'

'How I envy you your son, Jane,' I sighed, as Toby trotted off to play.

'You still have no interesting news then?'

I shook my head. And none expected if Robert continued to turn away from me every night.

'Don't look so despondent, Kate! Robert must be sick with worry about his parents and I'm sure it will all come right in time.'

'But will it?' I swallowed back a sob. 'Robert barely speaks to me any more. We haven't argued, but he comes home, eats a meagre supper and then retires early to bed. I hear him walking about the house at night, but he will never tell me what ails him.'

'Husbands rarely talk about what troubles them.'

I hesitated. 'I think it's something to do with Mr Hackett.'

'Gabriel has invested in one of Mr Hackett's schemes,' said Jane, a thoughtful expression on her face. 'He's building new houses in Rochester Court, which sound as if they'll be very fine.'

'Rochester Court? Isn't that where a house was burned?'

Jane nodded. 'I cannot like Mr Hackett, however much he professes to be such a benefactor.'

'There's something . . . ' I bit my lip. 'Something almost *savage* about him. I find it hard to breathe when he looks at me. But I never dare to voice such an opinion to Robert, who quite dotes on him.'

Jane sighed. 'And it never does to burden husbands with concerns of your own.'

I glanced at her. She looked tired and troubled, I thought. Selfishly, I had been too caught up in my own concerns. 'You can always talk to me, Jane.'

'Bless you, Kate!' She reached for my hand. 'Since Eleanor died all my friends appear so frivolous and there isn't anyone I care to confide in. I never expected to marry and perhaps I expected too much. Somehow I thought a husband would prevent loneliness, but Gabriel and I have little in common except for Toby. We're all alone in the end, aren't we?'

I nodded in agreement, thinking of my own despair. 'I've never had a friend before.' I smiled bleakly. 'Aunt Mercy never allowed that.'

'She sounds like a dragon! Why did she treat you so badly?'

I sighed. 'It's an old story. She fell in love with my father but he chose my mother, her younger sister. Aunt Mercy never forgave Mama for "stealing" him and when she became my guardian she visited her dislike upon me, keeping me a virtual prisoner.' I didn't tell Jane that when my dowry was being agreed with the Finches' lawyers, I'd discovered that Aunt Mercy had profited for years from the inheritance my parents had left for my care, enjoying choice cuts of meat and fine wines while I had suffered stale crusts and water. I'd been far too frightened of her to demand she made restitution.

Footsteps crunched along the gravel and I looked up to see Gabriel approaching.

'Is that Mistress Finche I can hear?' he called. He was as elegant as ever in a sapphire blue coat.

'Come and join us, Gabriel,' said Jane.

We sat in the autumn sunshine and talked of inconsequential things while I studied the lean lines of his long legs and how the sun lit up his wheat-blond hair. I felt sad for Jane that marriage to such a man had not given her the fulfilment she'd hoped for and wondered if Gabriel had been disappointed too.

'Tell me, how does the rebuilding in the city progress?' he asked me.

'I hear nigh on eight hundred houses will be completed by Christmastide and another eight hundred by this time next year. Some roads are levelled and paved and are a great improvement from before the Fire.'

'I heard that a new house in Canning Street collapsed the other day,' said Gabriel. 'It seems that the builder was too keen to turn a profit and used shoddy materials. I daresay many fortunes will be made and lost while the city rises again.'

I reflected briefly that Hackett must be only one of a number of builders grasping the opportunity to make themselves rich.

'But I still mourn the loss of the old city,' said Gabriel. 'I could walk almost anywhere before without becoming lost, but now all my familiar landmarks have gone.'

I left the House of Perfume a little while later and, as I walked, I attempted to imagine what a frightening and unfamiliar place the city must have become for even such a self-sufficient blind man as Gabriel Harte.

Another house was being built on the corner of Cheapside and Ironmonger Lane and the row of town houses opposite to my own were well under way. The roof was complete on the house next door and the perpetual sound of whistling and hammering came from the open windows. Perhaps, before very long, I would have neighbours.

My front door was sticking again. I wrestled with the key and heaved my shoulder against it until it finally grated open. It worried me that the long crack in the hall penetrated through to the front of the house, running from the corner of the bedroom window down to the parlour window. I'd tried to talk to Robert about it but he brushed away my fears with the comment that new houses always took time to dry out.

I spent the afternoon making plum jam and mint jelly. The mint in my little herb garden had grown well and there was sufficient for four pots of jelly, which pleased me a great deal. Afterwards, I went outside to water the rose bush I'd planted against the garden wall. The ground had taken a great deal of effort to clear but I was confident that, by the next summer, I should have my first blooms. I smiled as I remembered how shocked Robert had been when I'd gone out into the street one evening with a bucket to collect horse droppings. One thing I'd learned from Aunt Mercy's gardener was how good horse dung was for the roses.

Later, down in the cellar, I noticed a new fissure running down the wall as I arranged the pots of preserves on the cellar shelves. The shelf had begun to slope down at one end and I worried that the pots would slide off it. I cursed another example of the builders' poor workmanship.

Upstairs the front door banged shut and I hurried to the kitchen to check on the pigeons roasting over the fire but there was no sign of Robert. I found him in our bedchamber, lying on his back on the bed with his hands clasped behind his head. I was shocked by how tired and grey he looked.

'Are you ill?' I asked, touching the back of my hand to his forehead.

Mutely, he shook his head.

'Supper will be ready very soon.'

'Not hungry,' he mumbled.

'But you must eat . . . '

'Don't fuss over me, Kate!' He turned his head away.

Stung, I left the room.

I'd lost my own appetite by then and was left restless and out of sorts. Calling to Shadow, we went for a walk. My footsteps gravitated towards the river and I found myself following my old route past the Tower and the burned-out Custom House. The breeze off the river was chilly and I walked briskly to keep warm. Shadow trotted along beside me, tail all a-wag and making joyous forays onto the low-tide shore, barking at the seagulls until they lifted off the mud in flocks and wheeled overhead.

The sun had set by the time I arrived home but not a candle was lit in the house. Robert had undressed, dropped his clothes on the floor, and burrowed under the bedclothes.

I undressed and slipped into bed beside him. It didn't take long to realise that he was only pretending to sleep. Clearly he didn't want to talk to me. My thoughts churned miserably as I tried to work out how I had failed to be a good wife but, eventually, I drifted into uneasy sleep.

Chapter 17

The following afternoon I returned home with two bundles of night-shifts and one of petticoats. I had negotiated hard over payment with Dolly but now I would need to sit up sewing half the night for the foreseeable future until my commission was complete. Wearily, I struggled downstairs to the kitchen.

Robert was sitting at the kitchen table hunched over a glass of ale.

'You're early,' I said, suddenly anxious.

'I told Hackett I was sickening.'

Hurrying to his side, I touched his forehead.

He shrugged off my hand.

Suddenly, a deep rumbling sound came from the cellar and the table slid away from us. I screamed as the floor caved in, the boards splintering and groaning. The table disappeared into the pit that had opened up at our feet.

Robert snatched at my elbow and wrenched me to safety while plaster cracked off the walls and thumped to the ground, showering us in dust.

Then there was silence, only broken by fragments of plaster

scattering onto what was left of the floor. The terrible stench of the cesspit began to float up from the cellar.

Robert coughed, wiping grit from his eyes. 'Are you all right?'

I nodded, a hand pressed to my thudding heart.

Opening the cellar door, Robert peered down the stairs, stepping back hastily to avoid the rising cloud of dust. 'We'll have to let it settle before we can take a look.'

We skirted around the hole in the floor and went into the garden.

Coughing, I shook plaster out of my hair. 'Oh no!' I pressed a hand to my mouth. 'Look at my herb garden!'

Robert followed me as I ran to the patch of ground that I had laboured over for so long, clearing rubble and laying neat paths of reclaimed bricks. All the seedlings I had grown, the little rosemary hedge, the paths, had disappeared into a pit some ten feet deep.

'It's collapsed into the cellar!' said Robert.

'My preserves! I spent *hours* making jam to see us through the winter and now they've been buried.' It was all too much and angry tears began to well up. I kicked a stone into the hole. 'I hate Hackett!' I stormed. 'Is the house even safe enough for us to go into without risking our lives?'

Robert's face blanched. 'Stay here,' he commanded. He went back indoors.

I sank down on the garden bench and wiped my eyes. The evening sun slanted across the yellow brickwork and it nearly broke my heart that, although the house looked like the embodiment of my dreams, it was so flawed.

Robert, his hair covered in plaster dust, emerged from the back door carrying a brick in each hand. He held them up to the outside wall and studied them. 'Lord preserve us!' he whispered. 'Maundrell was right.'

'About what?'

He turned on me, his face shocked. 'Just leave me in peace for once, will you!' He flung the bricks over the wall then retreated to the end of the garden, where he paced back and forth.

Seething with repressed anger, it took me two hours to clean up the mess. Then I prepared a meagre supper of soup and bread, which we ate in silence in the dining room. As I cleared the plates, the doorknocker sounded.

I opened the door to find Ben Perkins on the step, twisting his hat in his hands. 'I wasn't sure if I should come by,' he said.

'Is it Nell?' Suddenly anxious, I wondered if she was ill.

'No, indeed. In fact –' a wide smile illuminated his face '– she's very well. We're expecting a happy event.'

'But that's wonderful news!' I experienced a sharp twinge of jealousy, but, of course, in our current circumstances it was a blessing that I wasn't with child.

'Is your husband at home?' His expression was uneasy again.

I called through the dining room door and Robert came to join us in the hall.

'I wasn't sure if I should come,' said Ben. 'It's just that I heard something today and I thought . . . '

'What?' asked Robert, rudely.

'I delivered a cartload of Portland stone today to a plot in Lombard Street. Nell told me you used to live there. It's a good location and now that the city is beginning to rise again, it's in a prime location. I'd heard that Hackett had sold on land there to another builder . . . '

'The old Finche house plot?'

Ben nodded. 'While I was unloading the cart I got talking to the foreman and, it being a warm day, we went to the tavern together to have our pie and a pot of ale. He told me that the new owner of the plot had paid fifteen shillings a foot for it.'

'Fifteen shillings!' Robert staggered slightly, reaching out a steadying hand to the wall. 'Fifteen shillings a foot? That can't be right!'

Ben shrugged. 'That's what the foreman told me. He was marvelling at how steeply prices have climbed in that location over the past few weeks. It's close to the main route out of the city towards the east, you see.'

'Fifteen shillings!' Robert shuddered and his face suddenly glistened with sweat. 'Hackett paid me four pence a foot for the Finche plot. Four stinking, measly pence!' He punched his hand against the wall. 'The bastard son of a whore!'

'Robert!' I touched his arm but he shook off my hand.

'Hackett lied to me! He said the plot would never be worth any more than four pence a foot. If he'd even paid me a *shilling* a foot I could have paid off all my father's debts.' Raging, he strode around the hall, kicking at the walls while Ben and I looked at each other aghast.

'I warned you Hackett was a tricky one,' said Ben.

'I daresay we'd have found out before long,' I said dully.

'Best be going. Nell will be wondering where I am.' He sidled towards the door and left.

Robert tore at his hair and punched the walls, railing against Hackett and his future issue all the while.

I made myself as small as possible in the corner of the hall until his fury dissipated and he slumped down on the bottom stair.

Finally, he caught sight of me and drew a shuddering breath. 'How could he, Kate? Has the man no decency at all? He *knew* that the Finche plot of land was all I had to release my father from the debtors' prison.'

'I suppose the land wasn't worth as much when he bought it from you.' I sat down on the stair beside him.

'I should have known it would increase in value as the city grew again. How could I have been so stupid? He tempted me with half-promises of making me his business partner, but I know now that will never happen. At least, not unless I embrace his passion for becoming rich by being as devious and scheming as he is and I've found that I don't have the stomach for it.'

‘Thank the Lord for that.’ I sighed. His face was so woebegone that I was overcome with pity for him. ‘You’re worn out, Robert. Come, let us go to bed.’

In the morning, Robert stirred and stretched. Yawning, he sat up and scratched his chest. ‘Make me some coffee,’ he said. ‘As strong and dark as you like, to give me courage. Despite your small size and soft voice, you are much braver than I. You stood up to Hackett right from the beginning and now I must do the same.’

‘Perhaps,’ I said. Without the constant threat of Aunt Mercy’s birch switch to keep me in check I knew I’d allowed myself to be recklessly impulsive with Hackett at times. ‘You’d be wise not to make an enemy of him, Robert. He’ll turn us out of this house. Shouldn’t you find other work before you challenge him?’

‘I’m not the man I want to be if I bow and scrape to his every wish. I’ll speak to him, man to man, this very morning.’

‘What will you say?’ I asked, uneasy.

‘First I shall ask him for the month’s wages he owes me and then I shall remind him of how he assured me that the Finche plot would never be worth more than four pence a foot. I’ll appeal to him to use a proportion of his profit to clear my father’s debts.’

I remained silent for a moment. ‘I don’t like the thought of you confronting him.’

‘I must regain my self-respect,’ he said. ‘I can’t do that while I remain in Hackett’s employ. Then I’ll ask Maundrell for my old job back.’

‘But you argued with him!’ What was Robert thinking of? Maundrell would never employ him again.

Robert shrugged. ‘If necessary, we’ll leave the city and seek employment in another town.’

‘But . . . ’

There was the steely light of determination in his eyes and I knew that whatever I said would make little difference.

❦

Heavy-hearted, I trudged across the city later that morning, wondering all the while how Robert's meeting with Hackett was going. Even though he'd spoken to me with confidence I fully expected him to come home early having been turned off without a reference. And in that case, we'd also be without a home.

Anxious that time might be short, I spent the afternoon walking the streets seeking new accommodation. A few hours later I was exhausted and despondent. The rooms we could afford were rat-infested or damp and anything halfway acceptable would be too expensive.

Dispirited, I returned to Ironmonger's Lane.

Robert wasn't there so, to keep myself occupied, I baked an apple pie for supper.

Later, a mutton stew simmered gently upon the fire and the golden apple pie, glistening with sugar, kept warm nearby. I sat down at the table to slice the cabbage, listening all the while for Robert's key in the lock.

The light began to fade. I carried a tallow candle upstairs, shielding the flickering flame with my hand until I reached the dining room and used it to light Gabriel Harte's lovely tuberose candle. Everything was ready.

Sitting by the parlour window with Shadow at my side, I watched the darkening street, waiting for Robert to appear. A gentle breeze from the open window stirred the air, bringing with it a faint smell of brick dust and damp cement, most unlike the smell of the old city. Before the Great Fire laid the city to waste, the air was as thick as soup. It had a scent all of its own, an odour that changed from day to day, but there had always been the underlying stink of rotting vegetables, drains, tallow, horse dung, sea-coal smoke and the sweat from a thousand bodies.

Now that the workmen had gone home there was little noise,

except the bark of a fox and the occasional rumble of cartwheels. The old city had never slept and the silence unnerved me. There were no lights in the half-built houses that loomed up out of the darkness. It was strange, and a little frightening, to know that I was alone in that part of the city. This hushed wasteland was sleeping, waiting for the people to move back and breathe life into it once more. Shivering, I closed the window.

The clock on the mantelpiece slowly ticked the seconds away. Anxiety gave way to annoyance. Robert knew I'd be counting out the minutes and worrying about the outcome of his conversation with Hackett.

Shadow whined and pawed at the door and I went downstairs to let him into the garden. He nosed around the edges of the crater into the cellar while I shivered in the breeze and imagined Robert lying in a drunken stupor in the alehouse.

The mutton stew had stuck to the bottom of the pan. Beyond hunger and in a sudden fit of temper I scraped it into Shadow's dinner bowl. Resentful and worried in equal measure, I went to bed.

Chapter 18

I awoke from a troubled sleep when the first light crept through the shutters. I'd had the old nightmare again, reliving my childhood terror of being locked in Aunt Mercy's freezing cellar in the suffocating dark with only scuttling rats for company. I stared at the ceiling for a moment and then rolled over abruptly to run my hand over the mattress on Robert's side of the bed. The sheet was cool and his pillow smooth. Barefoot, I ran downstairs in my nightshift, throwing open the door to each room as I went.

'Robert!' My voice echoed back to me as I ran through the hall.

Shadow loped along beside me, his tail wagging furiously as if we were playing a game.

It didn't take long to determine that Robert was nowhere to be found in either the house or garden. Breakfasting on stale bread dipped in coffee, I tried to reassure myself that he'd soon make a shamefaced reappearance. Anxiety made me queasy and I pushed my cup away while I considered my course of action. I sighed, facing up to the fact that I would have to visit Hackett.

Closing the front door firmly behind me, I set off at a brisk pace for Holborn before my courage deserted me.

Nat Hogg opened the door of Hackett's chambers and peered at me through narrowed eyes. 'What d'you want?'

'I should like to see Mr Hackett,' I said.

Hogg sucked his yellowing teeth. 'He ain't 'ere.'

Disconcerted, I studied Hogg's face while I tried to decide if he was lying. 'Where is he?'

Hogg shrugged. 'Out.'

Gritting my teeth at his insolent manner, I said, 'I must speak with him on an urgent matter of business.'

'Urgent business, is it? Well then, he's at Rochester Court off Fetter Lane.'

As Hogg began to close the door I put my foot in the crack. 'Have you seen my husband today?'

Hogg raised his bushy eyebrows. 'Lost 'im? Now that was careless.' He began to laugh, a sound as discordant as nails scraping down glass and I turned and hurried away.

The building site in Rochester Court was bustling. There were six town houses almost complete on one side of the court and a gaping trench of foundations opposite. Great heaps of sand and cement lay on the ground beside a forest of roof timbers. The air throbbed with the sound of hammering and sawing and shirtsleeved men wiped sweating foreheads as they hurried up and down ladders. I deduced from their close attention to their duties that Mr Hackett must be at hand.

I stood uncertainly on the fringe of all this activity until I spied Hackett, studying a set of drawings laid out on a wooden trestle. Holding up my skirts, I picked my way over the uneven ground, littered with bricks and offcuts of timber. I paused to stand at the edge of the foundations and peer down into the hole, while the sun beat down on the top of my head. Walls of dingy-looking bricks had already been built, dividing the cellars into separate storage rooms, ready to provide support for the floors above. It appeared that Hackett had learned from his mistake at Ironmonger Lane since the vault was very deep. It made me a little dizzy to look so far down.

'Mistress Finche.'

I gasped as a hand grabbed my arm. For one terrifying moment I lost my balance and teetered on the edge of the pit. My stomach lurched and a cold sweat prickled under my arms as I passed the point of no return but then the vice-like grip on my arm dragged me back to safety.

'Careful!' warned Hackett, a scowl on his face. 'You might have fallen.'

'I was just . . . ' I swallowed, a hand clasped to my breast while I attempted to steady my breathing.

'Why are you here? Is your husband still unwell?'

'Unwell? Have you seen him?' He stood too close to me and my nose wrinkled in distaste at the smell of his stale perspiration.

'Not today.'

'Oh! I had hoped –' I broke off, really worried now. 'But you saw him yesterday?'

'Said he was sickening for an ague but I suspected he was malingering. Damned inconvenient for me.' Hackett shrugged. 'Still, he was as pale as a bed sheet and clearly no use to man nor beast.'

'He didn't come home last night.'

'Did he not?'

A prickle of fear made me speak sharply. 'So where is he?'

'He's been in low spirits but that's no excuse for dodging his duties and I'm not happy about that at all.' Hackett grasped my elbow again in his hot, sweating hand and led me firmly away from the building site.

'Will you let me know if you hear of his whereabouts, Mr Hackett?'

He nodded curtly. 'And when he does come home, you tell him to hurry back to work. There are orders and accounts waiting for him to attend to. Lost orders cost money and I'll not give space to shirkers.' Letting go of me, he said, 'And, Mistress Finche, may I strongly advise you not to visit my building sites again? Far too dangerous.'

I rubbed my elbow. I should have bruises the next day.

Hackett bent to pick up a piece of timber from the dusty ground. A long nail projected from it and he tested the sharp point against his fleshy thumb while his eyes raked slowly over me, pausing when his gaze reached my breasts. 'As I say, no place for a lady. You never know what accident might befall you. It would be such a pity if you tripped and sliced open that pretty face of yours, wouldn't it?'

There was something in his tone and the penetrating expression in his dark eyes that frightened me. 'I shall continue to search for my husband,' I said, the colour flaring in my cheeks. 'And I'd be grateful if you'd send me a message if you have news of him.'

He flung the piece of timber away and I flinched as it flew close past my cheek, the nail flashing in the sunlight. 'Good day to you, madam.'

I watched Hackett stride off while my mind raced. Had I nearly fallen into the foundations or had Hackett caused me to lose my balance me as a warning? There had been an implied threat in his apparently solicitous words that unnerved me. And where could Robert be? He hadn't been ill when he left me, only anxious about confronting Hackett. I supposed his courage may have failed him at the last minute but he'd left home with the light of determination in his eyes. A horrible, hollow feeling grew in the pit of my stomach.

Undecided, I stood on Fetter Lane trying to decide which way to turn. I had no idea where to begin to look for Robert and suddenly I felt alone and frightened. But then I thought of Jane and turned and hurried towards Covent Garden as fast as my skirts would allow.

The air had become very close and I was breathless and overheated when I arrived on the doorstep of the House of Perfume.

'Is Mistress Harte at home?' I asked, stepping into the cool, scented hall, when Jacob Samuels opened the door.

'The mistress is indisposed,' he said.

'Oh!' I said, dismayed.

'I have instructions not to disturb her.' Pointedly, Jacob waited for me to leave.

'Please tell her I called and hope that she's soon recovered,' I said dully.

Then the Perfume Salon door opened. 'Is that Mistress Finche?' said Gabriel Harte.

'I came to see Jane,' I said, 'but I hear she is indisposed.'

'Another of her troublesome megrims. But, please, stay and take some refreshments.'

My spirits lifted at the thought of having his company for a while. 'I wouldn't wish to intrude upon your work.'

'Not at all.' He smiled. 'Besides, Toby would be disappointed to miss you. We shall sit in the garden to enjoy the sunshine while we may. Winter will be upon us before we know it. Jacob, will you set up a table in the arbour for us?'

'Very good, sir.' Jacob took himself off down the passage to the kitchen and Gabriel Harte offered me his arm and led me towards the garden.

'Mr Harte, I'm very anxious,' I said. I stopped as sudden tears threatened to close up my throat. 'Robert didn't come home last night.'

'Is he in the habit of staying out all night?'

'Not at all! I've visited Mr Hackett who told me that Robert felt ill yesterday morning and went home. But he never arrived.'

'Did your husband seem unwell to you?'

Gabriel Harte's calm questioning settled my nerves a little. 'He'd been worried about a particular matter and then he seemed relieved once he decided to confront Mr Hackett about it.'

'And did Mr Hackett mention if your husband broached the subject?'

'No. But I believe that if it had been discussed Mr Hackett

would have been angry.' A picture of Hackett testing the rusty nail against his thumb flitted across my mind, making me shiver. Then I heard quick footsteps across the gravel and Toby came running towards us.

'Mistress Finche! Have you brought me an apple today?'

'Toby!' Gabriel Harte's voice was stern.

'I beg your pardon, Mistress Finche,' said Toby with a cheerful grin. 'I'm not supposed to ask for things.'

'Next time I see you I shall bring you an apple.'

Jacob laid out the small table with a lace cloth and blue and white cups for Toby and myself with a glass of ale for his master. There was an apple and cinnamon cake and Toby was soon ensconced at the table with a starched napkin around his neck and a plate of cake before him.

'Now don't you spill greasy cake crumbs on your clean breeches, Master Toby,' said Jacob.

I glanced at him, surprised at his affectionate tone with the boy.

'Thank you, Jacob,' said Gabriel Harte.

The manservant gave a small bow and returned to the house.

'Jacob does so like perfection! You only have to feel the starched crispness of the lace on my shirts to see that. Why, the laundry maids are in terror of him!' Mr Harte smiled. 'As to your husband, could he have gone to stay with friends?'

'Robert is too ashamed of his parents' situation to keep up with any friends he had before the Fire.'

'Might he have gone to see his parents, then?'

I hesitated. 'It upsets Robert to see them in such a place and he rarely visits. I don't want them to worry. Nevertheless, I'll call on them tomorrow if I have no news.'

'Is your husband any nearer to clearing his father's debts?'

'We save everything we can. Robert works hard and I take in sewing . . . '

'You take in sewing? It has come to this?' His voice was shocked.

'I hope Robert Finche knows how lucky he is to have you for his wife?'

I glanced down at my fingers, counting the pinpricks. 'I do what I can but it's a mere drop in the ocean. We had thought that when Robert found a buyer for the Finche family plot in Lombard Street that the debts could be cleared. But Robert misjudged the market and sold it to Mr Hackett too soon. The price achieved wasn't nearly enough to clear Father Finche's debts. And then, the day before yesterday, we discovered that Mr Hackett had sold the land to another buyer for fifteen shillings a foot.' I swallowed, remembering Robert's distress. 'Hackett had bought it from Robert for four pence a foot.'

Gabriel Harte drew in his breath sharply and dropped his slice of cake.

'Robert was absolutely bedazzled by Mr Hackett before but the scales have certainly fallen from his eyes now. In hindsight, Robert's judgement was poor.' I sighed. 'It was a clever business decision on Mr Hackett's part but I cannot think he behaved like a gentleman.'

'Could your husband ask him to contribute some of the profit to clear your father-in-law's debts?'

'That's what he was going to do.'

'I see.' Gabriel Harte's fingers tapped on the table.

'The main creditors are paid off.' I smiled wryly. 'The remaining sum is not excessive but trying to pay for it by stitching petticoats will take me a lifetime.' I glanced up as a cloud passed over the sun. 'What has made me so anxious is that Robert went off so fired up to confront Hackett, but it appears he never discussed the matter with him at all.' I sighed. 'It's a difficult thing to say but I'm concerned Robert lost his courage and went to drown his sorrows.'

'Does he often do that?'

I hesitated. 'Occasionally he retreats to the alehouse if he feels life isn't treating him well but he always comes home at night and never drinks himself insensible.'

Gabriel Harte frowned. 'It's a conundrum, isn't it? I shall set Jacob to making discreet enquiries in the alehouses to see if there is news of your husband's whereabouts. We'll work together to find your husband.'

It gave me a great deal of comfort to hear him say 'we' since I didn't feel so alone. A sudden breeze flapped the tablecloth and I glanced up to see that the sky had turned an eerie purplish grey. 'I must go,' I said. 'I fear it will rain before long. Will you pass on my love to Jane and wish her better?'

'Of course.' He offered me the crook of his elbow and led me back towards the house. I noticed his faint scent of lemon balm and freshly ironed linen as we walked and reflected how refined he seemed by comparison to Hackett.

Jacob materialised out of the scented shadows of the hall and silently opened the door.

Gabriel Harte shook my hand but just then came a rumble of thunder and a second later a streak of lightning. 'Come back inside and wait until it passes,' he said,

'I had rather leave now,' I said. 'In case Robert has returned.'

'In that case ... ' He called over his shoulder into the hall. 'Jacob, have the carriage brought round to carry Mistress Finche safely home.'

'I shouldn't wish to inconvenience you.'

'Nonsense! The horses need exercise and the coachman has been twiddling his thumbs while Jane has been sick.'

'Has she been ill for a while then?' I asked.

'On and off for the past year or two, I'm sorry to say.'

The first heavy drops fell then and as we stood in the open doorway the rain grew heavier, hissing down onto the ground. A short while later the carriage drew up at the front of the house.

'Thank you so much for your kindness, Mr Harte,' I said.

'I shall come with you.'

'Really, there's no need.'

'I shall expire of curiosity if I am left wondering whether or not your husband has returned,' he said. 'Shall we make a run for it?'

I took his arm and we ran helter-skelter. The rain bounced up from the ground spattering my skirts. We slammed the carriage door behind us and sank down on the comfortably upholstered seat. Rain drummed on the roof as the carriage rolled forwards.

'I wonder the coachman can see where he is going,' I said, peeling my sodden hair from my cheeks and shoulders and shaking rain off my skirts.

The rain stopped as suddenly as it had started just as we turned into Ironmonger's Lane, where the dust had turned to a slippery and treacherous mud under our feet.

'I shall come in for a moment,' said Gabriel Harte. 'Perhaps even now your husband is waiting for you.'

I unlocked the door, but as soon as I stepped inside I knew by the stillness of the air that Robert had not returned. Mr Harte waited in the parlour while I ran upstairs to be sure. Shadow followed on my heels as I returned to the parlour with my stomach churning with anxiety.

'He isn't here,' I said.

Shadow inspected Mr Harte's breeches, sniffing them thoroughly, before settling down at his feet.

'I'm sorry to hear that,' he said gravely. He fondled Shadow's silky ears while he thought. 'Perhaps you would care to come and stay with us? I don't like to think of you all alone.'

'How very kind!' I longed to accept, dreading the possibility of spending another night by myself in this house. 'But I cannot leave Shadow.'

He smiled as Shadow nuzzled his hand. 'Bring him with you.'

'But what if Robert comes home?'

Gabriel Harte stood up. 'You're right, of course. Do send a message when you have news. And come and see us at any time if you need company.' His hand was warm as he shook mine and I was sorry to see him go.

Chapter 19

The night was long and magnified my anxiety. I dozed fitfully, waking at every small sound: a mouse scratching in the wainscot, the wind rattling the shutters and the mournful screech of an owl. The house creaked as it settled and I became overcome with dread that it was all about to collapse into the cellar.

As the sun rose I scolded myself for my night fears and went to sit by the parlour window again. The building sites woke up and before long the usual daytime sounds of whistling, hammering and sawing filled the air. Carts laden with building materials rolled along Ironmonger Lane and the workmen shouted across to each other from the other site, making the lane very different from the frighteningly lonely place it was during the long dark hours of the night.

I sewed by the parlour window all day while my anger at Robert grew.

Later, as the workmen on the building sites tidied away their tools and their voices faded away into the distance, anger gave way to dread again. Even if Robert had taken refuge in a tavern, surely he would have recovered by now? Drizzle began to patter at the windowpanes. Soon it would be time for me to light the porch lamp again but my limbs were too heavy with exhaustion to move. I yawned.

Some sixth sense awoke me. I strained my eyes through the rain and the grey twilight and caught sight of a movement. My heart began to hammer and I opened the window and hung over the sill as I saw a heavily shrouded man walking through the downpour towards the house. Relief flooded over me and I waved my arms and shouted Robert's name before running out of the house with tears of relief running down my cheeks.

Heavy rain soaked my hair and shoulders in moments and the road was muddy as I ran, slipping and sliding, heedless of the mire splattering onto my skirts. Then I stopped dead. It wasn't Robert. There were two men, draped in heavy cloaks, one very tall and resting his hand on the shoulder of the other who was very small.

Gabriel Harte stood before me and as soon as I saw his face I knew that something was terribly wrong. He took off his hat and held it to his chest, his expression grave. 'We must go inside out of the rain, Mistress Finche.'

Suddenly I was too afraid to ask what had happened.

Jacob Samuels stepped forwards, not meeting my questioning gaze, and took me by one arm and Gabriel Harte by the other.

I allowed myself to be led, unresisting, back to the house.

The front door was wide open, as I had left it, and the wooden floor was wet. I felt an inconsequential moment of annoyance that I would have to polish the floor again.

Jacob closed the door, shutting out the drumming of the rain.

I smelled the wet wool of the men's cloaks mingling with the dusky rose perfume of the pomander on the hall chest and waited for someone to speak.

'May we go into the parlour, Mistress Finche?' asked Gabriel Harte, taking off his cloak.

I noticed that he wore a coat of sober dark grey rather than his usual sea green or sapphire blue. Shivering, I wondered if it was a portent. Wordlessly, I led the way.

Dolly's petticoats lay in piles of half-finished, completed and not-yet-started heaps and I began to bundle them up, apologising all the while as I tidied them away, delaying the moment when I had to find out what had happened.

'Please, do not trouble yourself, Mistress Finche,' said Gabriel Harte with a half-smile. 'You forget, I cannot see them.'

I dropped the petticoats back on the chair and waited, a pulse beating so loud in my ears that I wondered he couldn't hear it.

'Mistress Finche, I asked Jacob to make enquiries as to the whereabouts of your missing husband.'

'Did you find him?' I couldn't wait any longer. I had to know immediately.

'I did,' said Jacob.

'Where?' I held my breath.

'He . . . ' Jacob stopped and looked at his master.

'I'm very sorry to tell you,' said Gabriel Harte, 'that he was found washed up under London Bridge.'

'Washed up?' A drop of icy water ran from my sodden hair, down my throat and into my bodice.

'Mistress Finche –' Gabriel Harte's voice was gentle '– your husband has drowned.'

I heard his words but had to repeat them to myself as I struggled to take in their meaning. Robert had drowned. He wasn't coming home after all, no matter how long I waited by the parlour window.

'Mistress Finche?'

'Where is he?'

'I have arranged for his body to be taken to the House of Perfume until the burial. Of course, I can bring him here if you prefer.'

Until the burial. All at once I became very cold and my teeth began to chatter. I sank down onto a chair. Robert was dead.

Somewhere, a long distance away, I heard Gabriel Harte sending Jacob to fetch the flask from his cloak. Someone began to rub the feeling back into my tingling fingers. A moment later I was enveloped in a damp cloak but the warmth of it didn't stop the terrible shivering that wracked my body.

Gabriel Harte's face loomed close to mine. 'Mistress Finche, drink this.'

A finger on my cheek, tracing a line to my mouth. The cold touch of metal against my lips. Obediently, I opened my mouth and sipped, then swallowed, a river of fire. I coughed and spluttered, while warmth filled my stomach. I shook my head and took a deep breath. 'My husband is drowned, Gabriel,' I said.

Then I was clinging to him with my head against his broad chest while he patted my back. He smelled of lavender-scented linen and warm, male skin.

Jacob Samuels coughed and I drew a deep breath and pulled away from his master.

'I'm sorry,' I said, scrabbling in my pocket for a handkerchief. 'I guessed something terrible had happened to Robert but, oh, I did so hope against hope that it wasn't so.'

'I wish I hadn't had to be the bearer of such unhappy news. Is there a friend I can call to stay with you tonight?'

'I have no friends. Only Jane and you.' My breath caught on a sob as I wished that she were with me at that moment.

'Unfortunately, Jane has taken Toby with her to stay with her aunt in Epsom for a few days.'

'Oh!' I clasped my hands to my breast. 'I shall have to tell Mother and Father Finche about Robert.'

'You must go to them in the morning, said Gabriel Harte. 'And I shall visit Hackett and persuade him to settle your father-in-law's debts. It's the least he can do. And then you can bring him out of that place.'

'I doubt if Hackett will listen to you, not if it will cost him money.

And my husband is of no use to him any longer.' I wiped my eyes. 'But why was Robert in the river?'

Jacob shrugged. 'The Thames is running high after the rain. The water is always dangerously turbulent under the bridge where the wider flow is forced between the piers. Perhaps he slipped?'

'But why?' My head felt as if it was stuffed with wool as I tried to understand. 'Why would he have cause to go to the river?'

'Might he have been crossing to Lambeth to visit his parents?' suggested Jacob. 'The public stairs are treacherously slippery.'

'But the current would have carried him in the opposite direction.' I rubbed my forehead, which ached with thinking about it.

'May I suggest you rest now?' said Gabriel Harte. 'We can do no more tonight. I've brought some of Jane's poppy syrup with me to help you sleep.'

I closed my eyes, imagining the luxury of being able to sleep without waking for a whole night. Gabriel Harte was right, there was nothing else that could be done tonight.

'Jacob shall check that all your windows and doors are safely closed and we'll warm you some milk.'

Jacob measured out a spoonful of poppy syrup into my milk and when I had drunk it, the two men stood up.

'Lock the front door behind us and go straight to bed,' said Mr Harte.

In the hall, he reached out for my fingers and his warm lips brushed the back of my hand.

I clung to him for a moment. 'You have been so very kind,' I murmured.

Jacob caught hold of his sleeve and guided him down the front steps.

I closed the door behind them and leaned against it. Then, wearily, I made my way to bed.

The sound of hammering close to my head awoke me. Startled, I sat up in bed, blinking in the bright sunlight. My head was muzzy and I couldn't think clearly. Several more hammer blows and the sound of whistling came through the thin wall to the adjoining house. The builders had started early. I yawned widely and swung my legs over the side of the bed.

It was as my feet touched the floorboards that I remembered. An icy cold shiver began in the small of my back and skittered up to the crown of my head. Robert was dead. I made a small mew of distress and shot to my feet, fingers pressed to my mouth. I stood motionless while I relived the events of the previous evening. And remembered that this morning I had to go and tell Mother and Father Finche that their son was dead.

A heavy weight appeared to have lodged itself on my chest, squeezing the breath out of me and my feet didn't want to move. I crept over to the basin and splashed my face.

Shadow uncurled himself from the floor, stretched and then sat, looking expectantly at me. I bent to stroke his head and then fell to my knees and wrapped my arms around him, burying my face in his neck. He suffered me for a few moments before politely extracting himself and going to wait beside the door.

I lifted the lid of the chest and slowly pulled out my green wool bodice and skirt. I should have to buy mourning clothes. Dressing seemed unaccountably difficult and my fingers fumbled with the laces and buttons. I sat on the edge of the bed to pull on my stockings and wondered why I didn't feel impelled to throw myself upon the tumbled sheets in a frenzy of weeping and wailing.

Lifting Robert's pillow to my face, I sniffed the cool linen and wrinkled my nose at the fusty smell of his hair. It worried me a little that it didn't distress me, but an unaccountable numbness had gripped me.

Shadow pawed at the door and I followed him down the stairs. Passing the parlour door, I glanced at the clock on the chimneypiece and was shocked to see that it was after noon. Gabriel Harte's poppy syrup must have been very strong. I mustn't delay. Locking the door behind me, I set off for Lambeth.

I spied Mother Finche almost as soon as I stepped into the courtyard. She sat huddled on a bench with her shawl wrapped around her head against the damp wind, like a beggar woman. There was a bundle at her feet.

'I was waiting for you, Katherine,' she said.

I hesitated for a moment, trying to summon up the right words to break the news of her son's death to her but couldn't find them. Sitting down beside her, I took her cold hand in mine.

'He's gone, Katherine,' she said.

'Who told you?'

She lifted her gaze from the ground and looked at me, her eyes bloodshot from weeping. 'I was at his side at the end. He coughed so hard that he couldn't breathe and the next thing I knew, he'd gone.'

I stared at her in horror. She wasn't talking about her son but about her husband. John Finche was dead. Silently, I rocked her against my breast, unable to imagine how I would find the courage to tell her that her son was dead, too.

After a while, she drew a trembling sigh and leaned back against the wall. 'Both my children have deserted me,' she said. 'I had thought you might persuade Robert to visit us more often and now he will never see his father again.'

'Mother Finche, I could not.' I drew a deep breath; best to cut clean and deep and finish it. 'It's a cruel business that brings me here today and you must be very brave.'

She looked at me, her wrinkled old mouth quivering. 'What is it, Katherine?'

'Robert had an accident. Mr Harte came to see me last night to tell me that Robert had slipped into the river and . . . ' I faltered and then continued, 'And he drowned.'

Mother Finche stared at me uncomprehendingly. Then she said, 'My lovely boy? Drowned?'

I nodded, too close to tears to speak.

'They buried my John at dawn this morning in the prison graveyard,' she whispered. 'And do you know, not an hour ago, Dobbs came to tell me that a gentleman had settled all John's debts. If he hadn't died, John would have been free to leave today. Oh, Kate, how can I endure it?' Mother Finche wept then as if her heart would break.

Gabriel Harte had been as good as his word then and persuaded Hackett to clear Father Finche's debts out of his profit on the Finche land. Bitterly, I reflected that neither Robert nor his father had lived to know it.

At last Mother Finche wiped her eyes.

'Father Finche is free of all his troubles now,' I murmured. 'There is nothing to keep you here and I shall take you home with me.'

'But now we must bury my Robert.' Mother Finche picked up the small bundle that contained everything she owned. 'Will you take me to him?'

A short while later, Dobbs unlocked the outside gate.

Mother Finche peered fearfully through the opening. 'I had not thought to see outside these walls again,' she said.

Dobbs opened the gate wide. 'There you go, my lady.' He grinned. 'And don't go doing nothing that brings you back 'ere again.'

Mother Finche clung to my arm all the while we crossed the river and then on the walk to Long Acre. She flinched and held me all the tighter every time a carriage rolled past or a costermonger shouted his wares.

'It's so noisy, Katherine! Shall I ever become used to the hubbub of the city again?'

'Of course you will! In any case, the house in Ironmonger Lane is much quieter than here.' But for how long would Hackett allow us to stay in the house? I pushed the thought away as too frightening to contemplate at present.

At last we came to the House of Perfume and Jacob admitted us to wait in the drawing room while he fetched his master.

Mother Finche glanced around her at the silk-lined walls and the embroidered window hangings, the decorative plasterwork on the ceiling and the ornate chandelier. She refused to sit on the beautiful damask-covered chairs. 'Katherine, I'm so ashamed,' she whispered. 'Look at my filthy and ragged clothes! And I need to wash. Even my fingers are ingrained with dirt.'

I squeezed her hand. 'Dear Mother Finche, Mr Harte cannot see your ragged dress.'

She sighed. 'I had forgotten.'

Measured footsteps came across the hall and the drawing room door opened.

'This is a very sad day,' said Mr Harte, holding out his hands to us both. 'I understand poor Mr Finche, too, has been released from his earthly cares. But now you will wish to see your son.'

Mother Finche let out a sob.

He led us into a small room off the hall. The curtains were closed but scented candles in candelabra stood on either side of the coffin, which was placed on a trestle table. Two chairs awaited us.

Quietly, Gabriel Harte withdrew leaving us alone with Robert's body.

We tiptoed forwards and stared down at his waxen face, as cold and remote as the marble effigies I had seen in St Paul's. His dark hair had been combed neatly and he was dressed in a shroud of fine linen, worked with tiny pleats and finished with lace. I waited to feel the grief that I was sure must come but there was nothing except pity for him, for a life cut tragically short and sorrow that our marriage had brought neither of us happiness.

Mother Finche drew in her breath and stretched out a finger to touch a dark bruise shadowing his temple.

'He must have knocked his head when he slipped into the river,' I whispered.

Mother Finche stroked his cheek. 'He looks so peaceful.'

We sat in silence, heads bowed, while we prayed for his soul.

Sorrow mixed with anger in my breast. I had longed to love Robert but the opportunity for fondness to grow between us had been snatched away. I wept then, slow tears oozing from my eyes and dripping off my chin, washing away all my hopes for a loving husband and a home resounding with the sound of our children's laughter.

At last, Mother Finche sighed heavily, leaned forwards and kissed Robert's brow.

I, too, kissed Robert's cold forehead for the last time, and then we left him.

Chapter 20

I purchased serviceable mourning clothes for Mother Finche and myself from one of Dolly Smethwicke's second-hand stalls and, after I'd altered them to fit, I was satisfied that we would appear fine enough to do Robert credit when he was buried. Gabriel Harte took care of all the other arrangements and paid for the burial, which was handsome of him.

There were few mourners, other than myself and Mother Finche, gathered in the churchyard of All Hallows on the appointed afternoon: Gabriel Harte, Jacob, Matthew Lunt, Nell and Ben Perkins and Mr Hackett. Jane was still in Epsom as she and Toby had contracted bad head colds and weren't well enough to travel. A gusty breeze lifted my hair and whipped it across my cheeks, while I battled to prevent my skirts from billowing up and exposing my petticoats. Hackett's heavy-lidded gaze was fixed intently on me all the time. It made my skin prickle.

Cinnamon-coloured leaves swirled around our feet and floated down from the great beech tree at the edge of the churchyard, reminding me of the loose pages of burned books that had floated over the city for days after the Great Fire. Poor Mother Finche wept silently beside me, a sodden handkerchief in her hand, while I chided myself for feeling nothing except exhaustion. Lost in a fog of thought, I stared at my feet and tried to ignore Hackett.

The wind snatched the minister's words away as he read the service and Gabriel Harte had to nudge my arm to catch my attention when it was time to sprinkle a handful of earth onto Robert's coffin. I soon forgot all about Hackett's eyes on me as Mother Finche fell, sobbing, into my arms.

After the burial, we returned to the house in Ironmonger Lane for a simple repast of cold meats, bread and cheese.

'I will speak with you,' said Hackett, cornering me as he loaded his plate with enough ham and cheese to feed Mother Finche and myself for a week

I gave him an enquiring look, with as much boldness as I could muster. The truth was, I'd slept little the previous night. Anxiety had gnawed at me as I considered my situation with regard to the house, now that Robert was no longer in Hackett's employ. I'd been unable to imagine how I could support not only myself but also Mother Finche. I'd discarded the thought of returning to Aunt Mercy as too terrible to contemplate.

But then Gabriel Harte joined us and saved me by asking a number of searching questions about his financial investments in Hackett's schemes.

One by one, the guests began to leave. Ben Perkins turned his hat awkwardly in his hands, shooting uncertain glances at Hackett, while Nell, growing rounded in her pregnancy, hugged me tightly and made me promise to come and see her when the baby was born.

I shook Gabriel Harte's hand and gave him my heartfelt thanks. Suddenly, I didn't want him to leave. His quiet, strong presence comforted me.

'Come and see us when Jane returns,' he said.

Only Hackett was left then and I waited for him to leave, too, and allow Mother Finche and myself to do our mourning in private.

Frail in her widow's weeds, Mother Finche looked up at Hackett, her eyes full of tears. 'My son thought very highly of you,' she said with quiet dignity, 'and I am grateful to you for purchasing the ruined Finche house to allow Robert to pay off some part of the debts. Katherine tells me that, more recently, you were the benefactor who cleared the remainder of the debts. I can never find the words to thank you enough.'

Hackett glanced at me from under thick black eyebrows. 'Paid off your debts?' He frowned and then smiled. 'I wish your daughter-in-law appeared to show the same gratitude as you do.'

Mother Finche flushed a little and I gritted my teeth together to prevent a sudden outburst of rage. If he'd only cleared Father Finche's debts at the time he'd made his extraordinary profit from the transaction then poor Father Finche might have been saved.

'You look quite done in, madam,' said Hackett. 'May I suggest you retire to your chamber to rest? I have a matter of business to discuss with your daughter-in-law.'

'I have no secrets from my husband's mother,' I said, anxious not to be alone with him.

'Perhaps not,' he said. 'Nevertheless, we would not wish to tire her, would we?' He stood between us as unyielding as a standing stone.

Mother Finche glanced at me and, reluctantly, I nodded.

After she had left, Hackett sat down heavily, his bulk making the chair creak alarmingly. He was beginning to run to fat, I thought.

'A matter of business?' I asked, remaining standing. At least that way we were on the same eye level.

He looked at me, his dark eyes running slowly all over me. 'You're too thin,' he said. 'I like my women to have a little more meat on their bones.'

Dumbfounded at his impertinence, I took a step back.

'But widowhood suits you,' continued Hackett 'Black makes those hazel eyes of yours appear more lustrous than ever.'

'My eyes are red from weeping for my husband,' I said.

A slow smile spread across his face, exposing his tobacco-stained teeth. 'Don't make that prim mouth at me, miss!' He leaned forwards and narrowed his eyes. 'I know you,' he whispered. 'There are fires that burn brightly beneath that tightly corseted bodice, if I'm not mistaken.'

Refusing to look away from his challenging stare, I said nothing but a pulse beat wildly in my throat.

Suddenly, he clapped a hand on his great thigh, making me start. 'Now, to business! This house.' He raised his hands, palms up. 'My house, to be precise.'

I swallowed as fear twisted my insides.

Leaning back, he crossed one ankle over his knee, grasping it with thick fingers. A piece of horse dung was stuck under the heel of his shoe and I stared at it while my heart beat like a drum.

'This is a fine house, wouldn't you say?' he said.

'Except perhaps for the cellar,' I said as coolly as I could, 'which has collapsed again, taking the kitchen floor with it.'

He raised an eyebrow. 'Ah yes! Finche did mention something about that. Still, that's a small problem that my men can put right in a trice. In fact, I'll put them on to it tomorrow.'

'Perhaps they could repair some of the cracks in the walls at the same time?' I smiled sweetly. 'And the stairs shake every time I walk up and down them. Might the crack as wide as my finger running up the stairwell indicate that they're about to collapse into the cellar, too? Then, there's a particularly bad fissure running down the outside and I'm concerned the whole corner of the house may fall away.'

Hackett scowled at me. 'Or perhaps I shall send in my workmen *after* you have packed your things and left?'

The silence between us was so thick I could have carved it with a knife. I dropped my gaze to the floor, refusing to let him see my fear. One thing I'd learned about Hackett was that he liked me to show a little, but not too much, spirit.

Smiling now, Hackett pushed himself to his feet and came to stand too close to me.

I held my breath, refusing to tip my head back so that I could see his face.

'Not so bold now, are you? The fact remains that I have found a buyer for this house and I've told him he can have it as soon as you've left.'

My mouth was so dry it was hard to speak. 'Has your buyer seen inside, I wonder?' I kept my voice as steady as I could but it still wavered. 'Will he still want it when he sees how poorly it's built?'

'He's seen the adjoining house that's nearly completed and he's satisfied. Besides, he doesn't intend to live in it himself, merely to put tenants in it.' Hackett gripped my chin with hot, moist fingers and forced me to look at him. 'So, you see, much as I think of myself as a charitable man it makes good sense for me to rid myself of this house, especially if it has the problems you mention, while I have an offer on the table.'

I shook myself free of his grip. My hands and feet had become icy cold and it took an enormous effort of will not to let him see me tremble. 'In that case,' I said, 'if you're turning my mother-in-law and myself out to fend for ourselves, I shall at least expect you to pass me the wages that were owing to my husband for the past month.'

'My dear lady,' Hackett said, amusement dancing in his eyes, 'I handed Finche his wages the other morning before he left my chambers. Joseph Hogg will attest to it.' He laughed, throwing his head back so that I could see the dark stubble on his neck.

Rage flooded over me in a scarlet wave. 'No! You did not! There was no money in his pockets when he was pulled from the water.'

He spread his hands wide, still chuckling with enjoyment at my distress. 'Is it my fault if that snivelling husband of yours drank away a month's wages before throwing himself into the river? I've been more generous to you than you know. If I'd disclosed to the minister of All Hallows that your husband had done away with himself, do you think he would have allowed Finche to be buried in consecrated ground?'

'Liar!' A red tide rose up in front of me and before I could stop myself, I began to beat upon his chest with my fists. 'Robert would *never* have taken his own life and you know it!'

Hackett grasped me around my waist in a grip of iron and lifted me clear of the ground. 'Stop that, you little vixen!'

'Put me down!' I kicked out and my foot connected with his knee.

He shook me like a terrier with a rat and then dropped me to the ground, all amusement gone from his eyes. 'Now listen to me!'

I stood still, my chest heaving with fear and indignation.

Hackett's eyes gleamed. 'You're even more of a hellcat than I imagined; hidden fires, indeed! As I said, I have a proposition for you.'

Terror clawed at me at the prospect of how Mother Finche and I would live without either any money or a roof over our heads. I waited, trembling and hoping there was a way out.

'I might be persuaded to allow you and the old woman to stay. Under certain conditions.'

I let out my breath in relief and stood as tall as my barely five-foot frame would allow. 'What conditions might those be?'

All at once he snatched hold of my hair, twisting it tightly around his palm, and dragged my face close to his. His breath reeked of stale tobacco and cheese.

Suddenly, I knew what those conditions would be. 'No!' I shouted, terror making me squirm in his grip.

'Don't be too hasty,' he said, licking his lips. 'I'm a reasonable man. You can choose to stay here in this fine house, if you like.' He smiled. 'Why, I might even repair the cellar for you. And, *if* you please me sufficiently –' his fingers trailed down my throat and lingered on my heaving breast '– I will buy you a red silk dress and ribbons for your hair. Oh yes,' he whispered, his breath hot and heavy on my cheek, 'I shall enjoy taming this little firebrand.'

'Let me go!'

He yanked my hair again and I yelped, tears starting into my eyes with the pain of it. 'Or you can go out and earn your living on the streets.' He shrugged. 'Of course, you may pick up a dose of the French pox and you might be found in an alley with your throat cut.' He shrugged. 'But it's entirely your choice, my dear.'

'Never!' I said again, but my voice quavered and I shook with dread.

'Tell you what I'll do. Being the generous man that I am, I'll let you have seven days to make up your mind. Come to my chambers this time next week and let me know if you wish to stay on in this house as my mistress.'

He wrenched at my hair again and then his thick lips were pressed wetly against mine and his slimy tongue forced itself, like an eel, between my teeth.

Gagging, I made a useless attempt to free myself from his grip.

Suddenly he released my hair and pushed me away from him. 'Until next Thursday,' he said. 'Believe me, by then you'll be *begging* me to bed you.'

Staggering away from him, I slumped down onto the window seat.

The front door slammed.

I was scrubbing my mouth on my skirt when the door opened and Mother Finche came in.

'He's gone,' she said.

Shaking, I looked at the floor, too ashamed to meet her eyes.

Tentatively, she touched my shoulder. 'I was listening at the door.'

'So, now you know the kind of man he really is,' I said bitterly.

'I don't understand.' She shook her head. 'Robert had such respect for Mr Hackett. And he promised that he'd make Robert a partner in the business.'

'He might have done, if only Robert had been happy to adopt Hackett's corrupt business practices.'

'But he didn't?' Mother Finche's eyes beseeched me.

'No,' I said.

'What shall we do?' she whispered. 'Where shall we go?'

I had no answer for her.

Mother Finche buried her face in her hands. 'I'm so tired, Katherine.'

'Then go to bed. And I'll think what to do.'

She nodded. 'You're such a good girl. I'm sure you'll find an answer.'

After she'd left the room, I curled up into a ball on the window seat and wept.

Chapter 21

October 1668

There was a chill in the air the following morning but the sun shone. Walking briskly with the bundles of petticoats in my arms, it was possible to persuade myself that the scheme I'd thought up overnight, inspired by Gabriel Harte's Perfume Salon, would solve our present difficulties.

Dolly answered my knock with her usual sour expression. 'Oh, it's you.'

I pushed past her into the workroom where the orphan girls were sewing industriously. I heaved my bundles of petticoats onto the table, sending up a cloud of cotton dust and pieces of thread.

Dolly hobbled after me and untied the bundles, then lifted each petticoat in turn and held it up to the window to look for blood spots or crooked seams that she could use as justification for not paying me what she'd promised.

'You know my work well enough by now, Dolly,' I said. 'This batch is as perfect as the last one.'

'Maybe.' Grudgingly, she rummaged in her pocket and withdrew a handful of coins.

I took them from her and counted them. 'A penny short,' I said, stretching out my palm.

Dolly cackled and felt in her pocket again. 'Sharper than you look, you are, for all your hoity-toity ways.'

'That's what I want to speak to you about,' I said. 'I have a proposition for you.'

Dolly raised one eyebrow and waited.

I saw the orphans watching me with open mouths, needles halfway into their sewing.

Dolly sent them a sharp look and they bent their heads over their work again.

'You may run a thriving business with your second-hand clothing and petticoat stalls,' I said, 'but you could do better.'

'There's nuffink I don't know about my market stall that you could tell me.'

'Perhaps not. But you could expand your business into a different avenue.'

She sniffed suspiciously. 'Waddya have in mind?'

'Let's be honest, Dolly. You're not exactly a lady of quality, are you?'

'Bleedin' cheek!'

'I *am* a lady of quality, however,' I said, 'and my proposal is this. You should set up a discreet little shop where you sell the best quality second-hand clothes you can find. The shop must be prettily decorated. There are plenty of ladies who wouldn't dream of buying dresses from a market stall but cannot afford to patronise a dressmaker. I would advise and alter the clothes to fit the customers and perhaps make a matching petticoat or trim a hat to complete the outfit. Refreshments could be served in dainty cups and the ladies could meet their friends for a gossip in pleasant surroundings while they look at your stock. I think you'd be surprised at how popular such a place could be.'

Dolly folded her arms over her ample bosom and tapped a foot. 'Might work,' she said, grudgingly. 'What's in it for you?'

'A room for myself and my mother-in-law over the shop and fifty per cent of the profits.'

'You're havin' a laugh. Fifty per cent!'

I held my ground. 'You can't do it without me, Dolly.'

'I'll think about it,' she said. 'Not saying I'll agree, mind. And maybe twenty per cent of the profit.'

'Not enough,' I said.

She shrugged. 'Shops is dear to rent. Especially with rooms above. Now, are you taking more petticoats away with you or what?'

I left Dolly's hovel feeling as if there was a heavy weight on my shoulders again. I'd been so sure that she would like my carefully thought out idea. It was Friday and I only had six days to find somewhere to live and a means of support.

Mother Finche was still in bed when I arrived home, her grey hair limp on her shoulders and the sheets tightly tucked under her chin. She glanced up at me with an unspoken enquiry.

Suddenly I longed to crawl back into my own bed and pull the blankets over my head.

'Dolly said she'd think about my idea,' I said. 'There's no point in hurrying her or she'll become stubborn.'

'Didn't Robert have any savings?' asked Mother Finche.

'Everything we saved went towards Father Finche's debts at the end of each week. It stopped the creditors from bothering us too much if they could see that something was coming in regularly, however little.'

Mother Finche sighed. 'It wasn't at all what you were expecting, when you married Robert, was it?'

'There's no point in looking at what might have been,' I said. 'There's enough money to feed us for about a fortnight, if we're frugal, but not enough to rent a room.'

'Katherine?' Mother Finche caught at my skirt, her eyes wide and afraid. 'I have no friends any more. In any case, I'm too ashamed of having been in prison to cast myself on their mercy. So I've been thinking. Maybe Mr Hackett is right?'

I caught my breath. 'What do you mean?'

'Hackett has every right to take his house back and no obligation at all to look after us. If you do as he asks . . . '

Incredulity made me gasp. 'You'd have me, your son's widow, be that man's mistress?'

'My son's destitute widow.'

'I'll do *anything* but that, even take a position as a servant if necessary.'

'And who would employ you?' Bright spots of pink flared in Mother Finche's cheeks. 'You're too fine to be a servant. No lady will want you as her maid in case her husband's roving eye should fall upon you and no cook will have you as a scullery maid because she wouldn't like to order you to scrub the floor.'

'But I'll work hard at whatever I do! I'm honest and . . . '

'You have no references, Katherine.' Her tone brooked no argument. 'I would never, ever, have employed a servant without references.' She wrapped her arms around her waist. 'So long as you please Hackett he'll look after you. If you make a little effort you may cajole him into buying you good clothes and giving you jewellery. Jewels are ideal as you can sell them later when he tires of you.'

'How dare you!' Shock made me shout.

Mother Finche's expression hardened. 'I've seen a side of life you have not,' she said. 'In the debtors' prison, girls who were not pretty, or willing to please, starved. Those who were more, shall we say, adaptable survived. Kate, the winter is coming. When Mr Hackett turns us out and we have to take shelter under a bridge somewhere, I shall probably die of the cold before long. You may last a little longer but, in the end, hunger will lead you to sell your body leaning up against a wall in an alley.'

'I will not!'

'My dear –' she smiled a cold, tight smile, full of pity '– until you have experienced hunger, cold and desperation as I have, you don't know what you'll do. I tell you now, you will do whatever you need to do to survive.'

I stared at her, too shocked to speak.

Her mouth trembling, Mother Finche reached for my hand. 'I will not judge you, my dear, for becoming Hackett's mistress. And it will buy us time. You can continue to seek other means of support. Indeed you must do so because he will, inevitably, move on to a younger or prettier mistress. Men like that enjoy the thrill of the chase but are easily bored. You must save everything you can, then, when he drops you, you can set up as a respectable widow in another town.'

I remembered Hackett's hot mouth and wet tongue forcing its way into my mouth and shuddered. I had to find another way. I must.

That night I lay on the bed with my mind running in circles while I tried to think what to do. If Jane had not been in Epsom I might have begged her for shelter but even that could only be a temporary measure. If Dolly didn't accept my proposition, the only long-term answer must be to find a position as a live-in servant.

Over the following days, desperation led me to haunt the markets, stopping any servant who would speak to me to ask if their mistress might have any vacancies. My hopes were raised, and subsequently dashed, as I followed two possible leads.

I returned home from the last humiliating interview to find a young woman on the doorstep.

'Can I help you?' I asked.

'I'm not sure.' She was plainly dressed in black and unremarkable brown hair peeped out from under her sensible hat.

I looked into her grey eyes and felt the tiniest flicker of recognition. 'I'm sorry,' I said, 'have we met before?'

'Never, but is it possible you are Katherine?'

'Why, yes!'

She held out her hand to me. 'Then I am your sister-in-law, Sarah.'

I clapped a hand to my mouth. 'Sarah? Robert's sister?'

She nodded. 'I searched the city after the Great Fire, looking for my family but could find no trace of them. And then your letters all arrived together. We'd moved, you see, to another parish and it wasn't until we received a visit from the new incumbent a few days ago that I had your letters.'

I clasped her hands in mine. 'Oh, Sarah, you cannot know how pleased I am to see you. And how very sorry I was to be the bearer of such sad tidings about both your father and your brother.'

'It was a shock,' she said, 'but since I'd heard nothing for so long I thought they must have all perished in the fire.'

'I think it fair to say that although he wasn't consumed by the flames, your father's life ended then. And your poor mother has endured the most terrible experiences in the debtors' prison looking after him. She refused to leave him even when we offered her a home.'

Sarah squeezed my hand. 'And now poor Robert has gone, too.'

'But let us go inside and find your mother.'

'Will she forgive me for not coming before?'

'She loves you, Sarah, whatever may have passed between you before. But you'll find her sadly changed.' I took her into the parlour and bid her wait.

Mother Finche lay on her bed, staring at the ceiling. She sat up as I pushed open her door. 'Katherine, did you find a situation?'

I shook my head, not wanting to discuss my most recent mortification. 'But I have a visitor to see you.'

'A visitor? Who is it?'

'Someone you haven't seen for a while.'

'Mistress Spalding? Or Mistress Buckley perhaps?'

'No,' I said, helping her to sit up. 'Come.' I held out my hand to her.

We went downstairs and I led her into the parlour.

'Mother!' Sarah stood up so fast she knocked the chair over backwards. 'Mother, is it really you?'

Mother Finche stopped dead still. 'Sarah?' Her voice quavered and broke.

And then they were locked in a tearful embrace as they exclaimed over each other, stroking each other's face and hair, as if they could not believe that the other was real.

'I'm so sorry,' sobbed Mother Finche into her daughter's shoulder.

'I was too hasty and quick to take offence,' wept Sarah.

I left mother and daughter to become reconciled and a little while later I returned to the parlour to find them holding hands with their faces wreathed in smiles.

'Katherine, you cannot imagine, I have nine grandchildren! And Sarah has come to take me home with her.'

'I'm so happy for you.'

Mother Finche didn't meet my hopeful gaze.

'I'm so sorry, Katherine,' said Sarah. 'Mother has explained that you have to leave this house tomorrow but I cannot help you.' Her expression was unhappy. 'Edmund and I are provided with only a small cottage with his living and, truly, we have no space. The two youngest children already sleep in our chamber with us and now that Mother is coming to stay we'll have three sharing a bed with her while the other four will have a mattress in the parlour.'

'I quite understand,' I said, hoping my frightened disappointment didn't show in my face. 'Besides, it'll be easier for me to find a situation if I'm alone.'

Sarah looked relieved. 'We'll make extensive enquiries to see if we can find a position for you in one of the larger households in the area,' she said. 'And then we'll send for you.'

But that will be too late to save me from Hackett, I thought, cold waves of terror washing over me. And there was only tomorrow before I had to make that irrevocable choice.

'We'll take the four o'clock coach from the Three Tuns,' said Sarah, 'but on the way I wish to pay my respects to my brother's and my father's graves.'

'Your father lies under the courtyard in the jail in Lambeth,' said Mother Finche, 'but let us visit All Hallows and say a prayer for him beside dear Robert's grave.'

In no time at all Mother Finche's few possessions had been packed into a small bundle and we stood awkwardly in the hall.

'Katherine, I cannot thank you enough for what you did for the Finche family,' said Mother Finche, kissing my cheek. 'And remember,' she whispered in my ear, 'I shall never hold it against you if you do as Mr Hackett wishes.'

'We'll send for you as soon as we can,' said Sarah.

I stood on the doorstep watching them as they walked down the street and out of my life.

Chapter 22

On Thursday morning I woke at dawn in a cold sweat after suffering the familiar nightmare of being shut in the cellar, where things scuttled in the dark and Aunt Mercy waited outside with her birch switch and spiteful words. Even the prospect of returning to that forbidding prison, without the cushion of my dowry to protect me from her bitterness and cruelty was unthinkable. I'd escaped the horror of that place once and *nothing* would ever make me return. Becoming Hackett's mistress was preferable to that. At least I should only have to endure him for a few unpleasant hours each week.

I screwed my eyes shut, refusing to acknowledge for as long as possible that the fateful day had arrived when I would have to present myself at Hackett's chambers. Shadow lay curled up on the end of my bed and I stroked his head as he regarded me from one sleepy eye, his tail stirring.

'My last day of freedom, Shadow.'

It was an effort to rise from my bed but then I became angry. Dammit, if I had to bow to the inevitable, I would go out in style. I threw back the bedclothes, washed and rubbed Summer Garden on my wrists and throat. Then I shook out my lovely topaz silk dress and laced myself into it as tightly as I could. My silken skirts rustled around my ankles as I let Shadow out into the street and set off for Dolly's house.

Dolly's piggy little eyes widened a fraction when she saw me in my finery.

'I came to see if you'd reconsidered my offer,' I said, as haughtily as I could, 'before I accept an alternative business proposition.'

'Who's that with then? Not Nan Tuttle, is it?'

'As I'm sure you'll understand, my plans are confidential, Dolly. And time has run out for you to make a decision. I'll have your final answer now, if you please,' I said crisply.

Dolly turned and swiped one of the orphan girls across the back of the head. 'Didn't give you leave to gawp, did I?'

I tapped my foot in my best impression of Aunt Mercy when she was waiting for me to own up to one of my sins. 'Now, if you please, Dolly!'

'Too much of a risk.'

'Not at all. No one else offers such a service.'

Dolly sighed. 'There's a small shop vacant on Pye Corner.'

'And?'

'One room over and twenty per cent of the profit.'

'I told you that wouldn't be enough.' I picked up my skirts and turned to the door.

Dolly came back, quick as a flash. 'Twenty-five per cent then.'

I kept on walking.

'Thirty!'

I turned. 'Forty.'

Dolly's face worked as if she was in extreme pain.

I waited, smoothing down the cool silk of my skirts, my face calm but my pulse racing.

'Thirty-five per cent, then. Last offer,' said Dolly, almost in tears.

I sighed. 'Thirty-seven-and-a-half per cent and we have a deal.'

'You're a witch and no mistake!'

'Are we agreed?'

An almost imperceptible nod of her head.

'Good,' I said, almost fainting in relief. 'And be grateful that I drive a hard bargain because you can be sure that I'll always arrange the best deal I can with our customers.'

'Make sure you do!'

I ignored her comment. 'I shall come and see you later this afternoon to inspect the new premises. Please ensure that they are prepared for the arrival of my furniture.'

'Don't think I won't be keeping my eye on you,' muttered Dolly, darkly. 'And I shall want to see your accounts reg'lar, mind!'

I stopped in the doorway and raised my eyebrows at her. 'Really? I didn't know you could read, Dolly.' Turning on my heel, I swept through the doorway, swished across the courtyard and walked sedately away. It wasn't until I was sure that I was out of Dolly's sight that I picked up my skirts and skipped down the alley laughing with relief.

Behind me a dog barked and I turned to see Shadow following in my footsteps. I stopped to pat his head and set off again. Overtaken by a rush of energy I made a mental list of all the things I would have to do but first I must call on Ben Perkins and beg him to help me pack my goods and convey them to the shop on Pye Corner. I laughed under my breath at the thought of Hackett coming to seek me out when I didn't arrive at his chambers, begging to be his mistress. All he would find would be his crumbling house swept bare.

My euphoria, however, was soon tempered by the recollection that, although I might be saved from Hackett's unspeakable embraces, I'd be working for a capricious employer, living on an unreliable income in one room over a shop in a less than salubrious part of the city. I cursed Hackett under my breath. If only he hadn't cheated me out of Robert's last month's wages I'd be in a far more comfortable position. There was no help for it; I would have to be brave and approach Hackett again to demand he pay what he owed me.

I called on Nell first. Ben was out on a delivery but expected back very soon.

'I'll leave my key with you,' I said. 'Ben can start to pack the furniture and I'll return before long.'

Shadow was still waiting for me as I left and I was glad to have his company as he trotted along beside me. It wasn't far to Hackett's chambers so there wasn't time for my courage to fail me. I shivered in the chill October wind, took a deep breath and rapped upon the door.

A clerk, barely more than a boy, let me in and said he'd tell Mr Hackett I'd arrived.

I waited on a hard chair in the anteroom with my hands folded tightly in my lap, listening to the scratching of the clerk's quill as he wrote in his ledger. Every now and again Hackett's rumbling tones rose to a crescendo behind his office door and I sat up straighter, muscles tensed and ready to rise to my feet.

More than half an hour later the door burst open and two men came out. Hackett's curled wig was jet black and he wore a coat of shiny buttercup yellow satin stretched across his stomach. His arm was draped around his companion's shoulder and a cloud of tobacco smoke drifted around them. I recognised the second man as the magistrate, Charles Clifton.

'We'll go to Rochester Court next week,' boomed Hackett, full of bonhomie, 'and you can take your pick of which house you'd like for your daughter, Clifton. Then I'll take you to dine at the Folly, afterwards.'

'The Folly?'

'You must have heard of it – the eating house on a barge moored by Somerset House? Leave your wife at home, though. Very accommodating serving wenches I've found.' He touched his nose and nodded meaningfully.

Clifton brayed with laughter and clapped Hackett on the shoulder.

It was then that Hackett saw me. 'Mistress Finche,' he drawled. 'I've been expecting you.' He turned to his clerk. 'You can go home now as I have some business to attend to.'

'Yes, sir.'

'And find Hogg and tell him to mind the office. I shall be busy with this lady for some time.'

The boy scurried away.

Hackett leered at me and gestured me into his inner chamber.

Reluctantly, I followed him.

The room was fogged with tobacco smoke, heavily laced with the sickly scent of rum and stale sweat. I glanced longingly at the firmly closed window.

'So, you've taken off your mourning and put on your finery to come and visit me,' said Hackett, looking at me with his heavy-lidded eyes. 'And as you can see, I've had a new coat made in honour of the occasion.'

He lifted one of my curls from my shoulder and rubbed it through his fingers.

'And what occasion is that?' I asked, stepping back.

'Hmm. I'm wondering whether to wait until tonight or if I shall have you now, right here on my desk.'

Appalled and repulsed, I was struck dumb.

Hackett pushed aside an inkwell and quill on his great desk, picked up a bottle of rum and poured generous measures into the two glasses that sat beside it. He pushed one towards me and I saw with distaste that the rim was sticky from a previous user.

'Drink up!' It wasn't a request.

'I haven't come to drink with you,' I said frostily, impatient to come to the crux of the matter.

He scowled. 'You'll drink with me if I tell you to.'

'I've come to collect my husband's wages.'

His mouth tightened in irritation. 'I've told you before that he's had them. Besides I'll settle your household accounts directly.' He turned his palms up and smiled. 'Now, you can't say I'm not generous, can you? And, maybe, if you please me –' his hot gaze raked up and down my body '– we'll buy you some pretty trifles tomorrow. A knot of ribbons, or somesuch thing. How would you like that?'

I pursed my lips to prevent me laughing aloud at the news I was about to impart that would wipe the complacent smile off his lips. 'I say that I have no intentions whatsoever of becoming your mistress.'

Hackett's smile faded.

'As I said, I have come here merely to collect the wages you owed to my husband. Since you say you are so generous, surely you would not deny his widow that?'

He was silent for a moment as an angry flush flared on his cheeks. 'Found yourself another protector, have you?' His tone was ugly and I gave an involuntary shiver.

'Certainly not!' I said. 'I intend to make my own way in the world. You may repossess your house this evening when I have removed my furniture.'

'You won't be needing furniture when you return to the gutter!' He came to stand so close to me that his tobacco-laden breath stirred a strand of hair on my cheek. 'I don't believe you've considered the matter carefully, my dear.'

'On the contrary, Mr Hackett, I assure you that I have considered the matter extremely carefully.' My heart was thudding like an anvil and I wished I'd never decided to approach him. 'I should like the money owing to me, if you please. Now!'

'No protector?' His expression was incredulous. 'Do satisfy my curiosity and explain.'

'What I intend is of no consequence to you since I shall not see you again.'

'Why, you ungrateful little jade!' He pushed his face close to mine. 'I've been exceedingly generous to you and this is how you repay me?'

'Generous!' The heat of anger rose up my throat. 'You refuse to settle your debts and then intimidate me into becoming your mistress? I'd rather die!'

'And indeed you might!' Spittle from Hackett's mouth spattered my face. 'Have you no conception of the honour I do you? I am a man of consequence and standing in this city. Far better to come willingly to my bed than lift your skirts in a back alley for every Tom, Dick and Harry who offers you a penny.'

I held out my hand and then hid it behind my back when I saw how much it was shaking. 'Give me what you owe me or . . . '

'Or what?' Hackett sneered.

The sight of his scornful expression made my temper boil over. 'Give me what you owe me at once!' I said, suddenly reckless. I was damned if he'd get away with it! 'Or shall I tell all your investors that you are a cheat and a liar who takes advantage of those weaker than yourself? And furthermore, your bricks are dangerous and your rotten houses are so badly built that they're impossible to live in.' By this point, I was shouting, with my fists clenched by my side.

'What do you know about those bricks?' Grasping my shoulders, Hackett shook me until my teeth rattled.

Fury rose up in my breast again and I pulled back my foot and kicked at Hackett's shin with all the force I could muster.

Hackett roared and swiped at me, his great fist hitting my cheek like a hammer blow.

I reeled back, almost fainting with the shock.

'Not so bold now, are you, you little baggage!' He grasped me by my waist, lifted me up and dumped me on my back on his desk. 'I shall have you now and you'll never forget it!'

Before I knew what was happening, he caught at the fragile silk of my bodice and ripped it apart.

I gasped and tried to cover my nakedness, but he held my wrists together above my head and his great mouth came down on my breast, sucking and biting as I fought against him. I screamed and he threw my skirts up over my head. Thrashing and kicking, I struggled to push the suffocating froth of silk and lace off my face as his hands groped between my thighs, forcing them apart.

Terror-stricken, I managed to free my face to find that Hackett hung over me, red-faced and sweating, as he unbuttoned his breeches with one hand, holding me down effortlessly with the other.

'Pointless to struggle,' he said, 'so you might as well enjoy it. I know I shall.' His eyes shone with lust. 'In fact, I like a fight; it'll add spice to our coupling.' He laughed. 'Spice with the spice merchant's little wife!' He undid the last button on his breeches and his monstrous prick burst free. 'What do you think of that?' He smirked. 'Believe me, you'll soon be begging for more.'

I screamed again, attempting to draw up my knees and pull away as he held me down. I felt him, hot and hard, bumping against my inner thigh and sickness and disbelief rose in my throat as I realised that I couldn't escape him.

Rolling my head from side to side I knocked over a glass of rum. Then I saw the inkwell. I snatched it up and flung the contents in Hackett's face.

He snarled and reared up, his face and the front of his vulgar yellow coat dripping with ink. Shaking his head, black drops spattered from his wig onto my face and breasts. 'You vixen! You've ruined my new coat.'

I saw the murderous glint in his eye and knew with cold certainty that my next breath might be my last. Wildly, my fingers fumbled across the desk until I caught hold of something cold. A quill knife.

Hackett's hands reached for my throat.

I didn't hesitate. Lifting my fist, I plunged the blade into Hackett's shoulder.

He bellowed but it didn't stop his hands tightening around my neck.

Gasping for air, I pulled the blade free and stabbed him again. And again and again. The pressure on my throat increased. I couldn't breathe and there was a roaring in my ears. Dropping the knife, I scrabbled frantically at Hackett's fingers, scratching at his face and gouging at his eyes with a desperation born of blind terror. Pain pounded in my throat and my swelling tongue protruded from my lips. My ears boomed with the drumbeat of my heart.

But then a strange calm descended on me and all movement became too much of an effort. There was nothing I could do to avert my fate. All I wanted was to sleep peacefully, all strife forgotten. My hands stopped plucking at Hackett's fingers as they squeezed ever tighter around my neck. I stared at his sweating, scarlet face with the purple veins bulging in his forehead and was overcome with sadness that such an ugly sight was the last thing I would see before I died. Then my vision grew spotted, darkened and faded away to nothing.

Chapter 23

Awareness came slowly. It was pitch dark. There was a throbbing pain in my throat. My face was pressed against something hard that smelled of ancient dust. I hurt all over. Was I confined in Aunt Mercy's cellar again? Gradually memory returned. Hackett's ugly face close to mine, his eyes hot with lust. The sound of tearing silk as he ripped my bodice. His mouth on my breast. I made a small sound of distress and lifted my head. The agonising pain in my swollen neck made me gasp.

Slowly, I inched myself up into a cramped sitting position, knocking my head. There wasn't room to stretch out my legs. A terrible thirst consumed me and my mouth was dry as ashes. I leaned back until my spine pressed against something hard and I reached out into the sooty blackness until my shaking fingers touched a flat surface. I ran my hands over it, feeling splinters snag against my palms. Stretching above me, I felt wood again, with narrow spaces between separate planks. Behind me the cold surface was smooth, like a wall.

As my eyes became accustomed to the dark I noticed that the tiniest line of grey light crept in, outlining a large square. I touched the wood in front of me, gently at first but then more firmly as it shifted slightly under the pressure of my palm. A door? I pushed harder but it wouldn't open. A locked door.

Then I realised; I was confined in a cupboard. Panic washed over me in an icy wave as I stared wide-eyed into the darkness. I was instantly transported back to the many times Aunt Mercy had shut me in the coal cellar, leaving me sobbing, cold and frightened, for hours at a time. But this was worse. And I could expect more than a thrashing with a birch twig if Hackett found out I was still alive.

I forced down the impulse to scream and bang my fists on the door. The air smelled of dusty old papers, mould and tobacco smoke. Each breath felt as if I was swallowing crushed glass. I don't know how long I sat there trying to control my panic while my heart banged in my chest and the blood sang in my ears. Unbidden, I thought fleetingly of Gabriel Harte, locked into his eternal world of darkness, and wondered if he ever experienced the same terror as I felt now.

And then I heard a noise. Voices. Tensing every muscle, I strained my ears, listening.

Somewhere a door slammed. Heavy footsteps approached and Hackett's voice called out, 'Nat!'

A moment later another voice replied, higher and more nasal in tone, 'Coming!'

I froze. The voices were coming closer.

The floorboards beneath me juddered. My breathing was quick and shallow.

Then Hackett spoke. 'Have you brought the carriage right up to the front door, Nat?'

'Just like last time. Beginning to make a habit of this, aren't you?'

'No choice. She knew about the bricks. We drowned that milksop Finche too late to stop him telling Wifey what was going on.'

Shock made me gasp. Hackett had murdered Robert!

There was a sudden rattling at the cupboard door and the click of a key turning in the lock.

Quick as a flash I huddled face down on the floor again.

The door creaked open and I glimpsed flickering candlelight through my half-closed eyelids.

'Shame. She was a pretty little thing.' Hackett nudged my hip with his foot. 'Didn't quite manage to have my way with her before she turned up her toes.'

'Wouldn't of let that stop me,' sniggered Nat. 'And it's not too late now.'

I felt him lift my skirts and had to grit my teeth to stop myself from flinching as he ran his calloused hands over my thigh.

'Give over, Nat. Let's get the business done with.'

Hands grasped me under my armpits and pulled me roughly from the cupboard. I smelled Hackett's sour breath and allowed my body to go completely limp.

Turned onto my back, it took every ounce of self-control not to cover my naked breasts with my hands.

'She's not stiff yet,' said Nat, cheerfully. 'In fact she's still warm.' Hands cupped my breasts, then he lifted my wrist and drew in his breath sharply. 'There's a pulse! Thought you said she'd snuffed it, Guv'nor?'

Hackett's wig brushed my cheek.

'Is she breathing?' asked Nat.

'Not for long,' said Hackett. 'Take her ankles.'

Overwhelmed with fear, I kept my eyes tight shut and remained limp as they heaved me from the cupboard and through the anteroom. My head thumped against the doorway and it was all I could do not to cry out.

Then there was a draught of cold air, the sound of wheeled traffic on the cobbles and the scent of sweating horseflesh.

'Wait!' murmured Hackett.

They dropped me to the ground like a sack of flour. Footsteps passed and then faded away. It appeared to be dark outside for no light penetrated my closed eyelids.

'Now!' said Hackett.

Hogg grasped my ankles again and lifted me off the ground, my petticoats falling back to my knees. The night air hit me, bringing my bare legs out in goose pimples. The two men dumped me unceremoniously into the waiting carriage with my skirts all anyhow and my face squashed against the leather seat. My arm lay uncomfortably trapped underneath me but I dared not adjust my position. Playing dead was my only hope of surviving.

'Are you going in with her?' asked Hogg, lifting up my skirts. 'Give you a last chance to examine her ladyship's secret delights?' he asked.

I shivered, imagining the sly grin spreading over his weasel face.

'I'm sure I saw her twitch!' said Hackett. 'Is she waking up?'

'P'raps we oughta finish her off now?'

'I'll not risk any disturbance. Give me your belt!'

A moment later my arms were wrenched behind my back and a belt, still warm from Hogg's skin, pulled tightly around my upper arms.

'I'll stay with her,' said Hackett. 'Take the reins but don't do anything to draw attention to us.'

The carriage door closed with a click and the horses pulled us forwards with a sudden jerk before setting off at a tremendous pace. Hackett slammed his hand against the window, swearing under his breath as I shot off the seat and thudded to the floor.

The carriage bounced and juddered over every cobble and pothole in the road, each jolt sending a new shock of excruciating pain through my throbbing neck.

Hackett swore again and banged on the ceiling of the carriage until it slowed down suddenly, sending me rolling back across the floor again. My mouth was dry and my tongue swollen. I lay as still as I could, imagining drinking cool water, each drop rolling down my parched throat like rain running down a window.

Then we gathered speed again, rattling along the street hell for leather while I thought about poor Robert, struggling against Hackett and Hogg while they drowned him. I hoped his death had been quick and he hadn't suffered too greatly.

I don't know how long I endured the violent motion; each agonising second seemed to me to be an aeon. Fear and thirst froze my mind and time was running out to plan how to escape; I couldn't think straight. All I knew was that the carriage was travelling much too fast for me to risk throwing myself out through the door.

After a while, I heard Hackett open the window and the seat creaked as he leaned forwards to peer outside. The cold air carried with it a stink I recognized: the tang of mud, decay, tar and a hint of fish. I could hear the rushing sound of water and guessed we were near the river. Gradually, the motion of the carriage slowed and, finally, it rolled to a stop.

Dread made my skin prickle. I would have to act any moment now or be lost forever, like Robert. The carriage rocked as Nat Hogg jumped down from the driving seat.

Hackett wrenched open the door and jumped out. 'God's teeth, Nat!' he said. 'What the hell were you playing at, you stupid bastard?'

I heard the sound of a slap and Hogg's aggrieved exclamation.

'You flung me about in there as if I were a sack of coal and my shoulder hurts like the devil. It's bleeding again. Didn't I tell you not to draw attention to us?'

Their voices echoed into the night as if we were in a large building but there was the sound of fast-running water close at hand.

'No one can see us in the dark,' Hogg protested. 'Don't often get the chance to drive a fine carriage.'

Slowly, slowly, I pulled my elbow under my chest and braced my foot against the side of the coach, ready to push myself up. My breathing quickened. If only they'd step aside from the carriage for a minute or two to continue their altercation I might be able to run away under the cover of darkness.

'You'd better learn to obey orders, Nathaniel Hogg, or . . .'

I shivered at Hackett's menacing tone and carefully drew my knees up ready to roll over and spring up.

'Or what, Hackett? I know plenty about you that the magistrate'd like to hear about.'

'You'll end up drowned under London Bridge like Finche and his missus if you go on like that. Now shut your trap and help me carry her.'

Shivering in fear, I realised that they intended to drop me in the river. London Bridge was notorious for the dangerous waters that funnelled between the piers. There'd be little hope of surviving.

'If they find her, won't it be suspicious that she drowned in the same place as Finche?' asked Nat.

'What, the poor grieving widow, who killed herself at the exact same spot as her hubby?' Hackett laughed. 'I'll put it about that she couldn't stand the shame of finding out he did away with himself after I'd caught him fiddling the books and making dubious deals on second-rate bricks.'

'Neat!'

Filled with sudden fury, I could barely restrain myself from hurling abuse at Hackett for defaming Robert's name. I peeped through the narrow gap of the carriage door with my heart banging. The carriage had stopped under the bridge and Hackett and Hogg stood in the shadows. The dank smell of mould pervaded the air. Cautiously, I pulled myself into a crouching position ready to sprint for freedom.

But it was too late.

Hackett turned and saw me as I inched the carriage door open. 'Well, look who's awake!'

I tumbled out of the carriage, already knowing it was hopeless but damned if I'd go to my grave without a fight. Then I was running and running with the wind in my hair, slipping and stumbling on the muddy ground.

I didn't get very far. Tripping over, I crashed headlong to the ground, unable to save myself since my hands were still secured behind my back. The wind was knocked out of me so I couldn't scream as Hackett's great hands lifted me up and whacked me across the face.

'You're putting me to a great deal of trouble, Mistress Finche,' he said. 'And I'm not having any more of it.' He snatched hold of my hair and dragged me back towards Nat Hogg. 'Let's get this over with, Nat,' he said, 'and then we can go and have our supper in the King's Arms.'

Yanking at my hair again, he hauled me along, pulling me up sharply if I stumbled. Our footsteps echoed as we returned to the bridge and the sound of racing water became louder.

Desperation made me struggle to twist myself free of his grip but tears started to my eyes as he pulled viciously at my hair.

'Now untie her, sharpish!' He turned me around and shoved my face against the slimy stone of the bridge.

Cold dampness seeped though the thin silk of my dress and I began to tremble uncontrollably. Rough fingers pulled at my upper arms and then they were free. I whimpered as the blood began to flow painfully back into my fingers. Nat Hogg and Hackett half lifted, half dragged me towards the water.

The torrent was deafening under the arches and spray splashed up at my face and drenched my skirt. 'Don't!' I said. 'Please, don't!' My voice was little more than a croak. Disbelief gripped me. Surely my life couldn't end like this, drowned like an unwanted kitten?

'You know what you are?' said Hackett, pushing his face close to mine. 'An ungrateful little madam, that's what you are. This is your own fault. You could have been my mistress and all would have been well.'

Before I could turn my head away, his mouth enveloped mine and his slippery tongue forced itself between my teeth even as he grasped my breast. I fought uselessly against him and then clamped my teeth together over his tongue, biting down so hard that I felt his hot blood run down my throat.

Yelling with rage, Hackett shoved me away. 'Bitch!' He cracked my head against the stone pier of the bridge. Stunned, my knees buckled beneath me.

Somewhere, a dog barked itself into a frenzy.

Then Hackett grasped me and suddenly I was in the air. I screamed as the roaring water came to meet me and then slammed the air out of my belly. Icy blackness engulfed me and my scream was drowned as I plunged downwards under the freezing water. The deafening noise of the fast-flowing river was silenced. Shock made me gasp and then choke on muddy water. Suddenly, my face burst out of the water and I heaved in a lungful of air.

Tumbled over and over, I was swept downstream by the rapids, unable to think or act, only my natural instinct for survival making me gasp for air whenever my mouth was above water. The cold gripped me, turning my limbs to stone. Suddenly, I received a crashing blow to the head. Pain blossomed, red hot, behind my eyes. And then the world turned black.

Chapter 24

Voices, murmuring. Darkness. The yellow light of a candle guttered in a draught. Stabbing pains in my head and neck. A moistened cloth touched my parched lips.

Sleep.

Pale sunlight played on a whitewashed wall, flickering and twisting in a spellbindingly slow dance. Somewhere far away angels sang, their sweet voices rising and fading again. Pain, too great to bear, gripped my head, throbbing in time with my pulse.

I slept again.

A church bell was ringing, slow and sonorous. Daylight sliced in through half-opened shutters, making stripes on the whitewashed wall. A cool hand gently touched my brow.

'Mama?' My voice was rusty and unused, my throat painful. My head ached.

'Drink this.' The voice was low and melodious.

I sipped the syrupy drink but it was sour with an aftertaste of bitter herbs.

Then I slept again.

A bell clanged, reverberating sharply through my head. I screwed my eyes shut against the light and cupped my hands over my ears to close out the clamour. At last, the noise ceased.

I opened my eyes. The room was small and white. A white sheet covered me on the bed. A barred window high up in one white wall and a closed door in another. Nothing else. I had not, as far as I could remember, ever been in that room before.

I looked down at the unfamiliar shift that I wore. Uneasy thoughts whirled, ghost-like, in my aching head but I couldn't quite catch them. Shouldn't I be somewhere else? My throat hurt and I was thirsty. Licking my flaking lips, I gingerly eased myself into a sitting position and then, taking my time, moved my legs over the edge of the bed.

Then I heard the singing again. Women's voices, floating clear and sweet on the breeze coming through the window. I reached up to rub my temples and encountered a bandage. I winced at the sharp pain caused by the slight pressure of my fingers.

There was something I had to remember.

I stood up and was assailed by such dizziness that I sank back onto the bed. Breathing deeply, I waited for the faintness to pass before trying again. Haltingly, I made my way, barefooted, to the door, each step pounding through my ears. The door was shut and I fumbled with the latch until it opened with a click.

There was an open walkway outside with arcading onto a small courtyard garden. I stepped onto the stone-flagged floor and felt the cold, rough dampness of it on the soles of my feet. I shivered and folded my arms against the chill wind. I looked both ways along the walkway but it was deserted. Muzzy-headed, I stood motionless.

Apart from the mournful cry of a seagull wheeling overhead and the faint sound of water running, there was silence.

The courtyard was edged with low box hedges. Gravel paths formed a cross and at the intersection was a small pool with a fountain. I tiptoed hesitatingly along the path and sat down on the edge of the pool to peer into the greenish water.

My wavering reflection stared back at me and, wonderingly, it reached up to touch the bandage wrapped around my head. How did I come to this place? Anxiety gnawed at me but I couldn't remember what it was I'd forgotten. The fountain jet sent ripples across the surface of the undulating water, dissolving and reforming the reflection of my face. I leaned closer. If only I could see my face properly, perhaps then I would remember who I was.

I reached down to my twin in the water and as my hand dipped into the green depths the splashing of the fountain seemed to become magnified. Transfixed, I fought rising panic as I struggled with fleeting memories.

Then, all at once I recalled the sound of rushing water in the blackness of the night and my terror as I sank below the surface of the river and how I had tumbled helplessly along with the raging torrent. I remembered gasping for breath and my drowning screams and the terrible blow to my head. And then nothing.

The cold water made my hand ache and I snatched it from the pool and nursed it, dripping, against my breast. Where was I? I glanced wildly around, my breath quickening with fear.

A movement caught my eye and a small figure dressed in white was hurrying along under the arcading, her habit billowing out behind her in the wind. A nun. Confused, I shrank back but it was too late to hide for she had seen me.

'What are you doing out here?' Her wrinkled old face was full of concern. 'I haven't spent a week nursing you back from Death's door for you to catch a chill from sitting in the cold in your nightshift.' The nun's scolding tone was belied by her smile. She took my wet hand. 'Come inside this minute! Look at you; your shift is all wet! And with such a biting wind as this . . . '

I allowed myself to be led back to the little room and put back into bed.

'I'm Sister Assumpta,' she said. 'I'll fetch a hot brick from the kitchen. Your feet feel like icicles. Now stay here!' She fixed me with a glare from her twinkling blue eyes and turned with a swirl of her habit and hurried away.

Shivering, I touched my temple again. If only my head didn't ache so abominably perhaps I'd be able to remember what had happened. I lay back on the pillows with my eyes closed and tried to concentrate.

A few moments later Sister Assumpta returned and tucked a hot brick wrapped in wool under my feet and a muslin shawl high around my neck and shoulders.

'Sister Assumpta –' I put a hand to my throat since it hurt to speak '– how did I come to be here?'

'I hoped you would be able to tell me that yourself. You were found unconscious on the mud at low tide near Falcon Stairs with a head wound. A passing waterman saw you and brought you to us.'

I frowned while frightening images chased through my mind. 'I was under the bridge. It smelled of mould and the sound of the racing water was deafening . . . '

'It must have been high tide then.'

Voices echoed in my head. *You know what you are? An ungrateful little madam, that's what you are. You could have been my mistress* . . . And then I remembered Hackett's thick lips coming down over my mouth and his tongue . . . 'It was Hackett!' I whispered, clutching the sheet to my chin. 'Hackett threw me into the river.'

Sister Assumpta drew in her breath. 'Someone threw you in the river? Are you sure? You've had a bad clout to your head, my dear.'

'He tried to strangle me.'

Shock and disbelief raced across Sister Assumpta's face. She rested a hand on my forehead. 'You must sleep again and in the morning everything will be well.'

I threw back the sheet in sudden panic. 'I must go before he comes for me.'

Sister Assumpta pressed me back firmly into the bed. 'You are quite safe here. Can I send for your family?'

I closed my eyes and leaned back against the pillow. Who could I send for? Certainly not Aunt Mercy. 'I have no family.' Tears leaked out from under my eyelids. 'My husband is dead. He drowned under London Bridge.'

'Ah! Now I understand. But drowning yourself will not help him and will damn your soul.'

'But I didn't . . . '

'Hush now! Drink this and we'll talk about it in the morning. Is there no friend who could help you?'

She pressed a cup to my lips and I had no choice but to drink the bitter potion again. Amongst the whirlwind of thoughts I remembered Jane. 'I have a friend,' I murmured as numbness began to seep into my bones. 'Jane Harte.' It became difficult to speak. 'The House of Perfume,' I whispered, as I plummeted into a spinning void of darkness.

It was the scent of orange blossom that woke me. The perfume lingered in the air, teasing at my senses as I arose from the depths of drugged sleep. My eyelids fluttered open.

Jane Harte leaned over me, worry creasing her pale face. 'Thank the Lord!' she said. 'We thought you'd never wake. I was worried that Sister Assumpta had given you too much poppy syrup.'

My mouth was dry as dust. 'Jane,' I whispered. I recognised the scent of orange blossom as her special perfume now.

She touched a finger to my cheek. 'It's all right; Gabriel and I are both here. Poor Kate! I wish you'd told me how desperate you were!'

My head began to clear and I turned my head to see Gabriel Harte on the other side of the bed. I lay still while, one after the other, the memories came flooding back.

'Kate, could you not have confided in me?' asked Jane.

'You were in Epsom. Besides, I was ashamed,' I said.

'Ashamed that you felt sorrow for your husband's death?'

Painfully, I shook my head. 'It was Hackett . . . ' My voice was still hoarse.

'I don't understand,' said Mr Harte.

'He gave me one week to leave his house. The alternative was to . . . ' I couldn't look at him.

'To what?'

'To be his mistress.'

Jane gasped and her husband swore under his breath. 'But still,' she said, 'to try to drown yourself . . . '

'I *didn't* try to drown myself!'

'Ben Perkins came to the House of Perfume looking for you,' said Mr Harte. 'He said you'd failed to meet him at a shop on Pye Corner.'

Jane gripped my hand. 'Kate, why did you imagine you could live above a horrid little shop in Pye Corner of all places?'

'Because that was a better alternative than Hackett's suggestion I move into his bed,' I said bitterly.

Jane shuddered.

'I went to see Hackett after you disappeared and he told me that he'd given you money and offered you the opportunity to live in his house rent free,' said Mr Harte. 'He said you were very cast down in your spirits since your husband had drowned himself and that you spoke wildly of following in his footsteps.'

'Hackett's a miserable liar!' I struggled to sit up, my breast heaving with indignation. 'I heard him admit he murdered Robert as he was going to discredit him. And then he tried to ravish me and after I stabbed him in the shoulder, he strangled me and shut me in a cupboard. Then he threw me into the rapids.'

Jane looked at me, her face expressionless. 'I see,' she said, at last. 'Kate, my dear, you've had a dreadful bang to your head. Perhaps you're confused?'

'You don't believe me,' I said flatly. I pulled aside the muslin shawl and bared my neck.

Jane gasped. 'I can see you're covered in bruises,' she said, 'but you could have received them when you tumbled about in the river.'

'But that *isn't* how they happened,' I said. 'I tell you, Hackett murdered Robert!' What more could I say to make her see the truth? 'Why doesn't anyone believe me?' I cried.

'I do believe you, Mistress Finche,' said Mr Harte.

'Thank you,' I said, sighing in relief. In that moment I could have kissed him. Gabriel Harte had faith in me.

He stretched out his hand and rested it on my wrist. 'Clearly you cannot stay here, but you must rest and recover. Jane, I believe the best course of action is to take Mistress Finche home with us for a while. Don't you?'

'Exactly my own thoughts.' said Jane.

I nearly wept with relief. My friends would help me and I was not alone.

Sister Assumpta brought me a bundle of clothing and ushered Jane and Gabriel Harte from the room while I dressed. The cream wool of the nun's habit was heavy and slightly scratchy but it was comfortingly warm. I slipped on the sandals Sister Assumpta had left for me and went outside.

There was a little sunshine peeping through the scudding clouds. I felt as light as thistledown and wondered if the wind would blow me away.

'Don't tell me you've decided to take holy orders?' asked Jane with a smile. She turned to her husband. 'Kate is dressed in a nun's habit, Gabriel. But she's far too pretty to be a nun.'

Gabriel Harte stretched out a hand to me. 'Shall we go?'

'But what if Hackett sees me if I leave this place?' Fright caused me to grip Gabriel Harte's wrist. 'If he sees me . . . '

'We have brought the carriage,' said Gabriel Harte soothingly. His thumb stroked the back of my hand and my sudden panic abated at his calm voice. 'We shall keep the blinds up as we travel so no one will see you.'

'But if he finds out I didn't drown after all . . . '

'No one in St Agnes's will speak of this since we are a closed and silent order,' said Sister Assumpta.

'But *you* aren't silent.'

Sister Assumpta smiled. 'God has other uses for me than simply to pray. I am the contact with the outside world, leaving my sisters free to concentrate on their devotions. Rest assured, I shall not discuss your stay here with anyone at all.'

Sister Assumpta led us to the convent gate and, as she unlocked it, there came the sound of joyful barking. A dog raced towards us, his tail thrashing.

'It's Shadow!'

'You know this creature?' asked Sister Assumpta 'He's been most persistent. However often I told him to go away, he would keep returning to wait outside the gates.'

'He was waiting for me,' I said, as Shadow whined in delight.

'We'll take him home with us,' said Gabriel Harte. He offered me his arm and I was glad to lean against him.

I thanked Sister Assumpta for her care of me, and then we were in the outside world again.

Chapter 25

We arrived at the House of Perfume without incident but, nevertheless, I was almost fainting with exhaustion by the time Jane put me to bed in a pretty bedchamber overlooking the street.

'You must sleep for as long as you wish.'

'What if Hackett –'

Jane held up her hand. 'No one will disturb you. I haven't felt well myself and have given Jacob instructions not to admit anyone.'

'What of Shadow?'

'He shall be given a bed near the fire in the kitchen.'

Her gentle but firm voice forbade me to ask any more questions and since all I longed for was to sink down onto the plump pillows, I didn't protest.

'You're so kind to me,' I murmured, unable to resist the lure of the downy pillow any longer.

'Rest now,' said Jane, drawing the bed curtains closed.

I was asleep before she closed the door.

I screamed as Hackett ripped my bodice apart and felt the heat of his hands grabbing at my breasts. He loomed over me, his thick red lips glistening and the coarse hair of his wig brushing against my naked skin.

'*Kate!*'

Hackett shook me by my shoulders and I screamed again, my eyes tight shut.

'*Kate!*'

My teeth rattled together as he shook me and then I opened my eyes to find Jane leaning over me.

'Kate, you were having a nightmare. I couldn't wake you and I was worried.'

I swallowed, while my galloping heartbeat began to slow. 'I was dreaming of Hackett.'

'He's not here, Kate!'

Slowly, I sat up, clutching the sheet with shaking fingers.

'It was only a dream.' Jane laid a skirt and bodice on the bed. 'I've brought you something more suitable to wear and, when you are dressed, Toby has been asking to see you.' She hesitated. 'I told him that you slipped in the river and hurt your head. I didn't want to frighten him.'

'Of course not.' I noticed then that Jane's face was pinched and drawn. 'But I've been selfish and too full of my own fears. Do you still have the headache, Jane?'

She shrugged. 'I hoped the waters at Epsom would improve matters but I cannot seem to be pain-free these days.'

'Have you visited the apothecary?'

Jane smiled briefly. 'He almost looks on me as a daughter now, since I see him so frequently. When the pain is bad nothing helps except poppy juice, but it gives me such horrid dreams and afterwards I'm so listless.'

'Does your physician not know what causes the pain?'

'Some imbalance of the humours, he says. But enough of that!

I've been practising a new piece of music on my harpsichord. Perhaps you'd like to listen to it?'

'I should like that very much.'

'Then come to my closet once you are ready.'

As I dressed in the plain black skirt and bodice that Jane had lent me, I mourned my lovely topaz silk dress. Sister Assumpta must have cut away what remained of it while I was unconscious. I would never have a dress as fine again. But then I shivered as I remembered the lust in Hackett's eyes as he ripped apart the thin silk of the bodice. Jane's unadorned black clothing would never attract that kind of attention from a man and I was glad of it.

We sat in Jane's closet and her maid, Ann, brought us tea. Toby came running in to find us, full of cheerful chatter. Jane played a pretty piece on her harpsichord, but it has to be said that she was not a natural musician.

Jane laughed as she played yet another wrong note. 'Gabriel is far more musically accomplished than I and he's so forbearingly patient with me that it puts me quite out of temper,' she said, a slight edge to her voice. 'He never accompanies me any more as it always leads to disagreements.'

Toby joined us in a game of spillikins and the time passed very pleasantly without me dwelling unduly on Hackett's duplicity.

After dinner, a simple repast served in the comfortable but old-fashioned dining room, Jane led Toby away, leaving me alone with Gabriel Harte.

'Are you sufficiently recovered,' he asked, 'to discuss how we should progress matters with Mr Hackett?'

'I am much improved, thanks to you and dear Jane.'

He sipped his wine and I noticed how the light burnished the strong planes of his cheekbones and jaw. 'Tell me the whole story again, right from the beginning,' he said.

When I finished the tale Mr Harte sighed. 'Unfortunately, I've come to the conclusion that there is little we can do.'

I stared at him, shocked. 'But surely we must tell the constable what Hackett did?'

'The constable could do nothing without proof of Hackett's actions.'

'But I have all these bruises on my neck!'

'Jane is right. You could have hurt yourself when you fell in the river.' Gabriel spread his hands. 'It would be your word against Hackett's.'

'And I am merely a woman who might have tried to drown herself after her husband's tragic death,' I said bitterly, 'while Hackett is a man of consequence with important connections?' Despair made me bury my head in my hands.

'I'm afraid so. But, meanwhile, I'll see what can be done to obtain proof of Hackett's wrongdoings. I shall make enquiries.'

'Thank you,' I said.

'By the way, Ben Perkins came by while you were asleep, seeking news of your whereabouts. He's very disturbed by your disappearance and his wife is vociferous in her view that you would never have "done away with yourself". I made the decision not to tell him we'd found you.'

'But why?'

'Hackett thinks that you're dead and I don't care to disabuse him of the notion at present. Should news of your miraculous return to life reach his ears I wouldn't be able to ensure your safety.'

'Poor Nell!'

'It's for your own protection, Mistress Finche. I've arranged with Ben that we'll store your furniture and effects and Jane will retrieve your personal possessions for your current use.'

I rubbed my forehead, sighing at the hopeless task of bringing Hackett to justice. 'There *is* one thing,' I said slowly. 'I didn't tell you about the bricks.'

'The bricks?' Gabriel's green eyes were steady as he stared sightlessly at my face.

'Robert's former employer, Elias Maundrell, came to our house and they had a disagreement. They were shouting at each other and I heard Mr Maundrell say something about dangerous bricks. He pleaded with Robert, saying that he'd never be able to live with his conscience if . . . '

'If what?'

I shrugged. 'I don't know. But it was after I mentioned the bricks that Hackett tipped over the edge of reason and tried to murder me.' I sighed, worn out with worrying about it.

Gabriel steepled his fingers while he considered the matter. 'I think I must pay a visit to Mr Maundrell and see what he has to say on the matter. And you should rest. You sound exhausted.'

'I am,' I said.

After he'd gone, I went upstairs to lie down. I heard shouts of laughter coming from the landing, where I found two small figures battling to the death with wooden swords.

Jacob Samuels had taken off his immaculately cut coat and rolled up the sleeves of his ruffled shirt. He wore high-heeled shoes with polished brass buckles and red tongues and I thought that he'd be quite the dandy if he wasn't so small and hunchbacked.

Jacob caught sight of me and hastily pulled off the black eye patch he wore and dropped his sword to his side.

Toby turned to me, breathless with laughter and his face alight with excitement. 'Jacob's a pirate and I'm Sir Francis Drake. I'm stopping him from stealing the Queen's gold.'

'How exciting!'

Toby slashed at the air with his sword. 'Come on then, Blackhearted Jake!' he cried.

Jacob shuffled his feet. 'I have duties to attend to, Master Toby.'

'Please, don't let me spoil your game,' I said.

'Well . . . '

'Please, Jacob!' pleaded Toby.

Jacob picked up his sword. 'Five minutes, then. Hah!' He raised his sword and I watched from my post on the stairs, cheering at each thrust and parry as the flaxen-haired boy and the black-haired hunchback hacked vigorously away at each other, grunting and taunting each other all the while.

At last Jacob allowed Toby to flick the sword out of his hand and pin him against the wall.

'Now I shall kill you!' cried Toby with glee.

I left them to their game and went to the guestroom, kicked off my borrowed shoes and curled up on the bed. Toby and Jacob's game had distracted me from my worries for a few moments but now they returned in full force. However kind my friends were, I couldn't stay in their home permanently and must find a means of supporting myself very soon. The tight band of pain around my head began to increase as I fretted about it.

Exhausted, I yawned. Gabriel, for I had started to think of him by his given name now rather than as Mr Harte, had believed my story, even if I had no proof of Hackett's crimes. I remembered the look of concentration on Gabriel's face as he listened to me. It was an unusual experience, at least since I'd been orphaned, to find that someone else was really concerned for my well-being.

I awoke later to hear a gentle tapping on the door.

Ann, neat in a starched cap and apron, came in and bobbed a curtsey. She handed me the small travelling trunk that I'd packed before leaving the house in Ironmonger Lane. I opened the trunk and took out my comb, toothbrush and the bottle of Summer Garden perfume. I wept a few tears at these reminders of a life now gone.

Supper was on the table by the time I slipped into the chair beside Jane.

'Kate, Gabriel and I have a proposition for you,' said Jane after the plates were cleared.

'What kind of proposition?'

'Toby's nursemaid has left us. I've seen how good you are with him and he likes you a great deal. It would do me a very great service if you would become his companion. He's not a baby any longer and doesn't really require a nursemaid, but if you would keep him out of mischief and help him with his letters, I'd be very happy. And I too, would relish your companionship.'

'We'd both be delighted if you'd make the House of Perfume your home,' said Gabriel. The rich timbre of his voice was kind and warm.

'There would, of course, be a suitable salary to accompany the position,' said Jane.

A great weight lifted off my shoulders and a tight knot of fear loosened somewhere in my stomach. 'It's most kind of you,' I said, 'and I can think of nothing I should like better.'

Chapter 26

Over the next few days my headache disappeared and the painful bruises on my throat faded from purple through to yellow. Even though my nights continued to be broken by frightening dreams, I never ceased to be thankful that my immediate future had been resolved.

Toby was a delightful child, full of energy and mischief, and kept me so occupied with his happy chatter and affectionate nature that it helped me to forget my troubles. Even Shadow fitted into the household as if he'd always been there, making a particular friend of Mrs Jenks, the cook-housekeeper. He soon trained her, by the skilful use of mournful expressions, to pass him titbits of ham and tasty bones and rewarded her with a wagging tail and adoring looks.

One afternoon Gabriel went out in his carriage and when he returned he called me into the Perfume Salon. He paced backwards and forwards across the silky carpet while I sat down and breathed in the lovely flowery scent of the room.

'I've been to visit Elias Maundrell,' he said. 'And he's told me a most disturbing tale.'

I folded my hands in my lap and watched his agitated pacing.

'Maundrell told me he was angry with Hackett because he'd reneged on the order for bricks he'd placed with him because he'd set up his own brickyard.'

'I overheard him remonstrating with Hackett on the matter,' I said.

'Maundrell couldn't sell the quality bricks stockpiled in his own yard because the market had suddenly become flooded with cheap bricks.' Gabriel ceased pacing and sat down opposite me. 'The poor man was at his wits' end. He visited Hackett's brickyard in St Giles in the Field but discovered it had been cleared out and abandoned.'

'Was it Hackett's bricks that had flooded the market?'

'It's not as simple as that. Maundrell visited the alehouse nearest to the brickyard. He fell into conversation with a man who said that Hackett had produced vast quantities of bricks very quickly. He hadn't hired local, experienced labour but taken on a raggle-taggle army of unskilled vagrants for the purpose.'

'It's hard to think of Hackett as a philanthropist.'

Gabriel's mouth curved in a wry smile. 'Of course, they were all turned off once the bricks were laid out in the sun to dry.'

'But Hackett saved money.'

'Undoubtedly. And then, out of the blue, Hackett closed the yard and the bricks disappeared. Maundrell couldn't understand it so he went back to Hackett's yard under cover of darkness and took a brick that had been left behind.'

'Why would he do that?'

'He said the hairs rose up on the back of his neck when he handled it and he knew there was something wrong. The following morning he studied it by daylight and confirmed his suspicion that it was a dirtier yellow than the usual London brick. He's been in the business for a long time and was shocked to suspect that the brick was made with clay from a part of the river that his father had always told him was unsuitable for brick-making. Sure enough, when Maundrell placed the brick under pressure, it crumbled.'

'That could have been catastrophic! But clearly Hackett had closed the yard once he knew that his bricks were unsafe?'

Gabriel shrugged. 'He'd have lost his investors if they thought he was using bad bricks. But then Maundrell heard a rumour that business was being done in the taverns and bricks could be bought at a knock-down price if you knew the right people. After making a number of discreet enquiries, he determined that the bricks being sold were from Hackett's yard.'

I caught my breath as I thought of all the rebuilding in the city and realised the dangerous implications of the discovery. 'Hogg,' I said. 'It has to have been Hogg. But I feel sure Hackett would only have been using him to do the dirty work.'

'I agree. There was little Maundrell could do but then a house in Canning Street collapsed. It was built by a reputable tradesman but Maundrell had his suspicions that Hackett's bricks could be at fault. He went to the site and, sure enough, the bricks were the same as the one from Hackett's yard. He was too frightened to confront Hackett directly so he went to Ironmonger Lane to enlist your husband's support.'

'And Robert turned him away,' I said bleakly. 'But surely Hackett will be ruined once his investors know about the bricks? So when will Maundrell go to the constable?' I was full of elation. Perhaps, very soon, once Hackett was brought to justice, I could come out of hiding and the world would know what kind of a man he really was.

Gabriel rubbed his nose with his finger. 'That's the difficulty. Maundrell's terrified of Hackett.'

'And with good reason,' I said, ruefully.

'No one ever saw Hackett himself selling the bricks in the taverns. I'm trying to persuade Maundrell to speak to the constable but he's still frightened of the consequences. I've offered to lend him my carriage, however, to convey him to safety at his sister's house in Bath while Hackett is taken up. Once Maundrell's had a little time to mull it over, I'll go and see him again.'

'Mr Harte,' I said, 'you cannot know how grateful I am for your support. It makes me burn to think of Hackett escaping justice while he destroys others.'

'We're in complete agreement on that, Mistress Finche.'

As the days passed, I came to value Jane's friendship more each day and I was sad to find that her health was even less robust than I'd believed. She rarely complained, but I could tell she suffered by the shadows under her eyes and the wan cast of her cheeks. Frequently she rose late, sometimes not until after dinner, and I understood why such a devoted mother needed a companion for her son and an occasional nurse for herself.

We were sitting in her closet one afternoon, working on our embroidery, while Toby arranged our skeins of silk in order of colour.

'Do you still grieve for your husband a very great deal?' she asked.

I made another stitch to the outline of a rose, while I considered how to answer her. 'Robert and I were married to suit the convenience of his parents and my Aunt Mercy,' I said carefully. 'It was no love match. Although –' I rested my sewing on my lap '– as a young girl I dreamed of love, of far more importance was to escape from my aunt. Once it was agreed that I was to marry Robert, I hoped that in time we would grow fond of each other. If it had not been for the fire, then perhaps . . . ' I sighed.

'But you stayed at his side after the conflagration.'

'I had no family left, apart from Aunt Mercy, who'd been glad to be rid of me. Returning to her house was out of the question. Besides, I hoped desperately that before long I'd have a baby and a home of my own. For me, that might have made up for the insufficiencies in our marriage. The truth is, Robert and I were not ideally suited.'

'Marriage is often an unspoken contract, isn't it? In my case,' said Jane, 'my father knew Gabriel's uncle, who was anxious that his ward should marry and produce an heir. I'm relieved that I've fulfilled my part of the agreement since I have given Gabriel the son he required. In return, I have a comfortable home and a position in life that I never thought would be mine. We're civil to each other and he troubles me not at all, allowing me to do as I please, which is to lead a quiet life with my son.'

I wondered if that explained why there was no evidence of Gabriel in Jane's bedchamber, not a single shoe, shirt or nightcap to suggest his regular occupation.

'Not many women would care to marry a blind man, while I . . .' Jane bit her lip. 'Plain Jane my sisters called me. And it was true.'

'You are not plain to me,' I said, moved by her wistful expression

'And Gabriel will never see how irregular my features are.'

'For me, kindness, inner strength and an even temper are the most important requirements in a husband,' I said, remembering how carefully I'd had to tread when Robert was in one of his frequent bad moods. My fair-weather husband.

'Gabriel *is* kind but I've long given up any girlish thoughts of romantic notions. Our marriage is merely a convenient arrangement and I'm content with that since I never expected to marry at all. But my love for Toby surpasses all other and brings me all the joy I could hope for.'

I was saved from making any comment when the door pushed open.

'May I come in?' asked Gabriel. He wore a dark blue coat with silver buttons and looked very fine. I hoped he hadn't overheard our conversation.

Toby ran to hug his father's knees.

'Toby, Shadow was looking for you. Why don't you go and find him?'

'Make sure you wrap up warmly, Toby,' said Jane. 'I don't want you to catch an ague.'

The door slammed shut behind him and his little feet pounded down the stairs.

Gabriel sat down and crossed his long legs. I noticed that the tongues of his brass-buckled shoes were scarlet; an identical, if larger, version of the shoes Jacob wore.

'I have a letter for you, Mistress Finche,' he said.

'It must be from Mother Finche.' I opened it and read that she'd received my note and was happy that I had found a new home since she'd been unsuccessful in finding a position for me. I realised again how very lucky I'd been to meet Jane and Gabriel Harte.

'I've been giving a great deal of thought as to how we can maintain your safety, Mistress Finche,' Gabriel said, 'and an idea occurred to me. I heard about a woman who had been pulled out of the river. Young and black-haired, no one has claimed her body, poor soul. It occurred to me that it might be a good idea to mention this to Hackett to allay any fears he might have that you didn't drown.'

Shivering slightly, I imagined the poor girl, unwanted and unclaimed. Her life was over but she could help me to start a new one. 'That would remove any lingering uncertainties,' I said.

'So I visited Hackett and said that, since he'd mentioned that he was fearful for you as he thought you might have followed in your husband's footsteps, I'd made enquiries and discovered the body of a woman matching your description drowned in the river.'

'What did he say to that?' asked Jane.

'He sounded peculiarly relieved. So much so that, when I suggested we share the cost of burying poor Mistress Finche, he agreed. He said he regretted that he'd thought Mistress Finche was being overdramatic when she wept inconsolably on his shoulder and threatened to hurl herself in the river.'

'How I hate that man!' Rage seethed in my breast. 'When I think how he really treated me that makes my blood boil.'

'The funeral is arranged for the day after tomorrow.'

Gabriel left to go to his laboratory and I stared out of the window, wondering about the identity of the woman who had drowned. Shivering, I reflected on my own fortunate escape.

Later that afternoon, I went to fetch Jane's shawl from the drawing room. As I passed the door to the Perfume Salon, Gabriel called to me. 'Is that you, Mistress Finche?'

I stopped. 'It is.'

He stood, smiling, in the doorway. 'I recognised your quick footsteps,' he said. 'I wondered if you'd be interested to see my latest formulation for perfuming gloves?'

I followed him into the laboratory, lit only by flickering firelight. Curtains were pulled tightly across the windows and then I noticed Jacob in the dim light, dressed in a homespun apron, washing bottles in a basin of water. He moved quietly about his business, and didn't acknowledge my presence.

The walls were lined with sturdy oak shelves filled with rows of glass bottles and below them were ranged cupboards and drawers. A marble topped workbench dominated the centre of the room and on it rested various pieces of equipment including a large pestle and mortar and a strangely shaped copper object.

'What is this?' I asked. 'It looks like an oversized coffee pot with a covered pan on the top.' I fingered the long tube that projected from it down into a canister.

'That's an alembic still for distilling flower oils.' He moved to the workbench and swiftly ran his hands across the marble until they reached a porphyry slab with a concave surface. A small mound of a dark, greasy-looking substance lay on the stone and he dipped a snippet of sponge into it, dabbed it onto the back of his hand and offered it to me to smell. 'What do you think of this?' he asked.

I leaned forwards and sniffed. It had a warm, earthy smell, powdery and sweet and yet I wasn't sure if I liked it.

'Well? What can you smell?'

'I'm not sure.' I sniffed again.

'Close your eyes and tell me what drifts into your mind. Be truthful, mind!'

'Leather, a horse's bridle after a long ride, sweaty and hot. Cloves.' Just for a moment I remembered the smoky perfume of the barrels of cloves and nutmegs burning in the Finche warehouse. 'Walking in the woods,' I said, 'kicking up the leaves and smelling mushrooms buried in leaf mould.'

'Good!' said Gabriel. 'Again.'

Obediently, I leaned over his hand. 'Chocolate!'

'I wondered if you'd notice that. What else?'

'Something fruity.' I screwed up my eyes in concentration. 'I know,' I said, triumphantly, 'it's pears. The sweet-sour smell of a ripe, sun-warmed pear, just plucked from the orchard.'

'Do you still dislike the perfume?'

'Yes. No!' I breathed it in again and underneath it all I smelled Gabriel's own particular scent, the aroma of warm, clean skin washed with Castile soap. It flashed into my mind that the perfume smelled of lovemaking. Heat raced up my cheeks as I suppressed the thought. 'It's strange,' I said. 'I wasn't sure if I liked it at first but I want, need, to keep sniffing at it.'

Gabriel laughed. 'Jane dislikes the scent intensely but it's seductive, isn't it?'

So he had felt it too.

'What have you put into it?'

'Musk and oil of Bems and powdered cloves amongst other things. But perhaps I should add the essence of rose or jasmine to make it more suited to a lady's taste? In any case, I recommend washing the gloves with rosewater, stretching them flat to dry and then rubbing the mixture into the leather. As the gloves become warm in wear, they'll release the perfume.'

'What a shame I have no gloves.' It was then I remembered that I'd been on an errand when Gabriel had called out to me. 'I have forgot the time,' I said. 'Jane sent me to find her shawl half an hour ago.'

'One thing, before you go.'

'Yes, Mr Harte?'

'I haven't forgotten Maundrell. I shall visit him again and attempt to persuade him to accompany me to the constable's chambers.'

'I shall never be truly free while Hackett goes unpunished,' I said.

'I do understand that.'

The light had almost gone and the room was lit only by the glow of fire.

'Shall I light the candles so Jacob can see what he's doing?' I asked.

'We always work in dim light,' said Gabriel. 'It makes no difference to me since I can only detect some misty shapes and many of the perfumed oils and essences spoil in sunlight. Jacob has learned to work in low light.'

'So you can see something, then?' I blushed furiously, wondering if he'd ever seen me staring at his face while he spoke to me.

'Not really. It's like looking through a pinhole in a black door with a gauzy curtain on the other side.'

How sad it was for him that he would never see his wife and child's face. 'I must go,' I said. 'Jane will be waiting for me.'

I closed the laboratory door behind me and hurried to find Jane's shawl.

Two days later, Jane put on her black velvet cloak and waited in the hall with Gabriel until Jem, the coachman, brought the carriage to the front door.

Gabriel wore the black coat and breeches he'd worn to Robert's funeral and an even blacker frown. 'It's a sorry day,' he said, 'that we should have to go through this piece of play-acting to ensure your safety. At least the poor girl we're burying will be laid to rest in comfort.'

The carriage arrived and I watched from the window until it disappeared from view, taking my friends to attend my funeral. I leaned my forehead against the windowpane but the chill of the glass wasn't as cold as the chill in my heart.

Two days later, Gabriel called to me as I came downstairs.

'Will you come into the drawing room, Mistress Finche?' he said, grim-faced.

'What's the matter?' I asked, once the door was closed behind us.

'I've been to Mr Maundrell's house,' he said. 'His housekeeper came home from the market yesterday morning and saw a man running away from the house. I'm sorry to tell you that when she went inside she found Mr Maundrell hanging by his neck from a beam. There were signs of a struggle and he was already dead.'

I sank down onto a chair, shocked at the news. I hadn't cared for the old man but he hadn't deserved to be murdered. 'Hackett has to have instigated this,' I said.

'I fear Maundrell was right to be frightened.' Gabriel sighed. 'In any case, there's little we can do now. I'll go to the constable but, without Maundrell, it's all hearsay. It's possible he'll investigate Hackett but I sincerely doubt it.'

'But Hackett must be brought to justice!' Angry frustration seethed in my breast.

'I'll make a point of meeting Hackett more often to discuss my investments and try to catch him off guard.' A sardonic smile hovered on Gabriel's mouth. 'It's surprising how often people will disclose their thoughts to a blind man since they consider him to be of so little account.'

'You must be very careful!' I said, suddenly fearful for him.

'I have prior knowledge of what Hackett is capable of so I am forewarned.'

October turned into November and, as the year waned, I watched and worried about Jane's frail health. Often, her face was pale and pinched and I knew she must be in pain again. I was concerned as I suspected she was resorting to the poppy sleeping draught almost every night.

One day, while Jane was resting, Toby sat at his desk copying his letters and I stood by the nursery window concocting wild and futile plans to bring Hackett to justice. Gabriel had visited the constable, but, just as he feared, without solid proof the constable had refused to listen to any suspicions of wrongdoing by Hackett.

The door opened and I smiled to see Gabriel. He often came by the nursery to talk to us. 'Toby is working very hard on his letters,' I said.

'I'm pleased to hear you are a diligent pupil,' he said, ruffling his son's hair. 'Mistress Finche, I came to tell you that Jacob and I visited Rochester Court with Hackett today.'

'Did you find out anything,' I asked eagerly.

He shook his head. 'Hackett wouldn't allow us to explore the whole building. He said it was too dangerous for us to go up and down ladders as the stairs aren't yet completed.'

My shoulders drooped.

'But I've brought you a present, Mistress Finche.' He delved into his pocket.

'For me?'

His lips curved as he held out the package.

I unwrapped the paper to find a pair of black kid gloves, finely worked with decorative stitching on the cuffs. As I slid one onto my hand it released a waft of perfume. 'How lovely!' I said.

'I've worked my latest formulation into the leather but added a little attar of roses to make the scent sweeter and more suited to a lady's taste.'

'They're beautiful and the fragrance . . . ' I held them to my face and breathed in with my eyes closed.

'I'm pleased you like them.'

'Thank you, Mr Harte. I shall treasure them.'

'And what do you and Toby have in mind for today?'

'Mistress Finche is going to show me how to make paper boats,' said Toby.

Gabriel smiled. 'I remember sailing paper boats on the Fleet ditch when I was a boy.'

'Can we sail my boats on the Fleet?' asked Toby. 'Please?'

'I have a delivery of two bottles of Rose of Araby to make to Wood Street,' said Gabriel, 'so perhaps we could make a detour? I am waiting until Jacob returns from the apothecary to guide me. He has a feverish cold today.'

'Could we not accompany you?' I said. All at once, the prospect of a walk in the fresh air was enticing. Fear of Hackett had kept me strictly confined to the House of Perfume, but now that he was convinced I was dead, surely it would be safe so long as Gabriel accompanied me?

'Then shall I meet you in the hall once you have made your boats?'

Toby grabbed his father in a fierce hug and I watched with a smile as Gabriel kissed him and threw him up in the air.

Chapter 27

Toby and I were waiting in the hall when Jacob arrived back from the apothecary, his enormous nose red and his eyes running with the cold.

'Mistress Finche and I are going out with Father,' said Toby, full of importance. 'We're helping him to make a delivery to Wood Street.'

'But I always accompany your father on his deliveries!' Jacob cast me a darkly malevolent glance, but before I could say anything, we heard Gabriel's footsteps.

I drew on my new gloves, the silky leather caressing my hands as they released their heady perfume. Jane had lent me her velvet cloak and I pulled up the hood to shroud my face. Hackett may believe me dead and buried but I wasn't taking any foolish chances. I simmered with excitement at the prospect of our outing, spiced with trepidation in case Hackett was out and about too.

Gabriel held his silver-topped cane in one hand and dangled a small box tied up with ribbon from a finger of the other.

'I understand we're making a delivery to Wood Street, sir?' said Jacob.

'You're not to come today, Jacob,' said Gabriel. 'You'll be better tucked up in the warm.'

'But . . . '

'I insist!'

Gabriel held out his arm. 'Mistress Finche, shall we go?'

Jacob's eyes glittered, but then he sneezed explosively. I tucked my arm into the crook of Gabriel's elbow, eager to start our excursion.

The cold air nipped my cheeks but, in spite of the November chill, the sun shone and I was filled with a wonderful sense of well-being.

Gabriel's long cane swung from side to side before us as we cut through to Covent Garden and Bow Street and then progressed along the Strand, bustling with costermongers, carts and coaches. Toby skipped along just ahead of us with Shadow at his side. I was amazed at how confidently Gabriel navigated the streets and couldn't help but comment.

'Uncle Silas taught me how important it was to be independent.'

'Did you always live with him?' I broke into a trot in an attempt to keep up with Gabriel's long stride.

'Not at all! My mother died when I was young, but my father married again.'

'Toby!' I called. 'Don't run too far ahead!'

'I won't!' he called back over his shoulder.

'Did you like your stepmother?'

Gabriel sighed. 'My father's marriage was a rackety kind of arrangement and before long she bolted with a gambler friend of my father's. He was relieved, I think, being too fond of wine and women to settle in one place for long. I wasn't the sort of son he'd expected, too bookish and serious. And it wasn't long after I left childhood behind that my sight began to fail.'

'How very dreadful for you.'

'I thought my world had ended. Father saw my impending blindness as further proof of his disappointment in me and packed me off to live with his blind brother. The blind leading the blind, he called it.'

'How cruel!' Indignation rose up in my breast. It was painful to picture the lonely little boy Gabriel had been. I felt a sudden kinship with him, as I understood very well how frightening it was for a child not to be loved.

'It was the best thing that could have happened to me,' said Gabriel. 'My uncle turned out to be far more of a father to me than my own had ever been. Once I'd stopped ranting and raving about the unfairness of God in visiting such a plight upon me, I became fast friends with Uncle Silas.'

'And he helped you to accept your blindness?'

'He showed me how to open up all my other senses and make full use of them; I learned to hear the rustle of silk petticoats as a lady selects her perfumed candles, catch the scent of a cat as it slinks silently by and feel the gritty texture of ground sugar on a fresh-baked jumbal. I would have noticed none of those things before. And, of course, Uncle Silas taught me all I know about making perfume.' He slowed his long stride, holding fast to my arm as a horseman trotted by.

As I listened to the story, the warmth of his hip was pressed close to my side and my senses swam as the perfume from my gloves permeated my every breath. Exhilaration coursed through my veins at the joy of being outside in the fresh air in such pleasant company.

'Uncle Silas trained to become a perfumer in Paris and made his fortune there. Once his sight failed entirely, he returned to London. He bought one of the houses recently built on Long Acre by the Duke of Bedford and so the House of Perfume came into being. And as his heir, I have been able to continue and develop his work.' He smiled. 'I'd love Toby to carry on the business.'

'So the loss of your sight has not been as terrible a thing as it might have been?'

'Not at all. Except . . . ' He sighed. 'I wish I could look upon my son's face.'

'Did you ever look in a mirror as a child?' I asked. 'If you remember yourself, you will have Toby's likeness.'

He smiled. 'But I am pleased to say that Toby is a happier child than I was.'

'Because both his parents love him and he is secure in the knowledge of that.'

'And now he has you, too,' said Gabriel. 'He's a lucky boy.'

I couldn't find the words to respond to that.

We arrived at Fleet Street and, before long, at the point that marked the extent of the Great Fire. 'Now you'll have to guide me,' said Gabriel, holding firmly on to my arm. 'I don't know my way about the new city.'

'It's so strange,' I said. 'If I look behind us, Fleet Street and the Strand, Essex House, Arundel House and Chancery Lane all look as they always did. But this way –' I turned around '– I can see down the new part of Fleet Street and Ludgate Hill and to the ruins of St Paul's.'

'I still see the city as it was in my mind,' said Gabriel, closing his eyes.

A short while later we reached the stream and Gabriel waited while Toby, Shadow and I ran along the bank, watching our paper crafts bobbing up and down as they floated downstream on the brackish water. My boat became caught in a clump of bedraggled reeds and Toby jumped up and down in glee as his won the race.

'I'll fetch your boat,' he said. He scrambled down the bank and slipped on the evil-smelling mud.

He squealed and I lunged forwards and caught him by his coat just before he fell into the water. I hauled him to safety and clutched him to my chest. The murky smell of the water reminded me of my terrible experience under London Bridge.

'Is everything all right?' called Gabriel.

'Toby slipped but I have him safe,' I called back. The little boy's thistledown hair feathered against my cheek as he clung to me and my heart turned over with sudden love for him. 'Your mama would never forgive me if I allowed you to fall in,' I said, my heart racing as I brushed mud off his breeches.

A dray drawn by a great carthorse rolled past, raising a cloud of dust. The scent of horseflesh hung heavily in the air long after the clip-clop of hooves was drowned out by the scrape of shovels and the shouts and whistles of men working on a nearby building site.

'The city is waking up again,' said Gabriel. 'Before long it will be as busy as it was before.'

'St Paul's is to our right now,' I said, glancing at the ruins, 'and we're coming up to Cheapside.'

'And Wood Street will be the third road on the left? I still have my own map in my head, but I used to be guided by the church bells, the cries from the market stalls or the smell of the ink from the printers around St Paul's. All these little reminders of my location have changed.'

I was saddened by his bleak expression. 'Then we must come here often to rebuild your map of scents and sounds to help you on your way again.'

'It took me many years to learn to walk confidently around the city.' He spoke quietly and I heard the note of despondency in his voice.

'It won't be as hard as the first time,' I said, suddenly conscious that Gabriel's own loss, caused by the Fire was, in many ways, much greater than my own. 'Toby and I will be happy to accompany you.'

'I should like that.'

'I'm not sure Jacob would,' I said, remembering the jealous glare he'd thrown at me when we left without him. 'He likes to keep you to himself.'

Gabriel gave a wry smile. 'Jacob is my loyal and trusted servant, but sometimes his devoted care is a little oppressive. Why, he even chooses my clothes for me!'

'You're always so handsomely dressed in rich fabrics and textures that perfectly complement your colouring that I assumed Jane helped you to select your wardrobe.'

He shook his head. 'Jane is indifferent to fashion, but Jacob considers it a matter of pride never to let me leave the house unless I am wearing the latest mode. He takes a great deal of interest in such things himself.' He smiled. 'I wouldn't dare to disappoint his high expectations of me.'

'Has he been your manservant for long?'

'Thirteen years. He was only a boy of fourteen when I discovered him. His father was a goldsmith and believed that Jacob had a crooked back because his mother was a Gentile.' Gabriel's voice was tight. 'I understand what it feels like to be rejected by your father for something that isn't your fault, so I brought him home with me.'

Another waif and stray, like myself and Shadow, I thought.

We stopped at the corner of Wood Street to allow a carriage to pass, and I saw that a number of new houses were already completed.

Gabriel stood still, listening. 'Children are playing,' he said, 'and I can smell bread baking and –' he sniffed the air '– pork roasting. It's good to know that there are families breathing life into the city again. Kate –' he bit his lip '– Mistress Finche, tell me what the houses look like so I can picture them.'

I coloured at his slip but it pleased me that he thought of me as Kate. 'The houses are built of brick with flat fronts, four storeys tall with fine large windows.'

Gabriel nodded. 'The style conforms to the Rebuilding Act in an attempt to reduce the threat of fire catching from one house to another. That reminds me, it's time I paid a visit to our friend Hackett's site at Rochester Court to ask for an account of his progress.'

‘Even the sound of his name makes me shudder,’ I said. ‘How many families will suffer by living in his poorly built homes?’

‘I, for one, will not accept poor quality building work,’ said Gabriel, ‘not when people’s lives and my investments are at stake. Jacob will come with me to act as my eyes and if there is any hint of malpractice then I’ll make contact with Hackett’s other investors.’

‘Mr Harte, which house are you visiting today?’

‘It’s the ninth house on the right.’

‘Then we must cross the road here. It’s next to an empty building plot.’

I called to Shadow and grasped Toby’s hand as we crossed the road. ‘We’ll wait while you deliver your parcel,’ I said. ‘The door is straight in front of you and there are two steps.’ I longed to guide him to the door myself but knew he would not allow it.

Carefully, Gabriel swung his cane in front of him until he located the lower step. After a moment a maid opened the door and he went inside.

Toby and I waited at the edge of the wasteland, shivering. Toby huddled up to me for warmth and I smiled as I stroked his hair. Then Shadow’s ears pricked up. He growled deep in his throat and suddenly shot off onto the empty building plot after a cat streaking along the ground.

‘Shadow!’ I called, but he was deaf to my command and intent only on the chase.

Toby slipped his hand out of mine and raced after him.

Sighing, I followed. The ground land was littered with lumps of stone and charred timber beams and full of dips and hollows. I stumbled along, catching my skirts on bramble bushes while my shoes filled with gritty dust.

The cat had disappeared, but Shadow raced around in circles, barking excitedly while Toby tried to catch him.

At last I caught hold of Toby and called Shadow to my side. ‘We must go back,’ I said. ‘Your father will be worried.’

'But he's coming to find us,' said Toby, pointing back to the road.

Gabriel was moving uncertainly across the rough ground, tapping the way with his cane.

Shadow loped off to greet him. He'd covered half the ground when he stopped, took a different route towards Gabriel and came to a standstill beside him.

Gabriel bent down and patted the dog's head before they set off towards us.

After a moment, Shadow began to act strangely. He sat down in front of Gabriel and each time Gabriel tried to push him away or walk around him Shadow blocked his path.

'What's the matter with this wretched dog,' Gabriel called, as we grew closer. 'I followed the sound of your voices but Shadow won't let me move forwards.'

I hurried towards him, Toby's hand clasped in my own. Suddenly, a few yards away I stopped abruptly. 'Careful, Toby!' I took another couple of steps forwards and peered at the ground. 'Stay where you are, Mr Harte! Don't move!'

'What is it?'

I stared down the deep hole in the ground. 'There's an uncovered well just in front of you. Shadow was trying to prevent you from falling down the shaft.'

Gabriel smothered a curse.

Toby dropped a stone into the well and I shivered as we heard a distant splash.

Carefully, I led Toby around the danger and took a firm hold of Gabriel's arm. I closed my eyes momentarily as I pictured him broken and bleeding at the bottom of the well.

'You're trembling,' said Gabriel.

'Shadow is very clever, isn't he?' said Toby.

'A prize specimen among the canine species,' said his father. 'But perhaps we should keep him tied up in future? We don't want him to be run over by a coach if he runs off, do we?'

Toby bent to hug Shadow around the neck. As if to lend weight to Gabriel's comment, a coach rattled into view and passed at a reckless pace, the horses tossing their heads and their hooves thudding along the road. It was then that a novel method of helping Gabriel to regain his independence sparked into being.

'Let's hurry home before we all catch our death of cold,' Gabriel said, offering me the crook of his elbow.

Holding Toby's hand firmly in my own, I maintained a running commentary on what I could see. Gabriel counted our steps and made a game of it with Toby, while my mind simmered with excitement as I considered the advantages and disadvantages of my unusual idea.

Chapter 28

Jane remained in bed the next day and sent Jacob for the physician. They were closeted together in her bedchamber for nearly an hour. I waited in my room across the corridor with the door ajar, watching Toby and Jacob playing soldiers in the garden below. I heard Jane cry out in distress and turned, hand on heart. Creeping across the corridor, I stood outside her door, wondering if I should knock to see if she needed anything. But then I heard the physician speaking to her in reassuring tones and retreated to my room.

As soon as he left I went to see her. 'I thought I heard you call out?' I said, watching her fingers plucking restlessly at the neck of her nightgown.

'It was nothing,' she said, avoiding my gaze.

'Jane, is there is anything I can do?'

'There's nothing anyone can do.' Her mouth quivered. 'I must think . . . '

I looked at her reddened eyes but forbore to question her further.

'Kate, I need to be alone for a while. It's a lovely sunny day, in spite of the hard frost,' she said with a wavering smile. 'Why don't you and Gabriel take Toby for a runabout in St James's Park?'

Tired of being indoors, I needed no further urging. I hurried downstairs and stood in the rose-scented hall, hand raised, ready to knock on the Perfume Salon door when I heard the murmur of women's voices, interspersed by high-pitched laughter. I hesitated. Since Gabriel was entertaining customers, I could hardly disturb him to ask him to accompany us on a walk to the park.

Toby called downstairs. 'Can we go now, Mistress Finche?' He peered down at me over the banisters, his little face so eager that I couldn't bear to disappoint him. After all, I reasoned, I should be perfectly safe as I would be walking towards the west, while Hackett's offices were in Holborn and his building sites further to the east.

A moment later, I pulled up the hood of my cloak around my face, just in case, and then Toby, Shadow and I set off.

A couple of hours later, invigorated by the crisp, cold air, we tumbled into the hall full of noisy chatter. Shadow growled as he and Toby engaged in a tug of war with my scarf, while I laughingly tried to stop it from being ripped to pieces.

The Perfume Salon door opened and Gabriel appeared. 'From all the noise I thought the French must have arrived to murder us in our beds,' he said.

'Shadow is very naughty and won't give me Mistress Finche's scarf!' said Toby.

Gabriel stood beside Shadow and rested a hand on his rear quarters. 'Sit, Shadow!' he said in a firm voice.

Shadow sat.

'Drop it!'

Reluctantly, Shadow released the scarf from between his teeth onto Gabriel's immaculately polished shoes.

Gabriel picked it up and presented it to me with an elaborate bow. His warm hands touched my frozen ones for an instant, making them tingle all the more. 'You smell delightfully of frost and fresh air,' he said.

'Thank you, kind sir,' I said, dropping into a curtsey.

Toby shrieked in delight and clasped his father's knees.

'What is all this terrible noise?' A quavering voice came from above us.

I turned to see Jane, still in her nightshift, clinging shakily to the newel post, her hair in disarray around her shoulders.

'I'm sorry if we disturbed you with our high spirits,' I said, suddenly concerned by the ashen tone of her face.

'Is it too much to ask to be allowed to rest undisturbed? A little consideration would be helpful, Kate.'

I stared. Jane had never spoken to me in that sharp tone before. 'I apologise,' I stammered. 'I'll take Toby to the kitchen for his dinner and then keep him occupied while you rest.'

'No! Toby shall come and keep me company after his dinner. We shall not need you this afternoon.' Her voice was cold as if I was a servant who had displeased her.

'Very good.' Should I address her as Mistress Harte? After all, even though she'd always treated me as her friend, what was I but her son's nursemaid? Confused and unhappy, I took Toby's hand. 'Shall we find you some dinner, young man?'

He glanced uncertainly at his mother and then his father, whose face was impassive.

I tugged gently at Toby's hand. 'Come now,' I said. 'You shall sit with Mama in a little while.'

After Toby had finished his dinner I made sure his face and hands were clean and then wrote the first letters of the alphabet on his slate. 'Your mama is tired today so you must sit quietly beside her and practise your letters,' I said, handing him the slate.

He nodded, looking up at me with anxious green eyes, his hand creeping into mine.

We went upstairs to Jane's bedchamber and I tapped on the door and we waited until her faint voice bid us to enter.

Jane lay against a nest of pillows with her hair in a tangle. I saw that her eyes were swollen from weeping.

'Would you like me to massage lavender oil into your temples?' I asked, full of concern for her.

'No. And I shan't need you this afternoon.' She didn't look at me but held out her arms to her son. 'Toby, come and sit on the bed by me, sweetheart.'

Toby glanced at me and I nodded encouragingly, trying not to show my distress at her fractious tone of voice.

Slowly he walked towards his mother and I closed the door softly behind me, feeling as if I had swallowed a stone.

Without Toby, I was at a loss as to what to do and with too much time to worry over Jane's unkind words. Suppose she had turned against me forever? The House of Perfume had become my refuge and if Jane turned me out what would I do then? I sat in my bed-chamber turning up the hem of a black skirt that she had given me a few days before. I was heartily sick of wearing mourning but it suited my mood that afternoon.

Later, I went to find Mrs Jenks and found her at the kitchen table gossiping with Ann, who was working her way through a pile of mending.

'Would I be in the way if I baked a cake?' I asked.

'Lord bless you, no!' Mrs Jenks's eyes crinkled up at the corners as she smiled at me. 'The dinner's washed up and the supper's not started yet.' She levered her plump body up from the table and smoothed down her crisp, white apron. 'Let me show you where everything is. Fancy a fine lady such as yourself baking a cake!'

The kitchen was warm and comforting as I mixed gingerbread at one end of the table while the two women chatted, reminding me of the kitchen of my childhood, the only safe haven in Aunt Mercy's house. While the cake was baking I sat in the rocking chair by the fire, listening to the kitchen talk and trying to ignore the hollow, unhappy feeling in my stomach. What had I done to upset Jane so?

The fragrant scent of ginger wafted around the kitchen and, once the cake was cooling on the trivet, Mrs Jenks prodded it gently with a stubby finger. 'That looks like a proper job to me,' she said. 'Master Toby will be down here in the shake of a cow's tail when he smells that.'

Ann, neat as ever in a clean cap, closed her eyes as she sniffed the steam arising from the cake. 'Smells like my mam's gingerbread that does.'

The cake was barely cool before I heard Toby's footsteps clattering down the passage.

Mrs Jenks nodded at me. 'What did I tell you?'

Two minutes later, Toby was sitting at the table beaming while I cut the gingerbread.

'Is Mama feeling better?' I asked.

He shrugged. 'Sometimes she hugs me too hard,' he said, his mouth full of cake.

I didn't feel it was right to ask him if she'd said how I'd upset her and was prevented from dwelling upon the matter when Gabriel joined us.

'There's a delicious smell in the air,' he said. 'Is it gingerbread?'

'Mistress Finche made it especially for me, Father,' piped up Toby.

'Would you like a piece, Mr Harte?' I asked.

'Possibly two.' He smiled.

Toby dropped a few crumbs and Shadow darted forwards to snuffle them up.

'You'd think that dog was starving,' said Mistress Jenks, 'instead of living a life of ease in my kitchen. He's quick-witted, though. Shame we can't find a way to put him to work.'

'An excellent cake, Mistress Finche,' said Gabriel, licking his lips. 'I shall always think of you now when I catch the aroma of ginger and nutmeg. Toby, why don't you take a piece up to Mama?'

I thanked Mistress Jenks for the use of her kitchen and went to the hall with Gabriel and waited with him while Toby, carefully carrying the cake, climbed the stairs and went into his mother's room.

Once the door had closed, Gabriel said, 'Please don't be angry with Jane.'

'I'm not angry,' I said. 'Only puzzled. What have I done that displeases her so?'

'I believe she spoke sharply because she was in pain.'

'But she's often in pain and she's never been short with me before.'

'Perhaps it's particularly bad today.' He sighed. 'I hear the distress in her voice and the more I ask her how I can help, the more she places a distance between us. Increasingly, we seem to have no common ground at all, except for Toby and even then . . . ' His voice trailed away.

'I'm sorry to hear that.' If Jane wouldn't discuss the matter with her husband then perhaps I shouldn't be so upset if she was irritable with me.

The following morning I stopped at the threshold of the dining room door when I saw that Jane was sitting at the breakfast table with Gabriel and Toby.

She glanced up to see me hovering uncertainly in the doorway. Her cheeks were bone white and her eyes deeply shadowed but her voice was calm. 'Come in, Kate.'

I said good morning to Gabriel, returned Toby's smile and slipped into my accustomed place. 'Are you a little better?' I ventured.

She nodded, her eyes not quite meeting mine. 'Jacob will take Toby for his walk today so will you sit with me for a while?'

'I'd be glad to,' I said.

Frost had painted delicate lacework flowers on the inside of the windows of Jane's closet as we sat huddled around the fire, trying to keep warm.

Jane put down her needlepoint, neatly worked in muted greens, blues and rose. 'Kate?' she said. 'I was unkind to you and it was unwarranted.'

I waited, not sure how to respond.

'I felt so down in my spirits that when I saw you and Toby come in from your walk, all rosy and glowing with health, I wanted so much for it to be me instead of you laughing with Toby and Gabriel,' she said. 'I can't bear it if Toby thinks that I don't love him because we don't have fun together any more. I was jealous and angry but I shouldn't have spoken to you in that way.'

'I'm sorry if it upset you,' I said carefully. 'But no one can ever take your place in Toby's heart.'

'Perhaps not.' Her expression was so anguished that I forgot my own unhappiness.

'Jane, truly, I'm not trying to steal your son's affections.'

'But you do love him, don't you? I see it in your eyes.'

I nodded. 'You know how much I longed for a baby. Robert's death and my current circumstances have denied me that. It's hard to accept ... ' My voice cracked and I swallowed before I was able to continue. 'It's hard to accept that I'll never have children of my own now. I have grown to love Toby and believe he returns my affection. But you, unquestioningly, are his beloved mother. The best I can hope for,' I said bleakly, 'is to be held in the same regard as an honorary aunt.'

Jane reached out to lift my hand to her pale cheek. 'Toby could not wish for a better aunt than you, Kate.'

'Should you ask another doctor for an opinion on your headaches?'

She stared at the frost flowers on the window for a moment. 'It isn't simply the headaches,' she said. 'I think perhaps they come because I'm so fearful. I remember my dear sister, Eleanor and I worry ... '

'But you are not Eleanor,' I said. 'You must try not to worry and perhaps your headaches will go away. And I promise you –' I squeezed her cold hand '– I only want to help look after Toby and keep him happy until you are well again.'

'Thank you, Kate. It means more to me than you know that you will cherish him for me even when I'm not with him. I want him always to feel safe.' She sighed and leaned back against the chair with her eyes closed. The tenseness began to drain from her face and eventually her eyelids twitched a little as she drifted into sleep. Her hand relaxed in mine.

I listened to her sleeping breaths and was moved by pity for her.

Later that afternoon, as I passed through the hall, I heard Gabriel's deep voice mingling with the higher tones of a party of lady visitors in the Perfume Salon. I stopped to listen and suddenly, the door opened and I started back.

Jacob and I stared at each other for a moment and I caught sight of our reflections in the mirror over the mantelpiece: me with one hand clasped to my breast and my mouth open in surprise and Jacob with his long nose and beady eyes black with suspicion. He closed the door firmly in my face. My cheeks flaming with embarrassment, I went to find Shadow and took him with me to the stables.

Jem, the groom, was sweeping the yard and looked up at me curiously as I approached.

'Good afternoon, Jem,' I said, 'I wonder if you will help me?'

Jem rested his hands on his broom and listened intently while I explained what I wanted. When I finished he scratched his head.

'Well, I reckon I could do that,' he said. 'Never heard the likes of it before, mind.' He cast a dubious glance at Shadow, who was sniffing around the manure pile. Then a smile broke out across his leathery face. 'I'll see what I can do, missus. Come and see me again tomorrow afternoon.'

'Thank you, I will. And don't say a word to anyone!'

As I hung up my cloak in the hall, I heard Toby's childish treble coming from the Perfume Salon. The visitors must have left. Tentatively, I pushed the door open and followed the sound of my young charge's laughter coming from the laboratory. In the dim light through the half-open door I saw that Toby stood on a stool at the workbench beside his father with an array of bottles and jars set out before them.

'Is Toby troubling you while you're working?' I asked.

'Not at all,' said Gabriel.

'I'm learning the different smells,' said Toby. 'Let her guess the last one, Father!'

'You must close your eyes, Mistress Finche,' said Gabriel, a smile in his voice.

'Are they shut?' demanded Toby.

'I'm opening the flask now,' said Gabriel.

I sniffed and then smiled at the scent of clean linen and heat-soaked summer days. 'That's easy; it's lavender,' I said. I wondered for a moment what it would be like to be Gabriel, blind but using all his other his senses to their full capacity. I was curious to know if he smelled and heard things that passed me by.

'Toby, I want you to learn a variety of scents,' said Gabriel. 'To create a good perfume you must call upon your memory. Imagine the scent of summer rain falling on a dusty road, or apple blossom in spring sunshine, or perhaps the aroma of apples stored in a dry, dusty outbuilding. All those scents can be used to inspire a new perfume but you need to know which of your repertoire of aromas to use. Now here is one especially for Mistress Finche. Close your eyes!'

I heard the sound of a cork being removed from a jar and then felt a slight disturbance of the air as he held the container under my nose. 'It's a spice,' I said sniffing again at intensely aromatic fragrance. A wave of sadness washed over me as, just for a moment, I was reminded of the pungent smell of burning spices in the Finche warehouse. 'Is it cardamom?'

'Correct!' said Gabriel. 'Now you smell it, Toby.'

I watched the tenderness in Gabriel's face as he spoke to his son and experienced a deep ache in my heart that I would never have a child of my own. I was thankful that Toby had the security of a father who loved him.

'That's enough for today,' said Gabriel. 'If you smell too many different things you won't be able to remember them.'

'I'm going to find Shadow,' said Toby, clambering down from the stool.

A moment later the door banged but I felt a curious reluctance to follow him.

Gabriel put the cork back into the jar of ground cardamom. 'I suppose it's never too early to train him in case he . . . ' He pushed the bottles and jars into a neat row, quickly running his long fingers over each one as he identified them. 'I don't know if he will become blind,' he said, 'but I need him to understand he could still have a rich and fulfilling life.' His face was impassive but there was the slightest suspicion of a tremor in his voice.

I swallowed as a pain as sharp as a thorn pierced my heart. 'I hadn't realised . . . '

'Uncle Silas lost his sight as a young man. I was fourteen. And there was a cousin of my grandfather's who had the same condition, so we cannot assume that Toby will be spared.'

'I see.' I realised the irony of my comment and bit my lip.

'I try to make my counting of steps a part of everyday life and will teach him how to recognise people by their voices, footsteps and natural perfume. Then, if the worst should happen, he will have already accomplished some of his training.'

'Then I'll be sure to continue your good work. We'll make a game of it.'

Gabriel's smile lit up his face. 'I knew you would understand. Jane . . . ' He sighed. 'She's a most dutiful wife but she's very frightened by the thought that our precious boy might suffer from my complaint and refuses to discuss that possible future with me.'

I ached for him that, especially in this, he and Jane were not of one mind.

'Bring Toby to me again tomorrow, will you?' he said. 'We'll continue our lesson.'

'We'll look forward to that,' I said.

I crossed the laboratory and stood for a moment in the doorway watching Gabriel unhurriedly returning the bottles and jars to their correct locations on the shelves. A shaft of light slanted through the half-closed shutters and fell on his face, outlining the strong line of his jaw and his sensitive mouth. I liked both Jane and Gabriel very much but how sad it was, in spite of the son they both loved and the life of ease they led, that they did not find joy and comfort in each other. Quietly, I closed the door behind me.

At breakfast the following day Gabriel announced that he was intending to call on Mr Hackett at his chambers.

I crumbled my bread, while unease made my stomach churn.

After Gabriel had left, Jane retired to her closet leaving me to amuse Toby.

'I have a secret,' I said.

'What is it?' asked Toby, his eyes round with curiosity.

'Fetch Shadow and I'll show you.'

A short while later, Toby and I walked through the garden to the stables with Shadow at our heels.

Jem was rubbing down one of the chestnut mares when we arrived. He put down his cloth and straightened up to greet us.

'Good morning, Jem! Did you manage to make what I require?' I asked.

He nodded his head and went into the stable.

'What is it?' whispered Toby.

'Wait and see!'

Jem returned, carrying a leather harness. He whistled to Shadow who romped up to him and sat patiently while it was fastened.

'Is Shadow going to pull a carriage?' asked Toby.

I shook my head and waited until the final strap was buckled into place and adjusted. 'There you are, missus,' said Jem. He lifted two struts fashioned from wood, each about two and a half feet long, secured at each side of the harness and joined at one end by a cross-member to form a handle.

I took it in my hand and motioned Shadow to move forwards. 'Look, Toby!' I said. 'When Shadow warned your father about the open well on that building site I had the idea that if he could be made to walk immediately in front of your father he could warn him about dangers in the streets. It would make walking through the city much safer for him.'

'But won't Shadow run away?'

'That's why he needs a harness. And he will have to be trained not to chase cats.'

'Can I train him?' His eager face was turned up to mine.

'Of course.' I'd taken the decision that it was safe for me to walk westwards to the park every day without Gabriel's protection. 'We'll take him in the harness every morning. I'll ask Mistress Jenks for some little pieces of cheese or meat to reward him when he's a good dog.'

'He's always a good dog!'

'Nearly always. But don't tell your father yet in case he's disappointed. I want to be sure that Shadow will do what is required of him.'

Toby nodded solemnly. 'So can we take him out now?'

We walked down Long Acre and along St Martin's Lane towards St James's Park. Sometimes Shadow pulled against the harness, lay down on the road or tried to wander off until I encouraged him with a morsel of cheese and an inordinate amount of praise to move forwards again at a steady pace. He scratched vigorously at the harness with his back leg once or twice but I was surprised at how easily he accepted it.

When we arrived at the park I unbuckled the wooden handle and allowed Toby and Shadow to run off their high spirits for a while.

Pink-cheeked and bright-eyed, Toby came trotting back to me with Shadow loping in circles around him.

'Shall we put on Shadow's harness again?'

'Can I do it?'

I helped Toby to harness the dog and we walked sedately back towards the park gates. I closed my eyes as if I were blind and allowed Shadow to lead me, delighted when he guided me around a fallen log.

'We still have a lot of training to do but we've made a good start, don't you think, Toby?'

He nodded his head vigorously.

'We'll bring him out with us again tomorrow. But remember, it's a secret!'

Later that afternoon Jane went out in the carriage with Toby and I was sitting at the nursery window, mending shirts when I caught sight of a man on a black horse trotting purposefully along the street. My heart began to thud as I realised with horror that it was Hackett and he was about to pay a visit to the House of Perfume. I shrank back from the window in a sudden panic. Had he heard I was living here?

I crept to the landing to listen. Down in the hall, Gabriel invited Hackett into the Perfume Salon and then all I could hear was the resonance of their voices.

Trembling, I slipped off my shoes and tiptoed downstairs. I stationed myself behind the partially open door to peep through the crack.

'As you're considering in investing in my Cornhill building site I came to speak to you before you heard the rumours,' said Hackett.

'Rumours?' said Gabriel.

'Wicked rumours that could destroy my reputation. I've been deeply disappointed by Robert Finche,' said Hackett, shaking his head. 'I went far beyond my Christian duty to him and I've discovered he repaid me by being a swindler and a thief.'

'Whatever makes you believe that?' asked Gabriel.

'A while ago I was forced to close my brickyard because I discovered the clay wasn't stable. Immediately, I instructed Finche to dispose of all the bricks in the river.'

'An expensive exercise.'

'Lost me a bloody fortune!' The floorboards shook as Hackett paced across the room. 'So you will imagine my outrage and dismay when I received complaints that bricks have crumbled, causing houses to collapse. It appears that Finche and his previous employer, Elias Maundrell, sold the bad bricks in taverns and back alleys at knock-down prices and pocketed the proceeds.'

I pressed a hand to my mouth to stifle a gasp. How dare he blacken Robert's name with such a lie!

'How do you know it was Finche and Maundrell?' asked Gabriel.

'Who else could it have been? Finche was desperate to pay off his father's debts and I'd already discovered he'd been fiddling the accounts. And Maundrell bore a grudge against me,' said Hackett.

'I suppose you'll be obliged to compensate builders who bought your faulty bricks?'

Hackett snorted. 'It's nothing to do with me! My only fault was taking on the son of a known bankrupt. Perhaps I should have expected Finche to be deceitful and corrupt but, nevertheless, I've been badly betrayed by the man.' His voice was aggrieved. 'I can't even go after Maundrell. He hanged himself the other day; out of shame, I suppose.'

'It *is* a shameful business,' agreed Gabriel.

'Knew you'd understand!' Hackett sighed heavily. 'I'd better be off. I need to explain Finche's and Maundrell's actions to all my investors.'

Hurriedly, I tiptoed away from the door and slipped into the drawing room.

'I'm relieved that little Mistress Finche never knew of her husband's perfidy before she drowned herself,' boomed Hackett as his boots clumped across the hall.

'No, indeed,' said Gabriel drily.

'In any case, let me take you to dine at the Folly very soon to discuss our next business venture together. Very accommodating serving wenches and good wine.' Hackett clasped Gabriel's hand. 'Good day to you, Harte.'

The front door banged shut and I came out of the drawing room.

Gabriel stood in the hall, an expression of disgust on his face.

'I heard him,' I said.

'What an unspeakably loathsome man!'

'I hope he's crushed by one of his own houses,' I said, my chest heaving with indignation.

'I was sorely tempted to tell him I knew the truth of the matter but, at present, it's better to keep my powder dry. But I shall keep close to him and find out what I can.' Gabriel flashed a brief smile. 'Meanwhile, I shall have to think of an excuse to refuse his invitation to dine at the Folly.'

Chapter 29

'Cedar wood has been used in perfume since biblical times,' said Gabriel. He rubbed a drop of cedar oil onto Toby's wrist then poured a little onto the back of my hand.

I listened to the gentle way he explained his craft to Toby and enjoyed how his long fingers gently massaged the oil into my skin, releasing the resinous fragrance. Would Robert have been so patient with any child of ours? I couldn't imagine it.

'Cedar is most frequently used in perfumes for men or added in small quantities to a ladies' perfume to prevent it from becoming too sweet.'

As he spoke, I glanced up and saw Jacob standing behind him, his watchful eyes taking in the scene. Blushing, I withdrew my hand sharply.

'And now,' said Gabriel, 'we're going to make Hungary water for perfuming handkerchiefs. He ran his finger along the shelves until he found a bottle, which he placed on the bench near a basin of rectified alcohol. 'Otto of rosemary,' he said.

He repeated the process, collecting otto of lemon peel, otto of Melissa, extract of orange flower and esprit de rose.

Gabriel passed me a glass measuring vessel. 'Mistress Finche, will you help Toby to pour in a measure up to the top?'

I removed the stopper from the bottle of greenish liquid and immediately an intensely aromatic scent of rosemary pervaded the air.

'It takes a hundred weight of rosemary leaves to produce twenty-four ounces of otto of rosemary,' said Gabriel.

One by one, Toby measured out the ingredients and poured them into the basin of alcohol, his tongue poking out between his teeth as he concentrated.

'Now stir it all very slowly, Toby. Can you smell how invigorating it is?'

'I remember my mother using Hungary water,' I said. 'It always smelled so clean and fresh.'

'This recipe is hundreds of years old but it remains popular,' said Gabriel. 'Mistress Finche, will you ladle the perfume into the bottles?'

A short while later a row of elegant bottles stood before us on the workbench, all stoppered with a cork sealed with wax and decorated with silk ribbon.

'Toby, would you like to give one of the bottles to your mama?' said Gabriel. 'Tell her it's a special gift as it's the first perfume you've made.'

'This one, with the pink ribbon?'

Gabriel smiled. 'Certainly. And Mistress Finche, please take one for yourself.'

Smiling with pleasure, I took a bottle with white ribbon.

Jacob began to move purposefully about, collecting up the basin and ladle to wash and elbowing me out of the way while he wiped down the workbench.

'I'll take Toby to his mother,' I said. 'Thank you for the lesson.'

Gabriel made me a small bow. 'You make a delightful pupil.'

I took Toby's hand and we left the laboratory.

Jane sat in her closet with her eyes closed but greeted us with a wan smile.

'Look what I've made for you!' said Toby, delight written all over on his face. 'I'm going to be a perfumer one day, just like Father.'

Jane's smile slipped, just a little. 'How lovely!' she said. 'Hungary water; just what I need to help my headaches.'

'Mr Harte has been teaching us to recognise different scents,' I said.

'That's all very well, but there are any number of professions that Toby might follow, if indeed he decides to take up a career at all,' said Jane, irritably. 'Our financial position doesn't demand that he earns a living. There's plenty of time for him to decide what interests him.'

'Of course,' I murmured.

'Don't you like my present, Mama?' Toby's face was crestfallen.

'Sweeting, of course I do! Come here and give me a kiss.' Contrite, Jane hugged Toby fiercely. 'And it's in such a pretty bottle, all tied up with my favourite pink ribbon. Will you run and fetch a handkerchief from my chest and I'll try it out?'

Toby hurried away and Jane sighed. 'I didn't mean to be ill-tempered. It's just that Gabriel refuses to understand my feelings.'

'Mr Finche explained to me that there was a possibility of Toby . . .'

'Don't speak of it!' Jane put her hands over her ears. 'I can never forgive him for not making it clear before we married that any children we had might become blind. He deceived me!' She sighed. 'And as Toby grows up I find myself watching him all the time, wondering.'

'It may never happen,' I said. 'But if it should, isn't it better to . . .'

'I am his mother and I don't need your interference, Kate. I will decide how to bring him up and I *said* I don't wish to speak of it!' She glared at me.

'I beg your pardon, Jane.' I bit my tongue but I felt quite out of temper with her. Could she not see that ignoring the possibility of Toby losing his sight could make it much worse for him? Poor Gabriel; no wonder there were difficulties between them when Jane was so intractable.

We sat in awkward silence until Toby's footsteps clattered along the passage and he burst into the room.

Jane opened the perfume bottle, poured a little onto the handkerchief and held it to her nose. 'Well!' she said. 'I declare that is the sweetest-smelling Hungary water I've ever found.' She pulled Toby onto her knee and covered his face in kisses.

'Jane, if you don't need me for anything,' I said, 'I shall go outside for a breath of fresh air before it grows too dark.'

Jane, her chin resting on the top of Toby's head, waved a hand at me. 'No, we don't need you at all,' she said.

Standing in the doorway for a moment I took in the picture of Toby with his arms entwined around his mother's neck while Jane stroked his cheek. There was a look of such naked love on her face that it made me catch my breath.

She looked up at me with hostility in her eyes and then turned her back on me. Stung, I retreated without another word.

I pulled the hood of my cloak tightly around my face as I hurried along Long Acre, without any clear idea of where I was going.

My cheeks tingled in the cold air and I broke into a trot to work off the agitation and bitterness that disturbed me so. Could Jane still not see that I had no intention of trying to steal Toby's affections? Might her changeable moods lead her to ask me to leave the House of Perfume? Anger, heartache and fear seethed inside me as I ran, pushing my way through the press of people returning home before dark.

At last I stopped to catch my breath at the end of Fleet Street and the scent of toasting chestnuts drifted towards me. A small crowd of people were warming their hands around the brazier in front of the Temple Exchange Coffee House and I joined them. Listening to the good-natured banter while I waited my turn to pay for a twist of paper containing half a dozen chestnuts, I read the notice on the wall of the coffee house.

> You see before you the Last House of the city in flames. The first of the city to be restored: May this be favourable and fortunate for both city and house, especially for those who are auspiciously building. Elizabeth Moore Owner of the site and Thomas Tuckey, tenant. 1667.

I took off the perfumed gloves Gabriel had given me, releasing their warm, earthy scent, and peeled away the hot chestnut shells. I stood in the shelter of the wall and thought that every time I ate roasted chestnuts in the future, I'd remember their comforting aroma mingling with the rich perfume from my gloves.

By the time I'd finished the chestnuts my unsettled mood had dissipated enough to return to the House of Perfume. I turned into Fetter Lane, the first part of which had been destroyed when all the houses, workshops and inns were blown up to make a firebreak at the westernmost extent of the conflagration. Now, new properties were springing up to replace them.

A group of workmen came out of a narrow alleyway carrying their picks and spades over their shoulders and it was then that I realised that the alley was the short cut through Rochester Court, Hackett's building site, to Chancery Lane and on to Lincoln's Inn Fields.

I had fled from the House of Perfume without thought and now found myself dangerously close to Hackett's offices. I stood on the corner of the alley, undecided as to whether I dared to walk through Rochester Court. If I didn't take the short cut I'd have to pass Hackett's chambers or take a much longer detour. Glancing at the darkening sky, I was anxious to return before nightfall. But the workmen leaving Rochester Court were on their way home, I reasoned, and surely Hackett wouldn't be on the site at the end of the day? Shifting from foot to foot in the cold I decided to risk taking the short cut.

The alleyway was dark now that the sun was beginning to set and I hurried along until I came into the open space of Rochester Court. The six three-storey houses on one side of the court loomed above me, casting dark shadows across the ground. For all that they gave the impression of being ready for occupation, not a single light glimmered inside any of them.

The brickwork of the houses opposite appeared to be complete but, in the gloaming, the gaping door and window openings, still without glass, were as black as an old crone's teeth. I tipped my head back and my hood fell to my shoulders as I looked up at the timbers outlining the skeleton shape of the roofs above. The court was uncannily quiet now that the workmen had left and I wondered for a moment if the poor mother and children who had died when they were trapped in their burning house still haunted the place.

Standing in the shadows, I steeled myself to stay long enough to look around the building site for anything that didn't ring true. Nearby was a large pile of bricks and I ran my finger over their rough surfaces, squinting at them through the gathering dark. Disappointed, as far as I could see, that they were standard yellow London bricks not the substandard bricks made in Hackett's brickyard.

Shivering in the cold, I remembered when Hackett had stood there beside me, testing the sharp point of a nail against the ball of his thumb. It had been madness for me to run to this part of the city without Gabriel to protect me.

The shadows were growing longer as the sun slipped behind the rooftops. I didn't want to be in that eerie place when it was fully dark. Hesitantly, I began to cross the silent court towards the alleyway leading to Chancery Lane. My echoing footsteps crunched over sand and gravel, sounding very loud. All at once a small noise behind me stopped me in my tracks.

Slowly, I turned my head. Muscles tensed, I glanced from side to side but the court appeared deserted. Stock still, listening, all I could hear was the singing in my ears, the distant drum of wheeled traffic and the mournful drawn-out cry of a rag and bone man. I took another tentative step and then stifled a gasp as I heard quick footsteps behind me.

Was it Hackett? Panicked, I began to run. My feet flew over the ground as I raced towards the alley. A man shouted, spurring me to run even faster. My heart rattled so fast that I thought it would burst. I'd almost reached the alley when the pounding footsteps behind me grew so close I could hear my pursuer panting. I screamed as he snatched at my cloak with grasping hands, dragging it half off my shoulders. He shouted again and I loosed the neckties of my cloak and pulled myself free.

The alley was in front of me and I hurtled towards it, losing a shoe in a pile of sand. As I threw myself into the mouth of the alley, another man stepped straight in front of me. I screamed and flailed in his tight embrace, terrified beyond reason. Fighting and kicking to free myself, another pair of arms captured me from behind, forcing my face against my assailant's coat. Still struggling, I smelled the sharp scent of sweat as my cheek grazed against the rough wool of his coat.

'Mistress Finche!'

Gradually, my screams turned to whimpers and the fight left me.

'Mistress Finche!'

I glanced up at the face of my unknown attacker. One side of his face, scratched and bleeding from my nails, also bore livid red scars.

'Sshh, now!' he said. 'I'll not hurt you.'

'Mistress Finche?'

I turned my head and saw that it was Ben Perkins who had imprisoned my arms from behind.

'Ben! Oh, Ben, I thought you were Hackett!'

I caught the flash of his smile in the gloom. 'Don't be frightened!' he said. 'Though I thought my time was up when I saw you.' His trembling hand held out the shoe I had lost. 'Thought I'd seen a ghost! Doesn't seem two minutes since Nell and I wept at your funeral.'

Slowly the other man let me go. 'I'm Dick Plumridge. Sorry for frightening you, missus.' He gave a tentative, lopsided smile, the scarred side of his face puckered. He would have been a well-favoured man, once.

'What are you *doing* here, Ben?' I asked, slipping on my shoe.

'I could ask the same of you.' He glanced around and pulled up his collar against the wind. 'This place fair gives me the creeps. Shall we go somewhere warmer to talk?'

We walked in silence, one man on either side of me. Dick Plumridge made slow progress since he had a severe limp but after a while we came to a tavern in Queen Street. The fuggy warmth and the noisy chatter as Ben opened the door were a welcome return to normality after the sinister quiet of Rochester Court.

The tavern keeper brought us a jug of spiced ale, then withdrew a red-hot poker from the fire and thrust it into the foaming jug so that it spat and fizzled. A few moments later, I had my hands clasped around a tankard of steaming hot ale.

'Now then, my lady,' said Ben, 'please explain why you allowed my Nell to cry herself to sleep night after night because you didn't tell us you were still alive?'

'I thought it was safer if everyone thought I was dead.'

'I guessed it was summat like that.' Ben scratched at his head. 'Spent days looking for you, I did. I knew there was something not right. Nell said you'd never have killed yourself over that husband of yours.'

I chose to ignore Nell's assessment of my marriage. 'Hackett tried to kill me. He threw me into the river under London Bridge.'

'Bastard!' Ben made a face. 'Sorry. I knew he was up to no good but there was no trace of you anywhere.'

'I nearly drowned but someone found me and took me to a nunnery. And, when I remembered who I was and what had happened, I sent for Jane Harte.'

Ben nodded. 'A kind lady, that one. But I wish you'd a told Nell and me.'

'Mr Harte thought it best you didn't know. He was concerned that you'd keep asking questions and put yourself in danger. While you only suspected Hackett, I *knew* he was a murderer. He killed Robert, too.'

Ben drew in his breath with a hiss.

'So, Mr Harte arranged a funeral for a poor drowned girl so that Hackett would be convinced I was dead and I'd be safe.'

Dick Plumridge looked up from his ale, his face pinched. 'Hanging, drawing and quartering is too good for that one.'

'Dick and I go back a long way,' said Ben. 'Dick used to live in Rochester Court. Hackett bought out the other tenants but Dick and his family didn't want to leave their home. So Hackett set it on fire. Dick's wife and four of his children died.'

My hand flew to my mouth. 'And you're sure it was Hackett?'

'I seen him,' said Dick. 'Him and that little runt, Nat Hogg, ripped off the shutters downstairs while we were abed and threw in turpentine and flaming brands. But by the time the fire had burned out, taking my Lizzie and four of the little ones, I was in no fit state to speak out about it.'

'Dick was badly burned saving two of the babies,' said Ben.

'No one will employ me now.' A single tear ran down Dick's ravaged face. 'And no one listened when I told my story because I hadn't any proof. Hackett is a mighty powerful man with friends in high places. He took my life away from me and I can never have it back,' he said, his head bowed and shoulders heaving. He looked up at me. 'But I *will* have revenge for Lizzie and my children.'

'That's why we were at the building site tonight,' said Ben. 'You know my opinion of Hackett's building methods and I hoped to find some evidence. Even if we can't prove he's a murderer, we could discredit him with his investors. Hit 'im in his pocket, I say!'

'I'm sure Hackett murdered Robert because of the bricks,' I said.

'The bricks?' Ben frowned.

I told him what Gabriel had discovered from Elias Maundrell. 'But now Mr Maundrell is dead, too, and we can't prove anything.

'I'd better get back,' said Dick. 'Mam'll be putting the babes to bed.'

'And I've been out far longer than I should.'

Ben stood up. 'I'll walk you home.'

I was glad of Ben's presence as we hurried through the darkness. The streets at night were no place for an unprotected woman, thronged as they were with roaming groups of drunken youths, beggars and whores.

When we reached the House of Perfume, Ben escorted me through the stable yard so that I could enter the house by the kitchen without disturbing the household.

'I'll let you know if Dick and I find anything,' said Ben.

'Thank you for bringing me home.'

Ben grinned in the darkness. 'Least I could do after nearly scaring you to death.'

I slipped into the kitchen, closing the door softly behind me.

Mrs Jenks backed out of the pantry carrying a bowl of eggs and nearly dropped them when she saw me. 'Lord have mercy! Where've you been?'

'I went for a walk.'

'A walk? At this time of night? You'd better go up and see the master and the mistress, straightaway. They're in the parlour.'

The drawing room door was ajar and light spilled out into the shadowy hall. I could hear angry voices within as I tapped diffidently on the door.

A fire burned cheerfully in the fireplace and Jane sat on one side of it, weeping into a handkerchief while Gabriel, legs braced apart, warmed his back by the flames.

'Mistress Jenks said you wanted to see me,' I said.

'Where have you been?' Gabriel's voice was like thunder and I flinched.

'I went for a walk,' I said.

'It's been dark for two hours! We thought, at the very least, that footpads had robbed you and left you for dead or more probably that Hackett had found you.'

'No. I . . . '

Gabriel strode over to me and caught me by the wrist. 'Come here!' He towered over me as he sniffed at my hair. 'By God! You've been in an alehouse! I can smell smoke on your hair and ale on your breath. We've been half worried to death and you've spent the evening in an alehouse?' His tone was incredulous.

'Yes. No! It wasn't like that.'

Gabriel's cheeks were suffused with pink and his handsome mouth tightened into a thin line. 'No decent woman goes into an alehouse unaccompanied. So tell me about the man you've spent the evening with. Where did you meet him? On one of your walks with my innocent little son in tow?'

I stared at him. His anger made him sound as if he were jealous. 'I've been with Ben Perkins,' I said. 'I went to Rochester Court . . . '

Gabriel became very still.

'What happened?' asked Jane. Her face was tense as she balled up her handkerchief. 'Was it my fault? I know I said I didn't need you but I only meant . . . '

'I walked further than I intended,' I said, 'and decided to take a short cut back through Rochester Court.'

'How *could* you be so foolhardy?' said Gabriel. 'Supposing Hackett had caught you? He'd break your neck without even thinking about it.'

'It was growing dark and the workmen had already left so I judged it to be safe.'

'But Hackett could so easily have been there!' Gabriel's knuckles were white as he clenched his fists together.

'But he wasn't. The building site was deserted and a strange, eerie place it is by twilight. Then I heard a noise and I'm ashamed to say I ran away. You see, I remembered Jane telling me about the family that used to live there before their house was burned down. A mother and her children died in the fire.'

'And you thought the place was haunted?' asked Jane, shivering.

'It wasn't ghosts at all, of course, but I had a bad fright when Ben and his friend, Dick Plumridge, caught me in the alley. Dick is the father of the four children who died when the house was set on fire.'

Jane gasped.

'Dick saw Nat Hogg and Hackett set the fire. He was badly injured but, just as I have no proof that Hackett killed Robert, Dick has no proof that he set the fire.'

'You must promise me never, never to risk your safety like that again,' said Gabriel.

Jane glanced at her husband, her face entirely expressionless. 'I think,' she said slowly, 'that Gabriel is right and you had better not go abroad again, Kate, unless he accompanies you.'

'An excellent idea,' he said.

'Kate, will you go and see if Toby is still awake?' said Jane. 'He cried for you at bedtime.'

At the door I turned back. 'I'm sorry if I worried you,' I said.

'We're so relieved you've returned unharmed,' said Gabriel. 'We were frightened for you.'

Jane said nothing, only stared at her hands folded in her lap.

Upstairs, Toby lay asleep on his back with one arm outflung and his little fingers curled over his palm like the petals of a rose.

I sat carefully on the edge of his bed and stroked the silky fronds of hair off his forehead, overwhelmed by tenderness for him.

He murmured and his eyelids fluttered. 'Mistress Finche?'

'I'm here, Toby.'

'You didn't come to say goodnight!'

'I came as soon as I could.'

'Will you tell me a story now?'

'It's too late, my sweeting. But tomorrow I'll tell you two stories to make up. Close your eyes now!'

His warm hand crept into mine and I bent to kiss the soft skin of his cheek. He smiled and sighed and, within two breaths, he slept.

Chapter 30

The following morning Jane took her breakfast in bed.

'I came to see if you wanted anything,' I said.

Jane lay back against the pillows, her breakfast untouched. 'Will you comb my hair for me, Kate? It pains me to lift my arms this morning.'

Gently, I combed the tangles.

'Gabriel was fit to be tied yesterday when he heard you'd gone out just before dark,' she said. 'I've never seen him in such a ferment.'

'I had no intention of causing any distress,' I said.

'He was angry with me and I cannot deny it, I *was* unkind to you.' She glanced up at me, tears in her eyes. 'I confess I'm still jealous of how much Toby loves you. But most of all I want what is best for my son. And sometimes that is not the same as what I wish for myself.'

There came a tap at the door and Gabriel and Toby came in.

Jane held out her arms to Toby and he ran to her.

'Good morning, Jane,' said Gabriel. 'And to you too, Mistress Finche.'

'Gabriel, don't you think it's time you addressed her as Kate?'

asked Jane. 'And Kate, as my closest friend and now part of our family, I believe it is appropriate for you both to be on Christian name terms.'

I glanced at Gabriel and saw that his mouth had curved into a smile.

'I agree,' said Gabriel. 'And Toby, how would you like to have an Aunt Kate instead of Mistress Finche?'

Toby frowned at me from the safety of his mother's encircling arms. 'Are you going away, Mistress Finche?' He clung to his mother, his eyes full of apprehension. 'I don't want her to go away!'

'No, no.' Jane smiled. 'But you may call her Aunt Kate.'

'She can stay?'

'Most certainly! Now go and give your Aunt Kate a kiss.'

I held out my arms and he clambered off his mother's knee and came to plant a kiss on my cheek.

'There, that's settled then!' Jane leaned back against her pillows again. 'Gabriel, I'm tired so perhaps you will escort Kate and Toby on their walk?'

'I shall be happy to do so.'

'Come and tell me all about it this afternoon, Toby.' She closed her eyes.

'I will, Mama.'

I followed Gabriel and Toby from the bedchamber but as I turned to close the door I saw that Jane was weeping. I hesitated, wondering if I should go to her but she glanced up and saw me standing in the doorway.

She wiped her eyes and gave me a tremulous smile. 'Go!' she said. 'I'll see you later.'

Downstairs, I wrapped Toby up warmly, making sure he wore his scarf. 'I think it's time we told your father about our little secret, don't you, Toby?'

He nodded his head vigorously.

Gabriel smiled. 'And what secret is that?'

'You'll have to wait a little longer. Toby, will you call Shadow?'

Toby ran off and I called out after him, 'And don't forget to count how many steps!'

Gabriel and I made more sedate progress through the garden to the stables.

'Have you quite recovered from your fright last night?' asked Gabriel.

'Perfectly, but I don't care to visit Rochester Court again,' I said. 'There's something uncanny about the place. Do you think I'm fanciful when I wonder if there are echoes of Dick's murdered family there?'

'Who knows? But I hope it's a lesson to you not to go wandering around at night on your own.' Gabriel stopped and turned to face me. 'Kate, you cannot know how anxious I was when I heard you hadn't come home.'

The concern in his face warmed my heart. 'Jane said you were angry with her.'

He rubbed at the side of his nose. 'Perhaps that was undeserved. But she was unkind to you. I couldn't bear that.'

I hesitated. 'Jane is my dear friend but you know how low her spirits are at present. She was concerned that I was trying to usurp her place in Toby's affections.'

Gabriel reached out and found my hand. 'Kate, you've enriched Toby's life by your presence.' He lifted my hand to his lips. 'And mine.'

His mouth lingered on the back of my hand and an unexpected shiver of desire ran up my arm. Then Shadow came bounding past us, followed by Toby. Gabriel dropped my hand.

'Aunt Kate, shall we tell Father now? Please?'

'Run ahead and ask Jem to make everything ready.' I still felt the imprint of Gabriel's mouth on my hand and a pulse beat erratically in my throat. 'We'd better hurry,' I said, 'before Toby bursts with excitement.'

Gabriel and I walked in silence to the stables, so close that his arm brushed against mine. I wondered if he, too, felt the vibrations in the air between us or if I only imagined it.

Jem had already buckled the harness onto Shadow and Toby was hopping from foot to foot in impatience.

'We've designed a harness for Shadow,' I said.

'To pull a small cart for Toby?' asked Gabriel.

'No, no, it's for you!' said Toby.

Nonplussed, Gabriel waited.

'Let me show you,' I said.

I took his hand, resolutely matter of fact, and guided him to find Shadow's head. 'Now run your hand down Shadow's neck until you feel his harness. That's it!'

'And what is this?' he asked, frowning a little.

'It's a handle. Lift it up.'

'Like this?'

'Perfect. We've started training Shadow but more work is needed yet. Let's see if he'll do as he's told, shall we? You need to give him a hand signal to make him move forwards.' I took hold of Gabriel's right hand again and placed it, palm down, by his thigh. 'Now lift your hand up to waist height in front of you and give him the command "Forwards!"'

Gabriel did as he was told and Toby let out a whoop of delight as Shadow stood up and walked forwards.

'We've been training him, Father,' said Toby. 'He'll walk in front of you and stop you from falling into potholes or tripping over things. We've been practising with our eyes closed.'

'What an ingenious idea!' said Gabriel. 'And the handle on the harness keeps Shadow at exactly the right distance in front of me so that I don't walk into him.'

'I know how important it is to you to be able to find your way around the city on your own,' I said. 'We'll walk with you and help you to map the new city in your mind but after that Shadow can accompany you.'

We walked briskly into the city and up Ludgate Hill, past the ruins of St Paul's and then on the route we had taken previously to Wood Street. I kept a continual lookout for Hackett, thankful that his considerable stature would make him stand out. It had frightened me when he arrived so unexpectedly at the House of Perfume and I shivered at how complacent I had been about leaving the house on my own.

Every now and again Gabriel stopped and told Shadow to sit, while he ran his fingers along a wall or listened to the cries of a shopkeeper advertising his wares. Toby, meanwhile, helped to keep a tally of the number of steps between landmarks and I reflected that anyone seeing us all together would think that we were a family.

At last we returned to the House of Perfume.

'My head is buzzing,' said Gabriel. 'I must go and sit quietly for a while and try to remember what I have learned today.'

'But you liked our surprise, Father?'

'I cannot think of anything better, Toby.' Gabriel caught his son up into a bear hug.

'Aunt Kate thought of it,' said Toby.

'And I'm truly grateful, Kate' he said quietly. 'It will take time to train Shadow properly and for me to learn my way around, but already I feel sure that it *will* happen. You cannot know how much this means to me.'

'I'm very happy for you,' I said. 'And now, don't you think Shadow deserves a tasty treat? Shall we go and see if Mrs Jenks has something special for him?'

Christmas and New Year came and went but Jane's health continued to be poor and she grew increasingly pale and thin. I was concerned that she sipped too often of the sleeping draught that Jacob regularly collected from the apothecary, seeking comfort in oblivion.

'Is Jane not coming down to supper again?' Gabriel asked one evening after I had put Toby to bed.

'She's resting,' I said.

'Then will you read some more of *Annus Mirabilis* to me after supper?'

Gradually, we had slipped into an easy informality and I spent my days looking forward to our evenings alone together. These times brought me a deep sense of peace and I was able to shut out the outside world as we talked about the day's events or laughed over something amusing that Toby had said.

After we finished our supper, Gabriel listened intently with a half-smile on his face while I read to him. This happy companionship, sitting on either side of the fireside was the embodiment of how I had hoped my married life would be.

'I visited Hackett again today.' Gabriel smiled. 'I'm enjoying stringing him along, talking about supposed investments I might wish to make. I've visited several of his building sites now but Jacob has seen nothing more than some poor workmanship to complain about.' He sighed. 'I've talked discreetly to other investors but apart from some undersized roof beams and continuing grumbles about poor quality bricks that Hackett refuses to be blamed for, there appears to be nothing untoward.'

'It makes me boil that he continues to escape justice.' Sighing, I picked up one of Toby's shirts to mend. 'I had a letter from Mother Finche today,' I said. 'Poor soul, her grandchildren exhaust her, I fear.'

'Do you never have a letter from your Aunt Mercy?' asked Gabriel, curiously.

'I've told you of the misery she inflicted on me when I was a child. We haven't communicated since I married Robert,' I said. 'She couldn't wait to have me off her hands and she doesn't care if I'm alive or dead.'

'She's a sad and embittered old woman. You should feel pity for her.'

'I still have nightmares about being shut in her cellar.' I shuddered. 'Even the thought of her frightens me. I never want to see her again.'

Gabriel reached out to me and found my hand. 'But you are not a child any longer and you have a new life now, where you are valued,' he said.

His hand enclosed my own for a moment and I wished that we could sit, hand in hand, in harmony by the fire every evening. I went to bed that night with the scented gloves Gabriel had given me hugged to my breast and slept without the nightmares that so often troubled me.

Gabriel, Jacob and Toby had gone out in the carriage to pay a visit to a supplier in Hampstead, leaving Jane and myself to have a quiet morning with our embroidery.

Jane sighed again and rubbed her temples.

'Does your head ache?' I asked.

She nodded. 'I hope Jacob won't return too late. I need him to fetch my medicine from the apothecary.'

An hour later Jane's face was grey with pain and she'd given up all pretence of working on her embroidery. I glanced at the clock and estimated that it might be another couple of hours before the others returned, longer if they stopped at a tavern for their dinner. I stood up.

'I shall fetch your medicine,' I said.

'But you mustn't go outside without Gabriel,' said Jane.

'I can't sit and watch you suffer.'

'I shouldn't let you go,' said Jane, blinking back tears, 'but, Kate, I do hurt so!'

'I'll avoid passing Hackett's chambers in Holborn and come straight back.'

Head down, I hurried along until I reached the apothecary shop.

I tucked the little bottle of medicine in my basket and set off again, worrying all the time about Jane. Perhaps it was time to call in another physician? There must be something that could be done to help her recover her health?

It was as I passed Chancery Lane that I saw him.

Hackett was standing on the corner of the street talking to two men. In the same moment that I was jolted out of my reverie by the sight of his familiar figure, he glanced up and his gaze passed over me. For a moment I thought I'd escaped his attention but then he froze and turned to stare at me.

I ran. Dodging pedestrians and horses, I ran like the wind, splashing through puddles, slithering in mud, my feet pounding along the cobbles. I glanced over my shoulder and whimpered as I saw his powerful figure lumbering after me. Spurred on by terror, I hurtled down a side street, my cloak flying out behind. Cutting along Great Queen Street the back of my neck crawled as I imagined his grasping hands reaching out for me.

An orange seller hawked her wares on the corner of Drury Lane and as I tore past her she stepped forwards and we collided. She gave a shriek of rage as her oranges tumbled to the ground, bouncing in the mud and rolling in all directions. A gang of street urchins descended in a screeching mass to gather up the spoils.

I caught a glimpse of Hackett bellowing at the urchins, lashing out with his feet and fists as he thrust his way through the heaving mass.

Ignoring the stitch in my side, I raced down Long Acre, swung myself around the gatepost of the House of Perfume and ran to the kitchen door. I thundered up the stairs and crashed into Jane's closet.

'What is it?' she asked.

'Hackett,' I gasped. 'He saw me.' Almost before the words were out of my mouth we heard a great hammering on the front door.

'He'll kill me,' I said.

Jane stood up. 'Take off your cloak and give me your basket!' She snatched the cloak from me and pulled up the hood. 'Stay here!'

I crept out into the passage and stood as close to the top of the stairs as I could without being seen from below.

Jane's footsteps hurried across the hall and as she opened the front door Hackett forced his way inside. 'Where is she?' he roared.

'I beg your pardon?' said Jane frostily, throwing back the hood of her cloak.

I edged closer to the gallery balustrade and peered down into the hall.

'Mistress Harte?' Hackett's voice was uncertain.

'As you see.'

'Where is Mistress Finche?'

'Mr Hackett, you know that Mistress Finche is no longer with us.'

'But I saw her!'

'You are mistaken,' said Jane.

Hackett scowled and narrowed his eyes at her.

Jane sighed. 'Mr Hackett, Mistress Finche did not run away from you. My eyesight is poor and I didn't recognise you. You frightened me and I ran away. I thought you were a cutpurse coming to rob me.'

'But I saw Mistress Finche!'

'You did not,' said Jane. 'Have you forgotten that we attended her burial? The poor lady drowned herself in the river, overcome with grief at her husband's death. Why, you told us that yourself! Clearly, you only *imagined* you saw her. Now, will you allow me to offer you a cup of camomile tea to steady your nerves?'

Hackett shook his head. 'I was so sure . . . '

'Then, if you please, I have matters to attend to.'

A moment later the front door slammed.

Jane sank down onto the bottom step and I ran down the stairs to join her.

Her eyes were sparkling and her cheeks flushed, even though her hands trembled as she pulled the stopper from her bottle of medicine. 'I was determined he wouldn't find you,' she said as she sipped it. 'Do you know, he slammed the door in my face! Apart from being a murderer, that man has absolutely no manners.'

I giggled and Jane joined in, both of us finding release from our fear in laughter.

Footsteps came along the kitchen passage and Gabriel came into the hall. 'What has caused you such merriment?' he asked, perplexed.

'You've just missed Hackett. He chased after me,' I said, 'but Jane saved me. And she offered him camomile tea!' I burst into laughter again.

'Hackett? That's no laughing matter,' said Gabriel.

I drew a wavering breath. 'No. I was terrified.'

Gabriel gripped the newel post, his knuckles white. 'He might have killed you. Didn't I forbid you to go out on your own for just that reason?'

'I went to fetch Jane's medicine.'

'Well, don't ever do it again!' Gabriel strode across the floor and slammed the door of the Perfume Salon behind him.

I bit my lip and looked at the floor. His anger had been so marked I wondered if Jane would find it inappropriate. I was already conscious that, in many people's eyes, Gabriel and I spent a great deal of time alone together. Jane would have every right to be jealous of his concern for me.

Jane raised her eyebrows at her husband's outburst. 'He's only angry because he was frightened for you.' She held out her hand to me. 'Shall we go and do our embroidery? I feel we've had enough excitement for today, don't you?'

A few days later I was reading to Jane while she reclined, waxen-pale, on the day bed in her closet when Gabriel pushed open the door.

'One of my customers tells me that there's a musical entertainment tomorrow evening in a private room over the George Tavern in Whitefriars,' he said, his face full of hopeful expectation. 'John Bannister will be playing his violin and we are promised an Italian singer and a concerto for harpsichord and lute.'

Jane was silent for a moment. 'I couldn't bear the noise and the chatter of company at present,' she said.

Gabriel's face fell and I confess I, too, was disappointed.

Jane looked at me and then back at Gabriel. 'But why don't you take Kate?' she said.

The following evening Gabriel and I climbed the stairs to the room above the George Tavern to find a number of people already gathered together. We took our seats and listened to the musicians tuning their instruments.

'I've looked forward to this all day,' said Gabriel. 'Since Jane's health has deteriorated we rarely attend parties and I do miss the music.'

I, too, had anticipated the outing with pleasure and could think of nowhere else I'd rather be. We sat so close together, I felt the warmth of him against my side and smelled the clean scent of the lemon balm that fragranced his linen.

The entertainment began and I listened entranced as the Italian lady singer's contralto voice filled the room. I had no understanding of the Italian language but, whatever the words meant, they heightened my emotions and brought tears to my eyes. The applause when she sank to the ground in a curtsey at the end of the aria was deafening.

'Wasn't that wonderful, Gabriel?' I whispered.

Gabriel slipped his arm through mine and my senses swam at being so close to him.

John Bannister, the leader of the Kings' group of twenty-four violinists, performed a solo and I watched Gabriel as he listened, rapt, with his eyes closed. I closed my own eyes and reflected that, in his enjoyment of this, Gabriel was no more disadvantaged than the next man. Perhaps that was one of the reasons he loved it so.

At the end of the piece Gabriel let out a sigh. 'I doubt I shall ever hear better,' he murmured. 'It's chastening to realise that however hard I practise I shall never achieve such mastery.'

As the sound of the harpsichord and lute concerto swelled to fill the room, Gabriel swayed slightly in time to the music, utterly absorbed in its ebb and flow. As I watched him, a great yearning took possession of my heart. I admired him for his courage in the face of great difficulties, his integrity and strength, but I was acutely aware that I had begun to feel much more for him than that.

Afterwards, in the carriage on the way home, Gabriel sighed. 'Sublime music such as that has the ability to transport me to another place,' he said. 'A different world where we could live another, more fulfilling life without hurting those we care for.'

I, too, craved such a world but I didn't trust myself to respond.

We spoke little after that. For my part, I was overtaken by melancholy that such a special evening would soon be over.

When the carriage drew up in front of the House of Perfume, Gabriel lifted my hand to his lips. 'Thank you for the pleasure of your company tonight,' he said, smiling in the silvery moonlight.

'A wonderful moment out of time,' I said.

He nodded and slowly let go of my hand. 'I don't want the evening to end but I suppose we must go in.'

It was hopeless, of course, but I couldn't deny to myself any longer that I had fallen in love with Gabriel Harte.

Chapter 31

The disagreement arrived out of nowhere. Jane, Toby and I were sitting in the drawing room the next day. My head still echoed with music from the previous evening and I pictured Gabriel's expression as he listened, spellbound. I was filled with the bittersweet knowledge that I had fallen in love with Jane's husband and there was nothing else to do but tuck the guilty knowledge away into the deepest recesses of my heart.

Jane, full of melancholy, stared out of the window at the frost-tipped garden with her embroidery untouched on her knee. Every now and again she sighed and rubbed her chest.

I watched her, wondering if she had indigestion. Meanwhile I kept myself occupied in letting down the sleeves of one of Toby's shirts.

'You've grown so quickly, Toby,' I said. 'I suspect you'll be tall like your father.'

Toby stood up and puffed out his chest. 'And I have long legs like Father. Look!' He walked across the room taking giant strides. 'See! Only ten steps this way and six the other.' He closed his eyes and held his arms out in front of him. 'And three steps to the door.'

Jane turned away from the window and frowned at Toby. 'Why are you counting steps?' she asked.

'Because Father always asks me to count the steps with him when we're walking.'

'I see.' Jane put down her sewing. 'Stay here with Aunt Kate.' Without another word she left the room.

A moment later I heard raised voices from the other side of the hall. Toby was lying on the floor occupied with his building bricks so I went to peep through the half-open door. Jane's shrill voice came clearly from the Perfume Salon.

'I will not have you teaching my son how to be blind!'

Gabriel's deeper tones rumbled something I couldn't hear.

'I don't want to listen to your explanations, Gabriel. I've told you countless times that I won't have it!'

A hand tugged at my skirt. 'Aunt Kate? Why is Mama shouting?'

I took his hand and closed the door firmly behind us. 'Shall we build a house with your bricks?' Keeping up a steady flow of chatter, I diverted his attention away from the continuing quarrel in the Perfume Salon.

Then a door slammed and light footsteps clipped across the hall and up the stairs.

I bit my lip, unsure whether I should go and see either Jane or Gabriel but then decided that it would be best to leave it be. I cared for them both but, in this, it seemed best not to interfere. Instead, I took Toby down to the warmth and safety of the kitchen and we baked a cinnamon and raisin cake together.

Later, when it was cool, I cut a slice and carried it upstairs for Toby to give to his mother. I tapped softly on the door and she called out for us to enter.

The room was in chaos. The doors of the press were open and gowns and petticoats spilled out in a flurry of silk and linen onto the floor. The lid of the storage chest had been thrown back and stockings and nightshifts trailed across the rug.

Jane stood before her travelling trunk on the bed. Bright spots of colour burned in her cheeks and her hair was in wild disarray.

'We've made you some cake, Mama,' said Toby, oblivious to the disorder.

She gathered him onto her lap, feverishly stroking his hair and kissing his cheeks.

'Have you lost something, Jane?' I asked. 'Can I help?'

'I'm planning to visit Aunt Tabitha tomorrow,' she said, 'and take the waters at Epsom again.' She hugged Toby so hard that he squealed. 'And you shall escort me, Toby. We shall have such a merry time, the two of us.'

'But Jane, should you travel when you are unwell?' I said. 'Shall I come too?'

'Jacob shall accompany me. I want to show Toby all the places his Aunt Eleanor and I loved when I was a little girl. We shall put flowers on her grave.'

I understood that Jane desired some time with her son without my presence and the prospect of spending a few days alone with Gabriel made my heart beat faster.

'Toby, take your father a piece of your delicious cake, will you?' Once he had left the room, her shoulders sagged and her bright smile disappeared. 'Kate, I'm so tired. Will you help me to pack?'

I set about picking up the crumpled clothes and folding them neatly into piles, while Jane watched me, slumped on the bed.

'Kate? You will look after Gabriel for me while we're away, won't you?'

I glanced up from the travelling trunk and saw that she was studying me intently.

'He's furious with me,' she said. 'But he refuses to understand how angry and frightened I feel about him continuing to act as if Toby is certain to become blind. It's tempting Fate and I will not have it!' Her voice was high and agitated. 'We cannot even discuss the matter without upset. But he thinks a very great deal of you and you can soothe him. Will you do that for me?'

'If I can,' I said, unsure how to respond.

'The truth is, Gabriel and I have so little in common these days that we cannot help each other any more.'

Disconcerted at such a confidence, I folded a nightshift with great care and placed it in the trunk.

'Gabriel only ever speaks of you in the kindest of terms,' I said, at last.

'But I cannot be the wife he needs or wants. Kate, he finds solace in your company and you must step into my shoes. Do you understand?' Her grey eyes were fixed on me, her expression serious.

A wave of heat began to flood up my throat. What did she mean; surely not what I thought she was hinting at? 'I'll keep him company while you are away,' I said. 'It's rewarding to see him making such good progress in learning the streets of the new city.'

She closed her eyes. 'I've done all I can for now,' she murmured.

'I've finished here,' I said. 'I'll pack Toby's clothes.'

Jane nodded. 'I know I can rely on you.' She opened her eyes again and caught my wrist, her fingers surprisingly strong as she gripped me. 'I *can* rely on you, can't I?'

I held her gaze for a long moment. 'Of course,' I said, not quite sure what I was agreeing to.

Quietly, I left the room.

After breakfast the following morning, Jem brought the carriage to the front of the house and stowed the travelling trunk.

Toby skipped in circles around me in impatience to be off, while Jacob glowered at me.

'You must heed your mama,' Gabriel said to Toby.

'Yes, Father.'

'I shall miss your assistance, Jacob,' said Gabriel.

'I'm concerned about how you'll manage without me,' said Jacob, 'but the mistress *insisted* I accompany her. I can't understand why she doesn't take Mistress Finche.' He sighed heavily, gloom and despondency written across his face. 'I've laid out your clothes for the next seven days and I suppose Mistress Finche may be trusted to help you keep order in the laboratory,' he said, looking up at me doubtfully.

A door opened upstairs and Jane came down, very pale but smartly dressed in a red velvet cloak with a fur tippet. 'Are you ready, Toby?'

'I've been waiting.'

Her smile belied the tragedy in her eyes. 'Then we shall leave straightaway to go on our adventure. Goodbye, Kate.' She kissed my cheek and whispered in my ear, 'Remember what I said, won't you?'

She released me and Gabriel reached for his wife's hand but she didn't take it. 'I'll see you next week, Gabriel,' she said.

He withdrew his hand, his smile frozen on his face. 'Send my best wishes to your Aunt Tabitha,' he said, his tone too formal.

Gabriel and I stood shivering on the front steps in the cold wind.

As Jane climbed onto the carriage step, she turned back. 'Gabriel?'

He stepped forwards. 'Yes, my dear?'

'Now that Kate has become such an important part of our family, don't you think it's time you created one of your unique perfumes for her?'

Gabriel's cautious smile froze.

Jane's bottom lip quivered slightly as she glanced at me. 'It should be a perfume of great significance, don't you think?' Then she climbed into the carriage and Jem closed the door behind her.

A moment later, Jem cracked the whip and the carriage rolled forwards.

Jane pressed the palm of her hand to the carriage window and our gaze met and held until the carriage turned out of the drive.

Once the others had departed Gabriel retreated to the Perfume Salon, with barely a word except to say that he was too busy for our usual walk through the city.

Since I had time on my hands, I asked Mistress Jenks if she would spare Ann to accompany me while I went out to make a purchase.

Ann, wide-eyed with excitement at the excursion, trotted along beside me, chattering all the way. Once we reached the New Exchange on the Strand we indulged ourselves by looking at the fancy wares displayed by the glove makers and mercers, marvelling at the variety of silk stockings and shawls. The object of the outing, however, was for me to visit the draper.

Resolutely, since I was still in mourning, I waved away the delightful prints and coloured cloths and asked him to show me what he had in black. I'd saved my wages and took pleasure in selecting a fine silky wool with a soft sheen. Giving in to temptation, I chose some black taffeta to make a petticoat because I loved the way it rustled.

Once safely home again, as I passed through the hall, I heard Gabriel playing his violin behind the closed door. The music was so savage and wild I could only imagine the hurt he must be feeling.

I set to work in my bedchamber, cutting out and sewing the cloth. It was a shame that Gabriel would not see the new gown, I reflected. All the while I was sewing, I relived my conversation with Jane, trying to understand what she'd meant by it. Surely I'd misunderstood her intention? And then, her suggestion as she left, that Gabriel should make a unique perfume for me, had astonished me. Clearly, Gabriel had been disturbed by her suggestion.

As darkness fell, Ann came to light the candles and tell me supper was ready.

'What do you think?' I asked, holding up the bodice to show her.

'You work so fast, Mistress Finche! And it's such fine stitching,' she said, stroking the soft wool.

Gabriel was already in the dining room as I slipped into my usual seat. The conversation was stilted and polite. Far from being able to enjoy this precious time alone with Gabriel, Jane's strange behaviour before she departed had left an uncomfortable atmosphere between us.

After we finished our cold meat and pickles, I pushed back my chair.

'Kate?'

'Yes,' I said, eagerly. I waited, hoping that he would ask me to sit with him for the evening. Perhaps he would play his violin for me?

'Would you help me in the Perfume Salon tomorrow afternoon?' asked Gabriel. 'I'm expecting Lady Dorchester and her friends.'

'Yes, of course,' I murmured, disappointed.

'Then, goodnight.'

I returned to my bedchamber with dragging footsteps to spend a long, lonely evening with my sewing. At last I put the dress aside, undressed and climbed into bed. I reached under the pillow to find the scented gloves that Gabriel had given me in their usual place.

The fire had died down to glowing embers and I lay watching the ashes crumble while I clutched the gloves to my breast and allowed the warm and sensual fragrance to envelop me until I finally slept.

The following morning Gabriel's mood was less sombre and he asked me to accompany him into the city as he had a delivery to make to Cheapside. He buckled on Shadow's harness without assistance and refused the offer of my arm. I missed the feel of him close by my side as we walked, but this privation paled into insignificance beside my pleasure in seeing his progress.

After he'd made his delivery, I guided us up Wood Street and along Aldersgate. Passing Pye Corner, I stopped dead.

'What is it?' asked Gabriel.

'It's the second-hand clothes shop that I was going to manage for Dolly Smethwicke,' I said, peering in through the window. 'There's a girl in there, sewing. Dolly must have found someone to replace me. How lucky I am that you and Jane rescued me from that dark little shop, working my fingers to the bone altering other people's cast-offs.'

'For my part, I can hardly believe that I've regained my ability to walk the city streets again with my only assistance from a stray dog,' Gabriel said.

Exhilaration glowed in his face and I had to restrain myself from hugging him.

'Dear Kate, I cannot thank you enough,' he said.

We returned to the House of Perfume, full of good spirits and with the spell of awkwardness between us broken.

Later that afternoon I ushered Lady Dorchester into the Perfume Salon.

Lady Dorchester was elderly, her wrinkled skin painted with white lead and decorated with black patches. Her two friends were similarly ancient, patched, rouged and dressed in the latest fashions. It amused me to see how the coven of old ladies fluffed up their hair and fluttered their eyelashes at Gabriel when he greeted them, even though he couldn't see them.

'I suppose it is too much to ask, Mr Harte,' said Lady Dorchester in imperious tones, 'for you to make me an exclusive perfume? You would make an old lady very happy if you'd oblige.'

'I regret that I rarely make exclusive perfumes any longer.'

'Even for me?' wheedled Lady Dorchester.

'Even for the Queen of Sheba, my lady,' smiled Gabriel. 'However, since I hold you in such high regard, I will allow you to be the first to try Song of India, which is made in a very limited quantity. It's a sophisticated floral with a hint of patchouli, perfect for a lady of culture and discernment such as yourself.' He picked up a small bottle from the mirrored table, removed the stopper and touched a drop of the perfume onto the old lady's wrist.

She sniffed at it. 'Divine!' she said.

Her friends crowded around her and proclaimed it 'exotic' and 'charming'.

'And I am the first to try it?' she asked.

'Most certainly.'

'How many bottles did you make?'

'Ten, only.'

'Then I shall take them all,' she said, triumphantly. 'Then this perfume will only ever be worn by myself.'

I wrapped up the ten bottles of perfume, along with the candles, scented sachets, handkerchief waters, pomades and soaps the ladies had selected and the party swept away, full of good humour.

'A profitable afternoon,' said Gabriel.

'I thought you didn't make exclusive perfumes any more? Surely, by allowing Lady Dorchester to buy your entire stock of Song of India that makes it exclusive to her?'

'There is a world of difference in being the only person to wear a perfume and in having a perfume made especially for you, to reflect your unique character and inner beauty. Such a perfume cannot be made without true knowledge of the recipient. And it must be made with passion.'

'I see.'

'Kate, I wondered . . . '

'Yes?'

'After supper tonight, would you continue to read Dryden's poem to me?'

A wide smile broke out on my face. 'I should be delighted.'

The following morning Gabriel disappeared into his laboratory and I was disappointed when he said that he didn't need my assistance. I continued with my sewing, however, and made excellent progress. My new bodice, skirt and petticoat were nearly completed.

That evening, we sat in the drawing room. I stared into the fire, unwilling to think about Jane, Toby and Jacob's imminent return. During the past few days I'd been living in a world cushioned from reality, revelling in being Gabriel's sole companion.

'This week is disappearing fast,' he said, echoing my own melancholy thoughts.

'But I look forward to hearing Toby's happy chatter again,' I said.

'Yes,' said Gabriel with a smile.

Neither of us mentioned Jane.

The clock ticked and I yawned.

'Time for bed,' said Gabriel.

I damped down the fire and we went upstairs. We stopped outside my bedchamber door.

'Goodnight, Gabriel.'

'Goodnight.'

I stood and watched him hurry away down the passage, while the heat of longing flooded my cheeks.

Sleep eluded me that night. I beat my pillow in a vain attempt to make it comfortable, then threw it on the floor in a temper. I pictured Jane's face and shame burned in my breast that I should have such powerful yearnings for her husband.

Finally I dozed but awoke later to hear stealthy footsteps stop outside my door. I knew it had to be Gabriel. I held my breath, but, after a moment, the footsteps continued along the passage.

I overslept the next morning and missed breakfast.

Gabriel had by then shut himself in his laboratory and didn't emerge until supper. Yawning and stretching, he said, 'I hadn't realised how late it is. I've been engrossed with creating a new perfume. I become so elated and absorbed in the olfactory experience that I forget time passing.'

'Is this a formulation to replace Song of India?'

'I have in mind something far more interesting. For some time I have wanted to make a unique perfume for you.'

I stood very still unable to find the words to convey my confused feelings.

'Kate?' His voice was uncertain. 'Would you like that?'

'What woman would not?' I twisted my fingers together in indecision. 'But Jane … I have no wish to … '

Gabriel's mouth tightened into a thin line. 'It was Jane's own suggestion and I feel no reservations in the matter. Tomorrow I'll continue my experiments to create a perfume worthy of you. Goodnight, Kate.' And then he went upstairs.

My own desire to sleep had fled, replaced by a seething excitement, tinged with unease.

Chapter 32

Gabriel remained in his laboratory the following day but it seemed to me that his presence throbbed all through the house.

By the time darkness fell I had finished sewing my new dress. Wearing an outfit of my own, rather than something borrowed, gave me a thrill of pleasure. The skirt pinned up at each side to expose the taffeta petticoat, which swished as I walked. Gabriel couldn't see how well I looked but I knew he would hear the silky rustle of my petticoat.

At suppertime I paused in the dining room doorway when I saw that Gabriel awaited me.

He stood up and pulled out my chair. Briefly, his hand brushed my shoulder as I sat down, his touch making me quiver.

'You must be tired,' I said, 'locked away all day in your laboratory.'

'The exhilaration of working on your perfume made me forget the time,' he said. 'Perhaps, after supper, you'll come and give me your opinion on how I progress?'

'I cannot imagine anything I should like better.'

We both ate sparingly and as soon as we'd finished made our way to the laboratory.

The room was dark, lit only by the glow of the fire. I breathed in the faint aroma of the traces of a thousand perfumes created there over the years that still haunted the very air. Gabriel lit a candle for my benefit and I saw that a number of bottles, flasks and bowls were neatly laid out on the workbench.

'My vision of the perfume I wish to create for you is complex,' said Gabriel, 'just as you are. I have tried a number of variations but there is still something lacking. And then, of course, it must be to your personal taste.'

'I have always enjoyed flower scents,' I said. 'I loved Summer Garden.'

'And it suited your natural perfume, but this perfume should illustrate other aspects of your individuality. So, yes, we will use some tuberose and lily of the valley, but also jasmine to reflect the sweetness of your nature, but it also has a surprising, darker, more animalistic aspect. Although you are small, you are fearless so we'll counter the prettiness of the floral essences with sandalwood and fix them with musk. You like the muskiness of your perfumed gloves, I believe?'

'As you know, I wasn't sure at first, but now I love it.' I couldn't tell him that I slept with the gloves under my pillow every night so that their heady scent enveloped me.

Gabriel smiled. 'Aromas are like paint,' he said. 'When you mix two colours together, say yellow and blue, the result is green. But an infinite variety of shades are possible, from the softest green of a new leaf to the deepest blue-green of a fir tree, depending on the proportions. I aim to mix these essences together in such a way that we will find the perfect combination for you.'

He ran his hands over the workbench and found the first flask. Uncorking it, he tipped it against a small square of white linen and then held it out to me.

I sniffed tentatively at the cloth. 'Jasmine and tuberose?'

'And lily of the valley. Pretty but too simple for you.' He picked up the next flask. 'This is the same mix of florals but with musk and sandalwood.'

I took the proffered scrap of cloth, feeling his fingers brush against mine. I breathed in the scent. 'This is less sweet,' I said, 'woodier, and the perfume richer.'

'But it disappoints you?' He smiled. 'I can hear it in your voice. But don't be concerned, we haven't finished yet.' He picked up another flask. 'This is the same mixture with some additions. See if you can detect what they are.'

'Oh, spices!' I said. The perfume at once reminded me of the aroma of the Finche warehouse. 'Ginger, nutmeg and . . . ?'

'Clove. Perhaps a little more ginger? But there is still something missing. May I hold your wrist?'

'Yes, of course,' I said, puzzled but eager for his touch.

He felt for my hand and turned it palm up. 'I need to smell your skin,' he said, lifting my hand to his nose. 'May I?' He breathed in deeply and then again more gently. Then he put his mouth against the inside of my wrist and tasted the soft skin with the tip of his tongue.

I gasped and quivered with a pleasure so sudden that it almost hurt.

His tongue flickered on my wrist again and, weak-kneed, I clung to the workbench with my other hand, my eyes closed and my mouth open, as ripples of sensation fluttered through my veins, coming to rest with an aching heat deep in my pelvis. His breath was warm as he sniffed and tasted my skin again and again with a feather touch, moving up my forearm little by little, finally burying his nose in the fold of my elbow.

After an aeon, he stood up again. He swallowed before he spoke, his voice unsteady. 'Vanilla and almonds, milky and sweet like the innocence of a child. And then cloves and ambergris for the underlying sensuality. It's the unexpected contrast that's so remarkable. I'm determined to capture and intensify the exquisite scent of your skin.'

My pulse was still racing and I didn't trust myself to speak.

'Kate, will you stay while I work?'

I let go of the workbench and walked to the hearth, my taffeta petticoat sighing like the wind in the trees. I sank down by the fire, languid with desire.

Gabriel took off his coat and I watched the firelight glow burnish the blond hair of his forearms as he rolled up his shirtsleeves. He moved steadily between his workbench and the shelves of bottles and jars, stroking his slender fingers slowly across the containers, counting along the row until he reached the one he wanted.

'I shall use ambergris,' he said. 'It's one of the rarest and most precious ingredients used in perfume making.'

A glow of pleasure warmed me because Gabriel thought me worthy of using such a costly item in my perfume. 'What is ambergris?'

'It comes from the sea. Some people find the smell unpleasant, but when you add it to other fragrances it loses its own scent and magnifies other perfumes. It's the closest thing in Nature to the natural scent of a woman's skin and adds something indefinable and addictive. When it's worn by a woman it's noted for its intoxicating effect upon a man's senses.'

Cocooned by the warmth and the semi-darkness of the room, I became heavy-eyed as I watched his every movement. Every now and again I caught a trace of tuberose or vanilla in the air. I slipped off my shoes and rested my toes on the hearth to toast by the coals, then pulled my silken petticoat up over my knees. I felt curiously wanton, exposing my legs to the heat of the fire in Gabriel's presence, knowing that he couldn't see their nakedness.

The hall clock struck eleven and still Gabriel poured and stirred and sniffed the formulation. Yawning widely, I closed my eyes.

I must have dozed, because when I awoke, the fire had died down to glowing embers on a bed of grey ashes. I stretched out my arms and yawned again.

'So, you're awake, at last.' There was amusement in Gabriel's voice. He sat on the chair on the other side of the hearth with his long legs stretched out before him and the shirt laces at his neck loosened.

I stared at the glimpse of bare chest, wondering how it would feel to touch the skin there with my lips, to lick the curve of his neck ... Hurriedly, I pulled my petticoat over my knees to drive away such thoughts. 'I must have drifted off,' I said.

'Your perfume is ready for you to try.'

I sat up straight, suddenly anxious that I might be disappointed.

'Come!' He stood up and held out his hand to me.

I slid my hand into his and he guided me out of the laboratory and into the Perfume Salon.

'Oh!' I breathed.

The fire had been stirred up into a merry blaze and the shutters closed to keep out the night. Candles flickered in the wall sconces, a six-branched candelabra shimmered on the mirrored table in the centre of the room and on the floor, all around the perimeter of the room, small nightlights burned.

'How beautiful!'

Gabriel pulled back one of the high-backed chairs from the table and I sat down. He opened the door to the perfume cabinet and took out a tall glass bottle with an elegant long neck and a pear-shaped glass stopper. Placing it on the mirrored table, he sat down close beside me.

I looked at the bottle of clear amber liquid and reached out with one finger to touch the cool curved glass, glimmering in the candlelight.

'I'm almost afraid to let you try it,' he said. He leaned forwards. 'Kate, promise me you'll be honest? If you don't like it I'll change the formulation. I couldn't bear for you to wear a perfume that didn't move your senses.'

'Then I promise I'll tell you the truth.'

'Good. You may not know how you feel about it straightaway. The success of a perfume often lies with the way it mellows on the skin.' Slowly, he worked the stopper out of the bottle. 'Allow me to apply it to your pulse points.' He tipped the bottle against his first and middle fingers. 'Give me your wrist.'

I held out my hand, palm up, and he stroked the inside of my wrist with the perfume.

'Wait!' he said as I began to lift it to my nose. 'Give me your other hand.' Gently, he massaged the amber liquid into the other wrist and the scent of tuberose floated towards me. He dabbed more perfume onto his fingers and trailed them up the inside of my forearms until he reached the warm place in the crook of my elbow and, one by one, he caressed the perfume into my skin. 'Now,' he said.

I bent my head to my wrists and inhaled. All at once my senses were assailed by an explosion of femininity. It smelled of the comfort of my mother's arms and the anticipation of a lover's touch. It reminded me of the earthy smell of menstrual blood and the aroma of a newborn baby's neck. Spicy and warm, it carried notes of creamy vanilla and tuberose with the peppery sweetness of lily of the valley after the rain.

'Oh yes,' I breathed.

'The fragrance will change as it warms on your skin,' said Gabriel. 'Come closer!' His green eyes were closed as he inhaled the perfume and the huskiness of his voice made me tremble with longing. 'The top notes will evaporate soon and then you'll find the heart notes.' He felt for my hair and ran his fingers up my jawline. 'I shall put some behind your ears and on your neck.'

I closed my eyes, swaying a little as his fingers caressed my throat. I leaned my head to one side to allow his fingers to stroke up my neck until his hands were in my hair.

'So very soft,' he whispered and kissed the curve between my neck and shoulder.

I trembled but had lost the will, or the wish, to protest.

He loosed my hair from its pins and it fell like a silken curtain over my shoulders. He tipped the perfume bottle against his fingers again and then touched them to the valley between my breasts.

Shivers ran down my shoulders and, melting with desire, I moved towards him, just a fraction.

I heard him release his breath suddenly and then he wound his fingers in my hair and pulled my face towards him. He bent his head to mine and we stayed motionless for an eternity, our lips but an inch apart, his breath feathering my cheek.

The spiciness of the perfume intensified as it melded with my skin and the exotic sandalwood, cloves and ginger came to the fore, intoxicating and passionate. I let it flood over me, wrap me in its embrace and penetrate every pore of my body.

Trembling, I touched my hand to his neck. Unbidden, my fingers slipped inside the loosened laces of his shirt and stroked his chest.

Making a small sound he pressed his mouth to my cheek.

Sighing, I turned my head and our lips met, gently, tentatively, at first, but then with increasing pressure. The tip of his tongue slid into my mouth, gently tasting and exploring, until there was nothing in my world but him and spinning darkness and the fusion of our mouths. Heat rose up within me and I became liquid with wanting him, softening and opening, crying out for his touch.

He clasped me fiercely to his chest and I felt the hardness of him through his breeches as I pressed myself to his groin. His hands grasped and kneaded my buttocks so that I longed to wrap my legs around his waist and pull him deep inside me.

At last he drew back, his breath ragged and uneven. 'Kate . . .' There was a question in his voice.

'Yes,' I said, not hesitating for a second, knowing only that he was my soul mate and it was meant to be.

He lifted me into his arms as if I weighed no more than thistledown and carried me over to the rug in front of the fire, placing me carefully onto its silky softness.

I reached up to him as he kneeled over me and held his face between my hands and kissed his eyelids. 'Come to me!' I whispered, sliding my hands beneath his shirt and stroking the taut skin of his belly.

Then his hands were loosening my laces and pulling off my bodice and shift, while he scattered kisses on my upturned face.

I dragged his shirt over his head and fumbled at the fastenings of his breeches. And then we rolled together, skin to skin, on the rug, our nakedness lit only by the glow from the hearth. His kisses fell upon my bare shoulders and breasts and my back arched as his mouth found my nipple.

I caught my breath as he slid his hand up my legs, stroking my inner thighs, until he found my secret place, dipping into the warm, moist depths and gently caressing me until I was ready to swoon.

He whispered words of endearment and his mouth, from kissing the perfumed skin of my throat and breasts, tasted sweet-scented with a feral undertone of musk.

I gasped as a ripple of throbbing sensation began to build up in my pelvis. 'Gabriel!' I cried, clutching his head and pulling his mouth to mine.

He turned on his back, pulling me on top of him so that I straddled him and he touched me there again until my breath came in short gasps as the tremors increased.

Then he lifted up my hips and lowered me again until I felt the hot hardness of him slide inside me. As I moaned softly, he caught my wrists and I rode him, my breasts brushing against his chest.

My eyes were closed and I was lost in our private, perfumed world of sensation as the tidal wave of tremors grew within me. Time became meaningless. I travelled on the crest of the wave until I could ride it no longer and was dashed against the shore in a feverish explosion of passion I could not deny. I threw back my head and let out a cry of triumph.

A moment later Gabriel sighed as he found his own release.

I sank down and rested my head on his chest, hearing the rapid beat of his heart echoing my own. Sated, we lay entwined, our limbs growing heavier and the heat of the fire evaporating the sweat and the musky, spicy perfume from our naked skin.

Gabriel's voice was husky as he stroked my hair. 'You cannot know how much I have wanted this. I think perhaps I made this perfume for myself as much as you. Before now I have only been able to catch the faintest, tantalising hint of your natural fragrance but now my senses are drowning in you.'

He folded his shirt into a makeshift pillow and pulled my taffeta petticoat into a rustling blanket over us.

My mind empty of all thoughts, I nestled my head into the hollow of his shoulder and he wrapped his arm around me and tucked it under my breast.

In the hall, the clock struck four.

Yawning, I closed my eyes. Soon I heard Gabriel's breaths become even and, a moment later, I slept.

Chapter 33

My limbs were cramped and cold and I reached down for the bedcovers but couldn't find them. My eyelids fluttered open and I stared at the unfamiliar room, the cold dawn light outlining the edges of the shuttered window.

As I moved, a waft of perfume was released from my skin, carrying with it the musky scent of sex, tuberose and jasmine. Turning my head, I saw Gabriel's handsome profile as he lay on the floor beside me, fast asleep, his hand on my naked hip. He looked curiously vulnerable and my heart swelled with love for him.

And then I remembered. I recalled his lips upon my breasts, my shoulders, my throat, smothering me with hot kisses.

What had we done? An icy shudder of self-loathing ran down my spine. Gabriel was my closest friend's husband. How could we have betrayed her so?

Holding my breath, I lifted his hand off my hip and slid away. Shivering uncontrollably, I gathered up my clothes, retreating to the corner of the room to scramble into them. I'd lost my hairpins and my curls lay in a tangled mass down my back and my taffeta petticoat was stained and crumpled.

I placed Gabriel's clothes beside him so that he would find them when he awoke. A wave of tenderness washed over me again and I longed to wake him with a kiss. Hardening my heart against the temptation, I stepped away. What had happened must never, ever, happen again.

Tiptoeing to the door, I opened it a crack and peered into the hall, terrified that I would run into Ann in my current state of disorder. To my relief, the hall was deserted and I fled upstairs.

I closed my bedchamber door behind me and leaned against it, shaking and nauseous. Hurriedly, I stripped off my clothes again, poured water from the ewer into the basin and splashed my face. Then I washed all over, scrubbing the washcloth and icy water over my skin until it was pink, washing away the last musky remnants of our betrayal.

Trembling, I dressed in the clothes Jane had given to me. I'd come to the House of Perfume with nothing. She had taken me into her home with open arms, given me even the clothes I stood up in and I had violated our friendship. I looked in the mirror at my bruised mouth and the pink rash of shame where Gabriel's stubble had grazed my face and felt nothing but abhorrence for myself.

Had Gabriel seduced me or was it the other way round? Or had the perfume seduced us both? What Gabriel and I had shared was extraordinary and I knew I would never feel such depths of passion with anyone else. I cried then, for the glimpse of ecstasy I'd experienced with my forbidden love, knowing that I must never lie in his arms again.

At last my tears were spent but the sharp ache of misery and guilt lodged under my breastbone nearly choked me. When Jane went away it had seemed to me that, in suggesting Gabriel create a unique perfume for me, she was encouraging him to have deeper feelings for me. But surely I must have misunderstood her, imagining that was what she'd meant because that was exactly what I wished for myself? There could be no justification for what had happened.

My only course of action now was to leave the House of Perfume, but how could I leave when I had not a penny to my name? And how could I bear to walk away from little Toby?

I stayed in my room all that day, too wretched and ashamed to face Gabriel, while I agonised over where I could go and how I would manage. And all the time a secret, base part of me expected Gabriel to seek me out, to tell me that he loved me and that we would find a way to be together. Of course, I would tell him that it could never be but I needed, how desperately I needed, to hear him say that he loved me. A deep hurt bloomed in my heart when he didn't come.

When Ann knocked on my door, I told her that I had a headache.

'The master's out of sorts as well today,' she said. 'I hope you haven't both caught an ague.'

The following day I continued to avoid Gabriel and in the afternoon, Jane and the others returned.

I heard Toby's excited voice first and then running footsteps clattering up the stairs. He burst into my room and threw himself into my arms.

'Hello, Aunt Kate! Did you miss me? Aunt Tabitha has a cat called Tom and he caught a mouse and left it in the kitchen,' he said, covering my cheeks with damp kisses.

I hugged him to me, burying my face in his flaxen hair so that he wouldn't see my wretchedness. I had grown to love him so much that it would be an agony to leave him.

'Are you crying?' he asked, looking at me with his father's green eyes.

I pinched his cheek and forced a smile. 'I missed you,' I said, full of dread at the prospect of facing Jane.

Jane and Gabriel were already in the hall as Toby and I came downstairs and my steps faltered. I was shocked by the extreme pallor of Jane's face and the bruised shadows under her eyes.

'I hope you enjoyed your visit?' I said, unable to look at Gabriel. Jane's eyes were fixed intently upon me and I bent to stroke Toby's hair, hoping she wouldn't notice my agitation.

'Travelling is always tiring,' she said. 'Will you amuse Toby while I rest? Then, at supper, I shall look forward to hearing your news.'

Relieved not to witness any more of Jane and Gabriel's reunion, I hustled Toby and Shadow out for a walk.

Watching the boy and the dog romping together in the park in uncomplicated happiness, I had to fight back tears. Toby, quite as much as his father, had stolen my heart, but my illicit love for Gabriel had destroyed my self-respect. The price of that was to deprive me of the joy of being part of his son's life.

That night, after I had put Toby to bed, I reluctantly joined Jane and Gabriel for supper.

'Tell me what has happened while we were away,' said Jane.

'Nothing of significance,' I said.

Gabriel turned his head towards me, his hand stilled in the act of transporting a piece of bread to his mouth.

'We went on a foray to the city,' I said, placing a small slice of roast chicken on my plate, knowing I'd be unable to eat it. 'Gabriel and Shadow are making remarkable progress.'

'Shadow has made the most astonishing difference to my life,' said Gabriel. 'The prospect of learning to find my way through the rebuilt city was daunting and at times I was in despair. But now, thanks to Kate's inventive mind, I can foresee a time when I'll be independent again.'

'Toby fretted at me all the while we were at Aunt Tabitha's,' continued Jane, 'asking me almost every minute when he would see his Aunt Kate again.'

'But he must have enjoyed visiting all your childhood haunts?'

Jane nodded. 'We placed snowdrops on Eleanor's grave and I told Toby about some of our childish misdeeds, which amused him very much.' She passed me a plate of buttered carrots. 'And, Gabriel, how have you progressed with making a special perfume for Kate?'

'I worked on several different ideas –'

'But I'm hard to please and I didn't like his samples,' I interrupted. I wanted to needle him with my barbed comments, to wipe the bland expression from his face. It hurt me that he appeared not to be suffering as I was.

Jane raised her eyebrows. 'I had hoped . . . '

'Really, Jane, I do not need such a perfume. I like the simplicity and freshness of the Hungary water that Toby made as well as anything.'

'Most women would give their eye teeth for Gabriel Harte to create a special perfume for them.'

'But then,' said Gabriel with a tight little smile, 'Kate is not as most women.'

I bowed my head over my plate, in case she saw the shame in my eyes.

'No, indeed,' said Jane. She pushed her plate away from her, most of her supper untouched. 'Kate, may I prevail upon you to help me to bed?'

I followed her from the room without a word.

Upstairs, I helped Jane to unlace her bodice, folded her skirts and petticoats and put them away in the chest.

She sat on the edge of the bed in her shift, arms folded across her chest and drooping with exhaustion.

I was shocked to see how thin she had become. 'Did you take the waters at Epsom?' I asked.

She pulled a face. 'Toby is quite right; they do taste nasty. And, since they do me no good, I rapidly dispensed with them.'

I took the pins from her fair hair and gently combed out the tangles.

'Kate?' she said. 'Do tell me you didn't argue with Gabriel while I was away?'

'Not at all,' I said.

'Your conversation was so strained. '

'I promise you, we didn't argue.'

She sighed. 'Will you rub lavender oil into my temples?' she murmured.

Soon after, she slipped into bed and I pulled the covers up to her chin. 'Are you warm enough?' I asked.

Her eyes were suddenly bright with tears. 'You're so kind to me, my good and faithful friend.'

I tucked the sheet carefully under the mattress, overcome with self-disgust again.

She caught my wrist. 'I don't know what Toby and I would do without you! Promise me, you won't ever leave us, will you, Kate?'

'I only want to see you well and happy,' I said, unable to promise such a thing.

She continued to cling to my wrist, trying to read my face.

Smiling brightly, I said, 'Shall I measure out your sleeping draught?'

Relaxing her hold on me, she nodded. 'And will you go and kiss Toby for me?'

'I always do.' I blew out her candle.

Toby was already asleep, all pink and gold like a painting of a cherub. I stroked the hair off his forehead and bent to kiss him. Nothing must be allowed to hurt this innocent child, I vowed. But what must I do? Should I leave the House of Perfume, taking the taint of sin away with me? Or should I stay and suffer the agony of loving a man and a child who can never be mine? Such suffering would be a just punishment for my actions.

I was still struggling with my confused thoughts as I crossed the hall when the door of the Perfume Salon opened.

Gabriel stood in the doorway. 'A minute, if you please,' he said.

'I don't think . . . '

He opened the door wide and gestured for me to enter. 'We can't ignore what happened,' he said, closing the door behind us.

I glanced over to the thick carpet before the fireplace, remembering how we had entwined our naked limbs together there at the height of our passion. 'We must never speak of it,' I said, close to tears. 'Never, ever.'

'But how can we forget?'

'It was an enchantment brought about by the alchemy of the perfume you created. We have to destroy it,' I said, 'before we destroy Jane and Toby.' I pushed past him and went into the laboratory. Scanning the shelves, I searched for the distinctive bottle but it wasn't there. I tugged open all the cupboards in a frenzy.

'Kate!'

Gabriel took the key from his pocket and held it out to me.

I snatched it from him and ran to the locked wall cupboard and wrestled the door open. The elegant bottle with the long neck and the pear-shaped stopper was there. 'I shall go out tomorrow and dispose of it,' I said.

Gabriel said nothing and I waited, expecting him to argue with me, hoping he'd tell me he loved me. But then he stepped aside and I left the room, carrying the bottle as carefully as if it contained poison.

Wind rattling the shutters woke me during the night. The embers of the fire gave me enough light to find my way to the window and I leaned out into the lashing rain to catch the shutter as it banged to and fro.

Shivering, I stirred up the fire. The bottle of perfume rested on the dressing table, the amber glow of its contents glinting seductively in the firelight. I trailed my fingers over the cool glass until they came to rest on the stopper. Unable to resist, I slowly twisted the stopper out of the bottle. I caught the faintest hint of tuberose and jasmine, spiked with cloves. I had expected the perfume to overwhelm me with its sensuality and experienced a peculiar feeling of relief when it did not. I reached a finger forwards to dip into the amber liquid and hesitated. It was when the perfume met with my warm skin that its potent magic was released. I snatched up the stopper, jammed it back into the lovely bottle and then jumped back into bed as if the hounds of Hell were after me.

The following morning I put on my cloak and slipped the bottle of perfume into my basket before leaving the House of Perfume. I hardly cared any more if Hackett saw me and hurried along the streets intent on my purpose.

The previous night's downpour had left the street drains running fast, swirling away the animal dung and other detritus. The Fleet was less sluggish than usual and I stopped on the bank and took the bottle of perfume from my basket. The power of the sensually beautiful perfume had seduced me with false promises, but by the cold light of day I knew how treacherous it was. I had believed Gabriel loved me but I understood now that what he felt for me was merely lust. Without pausing to think, I pulled out the stopper and poured the contents into the river. I deliberated for a moment as to whether I should return the lovely bottle to Gabriel. Gabriel, the only man I would ever love, but who had never said that he loved me. Sobbing, I swung the bottle out in an arc over the ditch. I watched it bob up and down and then fill with the filthy water. After a moment it sank.

I clutched the hood of my cloak tight around my face and hurried back to the House of Perfume.

Chapter 34

April 1669

Hackett began to disturb my sleep again, stalking me in my dreams. I ran down dark alleyways with his pounding footsteps behind me, concealed myself under shadowy bridges and fought against drowning as I was swept away by an icy torrent, tumbled over and over in the black of night to the sound of Hackett's cruel laughter. I awoke each time, sweating and shivering, with my heart hammering.

It wasn't long before a waking nightmare began to plague me, too, causing the bad dreams to fade into insignificance. My courses were late. At first I reassured myself that the anxiety of the previous weeks had caused a delay in the natural rhythm of my body but when I didn't bleed for the second month, I knew I had to face the terrible truth. My one night of passion with Gabriel had achieved what had been denied to me during my lawful marriage. I was with child.

One April morning I sat listlessly in Jane's closet, staring out of the window, worrying. Pride prevented me from telling Gabriel I was expecting his child. He didn't love me, but had already behaved with great generosity to me. I wouldn't repay him by asking for more. There was no choice but for me to leave the House of Perfume. But how could I? Even if I found a place as a servant, as soon as my condition became apparent I would be cast out into the street. There was no point in appealing to Mother Finche as I already knew there was no place for me there, especially now that I would have a baby to care for. That only left Aunt Mercy and I began to shake at the very thought of begging her for help. Sick with fear, I didn't know which way to turn.

'What is it, Kate?' asked Jane.

'I sleep badly,' I confessed. 'Hackett always seems to be waiting for me when I close my eyes.'

'Is that why you seem so unlike yourself, lately?' I was saved from answering as the door opened and Gabriel appeared.

'You're looking very fine today, Gabriel,' said Jane.

He wore a new coat of forest green with silver buttons and matching buckles on his shoes. The pale green of his eyes was intensified by the colour of his coat and I bent my head to conceal the sudden stab of longing for him.

'I've been visiting our friend Hackett at Rochester Court,' he said. 'The houses are nearly finished. Hackett's ready to sell or rent them and release the profit. He took us on a tour of the properties but neither Jacob nor I could ascertain anything out of the ordinary.'

'Nothing?' I asked, disappointed.

'No, except that the finish on the woodwork is poor.'

The door closed behind him and despair consumed me again as I turned over and over in my mind how I could leave the House of Perfume. At last I came to a decision.

Later, while Jane rested and Toby practised his letters, I wrote a letter of my own. It was time to release myself from the lonely torture of being regularly in Gabriel's presence and being mired in shame at my duplicity to Jane, but there was an enormous price to pay. I wrote to Aunt Mercy, asking her to take me in. Utterly wretched, I could think of no other way to ensure the safety of my baby. I explained that my husband had died and left me destitute, carefully omitting to give her the date of Robert's death. I asked Ann to take the letter to the post office and prepared myself to tell Gabriel, Toby and Jane that I was leaving as soon as I received Aunt Mercy's reply.

That night I dreamed that I was standing at the top of the stairs looking down into Aunt Mercy's cellar. Down below something monstrous waited for me in the dark, its breath rank and its eyes glowing red like coals. All at once a hand thudded into the small of my back and I pitched forwards, screaming in terror. Spinning down into the shadowy depths, I was dazzled by a shaft of light slicing across the cellar wall before the monster roared and leaped at me, fangs bared.

Then Robert's voice echoed in my head. *'Maundrell was right!'*

I sat bolt upright in the dark, shaking and shivering while I fumbled to light the candle. The wavering light restored my sanity and I paced across the floor while my heartbeat steadied. All at once, I became motionless as I realised the significance of what I had seen that day in the foundations of Rochester Court but been blind to ever since. I gave a little hiccough of laughter, sat down at the writing desk and reached for a pen.

'Dear Ben,' I wrote.

Two days later, Gabriel, Jane and I were in the drawing room after supper. Jane dozed, while Gabriel was lost in contemplation and I stared into the flames thinking about my child, Gabriel's child, growing within me.

I'd been so frightened and ashamed that I'd given little thought to the baby before but now that I'd determined a course of action I allowed myself a glimmer of happiness through the veil of worry. Aunt Mercy's strong sense of duty meant that I was sure she'd take me in, however onerous she found it. Of course, she'd extract payment by making my life a misery, but now that I'd accepted I had no other choice than to return to her house, at least I had the comfort of knowing that by the autumn I would hold my longed for baby. I was wondering if it would have Gabriel's green eyes, when we heard the doorknocker.

'Mistress Finche,' Ann said a moment later, 'there's two men to see you. A Mr Plumridge and a Mr Perkins.'

I rose to my feet, my heart thumping.

Dick Plumridge limped into the drawing room, followed by Ben Perkins.

Ben twisted his hat between his hands. 'Sorry to disturb,' he said.

'You received my note?' I asked.

He nodded and his face broke into a wide grin. 'You were right!'

I sat down abruptly.

'What is it?' asked Gabriel.

'We broke into the cellars at Rochester Court tonight,' said Ben, 'looking for proof of Hackett's villainy.'

'And we've found it!' Dick smiled in triumph, his poor, burned face cruelly puckered.

'Mistress Finche said she thought Hackett might of used the bad bricks in the cellars,' said Ben. 'And there they are as plain as day.'

'There's great cracks in the cellar wall,' said Dick. 'It's only a matter of time before those houses come tumbling down.'

'Why didn't you tell me?' Gabriel asked me.

'I sent the note to Ben because I remembered something,' I said, 'but I hadn't realised the significance of it before.'

'I don't understand,' said Jane.

'When Robert disappeared, I visited Hackett at Rochester Court. He gave me a fright as I stood on the edge of the foundations and I lost my balance. As I swayed on the edge of the pit I saw that the walls in the cellars were made of dingy-looking bricks. I was too worried about Robert at the time to realise how momentous it was.'

Gabriel cursed under his breath.

'And then I remembered the kitchen floor collapsing into the cellars at Ironmonger's Lane. Robert retrieved some bricks from the cellar and I heard him say, "Maundrell was right!" He was very distressed but wouldn't tell me why. It's taken me until now to understand that he'd just realised that the cellar was built with the unstable bricks. It's no wonder the walls were cracking so badly.'

'I suspect Hackett decided to use up the faulty bricks in places they weren't likely to be noticed,' said Gabriel, frowning. 'I wonder if he also used them for building internal walls in his houses. Once they were plastered over no one would be any the wiser. It would have been a very costly exercise to dispose of all the bad bricks in the river as he said he'd done.'

'So he knowingly used dangerous bricks in his building works?' said Jane.

'And he can't blame that on poor, dead Robert Finche!' said Ben.

'The question is, what shall we do about it now?' said Gabriel.

'There is something else,' I said slowly. 'On the day Hackett attacked me, the magistrate, Mr Clifton, was in Hackett's office. Hackett was going to take him to Rochester Court to choose one of the houses for his daughter to live in.'

'But, if the cellars are at risk of crumbling, won't that be terribly hazardous for her?' said Jane.

'And for any family that lives in Rochester Court. We must go and see Mr Clifton first thing in the morning,' said Gabriel.

The following morning, Gabriel called for his carriage and we set off for Mr Clifton's chambers. It was the first time we'd been alone for more than a few minutes since the night we had lain in each other's arms. His expression was remote and I was relieved that he didn't seem inclined to make conversation. I studied his face, engraving it upon my memory, knowing that before long I would never see him again.

'Kate?' He reached out to me. 'We can't go on ignoring each other. Can we not still be friends?'

I looked at his hand and the desire to raise it to my lips and smother it with kisses nearly overwhelmed me. 'No!' I said, harshly. Friends! How could he be content with mere friendship after the passion of the night we had spent together?

'As you wish,' he said.

My heart broke all over again as I saw the familiar remote expression settle upon his face.

We arrived at Clifton's chambers and Gabriel descended from the carriage and handed me down. The brief touch of his hand nearly made me cry out but he released me immediately.

'You'll have to guide me,' he said, 'if you don't find it too distasteful.'

'Don't make this any more difficult than it is, Gabriel.' I took his arm and led him towards the door, trying to ignore the bittersweet yearning that overcame me at his close proximity.

Once inside, a clerk showed us into Mr Clifton's office.

'What can I do for you?' said Clifton. 'Don't I know you from somewhere?'

'Gabriel Harte, perfumer,' Gabriel said. 'We were introduced at Standfast-for-Jesus Hackett's assembly last year.'

'Ah! I remember now. M'wife buys her perfume from you.'

'This is Mistress Finche, widow of Robert Finche, one-time employee of Mr Hackett's. We have a story to tell you of murder and deceit.'

'How very interesting!' Clifton yawned and glanced at the clock on the mantelpiece.

'Mr Hackett murdered my husband and attempted to kill me,' I said, irritated by his condescending manner and unable to hold my tongue.

Clifton's bushy eyebrows disappeared momentarily under his wig. 'Is that so?

I lifted my chin and looked straight back at him. 'It is, sir.'

He pursed his lips. 'What nonsense is this? I know Mr Hackett personally.'

'It's not nonsense!'

'And when did you say this unlikely event happened, madam?' He laughed in disbelief.

'On the day I saw you at his chambers. I heard Mr Hackett arranging to take you to see one of his houses in Rochester Court and then invite you to dine at the Folly. He advised you to leave your wife at home, I remember, since the serving wenches are so obliging.'

All traces of amusement left Clifton's face. 'And why should I listen to this tarradiddle of a story?'

'Because it's the truth,' said Gabriel.

'I know Mr Hackett better than that,' said Clifton, his voice hardening. 'He's a most generous man. Why, he even offered me a house in Rochester Court for a peppercorn rent for my daughter, a recent widow with five children.'

'That is the reason we are here today,' said Gabriel.

'I do hope he doesn't impose the same conditions upon your daughter that he imposed on me,' I said.

'Conditions?'

'He demanded that I become his mistress in payment for my accommodation.'

'Madam, you insult a man I respect!'

My temper rose and made me speak before I could curb my tongue. 'Then you are a fool, sir.'

Gabriel caught at my sleeve. 'Mr Clifton, I assure you that Mistress Harte tells the truth.'

'What are you to this woman? Her protector, perhaps?'

'I am not,' he said, 'and you insult this lady. I am, however, part owner of the properties in Rochester Court. Mr Hackett has not discussed with me any plans to rent out the properties at a reduced rent. I expect a full return on my investment and will be asking Mr Hackett some very pointed questions as to why he feels it necessary to agree such a peppercorn rent with you when he assured me that the highest rents would be secured for these properties. I wonder, sir, what it is that he wishes from you in return?'

Clifton became very still.

'It has come to my attention that Mr Hackett sometimes pays less attention to the requirements of the Rebuilding Act than he should,' said Gabriel. 'Perhaps it would suit him if the local magistrate were to turn a blind eye when, for example, he built without the proper permissions? Were you aware that he threatened the original tenants of the old buildings in Rochester Court, finally setting their home on fire? A mother and her children were burned alive.'

Clifton sank down on his desk chair, his face a peculiar shade of grey.

'Perhaps you will allow us to recount the whole story from the beginning?' said Gabriel. 'We wish your daughter to avoid becoming yet another of Hackett's victims.'

Clifton opened a cupboard beneath his desk and took out a bottle and a glass with trembling hands. He poured himself a generous measure and drank it in one.

'I don't know what to believe,' Clifton said, half an hour later, his head in his hands. 'If Hackett is indeed the monster you make him out to be then he must be brought to justice. But he has a great many friends –'

'And as many enemies!' I interrupted.

'*Important* friends.' Clifton frowned at me. 'To accuse him falsely of wrongdoing would be the end of me. I have no wish to risk my daughter's life but there's no proof that the new Rochester Court is unsafe.'

'You must see for yourself,' said Gabriel. 'I suggest Ben Perkins takes you into the cellars once all the workmen have left for the day.'

'The faulty bricks are a distinctive dirty yellow,' I said.

'I shall make my own enquiries,' said Clifton.

'Then I suggest we meet again after you've done so,' said Gabriel, picking up his hat. 'And please remember that Mistress Finche's safety depends upon you not telling Hackett that she survived his assault.'

In the carriage a little while later, Gabriel said, 'I'm not sure he's entirely convinced.'

'If we don't convince him, others may die,' I said. 'We *must* find a way to make him believe us.'

'He needs to hear Hackett admit to his crimes,' said Gabriel. 'But that's unlikely to happen isn't it?'

I sat in silence pondering Gabriel's comment for the rest of the journey.

Two weeks later I sat on the window seat in my bedchamber, full of anxious thoughts. I still hadn't received a response from Aunt Mercy and my apprehension increased every day that passed. Within the month I'd have to let out my bodices and then Jane would be sure to notice my condition. Once Aunt Mercy's letter arrived, and please God it would, I'd have to leave immediately if I was to keep my shameful secret.

A carriage drove into view and pulled up in front of the House of Perfume. Curious, I watched from the window and saw the portly figure of Mr Clifton step down from the carriage. A moment later I heard Jacob open the door and then Clifton's voice in the hall asking for Gabriel.

I hurried downstairs to find Clifton about to leave. 'Mr Clifton!' I called.

'Mistress Finche.' He made the smallest bow he could without being impolite. 'I understand Mr Harte is not at home.'

'Is there some news?' I asked. He hesitated long enough for me to say, 'Please, tell me what you have discovered.'

Jacob eyed me speculatively as I followed Clifton into the drawing room and closed the door behind us.

'I've been making enquiries about the house that collapsed,' said Clifton. 'Whilst the story about faulty bricks has been corroborated by various builders, they've all told me that Mr Hackett was cruelly deceived by your husband.'

A hot flush of anger flooded over me. 'But can't you see? Hackett has used my husband as a scapegoat.'

Clifton shrugged.

'Listen to me, Mr Clifton. There's no time to waste. Before long families will be moving into Rochester Court and their lives will be at risk because you haven't acted. Do you want their deaths upon your conscience?'

'Your dramatic skills might be better suited to the stage, madam.'

'Will you go and look at the cellars of Rochester Court? Please?'

'That is why I came to see Mr Harte. Mr Hackett himself took me to see them.'

'And?' I said, eagerly.

'There's nothing to see.'

'I don't understand.'

'The cellars are commodious with several store rooms and a cistern. The ceilings are of a good height –'

'But the walls?' I interrupted.

'The walls are neatly plastered and whitewashed.'

I sat down suddenly. 'You can't see the bricks?'

'Not at all. All the houses are plastered and freshly decorated ready for occupation.'

'So he waited until the last moment before sale to cover up any cracks by plastering over them.' I should have known that Hackett would find a crafty way to slide out of trouble.

'If such cracks exist.'

His cynical tone made me angry. 'So, you're prepared to risk the lives of your daughter and your five grandchildren because you're frightened to upset Hackett? I thought better of you. I believe I must speak with your wife and your daughter.'

'You will not!'

'If you take so little care of your family, then it is my duty to warn them.' I sighed, weariness overtaking anger. 'I must make Hackett confess to his wrongdoings.'

Clifton gave a snort of laughter. 'And how would you propose to do that?'

'If I lure Hackett there and flatter him into confessing.'

'Why would he?'

'Because he's unbelievably arrogant and because he already has cause to wonder if I didn't drown. He won't be able to resist the chance to remove any threat that I might incriminate him. If he believes I'm alone he'll plan to kill me.' A shudder ran down my back at the thought of it. 'He won't care what he admits and I'll encourage him to boast of his misdeeds. If you're concealed in the house where you can overhear us then you'll know the truth.'

Clifton frowned. 'If Hackett is as dangerous as you say he is you'd be at risk.'

'You can have your constables nearby and whistle for them as soon as you've heard his confession.'

'And you're prepared to risk your life to bring Hackett to justice?'

'I'm frightened half to death,' I said, 'but there isn't any choice, is there?'

We made our plans and, after Clifton had gone, I went to my bedchamber and wrote to Hackett. It took several attempts but at last I was satisfied. Sprinkling sand onto the wet ink I read it again.

Dear Mr Hackett

It may come as a surprise to you to receive this letter but I am alive and well, although not happy.

I regret most sincerely that I did not accept your generous offer last year to be my protector, not understanding at the time how much better you knew the world than I. I humbly beg your pardon. I wish I could turn back time, as I crave nothing more than to be your mistress.

If you will come to meet me at nine o'clock tomorrow evening at number 1 Rochester Court, I will endeavour to show you just how grateful I would be, should you offer me such an opportunity again.

In hope and expectation.

Katherine Finche

I hoped that my letter would appeal sufficiently to Hackett's monumental vanity to lure him to Rochester Court. After that it would be up to me to encourage him into boasting about his exploits.

After further thought, I scribbled a note to Ben Perkins, asking him to meet me in the garden that evening to seek his assistance in the arrangements for the following day. Then I asked Ann to deliver both letters.

Whatever happened, I couldn't let Gabriel have any inkling of my plans since I knew he'd never allow me to carry them out.

Chapter 35

I met Ben again at the kitchen door the following afternoon.

'It's all arranged,' he said. 'The back door of number one, Rochester Court will be unlocked. Clifton will be hiding in the pantry, ready for when Hackett arrives at nine o'clock tonight.'

'I'll be there by a quarter to nine.' I was numb with sudden fear.

'When you hear Clifton's whistle run to the pantry and lock yourself in.' Ben smiled. 'I broke in last night and fitted a strong bolt to the door.'

'And Clifton's men will be outside?'

Ben nodded. 'Dick and I will stay well clear of the house until Hackett's gone in, but then we'll be nearby too, so don't worry! Stay in the pantry until we tell you it's safe.'

'So we're ready then?' I felt anything but ready.

'You have great courage, Mistress Finche. There's not many ladies as would do this.' Ben held out his hand. 'Until tonight, then.'

'Tonight,' I echoed, feeling sick.

At half past eight I pleaded a headache and declined to join Jane and Gabriel in the drawing room. As I was placing a note on my pillow, just in case my plan failed, I heard Toby crying. Torn, I stood motionless at the top of the stairs, but the sound of the little boy's tears made me turn back.

He held his arms out to me and I wiped his tear-stained face and soothed him until his bad dream was forgotten. When his eyes closed again, I kissed his forehead and laid him back into bed, conscious that I was now very late.

I hurried downstairs and crept past the kitchen where Mistress Jenks and Ann were having a late supper. Shadow materialised beside me, thrusting his wet nose into my hand but I pushed him away. Donning my cloak, and lighting the lantern, I slipped out through the back door.

Dusk was falling as I ran along Long Acre. I passed Drury Lane where the whores displayed their wares in the doorways, every step taking me closer to the dangerous situation I'd set in motion.

Sprinting along the dark alleyway leading to Rochester Court, I heard a noise behind me and held up the lantern in sudden panic.

Shadow ran up to me, wagging his tail.

'You bad boy!' I whispered. 'You frightened me half to death.' I held up my hand. 'Now stay!'

Ears cocked, he watched me closely as I hurried to the end of the alley.

There was sufficient moonlight to see that Rochester Court was deserted. The houses were finished now, but, devoid of all signs of life, curiously menacing as they loomed above me. My mouth was dry and my stomach churned at the thought of crossing the open space. I wondered if Clifton's men were already watching me from the shadows. I took several deep breaths and, before I could change my mind, launched myself out of the alley towards the house.

At the corner of the building I stopped and peered around it. Clouds sailed across the moon as I hurried to the back door. I pushed it open with the tip of my finger and it swung silently inwards. Glancing over my shoulder, I stepped inside.

I stood still for a moment but heard nothing save the rapid beat of my heart. Counting the steps to steady my nerves, I made my way to the kitchen.

'Mr Clifton?' I whispered.

The pantry door opened a crack and my lantern illuminated his face.

'If I find that you've taken me on a fool's errand be sure you will suffer for it,' he said. 'It's damnably cramped in here and smells of mice.'

'Ssh!' I said.

We listened to the grating of a key being turned in the front door.

I doused the lantern, the pantry door closed swiftly in my face and I withdrew to the corner of the kitchen, shaking like a Quaker.

Furtive footfalls sounded across the bare boards of the hall above.

It was time. I was about to play a dangerous game and must act my part convincingly or risk the lives of yet more innocent souls. I swallowed, stood up as tall as I could and walked to the bottom of the stairs. 'Mr Hackett?' I called.

The footsteps stopped.

I forced myself to breathe steadily. 'Mr Hackett?' I called. 'It's Katherine Finche. Are you there?'

A wavering light appeared at the top of the stairs and the author of my nightmares emerged from the darkness. Hackett's lantern threw menacing shadows up onto the wall and it was all I could do not to turn and run.

'I trust you're alone?' he said.

Smiling boldly, I spread my palms wide. 'As you see. And I thank you for giving me the opportunity to show you how grateful I will be, should you make your previous offer available to me again.' I turned and walked away from him, glancing back coquettishly over my shoulder.

Hackett's footsteps clumped down the stairs and the back of my neck crawled as if his hot breath was already on my naked skin.

I waited for him in the kitchen, squeezing my hands together behind my back to prevent them trembling.

He shouldered his way through the doorway and planted himself in front of me. 'So, I *did* see you in the street that day and the Hartes have conspired against me. No one makes a fool of Standfast-For-Jesus-Hackett and gets away with it. But that's for later. Now, what do you have to say for yourself, madam?'

'I misjudged you, Mr Hackett,' I said.

Placing his lantern on the floor, he raised one eyebrow.

'Before I, shall we say, *disappeared*, I wasn't fully aware of what a powerful and influential man you are.' I leaned back, resting one foot against the wall and pushing my breasts forwards, just as I had seen the whores do.

Hackett's gaze raked up and down my body.

'Since then,' I said, looking up at him with limpid eyes, 'I've discovered that you let nothing stand in the way of your desires. Like Rochester Court for example.' I clenched my teeth together to stop them chattering.

'What do you know of that?' He narrowed his eyes.

I held his stare; I couldn't lose my nerve now and must play the game to the end. 'Only that you determined you would build your fine houses here and, a landlord reluctant to sell the land and a family that refused to leave, were swept away by the strength of your desire.' I laughed, low and throaty. 'You are invincible, Mr Hackett.'

'I do believe that I am,' he said.

'I find that extremely attractive in a man.'

Hackett smirked and it took everything I had not to show my revulsion. By God, he believed me! Was there no end to his self-conceit?

'I'd no intention of letting an old man and a handful of peasants come between me and my ambitions,' he said.

'How amusing it must have been when you threw the lighted firebrands in through the window as they slept!' I held my breath. Had I gone too far?

'Burned some of 'em alive!' Hackett's eyes gleamed in the light of the lantern. 'What a hullabaloo there was, like poking a stick into an ants' nest.'

Hackett had confessed to murder! I licked my lips and looked up at him with a brazen stare while I waited for Clifton to blow his whistle.

Silence.

Why hadn't Clifton called his men? 'Power excites me,' I said. I must keep him talking until help arrived.

'Does it now? I often wondered if there were secret fires burning under your meek exterior.'

'There's a certain frisson that comes from being entirely helpless in the hands of a strong man, who wishes to bend me to his will. My husband . . . ' I paused.

'Ah, yes, Robert Finche.'

'Even though I didn't realise it at first, you did me a great favour by removing him from my life.' Slowly I undid the ties of my cloak to expose my décolletage. Dare I encourage him into confessing he'd murdered Robert, too, before Clifton blew the whistle? 'You cannot imagine how I'd tired of his weak and ineffectual ways,' I said. 'Especially in the bedchamber.'

'Robert Finche was an arse-licker.' Hackett's gaze was fixed upon my breasts. 'And whatever made him imagine that I'd clear his father's debts? I heard later that Harte paid them off but Finche Senior paid him back by turning up his toes that very day. What a waste!' He sniggered. 'You should have heard Finche snivelling and begging me for mercy when I kicked him into the river.'

'And it was a masterstroke when, after he was dead, you blamed him and Elias Maundrell for the crumbling bricks you sold.' Why hadn't Clifton blown his whistle? My mouth was dry. How long could I hold Hackett off before he pounced on me?

Hackett smiled, his thick lips glistening. 'I did away with that whingeing Maundrell, too. A clever twist, was it not, to blame the men who threatened to expose me?'

'Diabolical,' I said, feeling queasy with dread. I *had* to get away before he touched me.

Hackett stretched out towards my breast and my nerve snapped. Terrified, I whipped off my cloak and threw it at him, enveloping his head and shoulders.

He gave a muffled bellow of rage as I took three steps across the kitchen and grasped the latch of the pantry door. I tugged at it but it refused to open. Panicking, I realised Clifton had bolted my safe refuge from the inside. I banged on the door with my fist but out of the corner of my eye I saw Hackett freeing himself from the cloak.

I turned on my heel but it was too late.

'Come here, you little slut!' Hackett caught my wrist and forced it up behind my back.

I screamed as red-hot agony shot up my arm like a trail of boiling lead.

'So, you like being helpless in the arms of a strong man, do you?' He pushed me against the wall and thrust his great knee between my legs, his rank breath in my nostrils. 'Then I'm about to make you a very happy woman,' he whispered.

His hold on me was so tight that it was pointless to struggle. I glimpsed the lantern burning on the windowsill. If only I could ... Suddenly, I let myself go limp and leaned back in his embrace so that I could look up at him. 'Kiss me,' I whispered.

Surprised, he relaxed his hold. I stared back at him with a half-smile and closed my eyes as his mouth came down on mine, trying not to retch as his slimy tongue forced its way between my teeth.

He freed my wrist and clasped my breast, kneading and pinching at it. My involuntary whimper only seemed to excite him further.

Slipping one arm around his great bull neck, I stretched out behind me with the other, fingers extended towards the lantern, but it was a few inches too far away. I moaned softly and arched my back as if in ecstasy, bending backwards. He moved with me, his wet lips sucking mine, while my fingers scrabbled behind me for the lantern. I flinched as the hot metal burned my thumb and fumbled until I found the handle. I had it! I grasped it and swung it in an arc, smashing it with force against the back of Hackett's head. The lantern went out and Hackett groaned and sank against me, his fingers releasing my breast. I slithered out of his grasp as he fell to the ground.

It was pitch black.

I reached out, panic bubbling in my throat. I had to find the back door. Eyes wide as I stared into the blackness, I took a hesitant step forwards, picturing the route. I counted the steps, bumped into the doorframe, turned a fraction and found the corridor. A cold draught played on my face and, as my eyes adjusted to the dark, I saw the lighter rectangle of the open back door at the end of the passage. I ran towards it, my heart lifting and then stopped dead.

Outside, a light glimmered and I caught a whiff of tobacco. I peered into the night and saw Nat Hogg. If I ventured outside, he'd see me. I bolted the back door so Nat couldn't come after me and unlocked the doors on either side of the passage. One led to a windowless storeroom and the other to a cellar. There was nothing for it, I'd have to creep back past Hackett and leave by the front door.

Hackett was breathing heavily as I tiptoed past, holding my breath. Suddenly, my ankle was caught in a hot grip. I screamed like a banshee and kicked out, driven by terror. My foot connected, Hackett grunted and pulled off my shoe as I dragged my foot free.

I ran blindly, careering into the walls, until I banged my hand on the newel post. I found the bottom stair and raced upwards, two at a time, with my skirts held up to my knees. Stumbling through the hall, I heard Hackett cursing and blundering about in the darkness below. I located the front door and fumbled with clumsy fingers until I found the handle. It wouldn't turn. Sobbing, I banged on the door but it was too late; Hackett was behind me.

'I'm not so stupid I'd leave the door unlocked,' he called out, a note of triumph in his voice. 'Come here, you minx. I'll have you in the end.'

Flattening myself against the wall, the air moved as he passed me. He must have sensed me because, as I whirled around, his fists rained down upon me, beating me about the head and shoulders. I sank to the ground, my arms over my head.

Hackett's laugh was jubilant and I screamed as his great booted feet kicked me again and again and then stamped on my fingers.

Downstairs, I heard a deep, rumbling growl and a volley of barks. There was a furious clatter of claws on the bare boards and fur brushed past my face. Then Shadow was snarling and snapping as he tore at Hackett's body and clothes.

Painfully slowly, I crawled to the top of the stairs and hung, sobbing, onto the banister rail listening to Hackett's yells. I dragged myself downstairs, every step an agony. There was no choice but to take my chance with Nat Hogg.

Shadow gave a sharp yelp and then there was silence for a moment before I heard Hackett cursing as he clumped down the stairs after me.

Feverishly, I dragged at the back door bolt but my bleeding fingers were stiff and unresponsive. I couldn't do it! I shrank back into the storeroom but then, as I listened to Hackett's footsteps approaching, I had an idea. I slipped off my remaining shoe and held it ready. When I estimated that he was about six or eight feet away I threw it across the passageway, into the open doorway of the cellar.

'I've got you now!' crooned Hackett. 'Come to me, my pretty! I know you're down there.'

Holding my breath, I waited until he'd descended several steps then threw myself across the passage, slammed the cellar door behind him and jammed the bolt home.

Hackett roared in fury and began to pound upon the door.

I lost no time in struggling again with the back door bolt, finally easing it free. I opened the door a crack and slipped outside.

Chapter 36

Head down, I scurried barefoot around the side of the building towards the court. I hadn't gone more than a few steps when I collided with a dark shape that appeared out of the shadows. A hand went over my mouth and stifled my scream.

'Ssh!' whispered a voice in my ear. 'It's Gabriel.'

Nearly fainting in relief, I sagged against his broad chest.

He crushed me so tightly against him that I cried out, the bruises on my body throbbing. I clung to him, allowing myself the momentary luxury of his arms around me, wishing I could stay there forever.

Carefully, he removed his hand from my mouth. 'Why in God's name didn't you tell me what you were planning,' he hissed.

'I thought you were Nat Hogg!' I said, my teeth chattering uncontrollably.

Angry voices broke through the night, followed by the sound of shattering glass. We hurried to the front of the building where a crowd of men were milling about carrying flaming torches and crowbars.

Dick Plumridge ran up to us and caught hold of my arm. 'Where's Hackett?'

'I locked him in the cellar.'

'Then we've got him!'

A roar of approval rent the air and Dick limped forwards and, with a great cry of triumph, lobbed a brick at one of the windows.

I watched in shock as another man threw a flaming torch through the broken glass and another followed suit.

'Gabriel! They're setting the house on fire and Clifton and Hackett are inside.'

'Clifton's there? He didn't blow his whistle so his men went home. We thought he'd decided not to come.'

'He locked the pantry from the inside when Hackett arrived and I had nowhere safe to retreat to.' I wrapped my arms around my bruised and aching stomach, fear that Hackett might have harmed my baby making me shiver.

'The lily-livered . . . '

I flinched as a brick flew over our heads and another window shattered, showering us in shards of glass.

'We must make them stop, Gabriel!'

Gabriel bellowed at the crowd. 'Hey! There's an innocent man inside!'

'Innocent! Hackett?' came a hoarse shout. 'He's a murderer!'

'Hanging's too good for him!'

The crowd laughed, the sound echoing around the court and mayhem broke loose. The men surged forwards, smashing windows and throwing their torches inside, yelling and whooping.

'Stop!' shouted Gabriel.

The men, consumed by bloodlust, paid no heed. They marshalled themselves into groups, armed themselves with timber roof beams and took it in turns to run up to the row of houses and batter the walls.

'They're completely lost to reason.' I gasped as flames leaped out of an upstairs window. 'Shadow's in there,' I said, close to tears. 'Hackett hurt him.'

'I don't give a damn about Hackett, but we can't let Clifton or Shadow burn alive,' said Gabriel. 'I'm going in to get them.'

'You can't!'

'Someone must and, since Clifton's men have sloped off, it'll have to be me.'

'I'll go.'

'Absolutely not! Now give me some guidance.'

I looked at the flames and smoke pouring out of the upstairs windows. 'The first floor is on fire!'

The men roared as they thumped their battering rams at the walls again and again.

Gabriel caught hold of me. 'How many steps to the kitchen? And where's the pantry?'

I closed my eyes while I thought. 'From the back door the cellar is two steps in on your left. Seven more steps and the kitchen door is on the left again.' I gasped as the battering ram crashed against the house once more.

'Go on!' Gabriel urged.

'Inside the kitchen, the pantry is on your right, four steps away, I think. Don't forget that your strides are longer than mine.'

'And the stairs?'

'Four steps from the kitchen door towards the front of the house, on your right. Fourteen stairs. But the drawing room is on fire. Perhaps I should go? I know where the pantry is.'

A battering ram slammed into the house, making it shudder again.

'No time to argue about it! Besides, you're as blind as I am in the dark. The sooner I let Clifton and Hackett out, the better. If Rochester Court doesn't go up in flames the men will batter it down.'

'Hackett's dangerous.'

'He's hardly going to harm us when there are so many angry people about, is he? But Ben is on the other side of the court with Jacob, tying up Nat Hogg. Will you ask him to bring a couple of men?'

'Wait here!'

I hurried through the jeering crowd, searching for Ben through the confusion as the men ran backwards and forwards in the dark pounding the row of burning houses, their angry faces illuminated orange by the flames. I found Ben and Jacob bending over Nat Hogg, who lay bound hand and foot on the ground.

'You're safe!' said Ben, smiling in relief. 'Did you find Mr Harte?'

'He's going back into the house. Clifton locked himself in the pantry.'

Jacob grabbed my bruised wrist and I winced. 'Surely, you didn't let my master, a blind man, enter a burning building?' he said.

'Have you ever stopped him from doing something he was set on, Jacob?' I shook him off. 'Ben, Hackett's locked in the cellar. Will you bring some men to restrain him?'

'Jacob, stay with this useless piece of horse shit, will you?' said Ben, poking Nat with the toe of his boot.

Nat wriggled but was so tightly bound and gagged he could do no more than glare venomously at us.

Jacob gave me a hard stare. 'If Mr Harte is harmed I'll lay the blame at your door.'

Before I could reply, Ben took off across the court and I hurried after him.

The roof of Rochester Court was well and truly alight now and the fearful crackling of the burning timbers sent shivers down my spine. It brought back to me with fearful clarity the horror of the Great Fire.

Ben called to three other men and we ran together to the back of the building.

As we turned the corner, Clifton erupted from the back door of the house, followed by a cloud of smoke. He came to an abrupt standstill when he saw me.

'I thought Hackett had murdered you!' he said, his hand clasped to his chest.

'Since you denied me a safe retreat, he nearly did,' I said, acidly.

Clifton had the good grace to lower his gaze. 'It would have been foolhardy to expose myself to danger,' he said.

'Shame on you!' said one of Ben's companions.

'I trust you heard enough of my performance to give you sufficient evidence to take Hackett up for murder?' I said.

Clifton nodded. He started as another thump reverberated through the building, followed by a resounding crash and then a loud cheer.

'Where's Mr Harte?' I asked.

Another crash came from the front of the building followed by surging smoke from the windows.

'I thought he was following me,' said Clifton.

Dread clutched at me. 'He must have gone to look for Shadow.' I didn't hesitate; all I knew was that I had to find him. I shoved past Ben and through the door.

The fire roared away upstairs and the passage was filled with swirling smoke. I snatched up my skirts to cover my nose and mouth. Gabriel was nowhere to be seen but Hackett's muffled shouts and curses drifted up from the cellar.

Coughing, I felt my way up the stairs towards the glow of the flames. Air rushed past me, sucked from the broken windows towards the fire. Images of the flaming warehouse roof kept flashing through my mind and I faltered, suddenly too frightened to go on. But there was still no sign of either Gabriel or Shadow through the swirling smoke and I couldn't leave them to perish. I'd found the courage once before and must do so again. I swallowed my fear and moved forwards.

I peered into the drawing room but shrank back at the intense heat. No one could survive in that inferno. Hurrying, I ran to the dining room at the other end of the landing, but that, too, was empty except for the raging fire.

'Gabriel!' I screamed, full of fear for him.

The battering rams intensified their rhythmic banging at the front of the house. The vibrations ran through the soles of my bare feet and I felt them in my aching stomach. A scattering of dust began to fall from above and, suddenly, a section of the ceiling detached itself. I screamed as the mass of plaster crashed to the floor. Choking dust filled the overheated air.

'Kate? Is that you?'

'Gabriel?' I looked up at the staircase to the second floor and, as the dust began to settle, I glimpsed him going upstairs. 'Thank God! Come down, Gabriel! Clifton is safe,' I shouted over the roar of the flames.

'God's teeth, Kate! Get out now!'

'But . . . '

'Now! Do as you're told!' he shouted over his shoulder. Smoke hung in a cloud at the top of the stairs and I heard him whistling for Shadow as he disappeared into it.

I raced up the stairs behind him. The front bedroom was ablaze and the passage ceiling alight. Then Gabriel, carrying Shadow in his arms, appeared out of the smoke.

'You found him!' I said, almost crying in relief.

'Didn't I tell you to leave?' Gabriel's voice was furious.

'Is he all right?'

'Just get out of here!'

'Not without you.'

He started to cough and I clutched his sleeve and pulled him to the top of the stairs. We were halfway down when there was almighty crash at the front of the house followed by the thunder of falling masonry.

'What's happened?' asked Gabriel.

'The whole front wall of the house has collapsed.' The cold night air rushed past us and the flames grew in strength, dancing even higher. 'Four more steps,' I shouted over the clamour.

We reached the bottom of the staircase but there was no escape by the open front of the house through the flames.

Dry-mouthed with fright, I grasped Gabriel's sleeve more tightly. I remembered crawling through the smoke and flames in the Finche warehouse, while the spices fizzed and popped as the barrels caught alight. I'd been lucky then but was it too much to hope to escape this time?

Outside, men shouted and cheered as they continued their onslaught on the building and pieces of burning timber rained down on us from the floor above.

I sobbed in relief as we reached the bottom of the last flight of stairs and set off along the smoky passage to the back door. Then the staircase groaned and began to tilt. I screamed and dragged Gabriel clear as it sank to the ground. Acrid smoke whirled around us.

A moment later, coughing and heaving for breath, we burst out of the smoke-filled passage into the night air. Ben pulled us clear as another deafening crash resounded through the building.

'It's going to collapse!' warned Dick.

'Hackett,' gasped Gabriel.

'Bugger Hackett!'

'You can't leave him,' I said. 'If you do you're as much of a murderer as he is.'

Dick stared at me, his scarred face twisted with emotion. Then he turned and limped through the smoke-filled doorway.

Ben ran after him.

Jacob appeared, casting me a look of hatred. His expression softened when he saw Gabriel.

Shadow staggered to his feet, shook himself free of plaster dust and limped to my side.

We withdrew and waited at a safe distance. Jacob and I watched the angry flames leaping from the roof and windows high into the night sky as the men, raging out of control, screamed encouragement to each other as they pounded the row of houses.

Gabriel's face was smeared with soot and blood ran down his cheek. 'Have Ben and Dick come out yet?'

But my gaze was fixed in awful fascination on Rochester Court as it began to shudder. Slowly, slowly, one end began to crumple. The rest followed like a pack of cards knocked aside by a careless hand. A great blast of heat and smoke made me gasp and turn my face away, my hands over my ears to shut out the thunderous crash. The earth shook and the vibrations shuddered through me, right into the marrow of my bones.

The men cheered and catcalled, hugging each other and dancing around by the light of the flames like savages from the New World.

'There they are!' I shouted, as Ben and Dick emerged from the dust and smoke cloud.

I ran to Ben. 'Hackett?' I asked.

'Dick unbolted the cellar door but then the building begin to shake and we legged it.'

'Hackett must still be inside,' said Dick, 'and I can't say I'm sorry.'

A whistle blew and a dozen men ran into the court with a fire engine, and set to work pumping water onto the flames. I saw that Clifton was giving them their orders.

'Hackett's inside,' I said.

'Can't do anything about that until the fire's out,' Clifton said. 'Besides, I'm not prepared to risk my men's lives for a thug who's going to hang.' He gave Ben a meaningful glance. 'And I shall have to round up those responsible for this terrible act of destruction if they're still here when the water engine is empty.'

Ben slipped away and I watched him spreading the word. Before five minutes were out, all the men had melted into the night.

I returned to Gabriel and explained from the beginning what had happened. Grim-faced, he listened, his fists clenching when I recounted Hackett's treatment of me. 'Why didn't you let me know what you were planning?' he said, at last.

'I couldn't. You would have stopped me.'

'Of course I would!'

'If Hackett hadn't been stopped, he'd have gone on ruining people's lives,' I said, refusing to discuss it further.

'Jacob came to tell me you were up to no good,' said Gabriel, 'so I followed you. And then Ben told me what you'd planned but I was too late to stop you.'

I began to shake. Now that we were safe I had time to feel my burned feet and the painful ache in my stomach. Exhaustion and shock made my knees tremble.

'We should go home,' Gabriel said. 'There's nothing more we can do here tonight.'

Wearily, we walked away with Shadow limping behind us.

Jane was beside herself with worry when we returned and her anxiety turned to horror when we described what had happened. She rose from her bed, bathed our faces and applied salve to our wounds.

Tears welled up in my eyes. I could hardly bear her kindness when I knew how I had betrayed her. I pleaded exhaustion and made my escape upstairs.

In my bedchamber, I pulled off my chemise and drew in my breath at the ugly bruises spreading across my abdomen and hips. It was then I saw the trickle of blood running down the inside of my thighs.

Curled up on the bed with my hands protectively wrapped around my stomach, I wept.

Chapter 37

I groaned when I awoke, every part of my body in torment. As I stared at the ceiling, the events of the previous night came back to me. I threw back the sheet in a panic but saw that I had lost no more blood.

Slowly, I washed away the acrid smell of smoke and dressed. The relief I felt that I hadn't miscarried was offset by renewed fears for the future. A letter still hadn't come from Aunt Mercy and now I was afraid it never would. I could hardly breathe at the thought of what might happen to me and my baby.

Gabriel was already at the breakfast table when I made my appearance.

'I'll go with Jacob this morning to discover if Hackett has been rescued,' he said.

'I'll accompany you,' I said, even though the thought of walking any distance at all was almost unbearable.

Gabriel opened his mouth and I steeled myself to argue with him but then he sighed. 'I daresay it would be a complete waste of effort to stop you,' he said.

'It would.'

'Shall we go then?'

A mountain of bricks and smouldering beams were all that remained of Rochester Court. The persistent drizzle that fell from a leaden sky steamed as it landed on the glowing ruins but I saw that Clifton's men had already started to dig away the wreckage.

Gabriel and I sat on a wall and waited as load after load of rubble was cleared away.

'Still no sign of Hackett?' asked Gabriel, pulling up the collar of his cloak against the rain.

'None.'

'Shall I take you home again?'

'I must know.'

We sat in silence, while I studied Gabriel's profile, remembering how he had held me the previous night. I suspected that with one encouraging word from me he would enfold me in his arms again. But I had no desire to be merely his mistress and my love for him threatened Jane and Toby's happiness. Loneliness and abject misery washed over me and I turned back to watch the excavations.

It was another half an hour before a shout went up.

We hurried closer to the men crowding around the exposed cellar entrance. Ten minutes later Hackett, moaning pitiably, was dragged free of the rubble.

'His leg's crushed,' said one of the men.

'Bring him to the jail,' commanded Clifton. 'And we'll send for the surgeon.'

Hackett shouted in agony and blood spurted from his leg as he was dumped onto a door retrieved from the wreckage. Then he caught sight of me. 'You duped me, you little whore!' he snarled.

Gabriel surged forwards, anger twisting his face and I grasped his sleeve.

'Don't, Gabriel,' I said.

'I'll come after you, Katherine Finche,' screamed Hackett, ' if it's the last thing I ever do! There'll be no place you can hide.'

It took six men to carry him away. After his curses had faded into the distance I was faint with exhaustion again and my hands trembled.

'Let's go home,' said Gabriel.

The following day, Jane fell ill again. I sat beside her as she lay on her bed, her face as pale as whey. I closed the shutters to keep the spring sunshine from hurting her eyes, fed her chicken broth and massaged her temples with lavender oil.

'You're so very good to me,' she whispered, clasping my hand.

Whatever small comfort I offered her could never be recompense enough to repair my terrible betrayal of our friendship. I lay awake each night, consumed with guilt, and each morning, as I dressed, it was impossible not to notice that my waist was thickening and my breasts becoming fuller. And still there was no letter from Aunt Mercy. Sitting in the sick room day after day, stroking Jane's hand and soothing her with comforting words, my fearful thoughts churned round and around in my mind like a chicken on a spit.

Time was running out and before long my condition would become obvious to all who looked at me except, ironically, Gabriel. I *had* to leave the House of Perfume before that happened. If Aunt Mercy turned me away then I'd go to the convent and beg Sister Assumpta to shelter me until the baby was born. Perhaps she could find a kind family to take the child. The agonising prospect of giving my baby away broke my heart but if I could not provide for him, what other option had I?

A week passed and Jane craved fresh air. On a balmy April morning, Gabriel carried her downstairs to sit in the garden, well wrapped up against the draughts. I too wore a thick shawl, not because I was cold but to conceal my expanding waist.

Shadow, who still limped from Hackett's ill treatment, dozed in the sunshine at Gabriel's feet, while Toby trotted around the garden on his hobby horse.

'I sent Jacob to enquire after Hackett,' said Gabriel. 'He's ill with a fever.'

'I hope he recovers,' said Jane.

'Then you are far more merciful than I,' said Gabriel.

'Not at all,' said Jane. 'I hope he recovers so that he suffers when they hang him.'

Toby galloped towards us on his hobby horse and came to sit at his mother's side.

'I do believe you have grown at least an inch this past week,' Jane said, stroking his hair. 'What a fine young man you will grow up to be.'

I noticed that tears beaded her eyelashes as she kissed his cheek.

'Mama, may we go to see the lions in the Tower? Jacob says they roar louder than thunder.'

'There are so many things I'd like us to see,' said Jane. She rested her chin on his head 'Perhaps your father and Aunt Kate will take you?'

'Will you, Aunt Kate?' Toby smiled winningly at me.

'Of course, I will.'

Ann came along the garden path carrying a tray. 'Hot chocolate,' she said, 'to ward off any chills. And there's a letter for you, Mistress Finche.'

And there it was, tucked down between the chocolate pot and the cups, with my name written on it in Aunt Mercy's crabbed hand. I had to stop myself snatching it up. I took it with an outward show of calm, just as if it didn't hold the key to the future of myself and my child. I broke the seal with trembling fingers.

Katherine,
Your letter was delayed at the Post Office so I write to you as soon as I rec'd it. I have never been found wanting when called upon to perform my Duty, however irksome, and therefore you will take the coach at your earliest convenience to Kingston. Your old room shall be prepared for you and the Child.

Since you are now without fortune you will earn your keep as my maid. I trust that you are fully conscious of my Charity and will show your gratitude in the meekness of your manner.

Your aunt
Mercy Lambert

I gritted my teeth. How very like Aunt Mercy to impress upon me that she would only perform the unpleasant task of taking me in purely in the name of Duty and Charity. But, nevertheless, she had thrown me the lifeline I needed. Besides, how terrible could it be after all I had endured?

'What is it, Kate?' asked Gabriel.

'It's from Aunt Mercy.' I swallowed, postponing the moment when I must say what had to be said. 'She's ill and has asked me to return to her house to care for her.'

Jane glanced at Gabriel, who had paused in the act of lifting his cup of chocolate to his mouth. 'But, of course, you won't go,' she said.

'I must.'

'But you can't!' Jane's face blanched. 'You can't go to *her*! She made your life a misery for years.'

'She's old and has no one else.'

'But *we* need you! Gabriel . . . ' Jane appealed to her husband.

'Must you go, Kate?' asked Gabriel. His voice was cool and dispassionate and it cut me to the quick.

'My mother would have expected me to do my duty.'

'Then we shall not hold you back.'

'No!' Jane, shaking with distress, pushed herself to her feet. 'You *must* stay, Kate.' She reached for Toby. 'Toby, tell Aunt Kate not to leave us!'

Toby's eyes were wide and frightened as he looked at me. 'But you said you and Father would take me to see the lions in the Tower, Aunt Kate.'

'But I didn't know then that Aunt Mercy was ill.'

'You *promised*!' Tears welled up and rolled down his cheeks.

'I'm sorry,' I said, wretchedly, 'but I must go.'

'How could you, Kate?' Hectic spots of colour burned in Jane's pale face. 'After all we've done for you!'

'Jane, I'll never forget your kindness . . . '

'Does it mean *nothing* that we took you in when you were destitute and welcomed you into our home? We made you one of our *family*,' she wept. 'Do you care so little for us that you will abandon us now?'

'Jane!' Gabriel halted her tirade. 'That's enough!'

'But we need Kate! Toby, especially, needs her, don't you, sweetheart?'

Toby began to cry in earnest, clinging on to me and howling, 'Don't go!'

'Jane!' said Gabriel. 'You are overwrought. If Kate must go to her aunt then we shall find another companion for Toby.'

'No one else will do!' Jane raged. 'Everything hinges on Kate. You can't just let her go!'

I couldn't bear it. It was hard enough to leave without this. 'I'm so sorry, Jane, but I have no choice . . . '

She stared at me for a long moment and then sank down onto the bench, trembling from head to toe. A pulse beat in her throat and she was deathly pale. 'No choice?'

I was unable to meet the intensity of her gaze. 'No.'

'I see,' she said, quietly. Suddenly all the rage left her. 'What have I done?' she whispered.

'How could I ever cease to be grateful to you for all you have done for me?' I blinked back tears. 'But Aunt Mercy is the only family I have.'

'But you will return to us?' asked Jane.

I said nothing, unwilling to make a promise I couldn't keep.

'When will you go?' asked Gabriel.

Toby climbed onto my knee and clung to me like a limpet, while I kissed his hair and wiped his tears away.

'The day after tomorrow,' I said. 'I shall delay my departure to take Toby to visit the lions in the Tower, as promised.'

The day after tomorrow came all too soon. I packed my meagre possessions into a canvas bag and said my goodbyes to the servants.

Jane sat in bed, her eyes hazed with pain and poppy juice. 'Don't go,' she murmured.

'I must.'

She turned her back on me and I crept from the room.

Gabriel, Toby and Shadow waited for me in the hall.

'You're not going to take Shadow away, too, are you, Aunt Kate?' said Toby.

'No, sweetheart. He'll stay to look after you and to help your father find his way around the city.'

We walked in near silence to Lincoln's Inn where the public coach already waited at the stand. Gabriel had offered me the use of his carriage but I'd refused. Neither he nor Jane knew Aunt Mercy's address and I wouldn't take the risk of them calling on me to find me heavily pregnant or with a babe in my arms.

Gabriel handed my baggage to the coachman and we waited while the other passengers climbed aboard.

'Time to go,' I said, my heart breaking as I bent to hug Toby, who smothered my face in damp kisses. 'Be good for your mama.' I couldn't look again at his woebegone face, afraid I'd weep. 'Goodbye, Gabriel.'

A muscle flickered in Gabriel's jaw but otherwise he showed no sign that he was sad I was leaving and my heart broke all over again.

'Goodbye, Kate.' He lifted my hand briefly to his lips and it took all the strength I had not to throw myself against his chest and beg him to kiss me and tell me that he loved me. But he remained silent and impassive.

I pulled my hand away and climbed into the coach.

Half blinded by tears, I stared out of the window as the coach began to move, straining to catch a last glimpse of Gabriel with Toby sobbing in his arms.

The burning pain of their loss seared my heart, the agony of it rendering me momentarily unable to breathe. I huddled into my seat, arms tight around my waist, frozen in despair.

Chapter 38

July 1669

Aunt Mercy's parlour was shuttered against the oppressive heat, allowing only a crack of sunlight to penetrate the shadowy room and illuminate the Bible on my knee. Aunt Mercy had fallen into a doze as I read to her and, even in sleep, her mouth was pursed in constant disapproval. Her bony hands were clasped like claws in her lap.

The clock ticked on in its measured way and I sighed. How many childhood hours had I spent listening to that clock ticking? But, however difficult it had been to return to Aunt Mercy's house, this time I had something wonderful to look forward to. Resting a hand on my abdomen, I smiled. In only two months I would hold my baby, Gabriel's baby, in my arms. If I had lost the man I loved, at least I would have his love child.

Aunt Mercy let out a soft snore.

She was smaller and frailer than I remembered her. Her tongue still dripped vinegar and I hated her for what she had done to me, but I remembered what Gabriel had said, that her life had been wasted in bitterness.

I arched my back, which had ached all day, and kneaded it with my fists. Yawning, I leaned back and closed my eyes. Perhaps I could snatch a few moments rest before Aunt Mercy found another task for me.

I listened to the soporific ticking of the clock and the distant rumble of traffic, hoping I would feel the baby move within me but it seemed he was sleeping, too.

'Katherine!'

My eyes snapped open and I blinked, disorientated. I must have dozed for a moment because Aunt Mercy was wide awake and her cold blue eyes bore disapprovingly into me.

'Yes, Aunt Mercy?'

'You were asleep!' she accused. 'There's no place for laziness in this house. The laundry will be dry by now. Go down to the kitchen and help Mistress Kinross with the ironing.'

'Yes, Aunt Mercy.'

'And don't forget that the pewter on the dresser needs polishing.'

'No, Aunt Mercy.' I pushed myself to my feet, trying to ignore the dull pain that came and went in my stomach. I should have known it wasn't wise to eat the green apple I'd stolen that morning from a neighbour's tree that overhung Aunt Mercy's garden.

In the kitchen Maggie Kinross sweated over the fire, steam rising from the pan of Scotch broth and loosening tendrils of hair from under her cap.

'Aunt Mercy has sent me to do the ironing,' I said.

'Has she now?' Maggie rested her hands on her hips. 'It's too hot today for anyone to be doing the ironing, never mind a woman in your condition. You look tired and you're too thin. Baby keeping you awake?'

I shook my head, wondering if I should tell her about the trickle of blood I had found between my legs again that morning but, since it had amounted to nothing, decided against it.

'I'll do the ironing this evening when it's cooler,' said Maggie. 'Sit yourself down in the shade by the kitchen door.'

'You're good to me, Maggie.'

'Aye.' Her gaunt face was softened by her smile. 'Well, someone needs to be kind to you and it isn't going to be Her Upstairs.'

It was too hot to eat much of the Scotch broth at supper that evening and once I'd helped Aunt Mercy to bed I retired to my little attic room and undressed, relieved to be free of my boned bodice. The humid air pressed down on me like a hot, wet blanket, making every movement an effort of will. It was too early to sleep so I watched the dying rays of the sun setting in a haze of gold behind the tower of All Saints in Market Place.

Later, lying in the half-dark with my hands clasped over the small mound of my stomach, I pictured, as I so often did, my last glimpse of Gabriel and Toby as the coach carried me away from London. I wondered if I'd ever lose the awful, hollow feeling of loss that still tormented me. And Jane, my dear friend whom I'd so cruelly betrayed, how could I ever forgive myself for what I'd done to her?

I turned on my side and pulled up my knees as discomfort blossomed in my pelvis. It faded after a moment and I relaxed again. Sighing, I closed my eyes and slept.

It was inky dark when the pain awoke me. A fierce convulsion gripped my stomach and I groaned and sat up. When the pain eased I lit the candle and threw back the bedclothes. I stared in shock at the blood on the sheet. Another ripple of pain began deep inside me and I gasped in horror as I realised what it meant. The baby was coming, but it was too soon. Much too soon. Another spasm came and I hung on to the bedpost, watching blood trickle down my inner thighs.

When the contraction passed, I hobbled out to the passage and banged on Maggie's door.

'What is it?' she asked, wiping sleep from her eyes. 'Is the mistress ... ' But then she saw my bloodstained shift and her face blanched. 'I'll fetch the midwife.'

I crept back to bed and curled into a ball as wave after wave of agony washed over me. Panic gripped as I realised that the baby was coming and nothing was going to stop it. Time seemed to slow down as I sweated and strained, my teeth gritted against the terror that engulfed me. Was it possible for a seven-month baby to survive?

My mouth was dry as dust and I craved a sip of cool water. Through a haze of pain, I saw Aunt Mercy standing in the doorway and reached out my hand in supplication. When the next contraction had passed I opened my eyes again but she'd disappeared.

The spasms came every minute now and I groaned as I fought an overwhelming urge to bear down. But it was too late. I screamed as the pressure inside me became too intense to resist and I pushed down with all my might. There was a rush of fluid and the baby slipped out onto the mattress.

Slowly, I picked her up and wiped the blood off her tiny but perfect face. Her eyes were closed and her skin strangely grey. She wasn't breathing. I cleared fluid from her mouth and rocked her against my chest, smothering her with kisses. If I loved her enough, surely she'd wake up?

Footsteps ran up the stairs and the door burst open.

'Sweet Lord!' Maggie stood in the doorway, her hand to her mouth.

The midwife pushed past her and stopped when she saw the babe in my arms.

'Isn't she perfect?' I said. 'Look at her tiny fingers!' I smiled at the two women through a blur of tears. There was a constriction in my chest, as if a heavy weight was pressing upon it.

'Let me take her, dear,' said the midwife, reaching out her dimpled hands.

'No!' I clutched my baby even more tightly to my aching breast. 'Who's a pretty babe, then?' I crooned, kissing the soft blond down on her head. 'I shall call you Rose, after the most beautiful of all the flowers in the garden.'

'You must give her to me now,' said the midwife, firmly.

'Don't touch her!' I hissed. I would not allow her to take my darling child, Gabriel's child, away.

'Hold her for now, then,' said the midwife. Using gentle words, she persuaded me to lie down and lifted my shift again. 'One last push, dear.'

Resting my chin on Rose's head, I closed my eyes and obeyed instructions.

The midwife caught the afterbirth in the sheet and bent over to examine it. 'Has Mother suffered an injury?' she asked Maggie Kinross. 'The babe's very small for seven months and the afterbirth is damaged.'

'Hackett,' I said, tears seeping through my eyelashes. 'Hackett kicked me. I thought his poisonous influence had gone from my life, but I was wrong. He's killed my baby.' I gulped in air as the pressure built in my breast. I cried out then, a raw cry of utter desolation at losing everything in my life that was precious to me: my family, my home, my husband, my best friend, the man I loved and his son. And now, most of all, my child.

Four days later, Rose was buried in the churchyard of All Saints. Only myself, Aunt Mercy and Maggie Kinross stood by the graveside as the sexton lowered the tiny coffin into the earth. My aching need for Gabriel heightened the anguish of burying the daughter he'd never know existed. Still numb with shock, I was dry-eyed and trembling as Maggie supported me while we listened to the minister intone the service.

The following two weeks passed in a haze of grief. Aunt Mercy kept me busy with household chores in the mornings: polishing, ironing and scrubbing floors under her close scrutiny. In the afternoons we sat in the stuffy parlour and I read to her from the Bible or did her mending, while she watched me all the time to be sure I wasn't daydreaming.

'Sit up straight, Katherine,' she said one afternoon. 'Didn't I always tell you that you'd grow into a hunchback if you slouch over your sewing?'

A picture of Jacob flashed into my mind and I regretted not coming to know him better. I'd glimpsed a surprisingly gentle side to his nature in his care of Toby.

'Are you listening to me, Katherine? Didn't I always tell you . . . '

'Yes, you did, Aunt Mercy.' I bit my tongue until it bled, overwhelmed with despair.

Frowning, she clicked her tongue. 'It's time you shook off that miserable face; I can't bear to look at you.' She rapped my knuckles painfully with her fan.

Suddenly it felt as if something shifted inside me and I looked at her, really looked at her. She was nothing but a wizened old woman, pickled in the acid of her sour disposition, her visage shaped by years of disappointment and unhappiness. Where was the terrifying ogre of my childhood and how could I have let myself remain in thrall to her all these years?

'You never could bear to look at me,' I said, my fingers tingling and my pulse racing. I was astonished at my bravery, but once tasted, it was like a drug and I couldn't have enough of it. 'Was it because I looked too much like my mother? Is that why you were always so unkind to me?'

'Unkind? I gave you everything you had!'

I grew bolder. 'Nonsense! My inheritance, held in trust for me, allowed you to live in great comfort.'

Aunt Mercy narrowed her eyes. 'What do you know of my financial affairs?'

'I know what your man of business, Mr Catchpole, told me when he arranged for my dowry to be signed over to my husband.'

'He had no right . . . '

'He was my father's lawyer first, don't forget. And when I asked him if you would be left with sufficient to live on he told me that my father had left a generous sum to you, quite apart from that set aside for my own care as I grew up, and it had been untouched for all those years.' I pointed a finger at her. 'You took money that was meant for me.'

Aunt Mercy pursed her mouth, but she looked away from me and I knew my remark had hit the truth of it. 'You bullied me for years, relying on my fear for you meaning I'd never dare to ask you to return it. Well, I'm not afraid of you any longer.'

'All I can say,' said Aunt Mercy, 'is that it's a blessed relief your child didn't live. I cannot imagine what kind of girl she would have grown up to be, with you for her mother.'

That was enough to release the stopper from the years of pent-up anger and the festering wounds of wretchedness that I'd buried deep inside me. A red tide of fury boiled up and clouded my vision. 'It's perfectly plain to me, and to everybody else no doubt, why my father rejected you in favour of your younger, kinder sister,' I said, 'but perhaps, you're right. A small part of me *is* relieved that little Rose will never have to suffer the cruelty that you regularly inflicted upon me.'

'How dare you say such a thing?'

I stared straight back into her outraged blue eyes. 'Because you know it's true.' Deliberately, I dropped her torn stocking onto the floor. 'You can do your own mending from now on. And I think it's time for me to take advice from the magistrate on how to recover my stolen inheritance, don't you?' I stood up. 'I shall retire to my bed-chamber since I cannot endure your presence any longer. Perhaps you might care to ponder on the shame you'll suffer if you are called to the court to answer the charges I shall make against you?'

Aunt Mercy shrank back into her chair as I stood up.

Scarlet with rage and trembling right down to the tips of my toes, I swept from the room.

The following morning I stared at myself in Aunt Mercy's spotted mirror and saw how thin I'd become and how sorrow shadowed my eyes. Rose had been so tiny and born so early that, with tight lacing, there was no longer any outward sign that she had ever existed at all.

I'd lain awake most of the night, hollow with anger after my spat with Aunt Mercy, lonely and overwhelmed with grief for all I had lost. The one shining light in the depths of my misery, was that my love for Rose had guided me towards facing up to Aunt Mercy and now I experienced a strange lightness at suddenly being free from my fear of her.

Later, I made my appearance at the breakfast table. 'I shall be away today and will not return until late, Aunt Mercy,' I said.

'Where are you –'

'That need not concern you.'

She gave me a frightened glance and bowed her head over her plate.

We ate our breakfast in silence and afterwards I set off for the market square and boarded the public coach.

As the coach jogged over the rutted roads, my conscience pricked over my unkindness to an old woman. Of course, I had no intention of speaking to the magistrate, but her cruel words had pushed me beyond the limits of my endurance.

I stared out of the window, watching the world pass by and thinking of Rose. I gripped my fingers together, not wanting to cry in front of the other passengers, wishing that she had breathed and lived long enough to open her eyes and see her mother. But perhaps then it would have been even more painful to let her go. 'Sleep in peace, my darling,' I whispered.

The day's outing was madness and I knew it but I missed Toby. Denied a child of my own to love, I needed to hold him in my arms and bathe in his uncomplicated love. So, upon a whim, I'd decided to call at the House of Perfume and take a cup of tea with Jane, and Gabriel too, if he was at home.

The coach rolled into Lincoln's Inn and I alighted and made my way through the busy streets to Long Acre. But when I stopped outside the House of Perfume, my courage failed me. What right had I to come back into the Hartes' lives and upset them all again? Perhaps Toby had a new companion and it would unsettle him if I visited for an afternoon and then went away again. And Gabriel. Could I trust myself not to let Jane see how I yearned for him?

But I couldn't find the strength to walk away. I crept through the side gate and sat on the bench under the arbour. The sweet scent of honeysuckle and roses drifted on the breeze. Running my fingers over the sun-warmed wood of the bench, I recalled all the times I had sat there chatting to Toby while he played in the garden. But those days had gone.

'Aunt Kate!'

I saw Toby running towards me and my heart turned over.

'You've come back!' he cried, clambering onto my knee.

Dismay gave way to joy. He hadn't forgotten me then. I wrapped my arms around him and buried my face in his hair, breathing in the little-boy smell of him.

'Kate?'

My heart skipped a beat and I looked up to see Gabriel, with Shadow at his side. 'Kate, is it really you?'

There were new lines on his handsome face and I wanted to run to him and smooth them away. 'I was passing,' I said, politely, just as if we barely knew each other.

Gabriel bent to unbuckle Shadow from his harness. 'Toby, will you ask Mistress Jenks to give you some dinner?'

'But I want to talk to Aunt Kate!'

'I'll come and find you very soon and then you can tell me all your news,' I said. I watched him run away with Shadow at his heels.

'Is your aunt well again?' Gabriel asked. 'Have you come back to us?'

'How can I,' I said, my lips trembling, 'after what we did? I will never forgive myself.'

He bowed his head. 'The blame is mine, Kate. But that's in the past and suffering guilt will not eradicate the sin. Won't you come back to us now?'

'I cannot,' I said. He had never said he loved me and I wasn't prepared to make myself even more vulnerable by letting him know that seeing him again had torn open the wound in my heart. I stood up to leave.

'Jane is very ill,' said Gabriel. 'The physician comes every day but there is nothing he can do except bleed her and give her poppy syrup to ease her pain. She's dying, Kate.'

I stared at him, horrified.

'I should have guessed that it was more than indifference when she denied me access to her bedchamber two years ago.' His expression was wretched and it was painful to comprehend that he loved Jane more than I realised.

'She has a canker in her breast,' he said, 'like her sister and her mother before her.'

I sank down onto the bench, my knees weak with shock.

'The physician says she shows great strength of will. He's dumbfounded that she's survived so long. Kate, she calls for you constantly. Please, I beg you, come to see her!'

Only a heart of stone could resist such an impassioned plea and I allowed Gabriel to lead me to the sickroom.

Jane lay like an effigy with skeletally thin arms folded across her chest. I stared down at her, shocked beyond measure at how she had

deteriorated. Her cheeks were sunken, her skin a waxy yellow and she laboured for breath.

'Jane?' I breathed.

Her eyelids fluttered open and she turned unfocused eyes towards me. 'Kate? Thank God you've come!'

Tears filled my eyes. 'Gabriel, I'll sit with Jane awhile.'

He nodded and a moment later the door closed behind him.

'Did Gabriel tell you I'm dying?'

'You must rest now.' I smoothed the tangled hair off her brow.

She snatched hold of my hand. 'There's no time to humour me! I have to make you understand.' Pulling aside the neckline of her nightshift, she exposed a folded pad of linen and, grimacing in pain, peeled it away. Her exposed breast was reddened, weeping and ulcerated, the skin rotting.

I gasped and put my hand over my mouth.

'It's not pretty, is it?' said Jane, laying the pad back in place. 'The doctor tells me the canker has eaten into my lungs.'

'But why didn't you tell me?' I could hardly speak. The terrible sight of her cankered breast hurt me almost as much as the knowledge that she hadn't confided in me.

'Since you left I've prayed every day that you'd return. I thought it might be a month or two yet but I knew you'd come back.' The breath bubbled in her chest and she fought to breathe, her eyes as frightened as those of a wounded animal. 'You cannot know the effort of will it has taken to stay alive until you returned.'

'What can I do?'

'Don't you know?' Her pale lips curved in a small smile. 'You love Toby, don't you?'

'You know that I do.'

'Would it be so very hard for you to love him after I've gone; to guide him as he grows up and to remind him now and then that his mama loved him beyond all the treasures of the earth?'

'Jane, I –'

'Let me finish! You *know* that the worst fate a child can suffer is to lose a mother.' She began to cough, her lips turning blue as she fought for breath. 'But if you will love him and nurture him as if he were your own, his loss will be lessened and I will go comforted to my grave.' She clutched at my wrist, her bony fingers made strong by desperation. 'But that isn't all. You must marry Gabriel to secure your position as Toby's new mother.'

'Jane!'

'I know you love Gabriel. Ssh!' She pressed a finger to my lips to still my protest. 'I've seen the way you look at him.'

'What madness is this?' I protested, the blood rising in my cheeks.

'Don't insult my intellect, Kate. I have so little time. I chose you to be Toby's new mother months ago. It was the most difficult and painful task I ever had to face, to step back and allow you to take my place in his affections and I wasn't always kind to you. But I know I made the right decision. Only *you* can do this.'

'It's impossible for me not to love Toby,' I said, 'but I cannot marry Gabriel.'

Jane touched my cheek. 'Why not?'

'Because he doesn't love me!' The words tore out of me before I could stop them.

Jane frowned. 'But I thought . . . ' She bit her lip. 'I wanted you to love each other so you would make a new family for Toby. I gave you both every opportunity possible to form an attachment. I even took Toby and Jacob away so that you would have the time and space to declare your feelings.'

'You planned that?' I stared at her in horror. 'You schemed for your husband and your best friend to be alone together, to fall in love? Is that why you were so cruel to him, so that he would turn to me for sympathy?'

'But my plan worked better than I expected, didn't it?' Her grey eyes regarded me steadily.

The flash of anger I felt at being manipulated in such a way was overtaken by shame. I had no one but myself to blame for yielding to my carnal desires. But how much did she really know? If Gabriel had said nothing to her, he and I were the only ones who knew exactly what had happened that night. And even Gabriel didn't know about our baby.

I couldn't meet Jane's eyes and looked down at my hands restlessly plucking at my skirt. 'I do love him,' I said quietly, 'but my love isn't reciprocated. I would never enter the married state again without love on both sides.'

'You must give him time, Kate! It nearly destroyed me when you went away and my plan didn't work as I expected. In this you've been a better friend to me than I wanted, when your guilt at loving Gabriel forced you to leave the House of Perfume.'

'My love for your husband is a terrible thing,' I said. 'The guilt of it burns into me like acid.'

'You mustn't let it. And when I'm gone –'

'Don't say it!'

'Look at me, Kate!'

Slowly, I lifted my gaze to meet hers.

'I give you and Gabriel my blessing,' she said. She touched her papery lips to my hand.

'Jane, I cannot . . . '

She turned her head away. 'Will you sit with me until I sleep?'

I listened to the harsh sound of her breathing as she dozed, my thoughts in turmoil. Seeing Gabriel again had increased my yearning for him, but he had given me no sign that he loved me. That enchanted night, for him, must have been motivated only by lust. Jane may have forgiven me for my treachery and given us her blessing but could I ever forgive myself?

Chapter 39

It was too late to return to Kingston that night, and after I had put Toby to bed, Gabriel called me into the parlour.

I sat on the edge of the chair, anxious about what he was going to say. Jane hadn't mentioned whether she'd told Gabriel about her scheme to make us fall in love and I couldn't bring myself to ask him. In the event, he spoke of something quite different.

'I thought you should know,' said Gabriel, 'that Hackett's crushed leg became gangrenous and the surgeon had to amputate. It was too late, however, and he died before they could hang him.'

I realised then that Hackett had ceased to disturb my dreams. 'I should be sorry for him,' I said, thinking of the beating he'd given me that had killed my baby, 'but I'm not.'

'His suffering and death was a just punishment, I believe.' Gabriel paced across the room and turned to face me, his expression uncertain. 'Kate, now that you have seen how very ill Jane is, will you stay with us? At least until . . . '

I was silent for a moment but I'd already made up my mind. 'Until then,' I said.

I wrote to Aunt Mercy to tell her that I would not return at present and resumed my role as Toby's companion and Jane's nurse. I avoided Gabriel, but was pleased to see that he and Shadow had formed a strong bond and they ventured out daily together into the city.'When will Mama be better, Aunt Kate?' asked Toby.

I hesitated, not wanting to lie to him. 'I don't know, sweetheart.'

'Is she ill because I was naughty?'

I gathered him onto my lap and hugged him so that he wouldn't see the tears start to my eyes. 'You're not naughty!'

Early that evening, while Toby was making jumbals with Mistress Jenks, I sat beside Jane. She had become even thinner and her pale skin was stretched tightly over her skull. Her lips were cracked and flaking and I dripped boiled water into her mouth from a spoon. Carefully, I soaked off the dressing from her breast, trying to shut out the sound of her sobs. She rolled her head on the pillow, moaning softly and my heart bled because there was so little I could do to relieve her pain.

When it was done, I applied a clean bandage. 'Will you have more poppy syrup?' I asked, wondering how long she could endure such torture.

'Later,' she gasped, the fluid wheezing in her lungs. 'Kate, it won't be long now,' she said. 'Will you bring Toby to see me? Quickly.'

I nodded, too distressed to speak.

'Bring me a clean nightshift first and prop me up a little higher. And I'll have some of Toby's Hungary water for my handkerchief.' Her smile was ghastly. 'I don't want to frighten him by smelling of the sickroom.'

I made her as comfortable as I could before running downstairs, suddenly frightened that she would pass away before I could bring Toby to her.

Toby was chattering happily to Ann in the kitchen. His face lit up when he saw me. 'I've made jumbals,' he said, proudly offering me a plate of sugar biscuits.

I forced myself to smile. 'They look delicious! I'll have one later, but your mama is asking for you.'

Something in my tone must have alerted Mistress Jenks for she stopped stirring the pan on the fire and looked up sharply. 'I'll fetch the master,' she murmured.

I nodded, took Toby's hand and hurried him upstairs.

Jane held out her arms to him. 'There you are, sweetheart! Come and tell me what you've been doing today. Kate, will you ask Gabriel to come?'

I glanced back as I left the room. Jane looked up at me with tragic eyes, her chin resting on Toby's head and his arms wound around her neck. I pressed my hand to my mouth to suppress a sob and hurried away.

Gabriel was pacing up and down in the hall. 'Kate, is that you?'

'Toby is with Jane,' I said. 'She thinks it won't be long now.'

'It's time she was released from her pain. She's been so brave ...' He fumbled for his handkerchief and blew his nose.

'Will you go to her? I'll stay nearby, ready to take Toby away if necessary.'

'He'll need you in the coming days. You won't fail him, will you, Kate?'

'I will do whatever is necessary for the next few days,' I said, 'but I cannot make promises for after that.'

Upstairs, I waited outside the sickroom door, as the clock ticked the minutes by.

Eventually the door opened and Gabriel came out, holding Toby by the hand. 'Kate, I'm going to take Toby to bed.'

I glanced past him into the room and saw that Jane had buried her face in her hands and her shoulders heaved.

'I'll come and tuck you in later, Toby,' I said, kissing his cheek, 'but I'm going to sit with your mama for a while.'

Gabriel led Toby away.

'Kate?' Jane's voice was barely more than a breath. 'My sleeping draught?'

I carefully measured a dose and fed it to her, wiping her chin as she gulped greedily at it.

'Not long now,' she gasped.

The last rays of the dying sun slanted in through the windows and I adjusted the curtains so that the brightness wouldn't hurt her eyes. When the light dimmed, I closed the shutters, wondering with a shiver of apprehension if Jane would live to see the dawn. I lit the candles, noticing that they gave off the scent of Jane's favourite orange blossom.

I listened to her laboured breathing with every nerve strained. She muttered and cried out in pain now and again and I murmured soothing words until she quietened.

'It's so dark!'

'I'm here, Jane,' I said, stroking her forehead.

'Toby?'

'Fast asleep.'

'You must kiss him for me tomorrow.' Jane coughed again, fluid bubbling deep in her lungs. 'Kate? Tell Toby . . . ' Her body convulsed as great rasping coughs wracked her frail body. 'Tell him that I'll always love him.' Her hand gripped mine.

'I will.' Inside me, the ice-cold bubble of dread that I'd carried with me during the past days began to expand.

'Don't forget, Kate!'

'I won't.'

Her eyes opened wide and she smiled. 'Oh!' she whispered. 'I can see the light!'

I clutched her hand, full of dread.

Then the breath rattled in her throat and she exhaled in a long sigh.

'Jane?' I squeezed her hand convulsively, stricken with panic. 'No, don't go! You can't leave us!'

But her tight grip on my hand relaxed and all at once the bed-chamber was strangely silent. I squeezed my eyes shut, suddenly frightened.

When, at last, I opened my eyes again I saw that Jane still had a half-smile on her face and the lines of pain on her forehead had smoothed away.

A cold mantle of acceptance settled over me. Gently, I closed her eyelids. The body lying on the bed wasn't my dearest friend any more, merely a husk that had once been Jane. I glanced around the room, wondering if her spirit watched me. I sprang up and ran to the window, fumbled with the catch and threw open the shutters. 'Go in peace, my friend,' I said. 'May your soul fly free.'

The candle on the table by the window flickered in a sudden draught and went out.

The following days were full of sorrow as Gabriel and I did what we could to soothe Toby's desperate tears. I knew that, no matter what we said, nothing would ever entirely heal Toby's pain.

The sun shone on the day of Jane's funeral but I can remember little except the sea of sympathetic faces at the graveside and Toby's terrible fit of weeping as he clung to his father's hand. Gabriel seemed somehow diminished by Toby's anguish, his hair less shiny and his upright carriage bowed. It was shameful of me, but it hurt to see him grieving for Jane.

After the service, people I'd never met before arrived at the

House of Perfume to share the funeral meats and talk in hushed tones of Jane's sweetness and goodness and an illness so bravely borne. There was no place for me in the life that Jane had shared with Gabriel.

That night I awoke from my own troubled dreams to hear Toby cry out. I ran to his room and found that Gabriel was already there, rocking his sobbing son against his chest, crooning to him and promising that the dragon that lived under the bed had gone.

'He can't hurt you while I'm here,' he murmured.

I watched from the doorway as Gabriel, barefooted and in his nightshirt, paced the floor, with Toby's head upon his shoulder. It was a curiously intimate scene and I longed to go to them and enfold them in my arms. Love for Gabriel overwhelmed me again as I watched how tenderly he cared for his grieving son.

At last, Toby quietened and, finally, fell asleep. Gently, Gabriel laid him on the bed, kissed his forehead and lay down beside him, still holding the little boy's hand.

All at once I felt like an intruder in their private world and turned to tiptoe away before he sensed me.

'Goodnight, Kate,' whispered Gabriel.

I should have known that he had been aware of my presence. 'Goodnight,' I echoed. *Goodnight, my love.*

Toby had forgotten the dragons by the following morning and was thundering up and down the stairs with Jacob and Shadow, repelling French invaders from the castle, when I tapped on the door of the Perfume Salon.

'Sometimes I think Jacob is little more than a child himself,' said Gabriel with a half-smile as he opened the door.

'It's a relief to hear Toby forgetting his troubles,' I said. 'And that's what I wanted to talk to you about.' I needed to say what had to be said before I weakened. 'It's time for me to leave.'

'No!' He gripped the edge of the table as if to steady himself.

'I promised I'd stay until Jane was buried.'

'But Jane said that she'd spoken to you! That she'd asked you to stay at the House of Perfume to look after Toby.'

'I cannot.'

'Yes, you can! I understand that you're concerned for your reputation if you stay on in the house with me, but it will allay any gossip if we are married.'

'Gossip!' I said acidly. 'We deserve any condemnation that can be heaped upon us.'

'Kate, you're not listening to me! Jane intended us to marry and it would be the very best thing possible for Toby. He loves you already.'

'And I love him. But I will not marry you.'

Gabriel's face blanched with shock. 'But why not?'

'Because what we did was wrong.' I glanced at the carpet in front of the hearth, remembering the warmth of the fire on our naked skin and the musky perfume that drove us to the heights of passion that night. 'I cannot live with the guilty memories of that facing me every day.' *And especially not with a man who married me for his son's sake and not because he loved me.*

'But Toby needs you!'

'No, he doesn't, Gabriel. He has you.'

'I thought . . . ' He reached out blindly for me.

'Don't touch me!' I said, knowing my resolve would fade if he did. 'You both need time to grieve for Jane, as I do.'

He sat down and rested his head on his hands. 'I imagined, after all the pain and misery of Jane's illness, that the one good thing to come out of it all would be our marriage.'

'And do I have no say in this plan that you and Jane concocted?' Anger flared and my hands involuntarily balled up into fists, my nails cutting into my palms.

'When Jane gave us her blessing before she died, I knew it was the right thing to do.'

'Not for me,' I said. 'I married once before without love and it brings only unhappiness.'

There was a long moment of silence. 'I beg your pardon,' said Gabriel at last, his tone one of deadly courtesy. 'In that case, allow me to call for the carriage immediately and Jem will convey you to your aunt's house.' He opened the door and strode into the hall.

Toby, sitting on the bottom stair with Jacob, glanced up at his father with a smile.

'Jacob, tell Jem to bring the carriage to the front straight away, please. Mistress Finche will be travelling to Kingston this morning.'

Jacob raised his eyebrows and his dark eyes bore into me as I tried to still the fit of shaking that had gripped me. 'Yes, master,' he said and scuttled off.

I sat down beside Toby and put my arm around him.

'You're not staying with me?' His green eyes were wide and anxious.

'I cannot, sweetheart, but your Father and Jacob will look after you with all possible care. And I will write letters to you.'

'But who will read them to me if you aren't here?'

Toby's face was so woebegone it was all I could do not to weep. I swallowed back the tears. 'Jacob will read them for you. And if you ask him to help you with your letters, before very long you will be able to write back to me.'

He nodded and slipped his hand trustingly into mine.

Before long the carriage came to a halt outside the front door.

Gabriel stepped forwards. 'I thank you for your devoted care of my wife and son,' he said, politely. He offered me his hand and it would have been churlish not to take it. 'I trust you will have an uneventful journey.' A muscle tensed in his jaw, but there was no hint of regret in his voice.

I looked down at our clasped hands through a blur of tears. There was nothing I could say that would make it right between us.

I kissed Toby and a moment later I was in the coach.

Jem cracked his whip and we started off.

Toby waved wildly at me with both arms while Gabriel stood impassively by his side.

I leaned out of the window to wave back to Toby and saw that Shadow was running after the coach. Tears started to my eyes as he fell behind and then dwindled into the distance.

Chapter 40

August 1670

Grey clouds scudded across the sky and a warm, blustery wind snatched at my skirt as I walked across All Saints churchyard. I carried an armful of roses and stopped beside the small headstone that marked my daughter's grave.

'Hello, my sweet Rose,' I whispered.

It had been more than a year since she'd gone, her existence snuffed out even before it began and I still grieved for the life we would never share. I came often to the churchyard to talk to her, to conjure up a picture of her, rosy-cheeked and happy.

I removed the dying flowers from her grave and replaced them with a posy of pink roses, spiked with rosemary for remembrance. Closing my eyes, I sent up a prayer for her soul. Sometimes, in a fanciful moment, I liked to believe that Jane watched over her in the Kingdom of Heaven.

There were dead flowers on the neighbouring grave, too, and I placed a bunch of yellow roses there. Soon after I had returned from the House of Perfume, Aunt Mercy had taken to her bed with a summer chill that developed into a persistent cough. She was pathetically grateful when I nursed her and in her final days broke down and begged my forgiveness. She talked of her jealousy of my mother, her younger, prettier sister, and her despair helped me to understand how she'd allowed her life to be ruined by bitterness. After she died, I was surprised to find I missed her a little and even more surprised to find that she had left me her house and fortune.

I sat down in my usual place on the bench under the elm tree. The churchyard was deserted. I sighed. There was nothing and no one to hurry home for.

It was a year and a day since Jane had died. I didn't blame her any more for scheming to encourage Gabriel and me to fall in love. If I'd been in her shoes, perhaps I'd have done the same to secure my son's happiness. But I still missed Gabriel and Toby with a pain that never seemed to fade. Sometimes, in the depths of the night, I wondered if Rose's death had punished me enough for my betrayal of Jane and I regretted refusing to marry Gabriel, even though he didn't love me.

The breeze sighed in the elm tree, mingling with the whispers of the dead. Horses and carriages clattered past in the market place but the churchyard remained an island of stillness amongst the hustle and bustle.

I closed my eyes remembering, as I so often did, the first time I saw Gabriel. He had emerged out of the shadows into the sunlight, dressed in a feathered hat and a coat of sea green looking as cool as a mountain stream. He'd carried a long, silver-headed cane in one hand and a perfume bottle in the other. I think I began to fall in love with him the first time I saw him.

Somewhere, a dog barked. I sighed and opened my eyes. A black dog raced across the churchyard, heading straight for me.

'Shadow!'

He capered around my feet, whining in excitement.

'Where did you come from?' I asked in incredulous delight. Then I glanced up and froze.

A tall figure in a feathered hat and a coat of sea green walked hesitantly along the path towards us, a silver-topped cane in one hand and a perfume bottle in the other. Gabriel.

I surged to my feet, the blood rushing in my ears and my heart turning somersaults. Had I summoned him up out of my imaginings?

Shadow ran back to Gabriel, who felt for the handle to his harness and then advanced confidently. He came to a stop in front of me and I studied his familiar, beloved face. New lines were etched around his eyes but his expression was remote.

'Kate.'

'Gabriel. Will you come and sit beside me?' Lightly, I placed my hand under his elbow and guided him to the bench. I hoped he couldn't hear the thudding of my heart.

'Your housekeeper said you would be here,' he said, resting the cane against the bench and placing the glass bottle on the seat beside him.

'Why did you come?'

He gestured to his sea green coat. 'As you see, this is my first day out of mourning.'

'How is Toby?'

'He has . . . adapted. We've grown very close. But he still misses his mother. And you.' He sighed. 'As I do.'

'Why have you come?' Part of me wished he hadn't; seeing him again opened up old wounds.

'To apologise,' said Gabriel. 'You were right to say that we needed time to grieve. What happened on the night I made your perfume tainted us. And it's taken time to understand how insensitive it was to ask you to be my wife so soon after Jane passed away.'

The silence hung heavily between us.

'Looking back,' he said, 'after the sadness of losing Jane and suffering Toby's anguish, my thoughts weren't ordered.'

'It's been a difficult year,' I said, remembering the aching pain of all the lonely nights.

'All I knew was that if I lost you, too, I might lose my reason.'

I stared at him.

One corner of his mouth lifted in a brief smile. 'I think that, for a while, perhaps I did. But now it's time to look to the future. Can we not forgive ourselves for what happened, as Jane did? It's not my intention to distress you but, Kate, dear Kate, I know I'll always regret it if I don't ask you again.'

'Ask me . . . '

He found my hand and raised it to his lips. 'Kate, you would do me the greatest honour if you would become my wife.'

My breath caught on a sob and I pulled my hand away. 'I cannot,' I said.

He bowed his head. 'I had so hoped . . . ' His voice broke and he swallowed. 'I misunderstood. I hoped you loved me.' He gave a mirthless laugh. 'How stupid I've been! It wasn't love at all that you felt for me, only pity.'

I drew in my breath, shocked that he could think such a thing of me.

'If you can't love me I'll not trouble you any longer by pressing my suit.' He stood up, his face a mask of misery.

'I didn't say I couldn't love you!' I said, before I could stop myself. 'It's rather that you do not love me '

'Not love you!' His voice was outraged. 'Of *course*, I love you. What kind of man do you think I am? That night we spent together would never have happened if I hadn't been so in love with you that I couldn't even put my hat on straight.'

A tiny flicker of hope lit in my heart. 'But you never said . . . '

'How could I possibly declare my love for you while I was still married to Jane?'

Did he really love me after all? But it was the time for plain speaking and he wouldn't like it. 'I will not be merely a convenient replacement mother for Toby,' I said.

'Of course not!' He caught hold of my hand and lifted it to his lips. 'But after Jane died you ran back to Aunt Mercy so quickly that you never gave me the opportunity to tell you that I loved you.' He kissed the palm of my hand and folded my fingers over it to capture the kiss. 'Kate, my dearest Kate, I will love you until the end of time.'

'Oh, Gabriel . . . '

Then he was crushing me to his chest and his lips smothered my face with kisses and he mouthed words of love in my hair as I clung to him.

'You have brought light to my darkness,' he whispered. 'Can you not love me, too?'

'I do! I do love you.'

'Then, please, Kate, what reason is there for you not to marry me?'

I closed my eyes revelling in the safety of his arms around me. How could I bear to spoil it with what I had to say?

'Kate?'

'There should be no secrets in a marriage,' I said.

'I solemnly promise not to keep secrets from you,' said Gabriel, kissing my hair.

'But I have kept a very great secret from you,' I said, pushing him away from me. I twisted my fingers together, unable to find a way to tell him.

'What great secret . . . ' Then he drew in his breath on a gasp. 'Jane said something to me on the day she died but I dismissed it as the raving of a dying woman.'

'What did she say?'

'She said . . . ' Gabriel stilled my restless fingers with his hand. 'She said she thought you were with child and that was why you had been forced to leave us to go to your Aunt Mercy.'

'She knew?' I whispered.

'Sweet Lord in heaven, so it's true?' His face blanched. 'Jane blamed herself for encouraging us to be alone together.' He shook his head in disbelief. 'But if that night resulted in a love child, surely it would have been born last September? You were not with child when Jane died in August. '

'Gabriel –' I clung to his hand '– our daughter was stillborn last July.'

Overcome with emotion, he could not speak. At last he drew a shuddering breath. 'Tell me about her. Please, Kate, I must know.'

'I called her Rose,' I said. 'She never drew breath, but I held her in my arms and loved her. Her hair was blonde, like yours and Toby's. I come here every day to sit beside her grave.'

'She's here?'

'Just a step away.' I led him to the grave and placed his hand on the headstone.

He ran his fingers over the smooth white stone and then fell to his knees on the grass. Resting his hands flat on the small mound of earth that covered her coffin, he followed the shape of it until he came to the posy of roses. He lifted them to his nose and inhaled their perfume before carefully replacing them. 'How can you bear it?' he murmured, wiping away his tears with his thumb.

'Sometimes I cannot,' I confessed.

'How very frightened you must have been! Why didn't to come to me for help? It was such a cruel burden for you to bear alone.' He stood up and took me in his arms. 'Don't you think losing Rose is punishment enough for our sins, Kate?'

I leaned against his chest and felt the strength of his arms around me. Perhaps he was right. Had I been too immersed in my guilt? The heavy weight I'd carried for so long lifted, just a little. And what of Toby? Didn't he deserve to have the safety and security of a mother's arms?

'Kate, no child can ever replace little Rose, but we could have other children to gladden our hearts. The House of Perfume needs a family to fill the empty rooms with the sound of laughter. Dearest Kate, I love you with all my heart and again I beg you, please, will you marry me?'

This time I didn't hesitate. 'I will.' As I said the words it was if a cage door had opened and I soared free from the pain and misery of the past.

'Thank the good Lord.' Gabriel let out his breath in a long sigh.

His kiss was tender and I slid my arms around his neck, wanting nothing more than to spend the rest of my life in his embrace.

A child's shout made me look over his shoulder and I saw Toby running towards us with Jacob at his side.

'Kate! Kate!' Toby launched himself at us and I caught him up into the centre of our embrace as he smothered my face with kisses. He held my face between his hands and looked intently at me. 'I've been waiting and waiting. Are you coming home with us at last?'

I glanced at Jacob, standing with his arms folded and a sour expression on his face. 'Of course she's coming,' he said. 'I'll not stay at the House of Perfume to endure another year of my master's misery if she doesn't.'

'In that case, Gabriel,' I said, 'I couldn't possibly be responsible for your most loyal and devoted manservant's departure.'

Jacob's frown softened, just a little, and laughter danced in his black eyes. 'Master Toby, let us return to the carriage until your father and Mistress Finche have concluded their ... conversation.'

Gabriel kissed me again.

'I forgot,' he said a moment later. He wrapped his arm round my waist and we walked back to the bench. 'This is for you.' He picked up from the bench the flask of perfume he had brought with him.

I took it from him, resting it on my palm. It was a beautiful thing with a stopper fashioned like a rosebud, but I was fearful of opening it.

'Don't worry,' he said, with a smile. 'It's nothing like the last one. I've had a whole year to create this for you.' Taking the flask from me, he worked the stopper free. He tipped the bottle against his fingers and caressed the perfume onto the inside of my wrist.

I lifted my hand and sniffed the perfume. Immediately, my senses were transported to a sunny garden after a shower of rain. The dewy freshness of the delicate rose fragrance was as uplifting and innocent as the baby who bore its name. 'It's beautiful, Gabriel!'

'I'm pleased you like it. But –' he smiled knowingly '– once we are married, I shall create another perfume for you.' Slowly, he caressed the skin on the inside of my wrist with his thumb, making me shiver with desire. 'A perfume,' he whispered in my ear, 'made with jasmine and tuberose, ambergris and musk.'

I closed my eyes, the husky richness of his voice lapping over me.

'It will be a perfume so potent and so seductive,' he murmured, 'that you shall only wear it in the privacy of our bedchamber. On those nights that you breathe honeyed words in my ear, tempting me with the rustle of your silken petticoats, we shall close the door upon the world and allow the perfume to stir our senses and inflame our passions.'

He buried his hands in my hair and kissed me again, until my knees turned to water.

'Would you like that?' he asked a moment later, his breath warm on my cheek.

'Yes, Gabriel,' I breathed. 'I should like that very much.'

Historical Note

When I finished writing *The Apothecary's Daughter* I couldn't free my mind of the picture of the Great Fire of London sweeping through the city and destroying everything in its path. Thousands of people's lives were changed forever and every one of them would have a different story to tell. Katherine Finche, the spice merchant's wife's, is only one of them.

The Great Fire of London began in the small hours of 2 September 1666 after a scorching hot summer of drought. The city was as dry as a tinderbox and before the night was out the warehouses by the river below Thames Street had ignited and become an unstoppable inferno. The fire leaped from building to building, fanned by a fierce east wind. The populace, led by the Duke of York and Charles II, frantically pulled down houses to form firebreaks but to no avail.

After the fire had raged through the city for four days, the wind died down and the progress of the fire slowed and finally came under control. A smoking wasteland under a glowering red sky was all that remained. Almost everything within the city walls was destroyed, including an estimated thirteen thousand houses. Over a hundred thousand homeless citizens fled to camp out in Islington or Moor Fields with their few remaining possessions gathered around them. Something had to be done and done very quickly.

Incredibly, Christopher Wren, Robert Hooke and John Evelyn produced plans for the rebuilding of the city in a matter of days. Their vision for the new city was on a geometric plan with wide, straight roads, open piazzas and grand boulevards designed to reduce the traffic congestion that plagued the city even then. But it was not to be. The difficulties in registering the ownership of so many plots of land and the Crown's lack of funds to buy them resulted in rebuilding on almost the same higgledy-piggledy street plan as medieval London.

Every story needs a good villain and whilst researching the aftermath of the Great Fire, I discovered Dr Barbon, who ignited the fire of my imagination. Whilst Christopher Wren was designing cathedrals and guildhalls, Dr Barbon saw the rebuilding of the city as an opportunity to make his fortune. The son of a preacher called Praise-God Barebones, Dr Barbon had been christened If-Jesus-Had-Not-Died-For-Thee-Thou-Hads't-Been-Damn'd. Who could blame him if he asked his friends to call him Nicholas? He attended university in Holland but never practised medicine, preferring instead to turn his skills to property speculation.

After the fire, Barbon began to build his empire with astonishing speed and the extraordinary opportunities were there for the grasping. He began buying leases from landlords whose property had burned and who didn't want, or couldn't afford, to rebuild. New laws had been made for the rebuilding, which set clear rules. Houses had to be built of brick or stone with no windows or jetties projecting from the face of the house. A lesson had been learned and ramshackle and combustible wooden hovels would no longer be tolerated.

Barbon didn't have the funds to build all the new houses himself so he sought other investors, constantly borrowing money from one to start a project, delaying payments to another for as long as possible and only settling his large debts when the percentage of capital and costs were about half the cost of borrowing. A Member of Parliament, Barbon used his position to shield himself from the courts when he defaulted on payments and defrauded partners. His projects were often underfunded and he skimped on the quality of building materials. Some of his houses collapsed due to unsafe foundations. He didn't bother to apply for the necessary licences and simply moved onto a building plot, violently beat off any objectors, demolished what remained of any previous house and set to work to cram in as many new houses as possible onto the site.

In spite of his unscrupulous methods, Barbon and his property speculator partners built a great number of buildings, many of which are still standing today. Amongst others, he developed Red Lion Square, Devonshire Square, Marine Square, Gerrard Street, Conduit Street, Bedford Row in Holborn, Cannon Street, Fetter Lane and the Middle Temple Courts. The fine Essex Street Water gates, built in 1676 before the building of the embankment and the road on the north side of the Thames, prevented the tidal wash that often reached the buildings along The Strand and Fleet Street.

Barbon didn't care what people thought of him; money was all. He dressed in the latest fashions and lived as splendidly as a lord of the manor in Crane Court off Fleet Street, all the better to impress his investors. Although physically different, the character of my villain, Standfast-for-Jesus Hackett, is unashamedly based upon Barbon, the property developer everyone loved to hate.

My thanks go again to my editor, Lucy Icke, who patiently encouraged me while I struggled to cut a third of the manuscript and polish what remained, to Simon and my family who rarely complain when my thoughts are lost somewhere in the seventeenth century and to all the members of WordWatchers, my fabulous writing circle who have cheered me on and supplied me with cake.

I read widely while researching *The Spice Merchant's Wife* but found the following sources of reference especially useful:

The Phoenix by Leo Hollis
The Concise Pepys edited by Tom Griffin
Pepys's London by Stephen Porter
London – Rebuilding the City after the Great Fire by T. M. M. Baker
The Diary of a Nose by Jean-Claude Ellena
The Closet of Sir Kenelm Digby Knight Opened by Kenelm Digby
A Queen's Delight published in 1671 by E. Tyler and R. Holt

Toby's Favourite Cinnamon And Raisin Cake

Old recipes fascinate me and I enjoy trying them out in my own kitchen. Of course, we have it much easier these days. In the seventeenth century, newly milled flour had to be sieved free of husks and then dried, the preserving salt washed out of the butter, the spices ground in a pestle and mortar and the sugar cut from a block, ground and sieved. There were no thermostatically controlled ovens then and most houses had no ovens at all, only an open fire.

It surprised me to find that there were few recipes for cake as we know it and that those I did find were more like rich breads made with a yeast used in brewing ale, known as barm. I was amused to discover that the word 'barmy' derived from a 'sense of frothy excitement'.

The cinnamon and raisin cake that Kate made for Toby would have been a fruited bread similar to the Irish 'barm brack'. I have modernised and tested the recipe below. Do try it, this cake-bread is delicious cut in thick slices, spread generously with butter and downed with a mug of builder's tea!

9g fast acting yeast
300ml mixed milk and warm water
50g muscovado sugar
50g butter
300g strong white flour
300g wholewheat flour
pinch of salt
175g raisins, soaked for a few hours in hot tea
50g candied peel
2 eggs
2 tsp cinnamon (or more to taste)
1 tsp honey dissolved with 2 tsp hot water to glaze

- Stir the yeast into the mixed flours and rub the butter into the flour
- Stir in the sugar
- Pour the beaten eggs, milk and water into the flour
- Mix together to make a soft dough
- Knead for 10 minutes or use a mixer with a dough hook
- Place the ball of dough into a bowl, cover with cling film
- Leave in a warm place for about an hour until doubled in size
- Drain the raisins and blot dry. Gently knead into the dough
- Divide the dough into two and form into two round loaves
- Place on greased baking trays and leave in a warm place for one hour
- Bake at 200°C for about 20 to 30 mins until golden brown
- Cool on wire rack and brush the tops with the honey glaze